The fuse had about three feet left to burn.

Kicking the body of Moses from him and tucking up his legs, Tom strained with all his might to lift his part of the bench. He felt the other end move as John's massive strength came to bear. He glanced round.

Two feet to go.

He tried again. His whole body ran with sweat. The cord bit into his wrists. His fingers went numb. Knees shaking with the strain, he heaved upward. The bench lifted a fraction. As it did so, John's weight forced it down the room, pinning Tom against the far wall. He looked at the fuse.

Nine inches.

Terror seized him. He kicked and wrestled. Tears of frustration sprang from his eyes. His wrists started to bleed. But all was in vain. He was stuck fast.

For Delphine & Geoffrey —

ONE CROWDED HOUR

STEWART ROSS

With all love and wishes —
Stewart
6.1.94

WARNER BOOKS

A *Warner* Book

First published in Great Britain in 1994
by Warner Books

Copyright © Stewart Ross, 1994

The moral right of the author has been asserted.

*All characters in this publication are fictitious and
any resemblance to real persons, living or dead,
is purely coincidental.*

All rights reserved.
No part of this publication may be reproduced,
stored in a retrieval system or transmitted, in any
form or by any means, without the prior
permission in writing of the publisher, nor be
otherwise circulated in any form of binding or
cover other than that in which it is published and
without a similiar condition including this
condition being imposed on the subsequent purchaser.

A CIP catalogue record for this book is
available from the British Library.

ISBN 0 7515 0173 5

Typeset by Solidus (Bristol) Limited
Printed and bound in Great Britain by
Clays Ltd, St Ives plc

Warner Books
A Division of
Little, Brown and Company (UK) Limited
Brettenham House, Lancaster Place
London WC2 7EN

Sound, sound the clarion, fill the fife!
Throughout the sensual world proclaim,
One crowded hour of glorious life
Is worth an age without a name.

Thomas Osbert Mordaunt, 1791

ACKNOWLEDGEMENTS

I owe a huge debt of gratitude to the following for their assistance and encouragement during the preparation of this book: Burstead Manor Riding Centre, Martin Lloyd, Carl Parsons, Lucy Ross, Anne Roscorla, Graeme and Irma Stewart-Ross, Victor Tunkel of the Selden Society, Susie Wynn-Williams and particularly my editor, Barbara Boote.

One Crowded Hour is dedicated to an array of angels, without whose support it could never have got off the ground: Jenny Candy, Christopher Chandler, Carol and Christopher Cullen, Linda Deeley, Audrey Eyton, Marjorie Henderson, Rosie Pether, Charles Ross and Graeme and Irma Stewart-Ross.

Stewart Ross, August 1993

CONTENTS

PART 1 *So Prettily Accompanied*

1	The Green Man	3
2	Clement's Inn	30
3	Pickering House	63
4	Ebgate Lane	93
5	The George	123
6	Tyburn	154
7	Hampton Court	189

PART II *The Tailor's Daughter*

8	Milk Street	219
9	Newmarket	251
10	St Andrew Undershaft	280
11	Blackmore Street	310
12	Royston	337
13	Stratton Audley Manor	366

PART III *Our Beloved Subject*

14	Godington Grange	397
15	Moseley Hall	425
16	Old Tailor's House	457
17	The Bleeding Stag	485
18	The Four Tuns	516
19	The White Cliffs	544
20	St Nicholas, Southfleet	571

PART I

SO PRETTILY ACCOMPANIED

SHALLOW I was once of Clement's Inn, where I think they will talk of mad Shallow yet.
SILENCE You were called 'lusty Shallow' then, cousin.
SHALLOW By the mass, I was called anything. And I would have done anything indeed too, and roundly too.

From the second part of HENRY IV, Act III, scene ii

ONE

THE GREEN MAN

i

2nd September, 1622.

Potscombe stood silent and deserted as a plague village. Since the feast of St Bartholomew, when the great heat wave had extended its clammy grip south over the whole country, every able-bodied man and woman had been toiling in the fields from morning till dusk to gather in the precious harvest.

The stillness was eerie. On either side of the empty high street cottage doorways gaped like landed fish. The lead on the church roof cracked and wrinkled in the sunshine, while around the green the leaves of ancient oaks rustled in the whisper of warm breeze. Only the incessant buzzing of flies and the cries of children chasing lizards in the dust disturbed the heavy peace of late-summer heat.

As the chimes of five o'clock faded away, Jane Wagstaffe wrapped a thin shawl round her shoulders and slowly emerged from her hovel. With a toothless curse, she tapped her way along the baked ridge of the gutter to the King's Head and lowered her meagre frame onto a shaded bench. Her handicap and the frailty of age had rendered her unsuited to anything but token childminding, and while her thin, agile fingers stuffed tobacco into the bowl of a clay pipe, she argued absent-mindedly with a knot of scruffy girls on the opposite side of the street.

All at once her sharp ears picked out the sound of a horseman approaching down the road from Oxford. Breaking off her wrangling, she cocked her head like a sparrow. Soon the street was echoing to the slow, flat clop of hoofs as the rider carefully steered his chestnut mare between ruts. The children stopped their games and stared.

He rode with easy confidence, a well-dressed young man, no more than eighteen years old, powerfully built and above middle height. An embroidered jerkin was slung casually over heavy saddle-bags. Long brown curls fell from beneath the shadow of his broad-rimmed hat and bounced lightly against the shoulders of his linen shirt. His fresh and beardless face was marked by strong, well-formed features – a flattering painter would have had little trouble in making him the subject of a handsome portrait. A more honest or skilful artist, however, might have captured the hint of arrogance behind the small brown eyes and mobile mouth. Above all, it was the contradiction between lips hovering on the verge of an insolent smile and a frequently scowling expression that most marred Nature's efforts at perfection.

When the horse was almost level with her, Jane raised her head and demanded in a high-pitched screech, 'And who might you be, riding so pretty through Potscombe without so much as a word to poor Jane?'

The girls nudged each other and whispered. The old crone's abrupt confrontations with strangers were always worth witnessing.

Pulling easily on the reins, the traveller brought his horse to a halt and turned in Jane's direction. His brow furrowed as if he were troubled by the glare of the sun. 'I might ask the same of you, old woman,' came the curt reply. The voice was cultured, with barely a trace of an Oxfordshire accent.

'Oh! A young gentleman, are we? And one that believes himself so mighty, too!' Years of practice had made Jane expert at discerning the character and station of those who answered her abrupt challenges. 'And where might the likes of you be travelling this fine afternoon?' she went on. 'Youngsters with sap in their bones are chasing molls in the straw at such a time, not riding all high and haughty by themselves.'

The children giggled. They knew the routine well and waited eagerly to see what would happen.

When the stranger did not reply, Jane persevered with her goading. 'Got no wench then, sir? You takes your pleasure from a saddle does you? Or maybe it's lads as what you want?'

The rider's frown darkened in anger. Clearly unaccustomed to being addressed with such a lack of deference, he swung down from the saddle and strode towards his tormentor. 'Woman,' he muttered, 'mind your sluttish tongue! Or you shall feel ...' He paused, suddenly aware of Jane's affliction.

'You'll not strike poor Blind Jane, will you, sir? She means you no harm. By our saviour's holy blood she don't!'

The youth's anger subsided as quickly as it had arisen and there was genuine repentance in his voice. 'No, indeed, good woman, though I wish you would keep a more kindly tongue in your head. From my saddle,' he explained with a frown of contrition, 'I could not see your sightless eyes.'

Jane laughed and held out a thin, cracked hand in a gesture of reconciliation. As the youth took it, she drew him onto the bench beside her. 'Now, my gallant young man,' she cackled, 'I see all. Don't mock! Jane has no eyes, but she sees better than those that do. And you're a pinch like me, sir, aren't you?'

'How is that, old woman? I can see the world, you cannot.'

'Ah! I know. But you don't see it proper, do you? Not quite sharp.' She felt the stranger's hand stiffen.

'What do you mean?'

'I mean, sir peacock, that your eyes are weak. You have need of spectacles. Yet you won't wear them, will you? Or else you'd have seen my blindness, even from up there on your great horse.'

'There is some truth in what you say,' replied the youth in a voice that revealed a mixture of relief and irritation. 'But—'

'I know,' she interrupted. 'Jane knows all. But you're a vain one, aren't you? You won't wear them 'cause you don't want your pretty looks all spoiled, do you?'

'It may be so.'

'It is. We share the same curse. It took me stronger, of course. But it's the same. 'Now,' she went on, turning her sightless gaze towards the humbled stranger, 'I pray you tell me your name and whither you are travelling. Perhaps Jane can help you. I know much, as I have shown.'

The traveller was in no great hurry. He also had a superstitious desire not to annoy a woman gifted with such uncanny perception. Like most of his contemporaries, he believed in witchcraft — and feared it. 'My name is Tom Verney,' he began, 'of Stratton Audley, some miles from here.'

'I know where it is,' Jane replied quickly. 'So you're not one of the mighty Verneys then?'

'Sadly, no. They are cousins. But my father is Justice John Verney, a gentleman with lands and some wealth. We are no mean folk.'

'No, maybe you are not,' said Jane with a smile. 'I have heard talk of John Verney. But you, young Verney, what brings you to the high road?'

'I am travelling to London, where I am to study the law of Chancery at Clement's Inn. And I am to attend the court.' He spoke with pride.

'The court? The Scottish King James's court? By God's blood, sir! Hold fast to your virtues. I have heard tales of what happens to young men at court. It is not the place it was in Queen Bess's day.'

'That may be so. But I can look after myself.'

'Can you, sir? Can you? When you can't see fine?' She felt him wince. 'Well, you must be on your way. But before you ride on so proud, let Blind Jane say what she will. We share the curse, you see, Tom, and I would help all who suffer as we do.'

He was growing restless, and did not appreciate the blunt references to his short-sightedness, particularly in terms of a curse. As Jane had pointed out, his disability was something he preferred not to acknowledge. Creasing up his eyes, he glanced towards the children to see if they were listening. Then he rose to his feet, whistled for his horse and bade Jane be quick with what she had to say, for he had to be over the Chiltern Hills by nightfall.

'I have this to say, Tom Verney. Listen tight to Jane. Beware those hills before you. They say there's vagrants there. Good men and bad. The villains set on a man last week and killed him, and they haven't been seized yet.'

'I thank you for your warning – I will take care. Now I must be on the road. Farewell. And God be with you.' So saying, he walked to his horse and swung gracefully into the saddle.

'But hold a while longer, sir. I have more yet,' Jane called after him.

He paused. 'Yes? Not just robbers on the highway?'

'More than that, Tom vain Verney. Wear those spectacles, my boy. Watch the world close. Beware your vanity. I was young once and I could see then, too. But I didn't look. Jane knows. Blind Jane Wagstaffe knows all. Look all round – but most of all, look inside.'

Tom touched the side of his horse with his heels and began to move off down the street, calling casually over his shoulder, 'Farewell, old woman. I thank you for your words.'

'Farewell, Master Verney. Don't thank me. We cursed ones must stick fast. Mind you watch the world, or it will bite you!'

Jane sighed, running her crooked fingers along the bench to find her pipe and summoning one of the children to come and light it for her. By the time Tom had ridden out of the village and into the shimmering green-yellow quilt of the countryside beyond, she was drawing contentedly at rich Indies tobacco, sending clouds of white smoke into the spreading branches of the tree above. But between puffs she could be heard muttering disconsolately to herself, 'Watch, Tom Verney. Watch, or the world will bite you. Tom vain Verney.'

ii

From Potscombe, the London road – in places as much as fifty yards wide – meandered in lazy curves through rich, undulating farmland before rising steeply onto the chalky slopes of the Chilterns. Trotting steadily along, Tom pondered the words of Blind Jane. 'So the world will bite me, will it?' he said to himself. 'We'll see about that.' His father had given him more than enough of that sort of advice before he left home, and within half an hour of leaving the village he had all but forgotten the old crone's unsolicited warning.

He had received Princess as a parting gift from his parents. She was a strong horse, and despite the burden of her rider and his bulky saddle-bags, she seemed scarcely to notice the incline as the highway lifted from the vale towards the scarp ahead. By now the difficult surface of dried mud had given way to smoother chalk, and unfenced common had replaced arable land. The few trees, mostly great beeches whose leaves were already fringed with autumn bronze, stood in thick clumps where the ground was level enough for them to take root. All around a profusion of wild flowers released their scent into the evening breeze.

Leaning back in the saddle, he drew a long breath of cool, perfumed air. For two years he had dreamed of this moment. He was free, his own master. He could scarcely remember ever being so happy.

Half a mile or so below the summit, where the incline was steepest, the road narrowed and began to zigzag like a white lace up the emerald bodice of the hill. Tom dismounted and led Princess by the reins. Twenty minutes later they were at the top.

Ahead, the highway divided into several tracks before

entering a small wood. Behind, the Oxfordshire countryside lay like an immense pastoral tapestry, a glimmering wash of green, brown and amber. He screwed up his eyes. As the fine view was just a blur of colours to his myopic gaze, he looked round to see that he was not observed, opened one of the leather satchels hanging by Princess's flank and drew out his spectacles.

The effect was little short of miraculous. To the left, before the dipping sun, he could just make out the Vale of the White Horse, while on his right the rich Vale of Aylesbury stretched towards the darkening horizon. He smiled and lifted his hand to remove his spectacles – it would never do to be seen wearing them. Why, he might be mistaken for a schoolboy or, worse, a clerk.

Just then he heard a sound behind him. He turned quickly, his hand still raised to his face. For the second time in five minutes he was grateful that he could see clearly. In the trees, some twenty yards distant, he could just make out the figure of a man flitting through the shadows. What had Blind Jane said? 'Beware those hills...'

'Thank you, Jane,' he whispered to himself. 'A double debt.'

Remounting his horse, he took stock of the situation. As the evening was drawing on, the most sensible course of action would be to return to Potscombe and find accommodation for the night there. But as the village was a fair ride away he would be lucky to get there before dark; besides, he did not wish to confront Jane again and have to confess his debt to her in public. Knowing that he could find a bed at Stokenchurch, only three miles down the road, and telling himself that the figure in the trees was probably only a poor cottager searching for firewood, he decided to press on towards London. Only long afterwards did he realise what a momentous decision it had been.

He took a brace of flintlock pistols from their holsters, primed them and tucked them into his belt. Then, making sure that the hilt of his sword was uncovered so that he could draw it swiftly if the need arose, he chose what seemed the widest of the several paths, touched Princess's sides with his spurs and advanced slowly into the wood.

He had gone no more than a dozen yards before he realised that he had made the wrong choice. It was an ideal place for an ambush. Arching above the track like a church vault, the dense canopy of leaves and branches cut out all but a few splintered shafts of sunlight. On either hand the broad boles of the trees, deep in shadow, could have hidden a whole army, let alone a band of robbers.

His pulse quickened. Whispering to Princess to steer her own course, he laid down the reins and drew out one of the pistols and his sword. In front he saw the path growing narrower still. He glanced over his shoulder to see if there was room to turn.

Not a moment too soon.

Without his hearing, two men had slipped out of the cover of the trees and were running silently towards him. Their intention seemed clear. The taller of the two, a huge, bearded fellow, surprisingly well dressed for a common thief, yet with the 'V' brand of a vagrant burned indelibly into his forehead, carried a short, thick staff in his left hand. He ran like a bear, closing on Tom with long, lumbering strides. His scrawny and weasel-faced partner, clothed in rags, padded along a short distance behind brandishing a broken, rusty sword. When Tom turned the Bear was no more than six feet away.

Swinging round in the saddle, he levelled his pistol and

squeezed the trigger. As his arm jerked backwards, a loud crack reverberated through the trees, shattering the calm of the evening. Princess leapt forward, almost throwing him from her back. All over the wood rooks rose screaming into the air.

Through a cloud of caustic smoke, he saw the Bear drop his club and sink to his knees, clutching at his stomach. Blood oozed between his fingers from a dark rent in his doublet. Startled by what had happened, his crony stopped in his tracks. He stood there, waving his sword and cursing, calling on Tom to get down off his horse and fight.

'Christ's eyes!' he screamed, as Tom threw down his spent pistol and fumbled for the second one. 'Pox pizzle! May God strike you dead for what you've done, glass-eyed coward!'

By now Tom had managed to tear his other pistol from its holster. As he raised it to shoot, he noticed that his foul-mouthed target was not looking at him. Although still pouring obscenities in Tom's direction, his eyes were fixed on something further down the track.

With horror Tom realised that there must be others in the gang. Ignoring Weasel-face, who seemed more intent on throwing insults than blows, he turned, simultaneously spurring Princess forward and grabbing the reins with the hand already holding his sword.

As he feared, two more footpads were advancing towards him. Finding themselves discovered before they had reached their target, the men tried in vain to get out of the way of the horse's flying hoofs. Princess struck the man on the left head on, winding him and sending him spinning into the bracken beside the track. His colleague ran off into the trees before Tom could get within pistol range.

Bringing Princess up sharply, he wheeled round. The Bear lay groaning on the ground. Weasel-face had obviously had enough and was nowhere to be seen. But the third robber was struggling shakily to his feet. Once again Tom urged Princess into a canter. By the time he had reached the spot where his assailant had fallen, the man was stumbling back into the woods.

Tom halted and took aim. His second shot was less accurate than the first. The man grabbed the back of his thigh as the ball hit him, but he did not go down. A few seconds later he had limped further into the undergrowth and was out of sight.

Pursuit was out of the question. For all his confident rashness, Tom was not prepared to follow three desperate men into a wood which they must have known as well as their own filthy fingernails. His first thought was to get back into the open and ride to Stokenchurch as quickly as possible. The fight had lasted no more than a couple of minutes. During it he had acted instinctively. Now, as he sat breathing heavily, his heart pounding like a drum, he was overcome by a flood of conflicting emotions. Fear, excitement, anger and, above all, pride jostled in his brain. Single-handed, he told himself, showing great fortitude and not a little skill, he had beaten off four assailants. He could not wait to tell someone.

Low moans reminded him that he was not alone on the field of his victory. Watching and listening for any sign of a counter-attack, he replaced his pistol and rode cautiously back to the wounded Bear.

The huge fellow was in a pitiable condition, lying on his side, groaning and holding his stomach. Blood was still seeping from his wound onto the ground. Hearing someone approach, he slowly raised his large, shaggy head.

Tom looked down into the branded face. Above wide, surprisingly warm brown eyes, the man's brow furrowed with pain. Tom was unsure what to do. Should he ride off and leave the fellow? Perhaps he should dispatch him with his sword? Then, as he sat there trying to make up his mind, to his utter amazement the fellow smiled. It was a gesture of acknowledgement, even of admiration, and the moment Tom saw it his heart softened.

He dismounted and gathered up his discarded pistol. Kneeling beside the rogue who only minutes before had apparently intended to kill him, he asked, 'Is it grievous?', surprising himself with the gentleness of his enquiry.

'Maybe yes, maybe no,' the man replied in a deep, quiet voice tinged with an accent Tom could not readily place. 'When my time is come, my time is come. God alone will decide.' The effort of speaking brought flecks of blood to his lips.

'But in the name of the Holy Mother of Our Lord,' he continued, feebly moving fingers as if to cross himself, 'I pray you bear me no malice, young sir. These are racking times for the likes of us. I would fain have done you harm.'

Tom picked up the man's staff and held it before his face. 'No harm? Then what is this, you wretch?'

'A simple staff, such as all men carry.' A twinkle flashed across his pain-dulled eyes. 'A splinter from the true cross, perhaps?'

Before Tom could reply, a voice began calling in the woods to their left, 'John! Great John! Here, sirrah!'

Tom rose to his feet. 'So, Great John they call you, do they?' His victim gave a slight nod. 'Well, Great John, vagrant and blasphemer, young Tom Verney will not kill you, although he knows he should.' Conceit mingled with kindliness in his tone. 'Your ill-chosen companions will be here shortly and I have no wish to meet with them again.'

Staring at the wounded man one last time, he unfastened his water bottle and, with a gesture that belied the arrogance of his words, placed it beside him. 'Farewell, Great John. In future choose your company more wisely, even if it is only from among God's angels. Farewell.'

Seconds later he was back in the saddle and riding at a gallop down the path towards the security of the open countryside.

Half a mile beyond the woods he slowed Princess to a walk. Behind him the sky was blushing with the hues of a glorious sunset. Clouds of midges hung like smoke, and the soft evening air was filled with the familiar cacophony of bleating sheep and the raucous call of rooks.

Amid the pastoral sights and sounds he had known all his life, he felt deeply secure. His adventure already seemed strangely unreal. Only when he raised his hand to mop the sweat from his brow and found that he was still wearing his spectacles, was he convinced that he had not been dreaming. So, telling himself that he had noticed the world carefully enough for one day and that it was now the world's turn to notice him, he wrapped his spectacles in cloth, replaced them in his saddle-bag and rode proudly on to Stokenchurch.

iii

The Green Man was one of the more popular stopping points on the Oxford road. Built on a stout timber frame towards the end of Queen Elizabeth's reign, it boasted ample stabling, spacious rooms and excellent fare. But it was the personality of the landlord, Robin Goodfellow, that was most responsible for the hostelry's good name.

His reputation had spread even to Tom's home village of Stratton Audley, which was one reason why Tom had decided to run the gauntlet of the woods and make for Stokenchurch that evening.

He reached the village at dusk. As he reined in Princess beneath the painted sign, the windows of the inn were already aglow with candlelight, and from the open door the sound of lively conversation and laughter drifted into the street. He immediately warmed to the place. At least there would be an audience to listen to the tale of his recent prowess. Seconds later his feelings of approbation were confirmed when, as he jumped down from the mare and started to lead her towards the stables at the rear of the building, he was hailed by a voice as rich and generous as Canary wine.

'Sir! May we be of service?'

'Indeed, you may be able to assist me,' Tom replied, hesitating to commit himself until he was near enough to see who addressed him. 'I require a good room and plenty to eat, for I have ridden far, and not without adventure.'

'Then, sir, you need travel no further,' the voice exclaimed.

A short, flame-headed, barrel-bodied man approached out of the gloom and grasped Tom warmly by the hand. 'Robin Goodfellow, sir. Your host and servant. You will find the Green Man provides a gentleman traveller with all the comforts he may desire. "All the Comforts", that is my motto. And by the stars,' he concluded with a boastful chuckle, 'I have not been found wanting yet!'

Tom was suddenly aware how much the day's excitement had taken out of him. He was ravenously hungry. 'That being so, Mr Goodfellow,' he replied, 'I would be only too pleased to pass the night under your roof.'

No sooner were the words out of his mouth than his

host was bellowing like a bull for the ostler. 'Peter! Peter, come here you dung cake! What, Peter, I say! Are you deaf?'

A young lad came scurrying round the corner of the inn, tugging on a greasy cap with one hand and rubbing his eyes with the other. 'Yes, Mr Goodfellow?'

'Look sharp, Peter. This gentleman is to rest here tonight. Take his horse, groom her and feed her well. And if you do not, by the stars, I'll ...'

'You'll wrap me in a parcel and send me to the King of Spain, Mr Goodfellow?' Peter quipped, clearly having heard the threat many times before.

To Tom's surprise Goodfellow did not fly into a rage at the lad's presumption but roared with good humoured laughter. 'Peter, you know your master too well. Now, be off with you.' Without further ado, Peter helped Tom unfasten his saddle-bags and led Princess away to the stables.

'Too familiar by half, that boy,' Goodfellow observed with a grin as the ostler disappeared into the gloom. 'And now, sir, if you would be so good as to follow me ...'

News of Tom's exploit spread rapidly round Stokenchurch and by eight o'clock that evening quite a crowd had gathered at the inn to hear his story. After sending a message to the local justice, requesting him to call at the inn at his earliest convenience, he had handed over his baggage to the landlord, changed his riding clothes and come down to address the audience waiting for him in the tap room. Now he sat on the edge of a table answering questions, his legs swinging casually beneath him. Feeling it necessary to retell the tale of his victory for the benefit of every fresh arrival, he had delivered it four times, giving more or less the same version on each occasion.

Had he not been so carried away by his own eloquence, however, he might have noticed that the audience's reaction had not been quite as enthusiastic as he might have expected.

'How many do you reckon they were, sir?' an aged labourer asked, passing Tom's beaker back to Robin Goodfellow to be refilled.

Tom hesitated. 'Well, old fellow, four I saw for certain. But there were more, by God! I heard them shouting in the woods. But, yes, only four dared come out into the open.' He sat back and grinned.

'No bows?' a woman enquired quietly.

'No. Not that I saw.'

'Ain't that odd, sir, seeing as they was intended on killing you?'

The point had not occurred to Tom before, and it puzzled him. 'I would fain have done you harm', Great John had said. Yes, it was strange that they had not shot at him from the cover of the trees. Yet the sword and the cudgel ...

'Oh, for certain they wished to kill me, good woman. I saw it in their eyes.' He spoke confidently, for his own benefit as much as the questioner's.

'Ah!' sighed a thick-set fellow with hands like braised steak. 'Would you know them again if they was taken, sir?'

'Recognise them?' Tom replied without thinking. 'Of course I'd recognise them. Sure enough to see them hanged.'

As he spoke, so cocky and confident, John's sad smile floated before his eyes, and he heard again the deep voice pleading, 'These are racking times for the likes of us ...'

Tom took a deep draught of wine. Putting down his beaker, he added with a measure of uncertainty in his voice, 'At least, I think I would recognise them. It was quite dark in there. Most fled, and the one I hit, well, I didn't wait to pass the time of day with him.' The crowd muttered its approval.

Gradually realising that there was something he did not quite understand about the whole incident, Tom decided he had said enough. He rose, and the audience parted like the Red Sea to let him through.

Robin Goodfellow, red-faced and beaming, was waiting for him by the foot of the stairs. 'You'll be taking your supper now, sir?' he enquired, eager to make the best possible impression on his celebrated guest.

'I shall, landlord. Have it brought to my room directly. And when Justice Fuller gets here, please send him up so that we can converse in private.'

Aware that all eyes were still on him, Tom climbed the dark oak stairs with as much dignity as he could muster and crossed the landing to his room.

As soon as he had shut the door behind him, he was aware that he was not alone. 'Who's there?' he asked, peering round in the dim light of the two candles placed on a table by the fireplace.

'Only me, sir. Rosemary Searle, the chambermaid.' The young voice was gentle yet confident. 'I beg your pardon, sir, only Mr Goodfellow bid me as I was to make sure that your bed was all prepared and comfortable.'

As she stepped out from behind the bed hangings, Tom frowned to get a better look at her. As so frequently happened, the expression was misinterpreted.

'Oh, I pray you don't be angry, sir!' she pleaded, clasping her hands together. 'I was only doing my bidding and seeing to your comforts.'

Tom recalled Goodfellow's motto – 'All the Comforts' – and wondered if he detected a hint of playfulness behind her words. He stepped closer to the maid to see her better. She was a handsome girl, about his own age, with long dark hair, green eyes and an unusually clear complexion. Standing with her hands on her hips and meeting his gaze with a steady stare, she was patently aware of her attractions without trying to flaunt them.

'I am not angry, Rosemary,' he reassured her. 'And I, well, I am glad that you are attending to my comforts.'

The unsubtle boldness of his remark raised a flush of colour on his cheeks, for there was something about the girl's bearing which rather unnerved him — she was alluring, yet unapproachable on the terms to which he was accustomed. He wished he had had more experience with women.

'I do my best, sir.' A wistful smile played along her pretty lips. 'Especially as you're someone special here, aren't you, sir?'

Half flattered, half embarrassed, he blushed still deeper. 'That may be so,' he shrugged, aware of the bulge distorting the front of his loose-fitting breeches.

If Rosemary noticed this outward manifestation of his inner turmoil, she did not let it be known. 'I mean your fighting and all that,' she explained quietly, before asking permission to leave.

'Of course. Will you be bringing supper?'

'Yes, Master Thomas. As soon as it is prepared.'

Without another word, she walked slowly from the room. Tom watched her go, trying to imagine the body beneath her rustling, long white gown.

iv

To Tom's annoyance his supper arrived at the same time as the local magistrate, Justice Christopher Fuller, and he had no chance to pursue further his dalliance with Rosemary. He had met Fuller before, at a meeting of justices at Stratton Audley Manor. He had disliked him then, and this fresh encounter only served to confirm his antipathy.

Fuller was a tall, thin-limbed man of about forty. His hair and deep-set eyes were of equal blackness, and his long, yellow nose was sharply hooked, like the beak of a hawk. The harshness of his bodily appearance was complemented by sombre clothing and religious views of narrow-minded ferocity that were known throughout four shires. It was said that the only thing he ever laughed at was the story of the failure of the Gunpowder Plot. 'A damned mean-minded puritan skeleton', Justice Verney had dubbed him after one of their gatherings, and no one present had contradicted him.

Already irritated by Tom's presumption in summoning him to the inn, a place he instinctively disliked, Fuller left his young informant standing awkwardly before him while he sat stiffly in a chair and watched in disapproving silence as Rosemary laid a generous supper on the table. When she had gone, without a thought for the youth's hunger or the fact that his meal would be spoilt by the delay, he began his questioning. 'Now, Thomas Verney, tell me all, for this is a serious matter. God Himself will be on your shoulder, so be sure you remember aright.'

Tom went over his story again. Once more, he omitted his conversation with Great John and gave no description of his enemies. The justice's reaction was not generous. 'So, you saved yourself, yet killed no one?' he asked, looking contemptuously up at his informant.

'No, sir,' Tom retorted, hurt that his prowess should be challenged, 'I do not believe I killed anyone. But I scored two hits with two shots.'

Fuller snorted. 'A winged bird may yet fly, young sir. Two hits leave two devils to strike again. You needs improve your shooting if you are to play your part in upholding God's peace.'

'By Jesus,' cried Tom, whose irritation had been fanned to anger by the deliberate condescension, 'are you so certain, sir, that you would have hit either target?'

For a full minute the older man sat staring at the fat congealing on Tom's plate. When he raised his head there was a look of hatred in his eyes.

'Master Verney, you must learn another lesson, too. God's Third Commandment to Moses. Perhaps you do not recall it? "Thou shalt not take the name of the Lord thy God in vain". And in answer to your impertinent question, had I fired two shots, I would have killed two villains. And I would have pursued the others unto death. The Lord God would have steadied my hand and given me courage. Ask yourself why he did not bless you thus, and be ashamed.'

Clenching his fists, Tom made no reply.

'Now,' continued the justice, 'you did not see the faces of these varlets? Think, Verney. Think.'

'I did not,' Tom lied. 'There was no light in the wood.'

'Yet you say two slaves were close enough for you, with your inexpert shooting, to hit them?'

'I could not see their faces.' Even if he had studied his assailants close enough to paint their portraits, he told himself, he would not have said so now.

'Strange, Master Verney. But I heard your father say, when lamenting of your waywardness, that were you but able to see clearly you would be more troublesome than you were already. Ah! Perhaps you are in need of spectacles?'

Tom almost burst with rage. 'I can see well enough, I thank you.' The remark was not acknowledged until, with great reluctance, he had added 'sir'.

The interview was soon concluded. As the justice rose to leave, he broached the question of Tom's assailants yet again. 'Perhaps when you are refreshed,' he suggested, 'God will sharpen your wits enough for you to recall more clearly the details of your adventure. If it happened at all.'

Tom could hardly believe his ears. But before he could object, Fuller went on, 'There is one man we seek above all others, Master Verney. A murderous and false papist who goes by the name of John. To their enduring shame, the ignorant call him "Great John", a title he deserves only for the great and many crimes he has committed. I had him branded for a vagrant a while back. Now he has taken to the woods with other thieves and murderers. A tall, bearded, ox-bodied villain. Think on it. Perhaps on the morrow you will recall seeing such a slave?'

'I saw no such man,' Tom insisted. 'Is he so vile?'

His hand on the door latch, the justice turned and stared hard at Tom. 'He is, indeed, young man.' The puritan's righteous fury then drew from him words he might not have uttered in a calmer moment. 'My daughter is with child, sir. This John is the father. I would have him whipped, nay – burned!'

The door slammed and he was gone.

By the time Rosemary returned to clear the dishes, Tom's anger had long since evaporated. The better part of a bottle of French wine and Goodfellow's plentiful supper, excellent despite the efforts of Justice Fuller to ruin it, had restored his spirits to their former buoyancy. He lay back on the pillows of his bed, screwing up his eyes to watch the maid as she busied herself at the table.

'Is there some wine remaining, Rosemary?' he asked, knowing full well that there was.

'There is, sir. Shall you be wanting it now?'

'I have drunk sufficient. Perhaps you would care for a bumper yourself?'

'A bumper, sir? At this time of night?' Looking towards him, holding the neck of the bottle in both hands, she spoke slowly, seeming to address her questions more to herself than to Tom. 'I have to be careful about what I takes on board at night, for I needs be about my business with the cock-crow.'

Tom was out of his depth. Was she teasing him, he wondered, or was there genuine tenderness in her voice? His previous sexual experience had been limited to hasty, chaste kisses with Anne Hutchinson, a neighbouring landowner's daughter for whom he felt a deep affection, and half a dozen quickly consummated romps with the young wife of one of his father's tenants. He sensed that despite her lack of years, the maid was making the first moves in a game about which he knew very little. He hesitated, anxious, almost afraid – before now he had always regarded games as something to be won or lost.

For a few moments they gazed at each other, wrapped in their own thoughts. Rosemary was the first to move. With a long, deliberate intake of breath she picked up a glass from the table and moved over to the bed.

'Maybe you would pour it for me, sir?' she enquired. 'All the inn is talking of your steady hands.' Again Tom was taken aback by the beguiling mix of flattery and innuendo.

With fingers anything but steady, he took the bottle, poured its contents into the glass held before him and placed the bottle on the floor beside the bed. When he had done so, she sat beside him, her eyes light and honest. With her right hand she lifted the glass to her mouth and drank. As she did so, with a gesture of innocent, almost unwitting affection, she rested her other hand on Tom's knee. He thrilled at her touch.

When she had finished drinking, her lips were wet with wine. 'All gone,' she whispered with feigned childishness. She smiled and looked down at her hand lying on Tom's leg. 'What now, sir?'

He fumbled for words, his throat so dry that he could hardly speak. 'I don't rightly know.'

'Well, Master Verney, might I suggest something?'

'You may, Rosemary.' He felt sure the pounding of his heart could be clearly heard downstairs in the tap room.

She kicked off her shoes and lay down at his side, her lips close to his ear. 'No more games. And them that knows me well calls me Rosy. You wish to know me well, don't you?'

'I do, sweet Rosy. I do.'

'Then might I call you Tom in return?' As he smiled his assent, he felt her hand slide up his thigh. 'Tell me, Tom, about your fighting. About your pistol and all that.' Her tongue was playfully licking his ear as she spoke, sending tingles of delight throughout his whole body.

'My pistol ...?' She turned and closed his mouth with a kiss. He shut his eyes. The conversation went no further.

Rosy's lips were soft and moist and tasted of wine. She opened her mouth and Tom's tongue slid between her teeth in a movement the significance of which he barely understood. He had never known the simple act of kissing to be so pleasurable.

He was wearing only a shirt and breeches. With deft fingers Rosy untied the string at his waist and slipped her hand inside.

'Oh, Rosy!' he groaned, rapidly losing control of himself. Realising what was happening, she grasped him more tightly and eased him to a climax.

Long after the moment had passed he held her fast, half laughing, half crying with pleasure and relief. 'I do not know what to say,' he gasped, finally lying back and staring at the canopy above him. 'Oh, thank you, Rosy! I love you, dearest Rosy.'

'No you don't, silly boy!' she replied with a laugh. 'We're just friends.' An edge of seriousness came into her voice. 'Special friends, if you like. But gentlemen and chambermaids don't go no further than that, whatever their hearts may say. God has given us our places, and it is our duty to hold to them – or risk ruin.'

After a pause she shook her head, as if confirming something to herself, then looked down at his shirt front. 'Holy Mary! What's all that, lover Tom? You were much in need of a gallop, weren't you?'

'I had never felt the like, my dearest,' he said, taking off his clammy garment. 'I could not wait.'

'We'll make it longer next time, won't we? And, Tom, kindly don't forget me neither. Girls is allowed to ride as well as men, you know.'

With a chuckle she rose and stood beside the bed.

'Surely you are not leaving?' he asked anxiously. Although only vaguely aware of his feelings, he knew that the prospect of losing further sexual adventure was not what worried him most.

She smiled. 'Of course not, Tom love. Here, unlace my gown and we can play proper.' Kneeling with her back to him, she turned her head and kissed him. 'Why, you haven't shown me half what your pistol can do, have you, my brave boy?'

Soon they were both lying naked on the bed. The air

was warm, and through the open window the noises of the night came floating in.

Tom stroked Rosy's breasts in wonderment, feeling their nipples rise beneath his fingertips. As he stiffened against her thigh, he ran his hand clumsily over her stomach and pushed it between her legs. She winced slightly.

'Tom,' she whispered, 'you have not been with many women, have you?'

His first reaction was to boast of a hundred adventures between the sheets. But her natural sincerity had broken down his defences, and he found himself confessing, 'No, Rosy. It is a sport I have not much met with. I am an apprentice.'

A profound sense of companionship was growing inside him. He was with someone, alone, with whom he had no need to pretend, no need to assume an air of confidence, with whom he could be himself, as naked emotionally as he was physically. 'Perhaps,' he added quietly, 'you would be my teacher, Rosy?' It was the ultimate confession, an instinctive denial and acceptance of the adulthood he so urgently sought.

'Surely I will. That is what friends is for,' she said softly, taking his hand and drawing it from her. 'Now take heed, student Tom, and I will show you how to make me dance for you.'

She knelt astride him.

By the flickering light of the single candle still burning on the other side of the room, she introduced Tom to a new, mysterious and wonderful realm of joy.

Long into the night mistress and pupil lay this way and that, giggling one minute, panting the next, exploring, giving. When she clasped her legs about his neck, he kissed her tenderly and felt her quiver with delight. Later, as she responded with equal intimacy, he stroked her hair and softly called her name, over and over again, praying that the dawn would never come.

Once, as they lay in the darkness, temporarily exhausted by their loving, Tom felt an unexpected sense of loneliness. 'Rosy,' he asked, seeking reassurance, 'is it me, or is it just . . . just a man?'

She had been half expecting the question. 'Do you really need to ask me, Tom?' she sighed. 'No, my lover, you are not any man. Yet it is not fit we think like this, for it leads only to pain. Our paths lie across different fields. Tonight they meet, tomorrow they will be apart again.'

The words caught at his heart. He tried to pursue the subject further, challenging her sad, fatalistic realism. She had seen more of life than he, however, and would not be drawn.

But when he leaned over to kiss her, to show that he understood, he found her eyes wet with tears. Before he could remonstrate further, with a bitter-sweet gesture that said everything she could not put into words, she took him in her arms, guided him inside her and held him there. Slowly at first, then with mounting sensuality and affection they were lovers for one last poignant time.

Five minutes later, finally tired out by all that had befallen him, Tom was asleep.

'Farewell, my pretty rainbow,' Rosy whispered, rising from the bed and pulling on her gown. By the door she paused and for several minutes looked back to where Tom lay sprawled across the sheets. As she gazed, a fresh breeze stirred the curtains around his bed and the darkness began to melt into the light of a new day.

Tom dreamed that he was travelling along a level highway. Beside him Rosy and Great John walked arm in arm. With one hand John fondled Rosy's breasts, with the other he covered a vivid purple hole in his stomach the size of an apple. They were laughing at Tom.

Looking behind, he saw Justice Fuller at the head of a large crowd. He was screaming at Tom, calling him a liar and calling on God to strike him dead. Tom's father was in the crowd too, and his mother.

When he turned again to Rosy, she had become Blind Jane.

The brand on John's head turned into a cloud, obscuring the road. All was darkness. Tom cried out, 'But where is London? I must get to London.'

The sound of Blind Jane's stick came tapping towards him through the gloom.

Someone was knocking at the door of Tom's room. Opening his eyes, he saw sunlight streaming in through the casement. Before him stood Rosy, holding a tray of food.

'Good morning, sir,' she said pertly. 'I hope you had a good night, sir. Shall I put your breakfast on the table, or will you be taking it in bed?'

TWO

CLEMENT'S INN

i

By the time Tom resumed his journey the sun was already drumming down from a cloudless sky, drying the glistening grass in the pastures and swallowing up the last wisps of mist that lingered in the hollows beside the highway. The thin, white dust rising from Princess's hoofs trailed like wood smoke into the balmy air.

For a while he pondered the last twelve hours. He was troubled. On one hand, the night with Rosy had introduced him to a world he had previously encountered only in fantasy. It had thrilled him, filled him with an arrogant male pride. He longed to boast to someone of his prowess, of the pleasurable dull ache that lingered still in his loins. Yet somewhere deep within him he knew that the sensuous hours of love-making had been more than just a rite of passage. To brag of it as such would be to betray the soft-skinned girl who had lain with him so tenderly and whispered his name like a prayer into the darkness. It would be false to his own feelings, too. He had told her that he loved her — a conventional, almost meaningless phrase — and in her wisdom she had bade him take back his words. But what else could he have said to express the wonder of their instinctive intimacy? He had felt so close, so vulnerable, and yet so utterly at peace, his unashamed physical nakedness mirroring the transparency of his innermost thoughts. Now, for the first time since leaving home, loneliness welled up within him. With all his confused heart he wished that Rosy were riding beside him, a pretty, practical, comforting and true companion.

The events of earlier that morning, however, had confirmed that this could and would never be. He was 'Master Thomas' again and his attempts at intimacy were gently but firmly rebuffed. He reacted with conceited selfishness, at first sulking, half believing that Rosy's distant behaviour betokened a genuine change of heart. When this elicited no response, he became angry, meeting her reserve with childish scorn. Regretting the words as soon as he had spoken them, he muttered in a low voice as she cleared away his breakfast dishes, 'So, my gaudy weathercock, you face one way in the night breeze before swinging round in the morning, do you? Huh! I will find others more constant than you soon enough.'

She stopped what she was doing and bent forward, her head bowed, resting her hands on the table. For a while she stood motionless, her long black hair hanging down over her face like a veil. Beside her Tom sat at the table in silence. He had delivered a painful, foul blow and hated himself for it. As he waited in fearful anticipation, torn between apology and stubborn pride, he saw her tears fall in heavy drops onto the platter before her. His shame mingled uneasily with the thrills of victory and desire.

He put out his hand to take her arm. She moved away, still looking down. 'Please, Tom – Master Thomas – don't do this to me.' The words were softly spoken, little more than a whisper. 'It is not fair, not kindly. Recall what I said last night. It is true, it is. You will understand one day, even if you do not now.' She lifted her head slightly and gazed towards him with wet, sorrowful eyes. 'But do not think ill of me. And, dearest Tom, I pray you do not forget. For sure, I shall not.'

He opened his mouth to reply, but she shook her head and they spoke not another word to each other.

Minutes later, having paid his bill and bade farewell to the ever cordial Robin Goodfellow, Tom climbed into Princess's saddle and rode slowly away from the inn. After a few yards, he glanced back over his shoulder. Did he see a pale face pressed to the glass in an upper casement? Since he was not wearing his spectacles, he could not be certain. He cursed himself for his vanity.

ii

Within an hour he was making his way through the thick woods above Wycombe. Although the shade was welcome after the heat of the open road, memories of yesterday's encounter were still sharp in his mind and, casting anxious looks about him, he hurried down the hill through the beech trees, towards the security of the village in the valley below.

The Carpenter's Arms in Wycombe was an altogether seedier hostelry than Stokenchurch's Green Man. The peeling sign, loosened during a gale the previous winter and not yet secured, hung from the wall like a broken gallows. Soot-blackened window panes clung precariously to their rotten frames, and the dirty brown thatch of the roof was so tattered that it might have been gnawed by a giant rat – if any such creature could have found sustenance in such foul straw. Nevertheless, Tom's throat was as dry as powder, and after narrowing his eyes to get as good a look at the inn as he could manage, he decided that no harm could come of resting there a while to slake his thirst. Tying Princess to a rickety rail beside the road where he could keep an eye on her, he pulled the only serviceable bench he could find into the shade, sat down and ordered the unkempt-looking boy lolling at the inn door to bring him a quart of ale. The brew was better than might have been expected, and he drank greedily, draining the tankard in long gulps. Soothed by the liquor, he realised how tired he was. He lay back against the inn wall and relaxed. Seconds later, he was asleep.

'Young sir! I pray you wake up!' The voice was quiet yet urgent.

Tom opened his eyes, blinking at the brightness. Before him, holding a small brown palfrey by the reins, stood a short, middle-aged man dressed from head to toe in sober black. In stark contrast, his plump face and hands were chalk white, so that against the glare of the sun he seemed to have no flesh at all. For an instant, until his eyes accustomed themselves to the light, Tom thought he was looking at a ghost.

Spectre or not, the fellow's words were real enough. 'Ah! At last! Quick, to your feet, sir! Your horse and possessions – that is your horse I take it? – your horse is being led away yonder. By the saints, make haste! Make haste!'

Tom stood up and stared in the direction the man was pointing. Some thirty yards away up the street he could just make out the shape of a horse. He glanced at the rail to which he had tied Princess when he arrived. She had gone.

Bounding into the road, he called Princess's name. The animal recognised his cry and replied with a whinny. When he saw that he was discovered, the thief determined to hasten his escape.

'He's going to mount her!' shouted the chessboard figure who had alerted Tom to the theft. 'Stop! Thief! A padder, ho!' The voice was shrill and light. No one stirred. All along the street the doors of the houses remained shut tight.

Tom ran forward in pursuit, his spurs clinking like glasses against the flints beneath his feet. He could see Princess more clearly now. As her captor placed a foot in the stirrup, Tom halted in a swirl of dust and bellowed, 'Princess! Here! Come hither!' Confused by the contradictory commands of her master and the stranger at her bridle, the mare pranced sideways. The thief lost his footing and stumbled to his knees.

Yelling again, Tom ran nearer. When he was about fifteen yards distant he saw the robber pick himself up from the road and grab Princess's reins. Once more he prepared to climb into the saddle. Tom was desperate. The villain now seemed certain of getting away. Intending at least to get a clear sight of the man, Tom put a hand into his pocket and drew out his spectacles, still wrapped in cloth.

To his astonishment, this harmless movement was misinterpreted. Believing his pursuer had produced a gun, the thief panicked, dropped the reins and bolted off down the street. Seconds later he had disappeared.

'He has taken nothing,' Tom said with a grin of relief after he had checked Princess's saddle-bags and led her back to the pallid stranger, who was still standing beside his own horse outside the Carpenter's Arms. 'I am indeed fortunate. But I forget myself, sir. I beg your pardon. First I must thank you for saving my horse and all I have to call my own.' He extended his hand in a gesture of greeting and gratitude.

'Ah, well, it was as nothing. As nothing.' The man's hand was cold and limp. 'Simple Christian duty, sir. The Good Lord must be watching over you today. Perhaps you have done something which is pleasing in His eyes? Pleasing, eh?'

Tom was unsure how to take the note of good-humoured mockery in the man's voice. 'Perhaps, sir,' he replied, 'although for sure I do not know what it might be.'

'It is not for us to fathom the ways of the Almighty. Not for us.' He gave Tom a sideways look, one eye squinting downwards, as if drawn by a magnet set at the tip of his sharp, bleached nose.

'No truly,' said Tom, unwilling to offend anyone who had rendered him so kind a service, however odd he might seem. 'My name, sir, is Thomas Verney of Stratton Audley in the county of Oxford. I ride to London to take up residence at Clement's Inn.'

'Ah! Verney. Clement's. It is good. And I, Master Verney, am Doctor Abraham Chillingworth, Canon of Worcester Cathedral. I am journeying to London to meet with Archbishop Abbot.'

Tom's heart sank. The last thing he wanted was the company of a cleric on the road. Noticing his lack of enthusiasm, Chillingworth asked mischievously, 'I see you do not warm to the thought of riding with a man in holy orders?' Once more Tom was surprised by the wry amusement in the man's tone. 'You think my presence will .. um – how shall we say? – enfeeble your spurring? Scare away the game?'

'Indeed no. It would be a great pleasure for us to travel together.'

'Lesson one, Master Verney, if I may be so bold, is to hold fast to the truth. The truth.'

'But—'

'Come now, sir. I may be from the altar, but gentlemen of your ilk have not altered – ahem! – since the days of my youth. Try me. I am in need of a stout companion to fend off high lawyers, such as the knave who would have jarked your beautiful Princess. And you, if I surmise correctly, peradventure might benefit from a little worldly, and even heavenly, wisdom by your side.'

'Well, it may be so.' Tom was unwilling to submit to the extraordinary cleric without at least a token show of resistance. But the loneliness of the morning's ride and the shock of nearly losing Princess made him more amenable to Chillingworth's suggestion than he might otherwise have been. Besides, there was something about the eccentric canon, whose language shifted so easily from the pulpit to the privy, that fascinated him.

'Good. That is good,' Chillingworth concluded. 'Exceeding good. Let us leave with all possible haste this place which God has forsaken and be on our way to London.'

With these words the two men, as incongruous a pair as ever travelled the broad highway to the capital, mounted their horses and rode side by side out of the town.

iii

'Clement's, eh?' The canon was the first to break the

silence. 'So you wish to join that great company of, um, kites who pass by the name of lawyers, do you? Mmm? A lawyer?' He spoke in a high, clipped, sing-song voice.

'My father believes it best for me, sir. He is a justice and hopes that one day I will be called upon to follow in his stead.'

'Ah! I see. So you do what your father bids, do you? Most unusual in a young man, if I may say so.'

'There was no great choice in the matter, Canon. The parish, as my mother said, was too small for us both. My father is not an accommodating man.'

'Few fathers are. Apart, of course, from Our Heavenly Father, eh? He lets His children do what they wish. What they wish. Though He must grieve sorely at what they get up to.'

Tom did not reply.

'Bless me,' Chillingworth chirped, 'I clean forgot. My apologies, Master Verney, for venturing into realms which you, er, do not care to enter.'

'That is not so, sir,' Tom retorted, his cheeks colouring. 'I am as steadfast in our church as any man.'

'As any man, eh? Any man?'

'You know my meaning, sir.' Tom was beginning to regret his choice of company.

The cleric's voice softened. 'Indeed I do, I do,' he replied, turning to Tom with a smile. 'Now, let us leave the marsh of faith – where even I walk with halting steps, yes, halting steps, Master Verney – and walk upon the firm soil of life. Something we can grasp, see and touch, like the body of a bawd, eh?'

Tom looked at his partner in surprise, but found the man's gaze fixed on the road ahead. Chillingworth continued without a pause: 'So, young gentleman, tell me of this father of yours whom you believe to be so – what was it? – unaccommodating.'

Tom needed no second invitation. Drawn by the enigmatic canon's skilful questioning, for the next hour he spoke freely of the events that had led to the decision to send him to London to study the law. It was his version of the story, of course, and there were moments when the canon suggested as much with a shrewd 'It was really so, was it?' or a flattering 'Come now, Master Verney, we are both men of the world, of the hot-blooded world, and understand that matters are not always what they, er, seem, eh?'

Mary Verney, the patient, intelligent wife of John Verney Esquire, Justice of the Peace, had born her husband eight children, four of whom had not survived infancy. Thomas, the eldest, had inherited his father's hot temper, wilfulness – and myopia. Although Tom had been away from home attending the grammar school at Banbury for most of the year, from the age of twelve he and his father had squabbled with mounting bitterness. Both were stubborn, refusing to admit that their mutual animosity stemmed from the similarity of their strong personalities and their determination never to confess that they might be at fault. In the end, over a trivial argument concerning Tom's relationship with the hired hands who worked the Verney estates, whom John believed his son treated in too friendly a manner, the two almost came to blows. It was only the timely intervention of Tom's sixteen-year-old sister Elizabeth that prevented an ugly brawl. A week later Justice Verney had summoned his troublesome son and informed him that he was to leave for the capital at the earliest opportunity to take up residence at Clement's Inn, not the most fashionable of the legal Inns but one where, owing to the good offices of an Oxford attorney,

Gilbert Marshall, Tom could be provided with chambers. 'That way,' the magistrate had growled, 'you may come to learn the true meaning of order and obedience.'

Tom's first thought was to scorn the proposal because it was not of his own devising; but after a little reflection, and not a few wounding remarks about how delighted he would be to free himself from what he called 'this tyrannous state', he went along with his father's wish.

Once the decision had been taken, the atmosphere at Stratton Audley Manor lightened considerably. John Verney arranged for a local magnate, Lord Banbury, who customarily spent at least half the year at his town house in the Strand, to introduce his son at court. A place for Tom was found at Clement's Inn and even Mary Verney was surprised when her husband announced that he was going to give Tom the princely sum of twenty pounds to set himself up in London, with more to follow upon receipt of satisfactory reports of his son's scholarship and behaviour. The gift of Princess was the last and most touching of a number of gestures by which Tom was made aware of his father's obvious – though undeclared – pain at the impending departure of his son, who for his own part made sure that he did and said nothing to resurrect their former hostility. He found himself drawn closer to his mother and sisters, too. Hitherto he had taken for granted their patent love, or even found it irksome; now, as his departure drew ever closer, he understood for the first time what their affection meant to him. The only member of the family for whom he was unable to kindle much fondness, despite the proximity of their separation, was his fourteen-year-old brother, Lucius. Studious, pious, mean and invariably, irritatingly correct, in the family circle he was known with proud litotes as 'little brain'. To Tom he was simply 'little pain'.

The day before he left home, Tom had sat up with his father late into the night. It was the closest they had ever been to each other. While they did not actually apologise for their past behaviour, John's veiled hints about his tempestuous youth, disguised in the form of advice about what his son might meet with in London, and Tom's admission that what he spoke with his tongue and thought in his heart did not always quite marry, meant that their long parting embrace the following morning was charged with sincere warmth.

'Well, there's a life!' said Chillingworth enigmatically when Tom had finished explaining his presence on the road. For the next half-mile, as they ambled along between fields of yellow stubble, the cleric added nothing further. He whistled quietly to himself, not a religious tune but some lewd ditty Tom vaguely remembered hearing intoxicated labourers singing late one night towards the end of a harvest supper. He was hurt. He had not exactly bared his soul, but he had entrusted a complete stranger with an approximate version of his life story only to find that it elicited virtually no response at all.

Eventually he could stand the man's taciturnity no longer. 'Canon Chillingworth,' he began, 'do you find what I have to say so dull that it halts our conversation altogether?' The whistling stopped. 'Do you, sir, have no observation upon what I have said?'

'Ah! Well yes, of course. I do, I do. But where to begin? There's the rub.'

'Well where? You are the preacher, sir.' Although Tom would never have admitted it, not even to himself, he sought advice. And there was something about this canon which, for all his quirkiness, told him that here was a man who might have something useful to say to one in Tom's position. He rode on, waiting.

Chillingworth resumed his whistling. Tom was on the verge of spurring Princess forward, leaving the infuriating little clergyman behind him, when suddenly the man began to sing:

> 'And so young gentlemen out on a hunt
> Beware what you begin;
> For all that looks as sweet as a cunt
> Is bitter gall within.'

Tom was dumbfounded. He was no prude. It was not the obscene language that shocked him, but the fact that it came from the lips of no less a person than a member of one of the most illustrious cathedral chapters in the land.

'That is the text of my, er, homily, young man. Neat, isn't it? The only wise thing that Doctor Laud, whose brief sojourn as Dean of Worcester was as turbulent as it was, um, unwelcome, ever said to me was — now what was it, precisely? — yes, the words were, "Chillingworth, if you don't hold your flock with your opening phrase, then you might as well sit down." A wise observation for a, er, fool, don't you think, eh?'

'Surely. So that verse is your text?'

'It is. It is. Somewhat straight, perhaps. Yet pithy. As the psalmist so rightly says, "Out of the mouth of very babes" — and, one might add, the lower orders — " ... hast thou ordained strength." Truth too. You are not shaken by my lewdness?'

'No. I am not.'

'But of course you are. At least you should be. I am, I am. It is the last stanza, the moral, of a popular piece. Popular with ordinary folk, that is, although I dare say the king would appreciate it as well. You will, of course, remember it? No, you will not. No one ever does. That's the pity.'

'And its meaning?' enquired Tom, reining in Princess while a flock of sheep were herded to one side of the road to allow the horsemen to pass.

'Simple, Master Thomas, simple. Yet so difficult. Take care. That's all. Just take care. Play in the, er, mire – we all do, we can't help ourselves, we are fallen creatures, after all – roll in it, take pleasure in its wetness, its warmth. But make sure you can come out again. Once you are stepped in too far, you have no choice but to wade on, and you will drown. You don't want to drown, do you?'

'No.'

'Neither do I. Rather, well, stuffy.' He paused and took a deep breath, as if confirming to himself the truth of his judgement. 'So, that is my text. "Beware what you begin".'

How is it, thought Tom, that twice since leaving home he had been warned to watch what he did? First Blind Jane and now Canon Chillingworth. Did he appear so naive in their eyes? No, he told himself, I am no fool. I can steer my own course without their cautious pilotage. He straightened his back and threw back his shoulders.

The clergyman had been observing him closely, his bleached face peering out from beneath the broad rim of his hat like a watchful stoat emerging from his hole. 'Ah well,' he sighed, 'I see you have heard it all before. But perhaps you will listen to what remains of my sermon? Its messages may find a warmer welcome in a proud head such as yours.'

Before Tom could either accept or reject the offer, Chillingworth began a detailed sketch of London life. Tom was captivated. Not a single aspect was omitted. He was told where to stay if accommodation at Clement's Inn was not forthcoming, where to have clothes made, how to employ a trustworthy servant – apparently not an easy task in a city teeming with rogues and roisters of every description – and which companies presented the best plays. Of even greater interest and certainly more surprising, particularly as the canon insisted in continuing his 'sermon' in the crowded tavern where the couple stopped to eat in the early afternoon, was advice on how to avoid catching the pox and his belief that the most discreet strumpets were to be found in Southwark, on the southern bank of the Thames. He initiated Tom into a new vocabulary too. As a new arrival in 'Romeville', he would be viewed as a 'gull' or a 'cony' – easy prey, unless he took great care, to the tricks of the city's numerous 'cony catchers', 'shavers', 'nippers' and 'foisters'; and as to the delights of the various 'trugging houses' or 'pick hatches', there seemed no end to the variety of 'queans', 'traffics' and other 'Winchester geese' who would be only too delighted to 'vault' with him – and probably leave him with a dose of the 'French Welcome' to boot.

By the time Tom and his companion had diverted towards Chiswick from the Oxford road and arranged to stay overnight in a comfortable inn near the river – where Chillingworth was greeted warmly and provided with a room he had clearly slept in many times before, even though it meant moving an irate and partly clothed merchant who had just settled down for the night with his young wife – the youth's head was awash with stories and information. If he managed to remember one tenth of it, he told himself, London would surely be his oyster.

After a hearty meal, washed down with two bottles brought from the cellar at the canon's request and for which he insisted on paying, Tom bade good night to his new friend and was shown by a chambermaid to a room beside the canon's. Too exhausted even to notice whether she was pretty or not, he was overtaken by sleep the instant his head touched the pillow.

He had a hazy recollection of being disturbed in the small hours by the sound of laughter in an adjoining room. As he lay in the darkness, more asleep than awake, he believed he could make out two voices, male and female. Although there was something vaguely familiar about the shrill, cultured chuckles of the man, Tom assumed they must have emanated from the dispossessed merchant. But in the morning, when he remembered that the original occupants of Chillingworth's room had transferred to a chamber the other side of the inn, he decided instead that he must have been dreaming.

iv

'Shh, Master Thomas!' Chillingworth snapped loudly. 'Hold your tongue!'

Angry at being addressed so sharply, Tom was about to repeat his jibe about King James's proclivity for the company of handsome young men when, speaking in a quieter, more friendly tone, the canon explained, 'It is not prudent to utter such words in a public place, however, er, innocent of the ways of the political world you might be.'

They had left Chiswick about half an hour before and were now passing through the village of Chelsea. The road was crowded with other travellers, several of whom showed more than a passing interest in the attractive, haughty youth and the chequer-coloured clergyman trotting beside him. The couple's conversation might easily have been overheard.

'And what is wrong with repeating that which is on the lips of every ploughman in the kingdom?' Tom enquired, obliging his companion by keeping his voice down but refusing to let the matter drop. He remembered what Blind Jane had said about the court.

'You are not, as you know full well, a common ploughman. What may pass as innocent banter on the lips of a labourer, is something altogether different in the mouth of a gentleman. Listen.

'A kingdom such as ours may be likened to a great pyramid of Egypt — you might have heard of them? — except that it balances finely upon its point. That point is the king, supported by we few, gentle, well-born folk. Do you follow me? We are fortunate in many ways, but in return it is our duty to assist the king to bear his heavy load. Without our strength and loyalty the edifice cannot stand. If we crumble, the very kingdom itself will crack and fall to a confused jumble of, er, dust and stones. It follows that because of your place in the scheme of things, your utterances — even your thoughts — are of close concern to the government. It will mark them nicely, while those of lesser men may be happily ignored. They cannot shake the symmetry of the state, you can.'

'Perhaps it would be better, sir Canon, if the pyramid were stood the other way up? Then might it rest more secure on a broader foundation.'

'Oh, hot-headed sir, I pray you, for your own safety, do not entertain such thoughts. Have you been drinking at the well of Aristotle? You speak like a Geneva man. If that is truly what you think, it were better you took yourself to some German Presbyterian den, or to a dreary settlement in the vasty wastes of the New World.'

'I would not exchange the rule of law for that of priests,' Tom answered without thinking. 'Besides, I do not rightly know what I think of government matters, although I intend to learn.'

'I hope you do. Indeed I hope you do.' There was an edge to Chillingworth's voice which Tom had not met before, and although he tried to humour his mentor by asking his advice on a range of practical matters, including how he should conduct himself at court, he was unable to recapture their former friendliness before they parted company.

One passage of their subsequent conversation stuck in Tom's mind for some time. In reply to a guarded, tactful enquiry about the king, Chillingworth replied that James was not to be underestimated. 'You will learn for yourself, young Verney, not to judge the soundness of woodwork by its paint. In the meantime, I pray you heed what more experienced carpenters have to say.' Tom glanced sideways at the speaker, wondering what worms gnawed away beneath his pristine surface.

Showing no indication that he recognised the irony of his previous remark, the clergyman continued that even though the king was now elderly and not in good health, he retained his clear perception and shrewd judgement. He was no Elizabeth, of course, but that was not necessarily something to bemoan, for the Stuart court was a brighter place than its Tudor counterpart, a brilliant centre of art, music and drama. 'There may be,' he concluded, 'what some refer to as a less, er, seemly side – although I have no knowledge of that – but one cannot hold a banquet without some guests taking a tipple too many, can one?'

'No, I suppose not,' said Tom with a laugh. 'Yet you surprise me, Canon, by professing ignorance of what you term the less seemly side of life. After what you told me yesterday, I would have thought ...'

'Do not think! Yesterday we engaged in idle prattle on the road. It meant nothing. Mere travel talk.' For the second time since leaving home Tom felt a wave of loneliness washing over him. He seemed to have made and lost two friends in as many days.

The feeling of emptiness did not last. Within a few minutes it had been replaced by a prodigious sense of wonder, for they were nearing the sprawling suburb of Westminster, once a royal retreat from the troublesome city, but now swallowed up in the conurbation which King James complained would soon devour all England. It was not so much the buildings, little more than blurred outlines to his short-sighted gaze, as the sheer vibrant complexity of life around him that made the greatest impression on his provincial sensibilities: never before had he seen such a teeming mass of mankind, all jostling together between the ceaseless traffic of horses, carts and coaches of every size and description, while dogs, cats, chickens and other domestic creatures sniffed and scratched their way through the multitude, dumbly indifferent to the chaos about them. Having visited Oxford on many occasions, Tom was no stranger to city life. But this was a totally different experience, beside which the measured bustle of the university town, for all the self-conscious exuberance of its students, seemed the very personification of sleepiness. He was familiar enough with beggars, but never before had he set eyes on such wretched, misshapen creatures as now pitifully stretched forth their arms towards him from the gutters and dark corners beside the street, blessing him to heaven as he approached, then cursing him most foully as he passed by without putting his hand to his purse. Hawkers and street vendors were plentiful in any town, but here they infested the thoroughfare like flies, shouting, singing, crying their meagre wares in an unending discordant symphony of din. Bakers and blacksmiths, milliners and manservants, soldiers, apprentices, actors, ballad-sellers, puppeteers, water carriers, flower girls, city officials and cutpurses thronged the street, some urgently pressing ahead to distant destinations, others standing around idly in the September sunshine.

The warm weather had not yet broken and the further they rode into the easterly breeze the more overwhelming the stench became: a pungent combination of sweat, both human and animal, putrefying rubbish, dung, pitch and sewage, occasionally lightened by the aroma of spicy cooking as they passed an open tavern door. 'Here,' called Chillingworth, whose eyes shone with increasing brightness as they moved nearer towards the ancient city walls, 'pass me your handkerchief.' Tom watched as the canon deftly pulled out a small bottle of rosewater from his pocket and sprinkled some of its contents onto the linen square. 'Hold this to your nose. It will sweeten the stench of this glorious sink.'

Chillingworth was just drawing out his own handkerchief with the intention of providing himself with a similar barrier of fragrance, when a woman suddenly grabbed the bridle of his horse and brought him to a halt. Reining in Princess, Tom sat and watched to see what would happen. Once more, the unusual cleric surprised him.

From her appearance there was no doubting the woman's profession. Her long blue gown, torn and muddied at the hem, was cut away at the front to reveal most of her bosom. Red hair hung untidily over a grubby ruff, stained with make-up around the neck. The harlot's face might have been attractive once, but what the ravages of smallpox had begun, several seasons on the London streets had most cruelly completed. Only her eyes, gleaming brightly within a mask of white powder, showed that she had not yet totally despaired of her wretched existence.

'Mister Cannon! Here, give us a kiss you hoyting little slate-staining white minister you!' Her voice was loud and hoarse. As far as Tom could see, there were more gaps in her mouth than teeth.

'Molly!' Chillingworth answered with deliberate restraint. 'What, are you still at your wicked ways, you naughty child, eh?'

'And why not? When in the name of God's sweet pizzle have you been one to complain? You still requiring your shillingsworth?' The remark obviously caused the canon some embarrassment, for he glanced up at Tom with an insincere smile and closed his squinting eye in a rather feeble parody of a wink. Bending down, he whispered something in the whore's ear. She looked up towards Tom.

'Oh! Mister Verney, is it?' She took a couple of steps in Tom's direction, fixing him with a brazen stare. 'Quite a fine gull, aren't you, sir? And we all know as what young country' — she pronounced the word slowly, laying heavy stress on the first syllable — 'morts are after in Romeville, don't we?'

Unsure whether he should reply to this flamboyant greeting in like manner, Tom frowned in an effort to see the woman more clearly. Molly took his look as a rebuff.

'Suit yourself, Mister High-and-Mighty Cony,' she sneered with a toss of the head, turning back towards Chillingworth and calling over her shoulder by way of an afterthought, 'but when you finds yourself all lonely of a night and dreaming of something a bit softer than your own claw, try a trug with young Molly, won't you? She's just dripping for country lads, isn't she, Shillingsworth?'

Tom did not catch the clergyman's reply.

For a few seconds Chillingworth conducted a muted conversation with the lively strumpet, then sat up in the saddle and kicked his horse forward.

'Farewell, Cannon,' Molly shouted after him. 'I'm all a-quiver waiting to have you shoot again!'

The remark was followed by coarse laughter, which deteriorated into a fit of violent coughing. Tom glanced back to see the bawd on her knees, bent double and convulsed with the effort of catching her breath. One of her breasts had fallen out of her gown and hung quivering like a withered bladder before her. No one in the street was taking the slightest notice.

'The time has come for us to part company,' Chillingworth said after they had left Westminster, passed Inigo Jones' fine royal banqueting house at Whitehall Palace and the great stone cross at Charing and were riding between the fashionable dwellings of the Strand towards Fleet Street and Ludgate Hill. 'From here onwards my way is no longer your way. I need to cross the river to the southern shore, where lies the palace of Lambeth – and other matters.'

Tom was not surprised. He felt that he had already discovered too much about the canon for the man to feel comfortable in his presence, and the events of the morning had shown him just how wide was the gulf in thinking and lifestyle between them. Nevertheless, they parted in good humour. Tom thanked his companion for having come to his rescue the previous day and for his plentiful advice, and the pale cleric gave Tom careful instructions how to find Clement's Inn.

'And, Master Verney,' he concluded, 'should you ever

find yourself sinking into the mire of this wonderful, wicked city, I would be only too pleased to assist you, if it lies in my power to do so. Someone in the cathedral of St Paul should be able to tell you where to find me. If that fails, then, er, you might return whence we have just come and ask for Molly. You remember her? Of course you do. A sweet thing once, but now sadly fallen. A mere callet, no less. There is just a chance that she will know my whereabouts.' Again, the odd, unsuccessful attempt at a wink. 'I plan to remain here until the end of the year. Farewell, and God be with you.'

'Farewell, Canon Chillingworth. I thank you again for your assistance.'

'Think not of it, Master Verney. Think not of it. And I pray you, for your own sake, do not forget that I will be there should you require me.' He paused. 'Alas! Something tells me that you will.'

With these prescient words still sounding in his ears, Tom watched the mysterious canon steer his palfrey into a narrow lane and trot off towards the river.

v

Clement's Inn was one of the eight houses of Chancery, all of obscure and ancient origin. Standing within the jurisdiction of Westminster, the Inn's ramshackle assortment of medieval and modern buildings shared with New Inn a triangle of land between Clement's Lane and Wyche Street, a few yards to the north of St Clement Danes church and near where stocks set in the middle of the high street at Temple Bar marked the imprecise junction between Fleet Street and the Strand. Some sixty chambers, grouped about twenty-four staircases, shared the site with an antique great hall, in which inmates took their meals (or 'commons'), and an assortment of kitchens, storerooms and servants' quarters. Until late Tudor times the Inn had been bounded by broad fields, where the students had practised their riding and fencing; but now lanes and houses pressed it on every side, leaving only two formal walled gardens for the inmates' recreation. It was perhaps just as well, therefore, that in recent years the popularity of this Inn, like the others of Chancery, had declined in the eyes of aspiring young lawyers. The well-connected preferred one of the Inns of Court, leaving the Inns of Chancery to the likes of country solicitors and a handful of students who sought sufficient acquaintance with the law for graduation to the Inner Temple or succession to a provincial family practice.

Despite his handicapped vision, Tom found the weathered red-brick gatehouse opposite St Clement Danes easily enough. Leaning down from the saddle, he beat loudly on the door with his fist. He hoped it was an appropriately confident gesture, for after what Chillingworth had said he was determined not to be taken again for a gull. Molly's immediate recognition of his country origins had unnerved him, and the conspicuously old-fashioned cut of his clothes, the height of fashion in Oxfordshire, had drawn disparaging comments from urchins lingering by Charing Cross.

The sound of his knocking echoed through the vaulted passageway beyond the portal, drawing no response. He tried again. This time, as the noise died away, he heard the sound of wooden shoes clomping slowly towards the gate. A small grille in the centre of the left-hand door swung open and Tom found himself staring down at a pair of watery brown eyes set in a monstrously carbuncled face.

'Yeah?'

'My name is Verney.'

'Yeah?'

'I am to become a student at the Inn this Michaelmas term.'

'Yeah?'

'Well, I have arrived to take up residence.'

'Michaelmas term's four weeks off.' The glowing apparition began to withdraw.

'Wait!'

The face reappeared. 'Yeah?'

'My father has written arranging for me to stay here now. I wish to acquaint myself with Romeville . . .'

'Eh?'

'London.'

'Ah!'

The sun was beating down on Tom's back, making him sweat profusely. 'Listen,' he replied, his temper rising, 'will you be so good as to open the gate forthwith?'

'Maybe.' The man clattered back to wherever it was he had first come from. Silence. Then the sound of footsteps again and a letter was held up to the grille for Tom to inspect.

'This it?'

Tom dismounted and peered at the paper. 'Yes. That is my father's hand. He asks you to admit me on the day I arrive. That is today, I believe,' he explained ironically.

'If you say so. But no prancers.'

'I am not a prancer, I assure you.' His reply was greeted with a muffled guffaw.

'Prancers is horses. No horses.' Tom blushed and lost control of himself. 'Look here, fellow. Treat me like a gentleman, or when I get inside I'll . . .'

'Yeah?'

'Open the frigging door, you whoreson knave!' The

grille slammed shut, the footsteps rattled away and Tom was left fulminating in the street. He had no idea what to do. Hearing a steady tap-tap on the dry surface of the road, he looked round to see a one-legged beggar limping towards him on a crutch.

'Sir! You are a man with a kind heart,' the fellow began. 'God bless you for a gentleman, sir. Spare a penny for one that lost his leg fighting for Good Queen Bess.'

Tom's anger and frustration boiled over. The last thing on earth he felt was charitable, particularly towards some scurvy vagrant who epitomised all he detested in this confounded, humiliating city.

'Curse you for a filthy liar!' he bellowed, kicking away the man's crutch and sending him tumbling into the dirt with a cry. 'Try to cozen me, would you?' He drew his sword, intending to use it to beat the wretch.

'Help! Murder!' The man's screams brought a small crowd hurrying to the spot. Tom heard the grille opening behind him.

'False villain!' he yelled, waving his weapon over the beggar's writhing body.

'Mercy! In the name of sweet Jesus Christ, I cry you mercy!' squealed the pitiful fellow as he tried to haul himself beyond Tom's reach.

A tall, bearded man brandishing a stout staff stepped forward. 'Call yourself a Christian gentleman, do you?' he growled. 'We men of London have ways of dealing with country cuffins such as you.' He raised his stick.

Tom felt a hand on his arm. Looking round, he saw the door of Clement's Inn standing open and the brazier-faced porter swaying at his side. 'Come away, sir,' he urged. His breath stank of drink. Gazing blearily about him, he explained to the onlookers, 'One of my new students. A green gull. He means no harm.' The crowd murmured, unsure whether to believe him. 'You'll see. Mister Vergree will make amends, eh, sir?'

Tom made no move. 'Now, sir, wouldn't want your head broken your first day at Clement's, would we, sir? Be a good Christian and give the poor soldier a penny. We'll all respect you for it.'

With a show of great reluctance Tom put his hand in his purse and drew out two pennies. 'There,' he said, throwing the coins into the road beside the cripple, 'go and drink yourself into a better humour.' As the onlookers muttered their approval and began to disperse, Tom followed the porter through the gate towards the Inn, leading Princess by the reins.

'This way, Vergree,' bade his guide. He lurched towards a side gate.

'Where are you taking me?'

'Stables.'

'Why in God's name ...'

'Yeah?'

'It is no matter.' Tom realised that it would be some time before he understood the ways of the city. In the meantime, he decided, he had better watch and learn.

Nothing would persuade the surly porter to give anything but the curtest of answers. All that Tom managed to elicit from him was that he had assisted in the street not through kindness or regret for his cussedness but in hope of reward (at which Tom tipped him threepence), and that at present there was only one other student in residence, Master Cowley. When asked where this Cowley might be found, he offered no more than 'staircase twenty-one' before banging back to his bottle in the lodge. Tom stared vacantly around him at the dusty vastness of the deserted great hall where he had been left.

It was very quiet. The afternoon sun filtered through the coloured glass of the windows, throwing a warm blanket of brightness over the dull oak of the benches and tables. This is just as our hall looks at this time of day, Tom thought. Through hazy eyes he imagined his mother and sisters standing before him, smiling, asking him where he had been and what London was like. He sighed and sat down heavily at the end of a long settle, placing his saddle-bags on the floor beside him. What was his sister Elizabeth doing now? Perhaps she had been to call on Anne Hutchinson? Sweet Anne, why had he not paid her more attention? But did he really miss her, or sad Rosy, he asked himself, or was it just his present desolation? As he confessed his true emotion, his throat constricted and tears came to his eyes. His handkerchief still smelt of rosewater. He wished with all his heart that he were back home again.

'I ... I beg your pardon?' So lost was he in his own thoughts that at first Tom did not hear the quiet voice. 'I would not intrude, but I believe you must be Master Thomas Verney?'

At the sound of his name, Tom looked up, his eyes red with weeping. Beside him stood a frail young man about his own age. His short black hair was carelessly combed in no particular direction, as if his hat had just blown off. Had his mouth been less sorrowful, his large brown eyes and a beak of a nose might have made him a human owl; as it was, he resembled rather a startled calf, innocent and painfully vulnerable.

The question was repeated, less hesitantly this time. 'Master Thomas Verney?'

'Yes, I am Thomas Verney. And you, I presume, are Master Cowley? I am sorry, but that is all I know of you — the wretched porter would not tell me more.'

'Ah! The porter. Yes, he is not an easy man. There is supposed to be right of way through the Inn, but he keeps the gates closed in the vacations to save himself trouble. His name is Martin Callow, but we call him Mono' – he pronounced the word Moan-o – 'because he will utter but one word in a sentence, and that is a moan. It is truly a sentence to converse with him, is it not? On most days he gets through more bottles than words. Yet he will help a gentleman in trouble, although he is loath to admit as much. And yes, I am Cowley. George Cowley, of the county of Warwickshire.' He extended his hand and Tom grasped it warmly. Here, he thought, looking George straight in the eye, is a friend. He liked his openness, his unassuming appearance, the way he pattered innocently on, as transparent as a window. Such a contrast from the likes of Chillingworth and Callow.

For the rest of the afternoon the two youths chatted amicably as they wandered about the Inn. George made an excellent guide, although some of his comments about his place of residence – 'rather third-rate, I'm afraid' – made Tom regret that he had boasted so openly of his destination to those he had met on the road; while an 'Inn of Chancery' sounded so grand in Oxfordshire, among the community of judges and barristers it was hardly a badge to be proud of. 'It is now little more, Tom, than a convenient place for solicitors from our part of the country to reside and carry on their practice during the terms,' explained George as the couple stood before a faded notice announcing that the instruction customarily given in the vacation between the Trinity and Michaelmas terms had been cancelled owing to the Inn's failure to find a barrister prepared to conduct the 'readings', the lectures by which the basic tenets of the law were traditionally handed down from one generation to another. 'As you will see, legal education is at a low ebb here. It makes my task very onerous – and costly. I have to pay for private tutors. Alas, I sometimes think that we students are scarcely more than an irritation to Principal Edwards and the Ancients.' Tom gathered that these 'Ancients' – an apposite title in many cases – were the council or 'pension' of fourteen senior Companions of the Inn who assisted the Principal with its management.

Tom was not too distressed to hear of the parlous state of legal education at Clement's. Having no intention of following a career in the law, he had decided from the outset that the academic side of his stay would be of secondary importance. Nevertheless, he was unwilling to upset his new acquaintance, for whom study was clearly a priority, and he made what he believed was a suitably regretful answer. Then, remembering his father's remark that at the Inn he would be tightly controlled and instructed in the ways and manners of a gentleman, he asked, 'I have heard, George, that life at the Inn is all rule and regulation. Is it truly so?'

George drew in a deep breath. 'There too the evidence does not support the case, Tom. It is true that there are statutes circumscribing many aspects of our lives. They ordain, for example, that we may not wear beards, or take women into our chambers, or stay out after St Clement Danes has struck the hour of ten. We are obliged to take our meals in commons, conduct ourselves becomingly at all times, particularly at table, and wear a costly gown within the Inn. But seeing as we little-regarded students are so few in number – eight, I believe, in the coming term – and that the great majority of those in possession of chambers at the Inn are practising lawyers of mature years, the regulations are like the warships of Spain's armada, more frightening in appearance than in performance.'

Tom laughed, partly at George's patriotic metaphor, which reminded him of his father's endless stories of the heady days of 1588, and partly out of relief. His friend turned to him with a pained expression. 'What I have revealed may please you, Tom. But remember that the law is a guardian, not a gaoler. When she is asleep, all kinds of beasts may prowl.'

'And your meaning, George?'

'You will discover for yourself soon enough.' His voice became low and earnest. 'Not all apprentices of the law are fit to be here. Closet papists, some of them, who take pleasure in, well, you will see.' He paused, as if afraid to go on.

'Pray continue.'

'They have a secret test.'

'A test? Of the law?'

George snorted. 'No. Far from it. But I would rather not pursue the matter further.'

Intrigued though he was to know more, Tom did not press the issue, and their conversation turned to less sombre subjects. But when he learned later that George's scorn for his contemporaries extended even to the fencing and dancing lessons they attended, he could not help wondering whether his mentor's attitude was not slightly tinged with jealousy.

George Cowley was an orphan. Both his parents had died during a visitation of the plague upon his home town of Nuneaton some three years previously, and he was now under the guardianship of his uncle, Sir Walter Earle. Sir Walter had little time for George. While happy to enjoy the fruits of the small Cowley estates, which he was exploiting shamelessly during their rightful owner's minority, he allowed his nephew a meagre thirty pounds per annum and expected him to keep well away. As a result, George strove to build up his career in London, living at the Inn and supplementing his income by writing ballads. 'They are of no great worth,' he confessed. 'I am no Ben Johnson. But the populace like them well enough, particularly when I mock what I know best – the lawyers. I have to take care, of course, and so write in the name of G. Bulley. Good, isn't it?' He paused. 'I can trust you, can't I, Tom?'

'You may, of course.'

'The others here are such blockheads they do not see who is laughing at them, even when they buy my ballads and fly into a rage at what they read.'

Tom smiled. For all his earnest legal ambition, George was a man of spirit, and Tom liked him for it.

'Tell me, George,' Tom asked later, as they were sitting down to a meal at an 'ordinary' eating house in Clare Market behind the Inn, 'You spoke earlier of this test which some fellows devise. Why do you hate it so?'

Once more his shock-headed friend hesitated to answer. 'Tom,' he began after gazing into his steaming bowl of broth for a time, 'I suggested this afternoon that the students of our Inn are too lightly regulated and that this allows behaviour that is not wholesome. You may also have heard' – he glanced suspiciously around him and lowered his voice – 'that at court ladies are not always, well, sufficient for the tastes of everyone?' Tom nodded. 'Well, such things soon spread. Young roisters take in the heady example of their superiors like wine, believing it is all the rage to behave as they do.'

'And this test?'

'It follows from what they have learned. Do not ask me to explain, Tom, for the memory is painful still. However abhorrent they may find its practices, new students may be compelled to take it, by force if necessary, and in secret. I did so.' He looked down at the table. 'I failed, of course. On both counts.'

'You failed?'

'I did. I am not ashamed.' Tom made no comment. 'Some of those responsible have left the Inn. We will see whether the test has gone with them. But if it has not, and you are confronted with it, perhaps you will not be as squeamish as I was. You will have to decide for yourself.'

He would not be drawn further. The rest of the evening was spent getting mildly drunk at Tom's expense and swapping stories. Emboldened by the drink, on the way back to the Inn Tom asked about the bawdy houses in the vicinity. George responded evasively, saying that he had no money to indulge in such fancies. That is one furrow, Tom reflected, that I shall have to plough on my own.

The weather finally broke at about ten o'clock that night. As thunder roared and crashed over the city and darts of lightning lit up the dark panels of his room, Tom lay in bed unable to sleep. It was not just the noise outside but the seething within his head that kept him awake. There was so much to remember, so much to understand, as if his previous existence had been spent indoors with no knowledge of what lay beyond the walls. Now the portal had been thrown open and he had made his first tentative steps into the world outside, he already felt frighteningly lost.

He was still awake long after the eye of the storm had moved away and the thunder had dwindled to no more than an angry grumble in the distance. Listening to the rain splashing against the casement and rushing down the broad lead pipes from the roof, he thought about the obscene test which George had been so reluctant to discuss. Nothing, he determined with a shudder, would compel him to take it. His mind made up, he stared blindly up at the ceiling for a few minutes, before closing his eyes and waiting for sleep to carry him towards the dawn and his uncertain future.

THREE

PICKERING HOUSE

i

'Well, Tom, isn't that a fine building!' declared George, gazing up from the muddy street at the stone symmetry of the new banqueting hall, which stood out markedly from the remainder of the ancient, rambling palace of Whitehall.

Tom did his best to stifle a yawn.

'So clean, so uniform,' his friend continued. 'Odd that it should be erected for a court which is by all accounts managed in quite the opposite manner. But then' – he lowered his voice to a whisper – 'perhaps it is fitting that so contrary a figure as King James should tease us with a visible symbol of his paradoxical nature: the clash of refinement and licentiousness, order and disorder made manifest for all to see.'

He paused to see if his companion had anything to say, before adding, 'The hall is constructed, I am told, according to the rules of design Mr Jones learned while sojourning in Italy. Would you care to visit Italy one day, Tom?'

Lost in his own thoughts, Tom did not reply.

Ten days had passed since his arrival in the capital. Apart from Treasurer Maydwell, who had been quick to record Tom's formal admission to the Inn and demand from him a ten-shilling fee, no other official at Clement's had shown the slightest interest in him. No commons were provided, and the few bachelors in permanent residence made their own arrangements for meals and other necessities. Mr Marshall, the acquaintance of his father in whose chambers he was lodged, was not in town and, according to George, was unlikely to appear before mid-October, if at all. The Principal, Richard Edwards, and the majority of the Ancients were similarly absent. Even Maurice Green, the venerable lawyer who had been responsible for student affairs since the last decade of Queen Elizabeth's reign, was resting on his estate outside Coventry. Believing himself about to die, George explained, the superstitious old man excused his frequent absences by saying that they were necessary to fulfil a prophesy that he would pass away with the sound of cattle lowing outside his window. He had not been amused when, some five years previously, a group of aspiring students had bought a cow and tethered it beneath Green's window in a light-hearted attempt to keep him in residence for longer than the customary month or so. The enterprising jokers had been heavily fined. Green had left for the country at once, believing – incorrectly – that the shock of the insult would bring on his immediate demise.

Left to his own devices, Tom had used his free time to acquaint himself with his new environment. The unselfish George was his constant and devoted guide, showing him the sights of the city to the accompaniment of musing monologues full of quirky detail and philosophical analogy. While Tom was extremely grateful for his companion's time and expertise, knowing how much George's studies meant to him and realising that the hours spent away from his books would have to be made up by reading long into the night by candlelight, he was beginning to tire of so cerebral an introduction to what Canon Chillingworth had temptingly described as a 'glorious sink'. Fine buildings were all very well, but he was also keen to explore the city's less seemly side. He longed to gamble, to venture among the stews of Shoreditch and taste some of the more exotic fruits so openly on display. But all his efforts to steer George's vision from the intellectual to more earthly matters met either with awkward silences or with a rejoinder that such diversions were beyond the pocket of a mere student. Thus, when walking round the great cathedral of St Paul and its extraordinary twelve-acre churchyard, he had prattled on merrily about the building's history and aesthetic merits, seemingly oblivious to Tom's observations about the swarms of whores, cutpurses and rogues of every description whose ceaseless seethings about that human ant-heap fascinated him far more than the inert stones and mortar.

As George droned on about the symbolism of the new addition to the palace of Whitehall, Tom's mind had taken its own course. Although nowadays the older buildings of the draughty palace were rarely used by the royal family, their presence before him conjured up fantastic images of the court.

Court. The very word thrilled him. What, even at this moment, was going on behind those discreet, screening walls? What scandals were brewing? What policies were being tossed about between council table and bed-chamber? Tom longed to join these dangerous games, to move, both metaphorically and physically, from the outside to the inside. Ambition, like hunger, welled within him. He recalled Lord Banbury's offer of an introduction at court, and made a mental note to present himself to his lordship as soon as possible.

'Are you with me, Tom?' George asked patiently. 'I was asking whether you would care to visit Italy one day?'

'Oh! Yes, indeed. Italy. It would be a fine journey,' Tom muttered, guiltily struggling to the surface from the depths of his reverie.

He removed his spectacles and replaced them in his pocket. 'You are too kind to me, George,' he continued, hoping his inattention had not insulted his guide. 'In truth, you should write your own Survey of London, in the manner of Mr Stow. You must know as much as he. Besides, his volume, towards which you kindly directed me in the library, is already much out of date.'

Delighted by this little flattery, George turned to Tom and smiled. '*Cowley's Survey*. Yes, I like the sound of it. Perhaps one day I will do as you suggest. But until then I must extend my knowledge further, for scholarship must lie in the womb many years if it is not to be born deformed. It is so with the law, too, Tom—'

Unable to endure another lecture, Tom cut him short. 'But to the question of a manservant, George, if I may divert you for the minute. As I have said on several occasions, it is not seemly that two gentlemen such as you and I have to fetch and carry for ourselves. Surely we require a man, do we not?'

Accustomed all his life to the ever present company of servants, soon after his arrival Tom had suggested to his friend that they share the services of someone to take care of their menial chores. At first George had rejected the suggestion out of hand. He was, as Tom had been quick to apprehend, careful in all matters, but particularly so where money was concerned. Having learned to fend for himself, he explained, he saw no real reason to change his ways now. Besides, servants were often more of a trouble than a help. But Tom had persevered, half-consciously playing on the fact that he seemed to be George's only real friend and, although he was eager to make fresh acquaintances as soon as the other students returned, the earnest, studious George was unlikely to do so. Consequently, as Tom correctly surmised, he was loath to fall out with the socially ambitious new arrival over this or any other matter. But the question of cost still held him back. The last time they had discussed the matter, Tom had offered to pay three-quarters of the man's wages, since he would probably be making the greater use of him. Frowning anxiously, George had said he would think the matter over, and there it had rested.

A heavy shower was now falling from the overcast sky, swelling the black puddles in the street and making it impossible for them to walk back to the Inn without filthying their clothes. Tom glanced down at his dirty boots and the mire bespattering the hem of his cloak.

'Dear George,' he exclaimed jocularly, seizing on what he believed was a good argument, 'who is to clean our boots and dry and brush our apparel when we are back at the Inn? Not I, for one! And surely, on our return, you would rather be before the fire with a book than scrubbing away like a scullery maid?' It was a shrewd if unkind thrust.

'Oh, Tom,' George sighed, 'first you draw me from my studies to wander the streets like a gawping kinchin-cove.

Next you urge me to spend what I do not have. What is it about you,' he went on, taking Tom's arm with a gesture of sorrowful affection, 'that makes me so willing to please you?'

Tom felt remorse and pride at the unexpected adulation. However, sensing success, he allowed an impulse to get the better of him. 'This is the deal then, George,' he said quickly, as he was steered round a particularly quaggy patch in the centre of the road. 'I will hire a fellow and pay him for a month. During that time we will share his services. If you approve of what he does, join me in meeting a quarter of his wages thereafter. If he is not to your liking, I will dismiss him or find another with whom to share the burden of his remuneration. Come, you can't do better than that.'

George walked on a few paces without saying a word. Listening to the sound of their boots squelching through the mud, Tom recalled another of Chillingworth's phrases – 'sinking in the mire of this wonderful, wicked city'. Perhaps I am already mired? he wondered. I have money enough at present, but with a servant to keep . . . ? Ah well, he sighed, it's too late now.

Mistaking his friend's exhalation for exasperation, George said quietly, 'Don't despair of me, Tom. I am cautious, that's all. My life has been hard. Things have not come easily to me.'

For a moment, believing he would reject the offer, Tom determined to let the matter drop.

His relief dissolved when George went on, 'And yet, dear friend, how could I refuse so kind an offer? Yes, I accept.' He smiled at Tom with wide, innocent eyes. 'You win, you rogue, Tom Verney.'

'I win?' Tom retorted with a laugh. 'It was no battle, surely, George.'

The lightness of his words belied the unease in his heart. It had truly been a battle. And one which, the more he pondered it, he realised that he may well have lost. To himself.

ii

That evening the two youths drew up a notice advertising for a manservant. They referred applicants to Clement's Inn and wrote in large letters at the top *Si Quis*, as was the custom. After some discussion, they agreed to pay at a rate equivalent to ninepence a day, explaining that the man's services would not be required full-time. The following morning they fixed the paper beside the many others fluttering from the west door of St Paul's and returned to the Inn to await a response. On passing through the gate Tom explained to Callow, with whom he was now on slightly better terms, what they had done and asked him to show applicants to his chambers. This the hell-faced porter undertook to do, for a fee, then retired into his lodge muttering darkly about fools rushing in and the 'river of punk-buggers' he would be obliged to allow through his portals.

The first applicant appeared shortly after midday. Callow knocked and announced the man with an uncomplimentary 'Ancien' wore-out work-horse to see you, sirs. One day.' The fellow was so old and decrepit that he took a good quarter of an hour to ascend the stairs, and when he eventually arrived, pale, sweating and blowing like a pair of leaky kitchen bellows, he looked for all the world as if the climb had been his last. George dismissed him with a kindly remark about the demands of two sprightly young fellows probably being too much for him.

Ten minutes later the clatter of Callow's clogs heralded

the arrival of a second applicant, and once again the porter gave his opinion of the man before his would-be employers had a chance to set eyes on him: 'Sly roister outside. Seen 'im 'afore. Bottle on legs.'

Annoyed at Callow's presumption, Tom was prepared to look favourably on the man. But one glance at his dishevelled appearance and the way in which he stood swaying with one hand on the door post was enough to confirm the accuracy of the porter's disparaging introduction.

For the next hour and a half Callow ushered in a trail of unsatisfactory drunkards and ne'er-do-wells, until Tom and George began to despair of ever finding a suitable candidate. They were on the point of calling a halt to the business while they went to find something to eat, when through the open door came the sound of a voice rising from the foot of the stairway. 'Don't trouble yourself, old fellow. I can see myself up.' The accent was educated, confident, quite unlike that of any other they had heard that day.

'As yer wish,' came Callow's reply, followed, in tones clearly intended for the ears of the prospective employers, by a call of 'Gent what's fallen now comin' up!'

Tom and George looked at each other and smiled. The man who had spoken snorted and, as the noise of the porter's departure echoed away, began his ascent. He climbed the stairs swiftly but erratically, as if impeded by a limp.

'Here!' George cried when the stranger reached the landing. A minute later the man was standing on the threshold, nodding towards the youths with a mark of respectful deference which was not quite a bow.

Raising his head, he announced in sprightly tones, 'Will Clifford, gentlemen, one who has, as your porter so correctly surmised, fallen on hard times but who is willing to work to restore his fortunes.'

He looked towards the students with sharp, bright eyes which narrowed almost imperceptibly when they alighted on Tom. For a second his body stiffened; with his left hand he felt for the edge of the door, as if reassuring himself of its position.

The moment of tension passed as quickly as it had arisen. Within a few minutes, hat in hands, Clifford was standing in the middle of the room telling Tom and George that his Herefordshire family, of ancient Roman Catholic stock (though he had 'no truck with popery'), had been ruined by the recusancy fines milked from them by an enthusiastic magistrate, and he had been forced to come to London to make his own way in the world. Seated at the far side of the chamber and therefore unable to see the speaker very clearly, Tom was nevertheless able to judge that the man's appearance supported his story. Aged about twenty-five and of middle height, Clifford was dressed in an odd assortment of ill-fitting clothes. His breeches were of fine stuff, although rather too large, while his dirty, embroidered shirt had clearly seen better days. The fashionable, high-heeled shoes were scuffed and muddy.

George sat quietly, leaving most of the interview to Tom. Clifford's responses were quick and confident. So eager did he appear to please, there seemed nothing he was not prepared to do. References were no problem. He would take care of their linen, of course. And yes, he could provide young students with everything they might need, from books, paper and ink to 'less scholarly needs, if you take my meaning'. Tom did take his meaning, and warmed to him somewhat.

But for all Clifford's plausibility, Tom still felt an edge of unease. What was it about him that did not quite ring true? He appeared so familiar, as if they had met somewhere before, although Tom could not for the life of him remember where. He wished he had the courage to put on his spectacles and examine him more closely.

In the end, as the man waited outside the closed door, they decided that whatever misgivings they might have, Clifford was too capable to be passed over, and they hired him then and there. George wrote down the name of a Mr Arnot of Fish Street who would vouch for the fellow's good character and Tom gave him a week's wages in advance, a bundle of dirty laundry and sufficient money to buy him three new shirts. Undertaking to return the following morning, by which time he hoped they would have found time to call on Mr Arnot, Will Clifford placed Tom's money in his purse, shouldered his burden and limped off down the stairway, calling over his shoulder as he left, 'I thank you, gentlemen. I thank you kindly. You will not find me wanting, I assure you.'

On their way out to celebrate their success with a long-overdue meal, Tom and George called in at the gatehouse to thank Callow for his help. They knocked heavily on his door. After the customary wait, the porter appeared, a leather bottle swinging heavily in his left hand.

'Yeah?' he grunted, displeased at the disturbance.

'Martin,' began Tom, 'here's a penny for you. We are grateful to you for your assistance.' Callow took the coin and tucked it away inside his greasy jerkin.

'What erssistance?'

'You helped us to find a manservant,' explained Tom with a smile. 'We have engaged Will Clifford. The last fellow to appear.'

'I know. Limper.'

'And what did you think of him, Martin?' asked George, hoping to learn that their choice had met with the approval of one whose uncanny knack of character judgement was well known.

'Your things he was taking out of Clement's?' answered Callow after a pause, allowing himself the rare luxury of an eight-word sentence.

'Mine,' corrected Tom.

'Ah!' Another pause. 'Lost.'

'What do you mean?'

'Jarked.' Tom looked blank. 'Filched,' the porter explained with a twisted grin. 'Stolen. Gone.'

'This time, Martin, you are wrong,' retorted Tom good-humouredly. 'Will Clifford is an honest fellow. See here. We have a reference as to his good character.'

'You 'ave? Who?'

'Mr Arnot of Fish Street. A reputable merchant,' announced Tom with a note of triumph at having finally caught out the man who had vexed him so sorely only days before.

'Maybe he is.' The cries of a ballad seller drifted over the wall from the street outside. 'But not of Fish Street.'

Tom felt his anger rising. 'What do you mean?'

'There's no Arnot in Fish Street.'

The revelation was followed by an even longer, more awkward pause as Callow gave time for his information to sink in. 'I knows Fish Street. Limper's a sharper. And you, Master Vergree, 'ave been taken for a cony.'

Again the twisted smile.

Tom's heart sank. How could he have been so foolish? After all Chillingworth's warnings he had allowed himself to be caught by the simplest trick in the book. And he had given the rogue money, too. My God, what a fool he had been!

He turned to his companion. 'I'm sorry, George. What an idiot I must seem.'

George was looking at him kindly. 'It was my time, Tom. That can be made up. But it was your money,' he said with a wry smile.

'Gave him coin?' interrupted Callow. 'Ask about his leg?'

'Leg? No, I did not.' Tom almost spat the words at the ravaged face leering up at him. How he hated to be humiliated before this know-all, low-born porter! 'You did, of course?'

'Who wouldn't? Didn't open gate till he told.'

'Go on.'

'Shot, he said. Accident, he said.'

Tom began to feel sick as he realised what had happened. No wonder the fellow had seemed vaguely familiar!

Callow continued, 'Huh! Lies. Caught thieving, I reckons. Highway, most likely.'

'Maybe,' said Tom quietly. His anger had evaporated, burned up by the cruel truth that had been revealed to him. To be tricked into parting with a substantial sum of money and much of his linen was bad enough, but for the fraudster to be one of those who, only a fortnight previously, had tried to rob – perhaps kill – him was beyond endurance.

With the vestiges of a grin still shadowing his face, the porter opened the gate. Tom passed through without a word and stomped off down the street, kicking at the ground before him and ignoring the presence of George at his side.

Beneath his breath he cursed London, with all its corruption and sly ways. Deep in his heart, however, he knew that at this moment he disliked himself – the vain and impetuous side of his nature – perhaps more than the city which had made such a mockery of him. Consumed with self-pity, he allowed George to lead him to the Angel, where he sought to drown his misery in tankards of sweet, thick ale.

iii

Three days later, as Tom lay on his bed in the early evening trying to get to grips with the volume of Cowell's *Interpreter* which George had lent him, he was disturbed by a knock at his door. Bidding the visitor enter, he was surprised to see a young lad standing before him.

'If you please, sir,' the boy began nervously, 'my grandfather says as you're wanting a servant.'

'I may be.'

'Well ...' The tiny voice faded away completely.

'You have to speak, little fellow, before I can answer.'

'Well, my grandfather says perhaps as I'll do.'

Tom heaved himself onto an elbow and, remembering his last unfortunate interview, reached into his pocket for his spectacles. 'Your grandfather?' he enquired as the diminutive caller came into focus. 'And who, pray, is your grandfather that he is so solicitous of my welfare?'

The pixie-faced child, who could not have been more than eleven years old, stared down at his feet. Once more he was too overcome to speak.

'You must try to answer,' Tom said with a smile, noticing with concern that his young visitor was quaking with fear. 'I cannot employ a puppet.'

'I ... I don't ... well, I don't quite get your meaning, sir. If you please, sir.' The boy was now shaking so much that Tom was afraid his arms would fall off.

He repeated his question slowly. 'Who – is – your – grandfather?'

'Oh!' The child grinned. ''E's your porter. Martin's 'is name, sir.'

Tom was so startled he almost fell off the bed. Even if he lived to be a hundred, he told himself, he would never understand that drunken old codger. He certainly knew how to get a hold over people. Not only did he control their passage into and out of the Inn, but he also made sure that they were dependent upon him in other ways, too. He looked again at the quivering elf. He was presentable enough, despite his size, and was unlikely to indulge in serious knavery. Not for several years, anyhow. Furthermore, to reject him out of hand would be to upset his grandfather, and that, as he knew only too well, would cause untold problems.

The boy might do.

'Well, child, what is your name?' Tom enquired gently.

'They call me Martin, too, sir. 'Cept that I'm so small and do maid's work, so they call me 'Ouse Martin.' He lifted his head slightly and stared at Tom with vivid blue eyes. 'You see, sir,' he stammered, 'it's a sort of jest. I am like a bird. Small and always flitting about.' A tiny grin crept into the corners of his mouth. 'But I don't go away for the winter, sir. I work all the year.'

This remark, whether original or not, was enough to secure House Martin his position. He proved an excellent choice, willing, reliable and unfailingly cheerful. His presence about the gloomy Inn heartened Tom immensely and he even found himself inventing little chores for him to do just so that he could hear the lad's lively whistling and see his bright face. One of the first tasks he gave him was to carry a letter to Lord Banbury's house on the Strand.

iv

Master Verney

    Your greatings, kind remarks, plentyful news etc etc were recieved with pleasure by Lady Banbury and myself. Your worthy father will indeed take much hart that you are settling into the Univercity of Life with such ease, enjoyment etc etc, though no doubt if I remember my own youth correctly there is much which is best not set down in ink lest it fall beneeth the eyes of one who might take it amiss! You must, I pray, tell me all over a bottle of something special when you come to take supper with us on 23rd Sept as on that day we have other gests. Over the table we can arrange how best I can find a way to take you to court with me – I have not forgotten my plege to your father! This finds you in high spirits, good health etc I trust.

    Your ennobled naighbour of Oxfordshire
    Sir Julius Pickering Baronet (Lord Banbury)

Tom read over the letter again, laughing out loud as he did so. He then asked House Martin, who had been waiting patiently since delivering the bizarre epistle, to fetch him paper and ink. Having written a hasty reply, in which he said that he would be delighted to attend for supper three days hence, he commanded the boy to take it to Lord Banbury at once and, on the way out, to ask his grandfather if he could recommend a suitable tailor. Tired of the street jibes about his dress, he was determined to look as presentable as possible for his first social engagement in the capital. Buffoon his lordship might be, but he was too rich and influential not to be taken seriously.

The faithful bird-child returned two hours later with the news that the letter had been safely delivered and that

Oliver Simpson, who had a workshop nearby, was a popular tailor with students of the Inns of Chancery. Since time was short and he was bored with sitting in all day, Tom decided to walk to Simpson's without further delay. Taking up his cloak and bidding House Martin lead the way, he clattered down the stairs and out into the autumn sunshine. At last, he said to himself, things were taking a turn for the better.

Tom's feeling of well-being received a further fillip even before he had entered Oliver Simpson's house, for the door was opened to him by a most handsome young woman. She was about his own age, of less than medium height, with fair hair hanging in ringlets around a pale oval face set with wide green eyes and a slightly pouting lower lip. Her high-waisted green dress, fitting neatly about her full figure, was topped with a neat lawn ruff and cut away fashionably at the front to expose the swelling of her bosom. The confident bob of her curtsey and the unabashed manner in which she met Tom's surprised look told that she was well aware of her own charms.

Having explained the purpose of his visit, Tom dismissed House Martin and followed his shapely guide through the front room into the workshop beyond.

'Father,' the girl called as they entered a large, well-lit room strewn with rolls of cloth, scissors, pin cushions and off-cuts of every imaginable shape and colour, 'here's a young gentleman to see you.'

Bidding a pasty-faced apprentice take over his master's work for the moment, Oliver Simpson rose to his feet and came over to greet his customer. Elderly and silver-haired, he was the very personification of his trade: long-fingered, lean and stooping, with narrow spectacles perched on the end of a thin nose.

'Sir,' he began in a high-pitched, obsequious voice, 'you are most welcome. I trust my daughter Lucy has given you a civil greeting?'

'Indeed,' replied Tom. He turned to Lucy with a smile and was somewhat taken aback to find her studying him closely.

'Ah! Good. She is a spirited wench and not always as civil as I would wish. Yet she is good to me. Yes, she is good to me. For she is all I have since Mrs Simpson passed away these – let me see – eleven years ago come Christmas.'

Tom had not come to hear the Simpsons' family history, however attracted he was to the only surviving child, and he said quickly, 'That may be so, Simpson, but I am here about a new suit of clothes and time is precious. I am expected at Lord Banbury's three days from now.' He added, in what he hoped was a casual tone, 'I expect to accompany his lordship to court.'

The mention of the word 'court' had precisely the effect he had anticipated. It galvanised Simpson into action, and after half an hour of measuring and presenting of material, he assured Tom that a new winged jerkin and cloak-bag breeches, both of the finest workmanship and at the pinnacle of fashion, would be ready for him to try on within thirty-six hours. 'And now, if you will excuse me, Master Verney,' he concluded, 'I must begin right away. Lucy will show you out, won't you, my dear?'

'Of course, Father.' She turned and walked back into the house, casting a wide-eyed glance over her shoulder to see that Tom was following. In the front room she paused before the door and, looking at him steadily, explained, 'You must forgive my father, sir. He does gossip on so. But his workmanship is second to none. You will see, sir. He will make a handsome gentleman like yourself the envy of all London.'

Tom blushed. 'Thank you, Lucy. I may call you Lucy, may I not?'

'Of course, sir. It was our honour to be of assistance. My father will call at the Inn on Thursday, when you can see for yourself what he has created.'

'Very good, Lucy.' Their eyes met for a second, then she opened the door into the street without further conversation and Tom walked out into the cool evening air.

He felt as tall as St Paul's.

Inside the house, Lucy rejoined her father in the workshop. 'A handsome young man, eh, daughter?' Simpson enquired as she came in.

'Surely so, Father.'

'Well mannered and of means, too.' Lucy did not reply.

'Well, you are now eighteen,' he continued as he busied himself looking for sufficient material for Tom's breeches, 'and I cannot work all my life. One day soon, daughter, you must find someone who can take care of us both.'

Lucy took a deep breath. 'Father,' she began firmly, 'you will always be nearest to my heart, but I will marry for love, not money. How many times must I say that?' Gazing down at her father's lowered head, her tone softened. 'Yet love and money are not always enemies, are they?' She stretched out her hand and stroked the wisps of hair on the balding pate before her. 'You said that you would call on Master Verney at Clement's on Thursday afternoon, did you not?'

Simpson laid down the cloth he was holding. 'I did,' he answered quietly.

'But surely that is when you will be calling on Mr

Woodbridge about his new cloak? Have you forgotten?'

'No, daughter,' said the elderly man with a smile, 'I have not forgotten. But I thought as you might like to manage Master Verney's fitting for me.'

'Father!' the girl exclaimed. 'How could you! I will be so ashamed!' She spoke the words with such vehemence that not even the tailor guessed at the pleasure which they disguised.

Tom was so taken aback when Lucy Simpson appeared at the Inn, accompanied by an apprentice carrying the new clothes, that for the first few minutes of their meeting he was quite unable to come to terms with what was going on. But the girl's practical, no-nonsense manner and the ebullient good humour with which she recounted how she had persuaded Callow to admit her soon set him at ease, so that by the time he came to try on his breeches they were chatting as if they had known each other for months.

'Now, Master Verney,' she laughed, 'I will just step outside while Jack here helps you change.'

'Yes, that would be seemly, Lucy. We would not wish to bring scandal to an Inn of Chancery, would we?' There was a sparkle in Tom's voice which had been almost entirely absent over the previous few weeks.

'Of course not! But scandal, they say, finds its way into the most hallowed of precincts.' She paused at the doorway and turned back. 'Oh! I almost forgot. Beware the pins, Master Verney. They are placed in the most endangering of places.'

Such merry banter accompanied the rest of the proceedings which, as far as Tom was concerned, were concluded all too swiftly. His breeches and jerkin were magnificent and needed little alteration. Lucy, too, was obviously delighted with the way they had turned out and the caring, almost proprietorial manner in which she smoothed out the sleeves sent shivers of delight through Tom's whole body. She was careful, nevertheless, to leave attention to the lower garment to Jack. For all her openness, she made it clear that, for the time being at least, her relationship with Tom was one of business. Frustrated by this and the presence of the apprentice, throughout the encounter Tom tried to think of a way of getting rid of Jack so that he might have a moment or two alone with her. Only when the clothes had been carefully wrapped up again and she was on the point of leaving did an idea come to him.

'Lucy,' he began, 'I would like to discuss payment with you.'

The approach was misunderstood. 'That is generally my father's business, sir,' she replied.

'Of course,' Tom persevered, 'but there are one or two details I would like to get clear in my mind now. In private.'

Lucy glanced up at him, her face expressionless apart from a brightness in her eye. 'Very well,' she said. 'Jack, be so good to step outside. I will be with you directly.'

As soon as the door was closed Lucy's face broke into a broad grin. 'Master Verney,' she whispered, 'I am no child. But neither am I a strumpet.'

Tom shrugged his shoulders. 'Of course, Lucy. I did not think for one wink that you were. It is just that you ...' He swallowed hard as his voice trailed away into silence.

'Yes? It's just that I what?'

'It's just that you are so attractive. And so kindly. It is almost as if I have been with my sister this morning.' As he was speaking he walked towards her until they stood only inches apart.

'Your sister?'

'Well, not quite a sister.' He leaned forward and laid his lips on her forehead. In response, she raised her face to him and their mouths met in a long, gentle kiss.

'So that's your discussion of payment, is it, sir?' she said, breaking away from his embrace with a smile. 'I hope you do not treat your true sister thus?'

'Need you ask? Come—' He held out his arms to her.

'No, sir – Tom. This is neither the time nor the place. Besides, I am hardly acquainted with you.'

'We can soon remedy that, dear Lucy.'

'In due course, Tom, in due course. You will call again at my father's?' He nodded. 'Then I must go lest we do indeed bring scandal to your noble Inn.'

She rose on tiptoe to kiss Tom again, turned about and, lifting the catch of the door, walked quickly out onto the landing, calling to Jack as she went.

v

The London residence of Lord Banbury had, like its current owner's family, recently been rescued from seemingly terminal decline. The fortunes of the Pickerings of Rochdale had been saved by the astute business brain of Sir Henry Pickering, whose dealings in monastic property in the middle of the previous century had led to the accumulation of a considerable fortune. The fine old house in the Strand had been saved by the equally energetic dissipation of that fortune by Sir Henry's son, the present Lord Banbury.

That his lordship ever appeared on this earth to take possession of the property was in itself something of a miracle. Of almost obsessive parsimony, Sir Henry had refused to marry until, at the age of eighty, he had fallen in love with one of his serving maids, made her his wife and, to the intense surprise of all who knew him, fathered a child by her eighteen months later. Sadly for himself, though not for his wife, the effort of procreation had sapped the remarkable octogenarian's remaining strength, and he died shortly after Julius's birth.

Raised in luxury by a doting if somewhat scatter-brained young mother, from whom he had inherited a singular lack of wit, Sir Julius grew up obsessed with the idea of raising the Pickerings to the first rank of society. To this end he had made three great purchases: an ancient seat outside Banbury, soon renamed Banbury Hall; the town residence, Pickering House; and, finally, the baronetcy of Banbury from James I, which entitled him to a seat in the House of Lords. As an eminently eligible if not altogether attractive bachelor, just when he was beginning to find that his father's fortune was not inexhaustible, he was lucky to secure the hand of the only daughter and heiress of a successful City wool merchant. Five years later this unhappy woman, unable to endure life with her 'loathsome toad' of a husband any longer, had eloped with a burly lighterman and drowned in a shipwreck while crossing to France, freeing Sir Julius to remarry. The second Lady Banbury was seventeen years his junior. She brought him no pecuniary comfort – that solace he now neither needed nor sought – but wisely employed her youthful charms to soothe his bruised middle-aged self-esteem as the price of a life of considerable comfort. To outward appearances at least, the Banburys were a devoted couple, and Tom had been given no reason to believe the malicious gossip of those who said otherwise.

This was about all Tom knew of his hosts as he dismounted from Princess and stood before the extraordinary neoclassical portico of Pickering House — a riot of convoluted pillars, strapwork and overweight cherubs. Leaving Princess with an ostler, he was shown into a large room with tapestried walls and a ceiling of flamboyant plasterwork, and told that Lord Banbury would be with him presently. After a wait of thirty-five minutes, most of which he spent trying to decide which of the scantily clad unfortunates in a large needlework representation of the *Rape of the Sabine Women* looked most like Lucy Simpson, he heard his lordship's unmistakable voice calling from upstairs, 'Do not tarry, my sweetheart. Remember Banby's heart aches every tiny minute he is parted from you.'

Tom did not catch the more softly spoken reply. A moment later the door opened and Lord Banbury joined him. 'Ah! Master Verney, welcome to Pickering House! You are well, I trust?'

'I am, thanking your lordship,' answered Tom, making a slight bow. As he looked at his corpulent, bow-legged host, whose tomato face was punctuated with a puckered hole of a mouth and pig's eyes, he could not help thinking that the description of Sir Julius by his first wife had been rather accurate. 'And yourself and Lady Banbury,' he went on with impeccable civility, 'flourishing too?'

'In such health as physicians despair of, Master Verney,' spluttered the Toad, adding with a lascivious wink, 'nothing like a young wife to keep the husband up to the mark, eh?'

'Is it so?' Tom muttered.

Finding himself on unsure ground, he shifted the conversation to another track. 'I have been admiring your tapestry, Lord Banbury.'

'Have you now? The *Rape of the Sammine Women*, woven in Flanders especially for this room. Lady Banbury's choice, of course.'

'Indeed.'

'She is possessed of such taste, Master Verney. She says it is a continual rejoinder to us men of our base instincts, so that we can better learn to keep them down.' He exhaled heavily, as if contemplating a recent rebuttal of his own base instincts, and shouted for a servant to bring them wine.

For the next twenty minutes, prompted by Tom's occasional questions and well supplied with an excellent Bordeaux, Banbury drooled on about his latest acquisitions, the adventures of his youth – he too, Tom gathered, had attended an Inn, or the 'University of Life' as he insisted on calling it – and Lady Banbury, his 'sweet little Bessie'. The contrast between the baronet's lewd bragging of past adventures, larded with solecisms, and his fawning references to his wife, afforded Tom some unexpressed amusement. What sort of woman is this Bessie, he thought, that she has such a hold over the man? He was just beginning to feel confident enough to ask his lordship whether Lady Banbury knew what a rogue he had once been, when their talk was interrupted by the arrival of three more guests. Sir Archie Medley and Mr Christopher Wilson were the peer's habitual drinking companions, and the three men were soon guffawing together at the far end of the room, leaving Tom to manage as best he could with Wilson's unforthcoming, angular wife Jane.

When the company were summoned to supper half an hour later, Lady Banbury had still not appeared.

'Supper' at Pickering House was one of Lord Banbury's little jokes. Expecting a light meal, Tom was startled to find the candlelit dining table loaded with such joints, fowls, sweetmeats and vegetables as would have satisfied half a dozen dinners in most households. The host took his seat at the head of the table, his cronies on either side, and waved to Tom to sit beside Sir Archie and opposite the silent Mrs Wilson.

Indicating the vacant place on Tom's right at the opposite end of the long table, Banbury called out loudly, 'Master Verney, you are truly fortunate! Beside you will soon appear the most sweet, innocent, lively little creature that ever trod this earth. A veritable angel, Master Verney, a sherub!'

As if on cue, the dining-room door opened a fraction. 'Ah-ha!' sang out a deep female voice from behind it. 'Has my Banby not waited for me, then? Oh, Bessie is broken-hearted at his cruelty.'

With these words, a tall, red-haired woman in her late-twenties, dressed in the most stunning low-cut turquoise gown, strode into the room. She made straight for the Toad. A dull light came into his seeping eyes, his mouth stretched into a flaccid grin and he struggled to his feet. His chair crashed backwards to the floor and the contents of his wine glass spilled over the table.

The embarrassing ritual continued.

'Pray, Bessie darling, do not chastise me!' he whimpered childishly, lowering his eyes and swaying slightly from the effect of drink.

'Chastise my Banby! Who could be cruel to the kindest, most handsome gentleman in London? Come, you are forgiven.'

The baronet moved forward unsteadily and, closing his eyes, raised his florid face for a kiss. Lady Banbury duly bent down and brushed her lips chastely against the tip of his oily nose. Then, with a sigh that was supposed to have betokened affection but which to Tom's ears sounded more like one of profound boredom, she walked quickly to her place beside him.

During the course of the meal Tom learned that there were three Lady Elizabeth Banburys. The first was the playmate of the insecure and drunken slubberdegullion of a noble husband who was tippling his way towards oblivion fifteen feet away at the other end of the table. The second was the considerate hostess in whose company he felt instantly at ease as she listened attentively as he talked about his time in London and his escapade with the robbers near Stokenchurch. The third persona, however, was not revealed until the meal was almost concluded.

In response to an enquiry from his wife whether her 'honey husband' was enjoying his wine, Banbury stood up and leant forward, clasping the table with both hands to keep himself upright. Mr Wilson was sound asleep and his wife had left the room, professing to feel 'a little giddy'. This was hardly surprising, for she had quietly been matching her husband's consumption glass for glass. Indeed, everyone round the table, including Tom and Lady Banbury, was rather less than sober.

'This wine,' began the baronet, 'is the second love of my life.' He paused and stared blearily down the table. 'There is the first. That cornupokia of delight.'

The object of his adoration smiled serenely back at him.

'But when I lie abed at night,' continued his lordship, 'my thinking often turns to the little ships – holds bursting with tuns of ruby wine – fighting through the raging, rough and rrr – yes, roaring sea ...'

'Poetry!' cried Sir Archie. 'Fine words, Sir Julius!'

'I thank you, sir,' said the orator. 'Yes, poetry. Liquid poetry. That is what wine is. Now what was I saying?'

Lady Banbury's voice cut across the silence. 'Ships,' she said slowly and deliberately. 'Full of barrels. My love.'

'Oh? Was that it? Ships of barrels, barrels of ships, bringing wine to wet my lips!' He sat down heavily to the loud applause of Sir Archie.

Entering the spirit of the moment, Tom stood up and cried, 'A triumph of art!'

When he sat down again, he wondered whether it had been the correct thing to do. As far as his hostess was concerned, it was certainly not.

'Fawning puppy!' she hissed in his ear. Tom froze. 'Come, don't play the innocent with me, Tom Verney. You are no fool, and even in drink you can tell a sodden, stupid, feckless, impotent swaggerer when you see one.'

Tom glanced towards the other end of the table. He could just make out Wilson snoring in his chair, and his host and Sir Archie slumped towards each other, deep in conversation. 'Your husband?' he asked.

Lady Banbury's face was seething with suppressed emotion. 'Correct. That grease-bag.' She began to grow more agitated and, ignoring the presence of the butler standing by the door, grabbed Tom's hand and placed it on her thigh. 'Why, the bowsprit on one of his cursed Bordeaux vessels in a tempest is more upright than his flabby spar.' She pressed her thighs together, rubbing them against his hand.

'That must be hard,' said Tom. He was so confused that he hardly knew what he was saying.

'Ha! Hard!'

'I mean hard for you to bear.'

'Sweet Jesus! Sometimes I think I will go mad with desire. That tapestry. The *Sabine Women*. The Toad – yes, I know the name – believes it is an aid to chastity. Not so, Master Verney.' She placed her hands beneath the table and began to draw up the skirts of her gown. 'It is to remind me that there are still men in the world. Men of action, who do more than just fawn and slobber and drink.'

Tom's hand was now on her bare thigh. She pulled it higher, causing him to lean awkwardly across the table towards her.

'Master Thomas!' cried Banbury suddenly. 'Master Thomas, we have some business to talk over.' Tom sat up with a start and peered beyond the guttering candles to where his host and his companion sat. Noting that their heads still inclined closely together, he sighed with relief and looked quickly to his right where the original Lady Banbury, smiling sweetly, was now gazing lovingly down the table at her husband.

'Yes, Lord Banbury. You were so kind as to mention to my father that you might introduce me at court.'

Sir Julius sat up. 'And I have been as good as my word. I have let your name be known. Yes, Tom, King James knows of Tom Verney. I will send for you – when the time is right.'

'I am your debtor, sir.'

'So you are. But it is the duty of great men such as myself to be of assistance to those lower than us.'

Tom heard a low laugh beside him. 'Huh! Great men!' The aside entered his ear like scalding steam.

'There is one further matter, my lord, in which I crave your assistance.'

'Speak on, lawyer.'

'Since you have constant intercourse with Oxfordshire, perhaps I could entrust to one of your servants a letter I have written to my father?'

Banbury called to the butler. 'Peter! Take Master Verney's letter and see that it goes to Oxfordshire this week. To Justice Verney of – where is it now?'

'Stratton Audley, my lord.'

'Yes, Stratton Audley.'

The butler came over and Tom handed him the letter which he had produced from inside his jerkin. 'Make sure you take good care of it now, Peter,' he said with a laugh. 'It contains a matter of importance.'

'What's that?' interrupted his host. 'Important news for your father, eh? Come, Thomas – have you got some wench with child? That'll stir old Verney, as sure as I'm a peer of the realm of England!'

'Not that, my lord. Truly not. Since arriving in this city I have been entirely chaste.' The remark drew a scarcely audible grunt of disbelief from his right.

'Then it must be money,' roared Banbury. 'That's a pretty costume you're in, Master Verney. Don't expect old Verney will dance a quagrille when I informs him that you have been spending his guineas on such garb. I can't wait to see his face when I tell him.'

'I had rather you did not, my lord.'

'Oh, but I shall! I shall say how his probigal son is living the life of a lord in the city of wickedness. His face will be quite a picture, just you see.'

'But I have bought books. And have had to pay a servant . . .'

'A servant too! Better and better! Satin Audley will ring with the news!'

'My lord, while I am grateful to you for your kindness towards me—'

Sensing that Tom was going to say something he would later regret, his hostess came to his rescue. 'Banby, my Hercules, do not tease young Tom so. He is not such a man of the world as you.' She pressed her leg against Tom's as she spoke.

'Very well, my lambkin. But you know above all others how hard I find it to re-strain myself when there is fun to be had.'

'Try this time, soldier. Just for me.' The words slid down the table like melted butter. 'Please?'

'Very well. For you, my snowy dove, I will try. But Banby makes no promises.'

Lady Banbury turned to Tom. 'Well, Master Verney, you can always write again if your father is displeased with your request for further money. You can explain the truth of your situation to him if my naughty husband allows the wine to trick him into an indiscretion when he is in Oxfordshire.' She continued, her eyes burning, 'Although Lord Banbury goes into the country from time to time, I spend most of my time here in Pickering House and can arrange for your correspondence to be posted forward.'

'Thank you, Lady Banbury. That is good to know.' Tom felt the pressure on his leg increase.

'I am so sorrowful when I am parted from my Banby,' she mused, again gazing wistfully towards the Toad, 'that it would be a comfort to talk with one who knows well the countryside where my love is pining.'

There was no doubting what lay behind Lady Banbury's invitation, but later that night, as he rode unsteadily back to the Inn through the deserted streets, Tom was uncertain whether he dared or even wished to take it up. Within a week the city which previously had seemed to hold him like a gaol had been transformed into a landscape of delight. Already several tempting highways led across it. Shortly, with an introduction at court and with the legal term under way, no doubt others of equal allure would appear. Sometime soon he had to decide which way he wished to go. But that, he realised, meant knowing just who Tom Verney really was.

And the problem at the moment was that he simply did not know.

FOUR

EBGATE LANE

i

October was dreary and overcast, as if Nature were taking a callous revenge for having allowed the summer to last beyond its customary span. A steady drizzle fell almost every day. The unpaved city streets, already softened to mud by September storms, soon dissolved into trails of filth and ordure. Every day from a thousand chimneys a vast, dirty fleece of smoke hung above the spires and towers, a lowering remembrance of the country's principal source of fortune. Around the elm piers of Temple Wharf the swollen grey river sucked and gurgled like a nursing child before moving on to pull at the narrow arches of London Bridge. A pall of unusual quiet lay over the capital. Unless venturing out to church or on some pressing business matter, when, where practicable, those who could afford it travelled by water to avoid the dirt, citizens stayed within doors. Even the cries of the hawkers peddling their mildewed wares along the slippery thoroughfares lost their customary enthusiasm. The hours of daylight shrank. By the third Sunday of the month, with the weather showing no sign of breaking, the entire metropolis lay wrapped in a heavy cloak of autumn depression.

The entire metropolis? Not quite. To the area around the Inns of Court and Chancery the approach of the Michaelmas law term had brought a new lease of life. A swarm of students, plaintiffs, witnesses, judges, barristers, clerks and benchers had descended on the quarter like locusts. After weeks of underemployment the inns and ordinaries, stalls and stews, churches and workshops of the neighbourhood were all teeming once more. Even the rather dull atmosphere of Clement's Inn had perked up somewhat. Most of the chambers were now occupied, obliging Callow to leave the precinct gates open during the day, and commons had recommenced, dinner and supper being announced with a loud blast on the horn by the bald-headed butler. To George Cowley's amazement, even the venerable Maurice Green – still very much alive, to no one's surprise but his own – had turned up and begun to make arrangements for the educational work of the Inn. When he remembered, a writ was read at meal times for the Companions to discuss. Less frequently, as it tended to empty the hall quicker than a fire warning, a case was put to one of the tables and the diners expected to deliberate over it at length. In theory the clerk of the Inn levied a fine on students who arrived late for commons or failed to turn up at all. Tom soon learned, however, that by slipping the easy-going official a shilling he was prepared to develop a selective and convenient blindness.

It was shortly after Tom had made this useful discovery that the clerk approached him one morning after breakfast with the words, 'Excuse me, Master Verney, but Mr

Green bids you step up to his chambers for a few words.'

'Me? Are you sure, Cripps? I did not know that Mr Green was aware of my existence.'

Assured that he was mistaken, Tom made his way to the chambers at the foot of staircase eight, conveniently near the hall, and knocked upon the door.

'Pray enter!' The voice was thin and nasal. Tom pushed open the heavy door and found himself in a spacious room overlooking the Garden Court. A coal fire blazed in the grate. To one side of the hearth, wrapped in a thick cloak, sat the frail frame of Maurice Green.

'Mr Thomas Verney of Oxfordshire?'

'Yes, Mr Green.'

'Good. Very good. Your father has land and, um, cattle?'

Taken aback, Tom stared at the skeletal figure before him without replying.

'I take it there are cattle in Oxfordshire, Verney?'

'Yes, sir,' he stuttered, recovering his voice. 'Plenty.'

'Ah. And your father possesses a goodly number, no doubt?'

'He does, Mr Green. Noble beasts they are too,' he added proudly.

The most ancient of the Ancients closed his eyes. 'Then they must low. It is a most soothing sound. One day soon I will breathe my last to the accompaniment of such music of Nature. I will meet my Maker with the lowing of beefs echoing in my old ears.' He paused. 'That is why I must return to the country soon,' he explained, opening his eyes again.

'Oh!' exclaimed Tom, completely at a loss for anything more constructive to say.

'You are disappointed, of course. But it cannot be helped. Yet before I leave it is my duty to see that you are well settled into your studies.'

'Thank you, sir.' Tom's voice carried little enthusiasm.

'You attend commons, Verney?'

'I do.'

'Ah! What was the writ we discussed yesterday at dinner, eh?'

Jesus! thought Tom. On the pretext of needing a minor adjustment to his new jerkin he had called at tailor Simpson the previous morning and had been invited to stay for a simple dinner. This was his fifth visit to the household, and although he continued to find a sartorial excuse for his expeditions, the real reason for them — the chance to exchange a few words and kisses with Lucy — was now patently obvious.

'The topic of our deliberations, Verney?' Green cut in. 'Come, it was but yesterday!' The old man's voice had an unexpected edge to it. He did not appreciate being lied to.

'Um, yesterday.' Tom reddened. 'Of course! Yesterday, Mr Green, I was at divine service.'

'At dinner time, Mr Verney?'

'Yes. It was a special service, called by' — he searched for a name — 'yes, Canon Chillingworth. At St Anne's, Blackfriars.'

'I see.' Tom breathed more easily. 'Very well. But do not absent yourself from any more commons, Verney. Pay close attention to writs, moots and bolts. Attend the courts. Read. That is the modern way of learning the law. Read books. You have a purchased a copy of the *Attorney's Academy*?'

Tom was not to be caught out a second time. 'No, sir. Not yet.'

'Remiss of you. Please do so. We ask but little of our students at Clement's Inn, but we do expect them to undertake the minimum that is required.'

'Yes, Mr Green.'

'Very well. You may go.' Tom turned to leave. 'By the way, Verney, you know that we have a little learning exercise in the Latin language, do you not?'

'Master Cowley has talked of it.'

'Good. Then prepare yourself. Upon my return I will call upon you in commons to speak in that language to the Companions. Do not fail me, I pray.'

'No, sir.' As Tom was closing the door, he was recalled a second time.

'By the way, Verney.'

'Mr Green?'

'The vicar of St Anne's is a friend of mine. He would, I believe, rather die than have Canon Chillingworth in his church.' Tom froze. 'I may be old, Verney. I may even be growing a suspicion absent-minded. But I am not' – he thumped his scrawny fist feebly on the table before him – 'I am not silly. Remember that.'

ii

During the fortnight previous to his interview, Tom's life had been radically transformed by the arrival at the Inn of the remaining six students. With four of them he had little contact. One, a consumptive looking man in his early twenties, found that the London air did not agree with his delicate constitution and returned to Leicestershire before the end of October. (A notice posted on the hall door a few weeks later announced that he had died; as Tom had a long-standing invitation to the Simpsons on the day of the memorial service, he chose to pay a penny fine rather than attend.) The other three were sons of prosperous shopkeepers in Hereford. Close friends before they arrived, the 'Three Tradesmen' — as George christened them — saw no need to widen their circle of acquaintance. They nodded to Tom in silent obsequiousness whenever they chanced to meet, but since they spent most of their time sampling the capital's multitude of religious services, taking notes on the sermons and drawing up a list of the best preachers, that was not often. Tom lost no sleep over this, for the company of the other two students, Silas Corbet and Leoline Williams, more than compensated for the Tradesmen's introversion. To George this pair were the 'Scylla and Charybdis of wickedness'. But to Tom, intoxicated with freedom, his friend's hostile epithet was simply the child of envy, and for six gaudy autumn weeks he accompanied his new cronies on a ceaseless round of irresponsible indulgence, telling himself that he was drinking from the spring of Liberty itself.

He was not surprised by George's antipathy towards Corbet and Williams, for they were not at all the sort of company he liked to keep. Silas Corbet was a straw-thin, fidgety young man, who disguised his premature hair loss by rarely removing his hat. He made no such attempt, however, to hide his disgust for the law and its institutions. 'A rotten game, played by corrupt persons for the preservation of their decaying commonwealth' was his private verdict. When Tom asked innocently why he continued to dwell at the heart of a society he so detested, he replied simply, 'To know it better.' Confused and even alarmed by Corbet's opinions, Tom still enjoyed the behaviour they gave rise to. Whether it were spent telling stories at a tavern or removing the pins securing the wheels of gentlefolk's carriages and hiding to watch the ensuing collapse, an evening with Corbet was never dull.

The squat Welshman Leoline Williams was an entirely

different character. He was less embittered than Corbet and more straightforward, but his loquacity, fiery temper and total inability to control his bodily appetites made him equally amusing. In the course of a single night, depending on which urge was in the ascendant at the time, he would take in half a dozen inns or as many brothels, and still come climbing over the Inn wall at cock-crow, complaining that there were 'not enough hours in the day for a man to take his pleasure in'.

These notorious reprobates, now in their third year of residence at the Inn, singled out Tom as a likely partner in revelry the moment they arrived and lost no time in initiating him into the drink and daring, fights and fornication that were the common fare of London's student underworld. Captivated by their vitality, wit and confident manners, Tom tagged along without dissent. Over the succeeding weeks the trio's insatiable quest for new pleasures became ever more wide-ranging and, to Tom's alarm, ever more costly. Some days they hired a boat and went on wild trips down the river, cutting up the ferryboats and abandoning their craft miles from its wharf for the unfortunate owner to recover as best he might. On other occasions they rode out of town and amused themselves by hassling country folk or poaching game from one of the many parks that dotted the landscape of north Kent.

There was something blinkered, almost deliberate in the way Tom allowed himself to be led along this dangerous path, for he knew it was almost certain to end in calamity. He made a point of not counting his money, while praying each day that his father would hurry to send more. There were aspects of his companions' behaviour, too, that he chose to ignore. He disliked their haughty, bullying treatment of social inferiors. More than once he found himself excusing their insolence to a humiliated House Martin, and he never dared tell them of his attachment to Lucy, a mere tailor's daughter. Corbet's ugly lust for young boys he found distasteful. Still more distressing was the thinly veiled contempt which both showed for the established church. Tom was certainly no fanatic, but his secure Protestant faith was rooted in a deep affection for the rituals in which he had been raised. No matter what else he did, he took communion at St Clement Danes at least once a week. It was a cleansing experience, which left him feeling that whatever the strength of the current of sin tugging at him, there was still solid rock beneath his feet.

He quickly gathered that both Corbet and Williams were among those George had described as 'closet papists'. In itself this was not too worrying. After all, the king openly accepted members of the Roman church at court, and his late queen had died a Catholic. It was only when popery spilled over into politics, particularly by recognising the authority of the Bishop of Rome over the king's, that it became a cause for concern. A mere seventeen years previously Guy Fawkes' plot to blow up James and his parliament had been uncovered in the nick of time. In the bloody aftermath of that event Catholics suspected of wishing ill on the state had been weeded out and dealt with. But some, of course, had survived to breed a new generation of potential subversives. In his more fearful moods Tom wondered whether Corbet, and perhaps even Williams, might not themselves be of that treacherous ilk.

Every so often, awaking with a head beating like a blacksmith's hammer and feeling the weight of his depleted purse, or when his mentors' behaviour moved over the bounds of humour into cruelty or even sedition,

Tom resolved that the time had come to sever all ties with them. But he was young and high-spirited, and his resolution never lasted long. By choosing his own company, however unsound, he felt he was making a statement about his new-found independence.

Sometimes, when drunk and behaving in a way he knew his father would disapprove of, he saw the magistrate's stern face looming before him. 'Well?' he would whisper harshly to the apparition. 'What do you want with me? This is Tom Verney's life, not yours. You cannot touch me now. Go back to your narrow village life and frown till your face folds like a blanket!' After these bouts of heartless defiance he drank still more heavily to submerge the painful memories and feelings of self-reproach which threatened to overwhelm him.

His longest period of restraint followed his unnerving interview with Ancient Green. Guilt stricken and seriously concerned by the rate at which his funds were declining, he made a determined effort to rein himself in. Upon George's suggestion, he sent House Martin to buy him a commonplace book in which he wrote down interesting and useful snippets of legal information. He bought a copy of the *Attorney's Academy* and worked hard to come to terms with the *Interpreter*. In the mornings he attended the law courts, sitting at the back of the hall, forcing himself to concentrate on the obscure drama enacted before him. To the great amusement of Corbet and Williams, he even walked about the Inn wearing his spectacles, making a public show of his scholarly intentions.

But this reformation lasted only a while longer than the others. There was still no sign of Mr Marshall, and Tom was easily bored with his own company. Before long his silken bookmark (a parting gift from his sister Elizabeth) lay marooned three-quarters of the way through Cowell's masterpiece. Dust gathered on the leather-bound commonplace book and his visits to the courts dwindled. When he did turn up, invariably hung over and dreadfully tired, it was all he could do to stay awake. Several times he fell asleep on his bench and had to be woken by a clerk long after the day's proceedings had finished. Once, to his acute embarrassment, he had started muttering in his sleep and was ordered by an irate judge to leave the court. When he told George what had happened, his friend simply smiled and said, 'It will soon be forgotten, Tom. Yet I hope that when you are done with roistering you will join me in serious study once more. Your new friends are not mine, and I enjoyed our former times together.'

The remark upset Tom deeply, for he liked and respected George, and would always be indebted to him for his kindness. 'Of course, George,' he had replied, suggesting they go out to a tavern together that afternoon. But his erstwhile guide had replied that he was too busy, and although thereafter they often exchanged a few sentences, Tom felt a regrettable wall of estrangement rising between them.

iii

'And where, my fine blind friend, do you think you're off to this dank day?' asked Williams one afternoon in late October. He had caught Tom leaving his chambers to visit Lucy.

'Off to?' replied Tom with a shrug, inwardly cursing himself for not having managed to slip out unobserved. 'I am not, as far as I am aware, off to anywhere. Just eager to get out of this Inn.' A passing lawyer looked at him with disapproval.

'"Out of this Inn", in of this out, in and out, round

about – hark what a twisted knot you make of our language, Thomas.' Williams might have made a competent barrister if he had been blessed with more drive and application. 'Well,' continued his lilting tone, 'allow me, sweet youth, to guide your drifting footsteps down a track of supreme delight and interest.'

'Then lead on, Leo,' said Tom, stifling a sigh and hoping that Lucy would understand his absence.

Williams took Tom to a tavern he had not seen before, a dilapidated, half-timbered structure at the river end of Ebgate Lane, near Old Swan Stairs. The whole place smelled of damp, even the first-floor room to which the couple were immediately directed by the shifty-eyed landlord. Williams opened the door with a flourish, making a noise like a trumpet as he did so.

'My lords, ladies and gentlemen,' he announced from the threshold, 'from the goat-tracked, green-valed, grizzly mountains of Wales, may I introduce to you the legendary Llewellyn – as he is rightly known – Williams, emptier of hogs' heads, collector of maidenheads, cracker of boneheads!'

The room erupted with laughter and clapping. Williams advanced, leaving Tom in the doorway. 'And now,' he went on, 'may I introduce to you a new recruit to this army of strumpet-straddlers: from deepest Oxfordshire, in whose principal city it is said that true scholars are found' – groans from the assembled company – 'Mr Thomas Verney, occasionally bespectacled, usually booze-befuddled and soon to be pox-riddled!'

The laughter began again. Tom made a low, mocking bow and stared around him.

'Oh, Verney!' called a drawling, cultured voice. 'Don't frown on us before you have made our acquaintance!'

'Don't take it amiss, James,' piped up Williams, 'he's as

blind as a stake-eyed Cyclops. Without his spectacles he can't see without screwing up his face like a bloodhound.'

'A vain one?' replied the man who had spoken first. 'Come, Verney. Tap with your stick towards me. Here.' Tom could just make out that the drawler was indicating a vacant chair beside him. Blushing deeply, he walked over and sat down.

The room was furnished with a rough table, several chairs and a straw mattress in the corner beneath the shuttered window. Light was provided by half a dozen candles, warmth by a small fire spluttering in a brick hearth. The air was thick with tobacco smoke. Apart from Williams and himself, Tom could make out three other people. Through the gloom he discerned the outline of Corbet, wearing a close-fitting cap and sitting cross-legged on the mattress with the head of a fair-haired youth resting in his lap. The lad was lying on his back with the front of his shirt unbuttoned, drawing inexpertly at a long clay pipe. As Tom watched, Corbet ran his thin fingers over his partner's chest and stomach. When from time to time his hand reached further down, he was obliged to lean over so that he lay almost on top of him.

With a sweep of his arm Williams introduced Tom to the man sitting beside him: 'James Cranfield, Tom. You may have heard of his father?'

'Oh, come now, Leo. I am my own man,' came Cranfield's languid rebuke.

'You mean,' Tom interrupted, 'the lord treasurer, recently created Earl of Middlesex?'

'Yes, Tom. That is he. My great and mighty father—'

'Who provides his roistering son James with a small fortune to avoid his company,' concluded Williams with a laugh.

That, thought Tom, explains much. Now he knew why, when Williams and Corbet fell foul of the law, a few quiet words in the ear of the officer who had charged them were sufficient to ensure their liberty with no more than a cautionary word. If they were in the circle of the eldest son of the Earl of Middlesex, whose sensible efforts to restore some semblance of order to the royal finances had made him one of the most powerful men in the kingdom, no wonder they managed to get away with things for which lesser men would be before the courts. No wonder, either, that the Pension was prepared to turn a blind eye to their open flouting of the Inn's statutes. To be within the sphere of the mighty Middlesex, even at its periphery, was to be well connected indeed.

'You are surprised to find me here, Tom, in this hovel?' enquired Cranfield, uttering the last word with total disdain. His sleek black hair so reminded Tom of crow feathers that he half expected to see droppings on the man's velvet shoulders.

'Why, yes, sir ...'

'Oh, for God's sake! Who are these peasants you produce, Leo?'

'Tom's no peasant, James,' replied Williams. 'Father's a justice of the peace. A proper piece of justice, if you please.'

'Is that so?'

'And he calls on the Banburys, too. Very well connected, he seems. But I hear that many who call on Lady Banbury are well connected. Like a piece of plumbing, pipe to pipe.'

'Then why in the name of God and all the angels is he so doltish?' asked Cranfield. 'Listen, Tom Verney. In this place there are no "sirs". I am Cranfield, or even James, if you wish. And you are Tom, with or without spectacles.

Come, take a pipe and mug of wine.'

As the afternoon wore on Tom learned that Cranfield, for all his democratic professions, was very much the leader of his little gang. 'James' he might be, but neither Williams, Corbet nor the anonymous catamite – referred to simply as 'Sodda' – ever went against his wishes. He paid the rent for the den they were in and kept it supplied with tobacco, drink and – as Tom was to discover – other pleasures. He also guessed from a number of passing remarks that Cranfield's hold over the students was not just pecuniary. At some time in the past he had used his influence to rescue Williams and Corbet from serious trouble – not simply a brush with a zealous constable – and he was not slow to remind them of this.

'Pray remember, sweet Leo,' he said lazily in reply to a tactless jest about his strained relationship with his father, 'you are my debtor in more ways than one. Do not see how far you can go, lest your test prove as ill-fated as the last. You remember Luke Cropley, I trust?'

Tom had gathered from idle talk about the Inn that Cropley had been dismissed the previous year for immoral acts. This linking of his name to the test had added a key piece to the puzzle which George had left so infuriatingly blank.

For once Williams seemed at a loss for words. 'Holy Mary!' he said at last. 'Forget? It is written on my heart in letters as large as horses: "I owe my liberty to James Cranfield". And yonder arrow-bodied citizen of Sodom has the same, except that his is written on his prick, which appears to be more important to him than his heart.'

Cranfield laughed and looked towards the window. Corbet, his breeches round his ankles, was carefully anointing the youth with oil from a small bottle.

'Leo,' requested Cranfield after he had watched the

display on the mattress for a while, 'prove your love for me by stepping outside and finding out what has happened to our own little baskets of juicy fruit.'

Williams did as he was asked, returning five minutes later with two girls, one of whom appeared not much above the age of fifteen. The older one removed her cloak as she entered the room. She wore no ruff and her dress was cut away from the shoulders to the waist to reveal her large breasts. Her casual manner and easy smile told that she had been here before and knew the company. Her young partner, however, was less confident, and modestly pretended to struggle with the fastening at her neck.

Williams sprang to his feet. 'Shy, my little ferret's nest?' he said, moving round behind her. 'Watch here.' With a quick movement he pulled the cloak to the floor, leaving the girl as uncovered as her friend.

'Ripe for plucking,' muttered Cranfield, his eyes narrowing. Tom did not like the man. Neither did he enjoy what followed.

For all his fantasies and braggadocio, Tom's limited experience had left him feeling that sexual relations ought to be, for him at least, a manifestation of friendship, if not of love. That had certainly been the case in his innocent fumblings with his childhood sweetheart, Anne Hutchinson. His brief, bitter-sweet night with Rosie at the Green Man had touched his heart, and his flourishing relationship with Lucy Simpson fed on a similar confluence of attractions. He could even contemplate taking up Lady Banbury's challenge because her fascination was not merely raw animal magnetism. On the only occasion when he had accompanied Williams into the stews of Shoreditch, hopelessly drunk, he had passed out as soon as they reached their destination, and the following day had been unable to recall what had happened. The

Welshman had said it was 'wonderful nought!' But now, in this sordid little room by the river, where there was nothing private, nothing personal, and where there was no way out without losing face, he was confronted by cold lust. For the first time since adolescence he began to understand why the church deemed fornication a sin.

'My sister,' said the taller of the two strumpets, nodding her head towards the timid girl at her side. 'Pretty little dell, ain't she, gentlemen? Fresh to the bawdy game. Tight as a Jew's fist.' As she made the introduction she walked round the girl like a stall-holder talking up her wares. 'Come, Lettie, show the men as what you've got for them.'

Prompted by her sister, Lettie began a sad little routine that the more experienced harlot had recently taught her. With a fixed smile on her painted lips, she first ran her hands over her small breasts until the nipples rose like mole hills. Next, placing her legs slightly apart, she slowly drew up the hem of her gown.

'More!' called out Williams as first her thin ankles and then her calves came into view. Momentarily diverted from his exertions on the mattress, Corbet looked up disinterestedly, then went back to work on Sodda.

The gown rose higher, gathering in folds about the girl's waist. On her left thigh Tom noticed a livid bruise.

'Ah-h!' sighed Williams when there was nothing left for his imagination to work on. 'Pretty!' He fingered the front of his breeches.

'You like it?' said the girl, looking nervously up at Williams.

'Heaven in a fur hat,' Williams grunted.

Lettie squatted down, exposing herself fully, and began stroking her thighs. Slowly her fingers moved higher and she closed her eyes in feigned enjoyment. Tom was aroused by the display, but his heart was full of sorrow.

'What a charming sister you have, Doll,' said Cranfield slowly. 'Come here, child. Don't waste your passion on yourself.'

Lettie stood up and walked over to him. 'Kneel!' he commanded. 'Now, see what you can find in here.' He waved a fist-hand airily over his velvet breeches.

Doll approached Williams and laid her hands on his shoulders. 'So I'm for the goat, am I?' she smiled, pushing her hips towards him.

'You are his manna from heaven, all wet with morning dew, I trust?'

'How could I be otherwise at the thought of a ride with a Welsh pony?'

'One ride, Doll? Oh no! We'll canter the hills till we drown in our own sweat!'

So saying, he began pulling off his lower garments while Doll slipped out of her gown. Unprepared for such a public performance, Tom looked on in amazement.

Williams spread his cloak on the boarded floor and Doll lay upon it, her hands clasped behind her head and her legs raised. 'There,' she chuckled, 'the mountain cave of sweet treasures!'

'Which I will devour!' muttered Williams, roughly placing her calves over his shoulders before lowering his head.

Doll, ignoring these preparatory ministrations, stared about her with a look of bored resignation. Her eye caught Tom's and he looked away quickly, pretending disinterest. 'You next?' she asked casually, placing her feet on the floor as Williams pulled himself forward.

'I suppose so.'

'Very well. The goat won't be long now. Never is.'

Suddenly Williams' grunts were interrupted by a cry

from Cranfield. 'Teeth! For Christ's sake, girl! Teeth!'

Tom turned to see what was happening. Cranfield was still in his chair, his breeches in a crumpled heap about his ankles. Lettie, her lips wet with saliva, knelt at his side. 'I am sorry, sir,' she stammered, gasping for breath. 'Maybe you would like to occupy me? I'm better at that.'

'No, whore. I pay for what I want. 'Here—'. He pushed himself towards her again.

Whatever confidence Lettie might have had was now gone, and Cranfield shoved her away again with a shout of pain and anger. 'Doll!' he called. 'Come and drink with me! This sister of yours has no education in her trade.'

Williams had now finished and was sitting on the floor with a contented grin on his face. Doll stood up. 'Lettie, how could you shame me so? Come and please this other gentleman while I give Master James a proper tongue-wagging.'

Lettie took Tom's hand with a coquettishness that was betrayed by the tears in her unhappy eyes. Raising a finger to her lips then running it down over her breasts to below her waist, she asked, 'Here or there?'

Tom glanced at Williams. 'There, Tom lad. There. Beware the cannibal.'

Lettie pulled her gown from her shoulders and let it fall to the floor. Tom lowered his breeches. Shamed by his aroused nakedness and depressed by the vulgarity of the proceedings, he wanted to leave. He thought of George, poring earnestly over his books, and of Lucy, gazing out of the window wondering what had happened to him. Wincing, he wondered what would they say if they could see him now.

'Go on, use my cloak,' called Williams. 'It needs a pressing.'

The whore kissed Tom roughly on the mouth, frantically searching his mouth with her tongue. He put his arms round her, feeling her thin, bony body.

'Hurry! I feel the urges rising again,' cried Williams. 'Don't keep a Welshman waiting for his gallop!'

Lettie's body was dry and unyielding. Gritting his teeth, Tom pushed at her roughly, forcing a cry from her lips. Her eyes were closed.

'I'm sorry,' he whispered so that Williams would not hear. At the words she opened her eyes and for a fleeting second Tom saw a look of relief pass across her face.

'Let me take the saddle,' she said, wriggling to one side. Tom lay back on the hard floor and she lowered herself slowly onto him.

'Variations!' cried Williams. 'I can hold back no longer!'

Tom heard him spit into his hand, then felt Lettie stiffen. Williams' hairy arms reached to the ground beside Tom's face. Lettie began to quiver and sob. Cruelly elated by the pain he was inflicting, Tom rose to a climax then lay there while Williams had his way.

For his weakness, cowardice and unkindness, Tom despised himself utterly.

iv

'Tom?'

'Yes, Lucy?'

'What is lying on your mind, my dearest?' As she spoke, Lucy leaned across the table towards Tom and took his hand affectionately. He responded by sliding his fingers between hers, but said nothing.

It was the middle of a foggy afternoon in the second week of November. The maid had retired after clearing the dinner dishes, and shortly afterwards, with a discreet wink to his daughter, Oliver Simpson had excused himself to complete an urgent piece of work, leaving the young couple sitting alone in the parlour. Outside the window the street was deserted and still. Within, the cosy silence was broken only by the crackling of the fire and the reedy whistling drifting in from the workshop where the tailor snipped and sewed by candlelight.

'A burden shared is half the weight,' Lucy coaxed.

'I know. But I am not sure that I wish to share my burden with you. I am not proud of it.'

Lucy mocked him amiably, 'You, not proud? Why, Tom Verney, you are one of the proudest young men in all London!'

'Am I? Perhaps so. But maybe it is only to cover what I am ashamed of.'

'I am lost, Tom. Riddles are not my way.' She spoke no less than the truth, for she was a straightforward, trusting girl who neither liked nor understood deceit in any form.

'Well, see here.' Fumbling in his pocket, Tom drew out his spectacles and put them on.

'Is that all?' Lucy laughed, squeezing his hand. 'Why, my affection towards you would not change even if you had no eyes at all! Besides, spectacles become you, give you an air of distinction. A proper scholar you seem.'

'But I am no scholar, Lucy. I am a wastrel. I have betrayed my father, myself – even you.' He took a deep breath. 'You remember when I failed to call on you two weeks ago?'

'Yes.'

'I said I was sick. It was not so.' Lucy withdrew her hand. 'No, listen to me. Please. If I cannot talk to you, I can talk to no one.'

Lucy's lips parted in an uncertain smile. When her relationship with Tom began, she had warned herself that the social gulf between them would be hard to bridge. They came from different worlds. Aware, whatever her father said, that it would be hard, almost impossible, to secure the genuine affection of a man who had been raised from birth to regard people of her station in life as lesser mortals, she had deliberately held herself back. Now Tom acknowledged that he had deceived her, she told herself she had been wise to do so. But at the same time she was comforted by his wish to confess. Perhaps it was a sign of genuine concern?

'Continue,' she urged. 'We know each other too well for secrets, don't we, Tom?'

And so, over the next half an hour, Tom opened his heart. Sparing the sordid details, he outlined his life with Williams and Corbet. He told how he had recklessly gone through his allowance, and of his repeated failures to settle to serious study.

'By God, Lucy,' he concluded, 'I have been such a fool. Such a weak-willed fool. And yet,' he added, looking across at her with a smile, 'talking thus has lightened my heart more than taking the sacrament, though it is probably blasphemy to say so. Perhaps the papists are not so foolish in requiring confession. It is like bathing – I feel cleaner already!'

'Have you told me all, Tom?'

'Everything of importance. Do you hate me for it?'

Standing up, she walked slowly round to Tom's side of the table and stood with her hands on his neck. 'Hate you? Why, do you believe I am about to throttle you for your sins? No.' She caressed the back of his head, then drew up her father's chair and sat beside him, looking closely into his face.

'Listen, Tom. You are not wicked and you are not weak. Wicked men are not troubled as you have been by the wrong they do, and weak men dare not admit their faults.' Tom shrugged, hoping she was correct.

'But now, Tom Verney, dear Tom Verney, perhaps you will swallow your pride sufficiently to allow a mere woman to help you?'

'"The weaker vessel" we are taught. Yet sometimes I believe it is a phrase devised by frightened men to hide their own, greater failings.'

'Ha! We are all as frail as one another, Tom. All sinners at heart. But the way of the world being what it is, we women are obliged to control ourselves more than men. Someone's hand has to rock the cradle, or where would the future lie? Listen close.'

'I am all yours, Lucy. The baby in your cradle.' Now that he had unburdened himself, he felt relaxed and happy again.

'First, Tom, you must control your purse. Start by ordering no more clothes from my father.'

'But how will I see you? I use his services only that I may be with you.'

'I know. But it is a pretence which no one is blind to any longer. You must be open with my father – tell him of your feelings towards me. He will not drive you away, I assure you.'

Tom felt a shiver of unease run through him. Publicly to announce himself as Lucy's gallant would be to throw up all kinds of problems, not the least of which would be the certainty that sooner or later news of his attachment would reach the ears of his fellow students, perhaps even the Banburys, or, worst of all, his father. Yet, that afternoon he had recognised Lucy as the one fixed point in his spinning universe, the only secure stanchion to which he could attach himself. He could not leave her now.

'Yes,' he replied, overriding his doubts, 'we must tell your father. Today.' Even as he spoke he was aware of a warning at the back of his mind that such decisions ought to be taken after much thought, rationally and certainly free from all compulsion.

Perhaps Lucy read his thoughts, for after they had stood up and sealed their pact with a long embrace, she said, 'Tom, you do not have to.'

'But I want to, Lucy, my guardian angel.'

'Very well. But you are a suitor, nothing more.'

'Nothing more.' He kissed her.

'And, Tom, I understand that the life of a young man in this city is full of temptations. You are no saint – thank God! I cannot bind you to me with iron bands. That would not be fair, or wise.'

Relieved to find that she knew him so well, he smiled, 'Lucy, I am bound to you alone.'

'No, Tom. You are not. But if we are to grow to—' she hesitated, 'perhaps to love one another, then no more secrets.'

'I promise, no more secrets, Lucy. That way we may grow to – what was the word you used?'

'You know very well what it was, Tom! Come now.'

Laughing, she took his hand and led him towards the workshop.

Two days later House Martin brought Tom a letter from Lady Banbury informing him that a packet and two letters awaited his collection at Pickering House. Written in a broad, confident hand, it ended:

I would have bade a servant deliver these to you, yet
no one is to be trusted in this city. Besides, Master
Verney, my dearest Banby is away from home again
and – as I believe I said when we supped together –
to speak (?) with an Oxfordshire man would ease
my sorry, lonely heart. Do not, I pray, fail a lady
who languishes alone.
   Elizabeth Banbury

Well, here's a fine puzzle! said Tom to himself as he folded the letter and placed it in a drawer. He had to collect the packet, for it undoubtedly contained much needed money from his father. And he was keen to know who else had written to him. But could he climb the spider's web without getting caught by the ravenous creature who dwelt there? Indeed, might he not enjoy falling prey to such a delightful predator? Memories of supper at Pickering House came flooding back. His hostess had hardly been dull company, and when he recalled her eager groping beneath the table he was so aroused that he was tempted to call at Pickering House at once.

But what of Lucy? He was more taken with her than he liked to admit, and had been deeply touched by the obvious happiness she took from telling her father of their mutual affection. But his feelings towards her stemmed partly from admiration for her insight into his weaknesses. What had she said? 'I cannot bind you with iron bands.' Did she really mean it? He had promised to keep no secrets from her. Would she understand a betrayal – for that is what it would be – so soon after the formalisation of their liaison? Torn by such thoughts, Tom passed the rest of the day glancing though a Latin grammar, wondering whether Ancient Green would remember his threat to test him on the language when he returned to the Inn.

When he awoke the next morning, Tom was still haunted by the image of Elizabeth Banbury, sitting back in her chair in that darkened dining room, her gown about her thighs and a look of uncontrollable passion on her face. Eventually, he could hold out no longer. Telling himself that if things turned out the way he thought, or hoped, he could always tell Lucy that he had been seduced – which would, after all, be the truth, or at least a fair approximation to it – he made his way to the stables and was soon spurring Princess down Clement's Lane towards the Strand.

Having announced his arrival, he was kept waiting in the hall of Pickering House for ten minutes. When eventually a maid told him that Lady Banbury was indisposed, but that 'the things as what he had come about' were waiting for him upstairs, he received the news with a mixture of relief and disappointment. He was taken to a room on the first floor, which he assumed from the scented air and exquisite furnishings to be some sort of antechamber in her ladyship's apartments, and shown a leather pouch and two letters lying on a low table near the window. As soon as the girl had withdrawn, Tom knelt down and eagerly pulled open the pouch. Inside, carefully wrapped in cloth, were thirty-five gold sovereigns.

'God be praised!' he whispered as he counted the money. 'Oh, Father, you are too good to me! I do not deserve such kindness.' He picked up the purse and kissed it. The faint smell of tobacco still lingered within, evoking such a legion of memories that a sob rose in his throat. More than fifteen pounds! He had not expected such generosity. It suggested that his father understood his needs better than he had dared hope and that the Toad had not betrayed him. Upon breaking the seal on the bulkier of the two letters, however, Tom found to his dismay that he was wrong, on both counts.

After a short greeting and an expression of relief that his son had not succumbed to the plague, which had lingered on in the capital longer than usual owing to the protracted spell of hot weather in September, Justice Verney went on to chastise Tom for not writing home more often. 'Since your arrival in London we have received but two letters, and those little more than hasty scratchings', he complained. 'Are you so deep in study that you forget your mother, brothers and sisters? I think not.' This ironic shot opened a volley of criticism. John Verney revealed that Lord Banbury had painted a lurid picture of Tom's new life, and although the justice admitted that 'his lordship's tongue may embellish the truth somewhat', he was shrewd enough to see that Tom's request for money and his brief, infrequent communications lent credence to the garrulous peer's malicious gossip. He continued:

> Even if we believe but one part in ten of what his lordship reports, then it is clear you are not living as becomes one of your station or your means. I do not expect my son to bring scorn upon the family.
> Even so, I am sending you further money. I pray do not lose it as easily or as swiftly as you did my last endowment, for there is no more. As it is, remember that in order to meet your needs your mother and sister Elizabeth will have no new gowns this Christmas and the refurbishment of the hall – for which, as you will remember well, I had great plans – must now wait another year.

When he had read through to the end of the letter, to which was appended a short paragraph from his mother, full of kindly concern and poignant domestic detail, Tom remained kneeling and uttered up a short prayer.

'Dear Lord,' he whispered earnestly, 'forgive, I pray, the wrong I have done to You and to those dear to me. I have erred and strayed from the true path like a lost sheep. Give me strength, I beseech You, to turn back from my wickedness, for without Your help I am but a frail fallen leaf at the mercy of cruel winds. This I ask through Jesus Christ, Our Lord.'

He remained on his knees a while longer, half wondering whether the self-pitying phrase about 'cruel winds' had not contained an element of excuse for further failings, then stood up. As he did so, his eyes alighted on the second letter lying untouched on the table. It had been addressed by his sister Elizabeth. However, as soon as he had broken the seal and glanced inside, he saw that the contents were the work of a different, less familiar hand.

My dear Tom – Pray forgive my forward presumption in writing to you, but I hear from your sister Elizabeth, with whom I converse almost every day, that all is not well between you and your father, and I hope that a less critical communication from one of your old companions may lighten your spirits somewhat.

Glancing to the foot of the letter to discover who was showing such concern for his welfare, Tom was surprised to read, 'Your affectionate friend, Anne Hutchinson'. His heart jumped. Anne! Why, he had almost forgotten of her existence. Dear Anne, he thought, how like you to seek to comfort me now. Once or twice in the past, after furious arguments with his father, he had found her a sympathetic and wise councillor, and he recalled with innocent pleasure their few moments alone together, particularly when, with Elizabeth's connivance, they had met in his father's orchard for an hour shortly before his departure. But, as on previous occasions, he had been slightly disconcerted by her unwillingness to respond openly to his eager advances. 'Tom dear,' she had said with an unconvincing jollity, slowly removing his hands from about her waist and standing slightly back from him, 'soon you will be far away and we will not set eyes on each other for long months. Whatever I say or do, you will meet many people and have many adventures. Of course, I hope you will not forget me entirely. Yet I would have you picture Anne Hutchinson not as a river crossed, truly not as a challenge at all, but as a friend to whom one day you might be pleased to return.'

Although Tom understood the wisdom of such sentiments, at the time they had irritated him. Inspired by the romance of imminent departure, he had sought more than reassuring phrases before their separation. Besides, the reference, however oblique, to what might happen after his eventual return reminded him that a match between them had been discreetly mooted in both their households almost since the day she had been born, and he balked at the thought of going along with his father's wishes any more than he had to.

Wondering unkindly whether this letter was not just another ploy to get him to mend his ways, he continued where he had broken off.

We all miss your company and talk of you often.
Elizabeth and I knew you were going to throw

yourself into London life with the same vigour as
you showed when you were here, though we do
not believe the stories which Lord Banbury has
been telling of you. He is, I believe, not a man to be
trusted. Your father, too, understands this, but he is
so hurt by the calumny that he blames you entirely
for bringing his family into disrepute. We do not
know whom to pity most – Justice Verney for his
humiliation, or you for being the centre of
unmerited scandal.

Elizabeth and I say what we can in your defence,
though I fear it is to little avail. You may gather
from this that you are often in my thoughts. There!
Now I have admitted more than ever I did when
we were face to face! If our families knew that I was
writing thus I would be dubbed a shameless hussy.
Happily, Elizabeth's subterfuge will protect me
from such accusation, for she has undertaken to
address this letter as if it comes from her. Should
you wish to reply to me – which I doubt – then she
has undertaken to pass to me (unread!) any paper
you enclose within a letter to her. Such scheming! I
did not believe it was in my nature to be so devious.
I trust you do not draw out the unworthy nature in
other ladies you meet ...

Tom had just reached the end of the letter and was
trying to come to terms with the emotions it raised in
him when he was startled to hear his name being called
from an adjoining room.

'Master Verney! Is that you?' He recognised the voice
at once.

As if it were a magic window through which his
correspondent might see from Oxfordshire to London,

he hastily placed Anne's letter in his pocket and replied, 'Yes. It is Tom Verney,' staring about him as he spoke to ascertain where his interlocutor might be.

'Ah! Please enter. The door is behind the screen.'

Tom turned the gilded handle and found himself in a large bedchamber. Although the shutters were partly closed, in the gloom he could make out an ornate dressing table, several chairs, and, set against the far wall but reaching almost to the centre of the room, a huge four-poster bed. The side curtains were drawn fast, but those at the end nearest to him were tied back with thick cords of turquoise twist, framing the silken luxury within. And there, sprawling in a nest of rose-coloured pillows, lay Lady Elizabeth Banbury.

She was completely naked.

FIVE

THE GEORGE

i

'No, Father! He is not to be excused any more than he is to be trusted.' Lucy's shrill voice passed from a scream to a wail. 'How could he have been so cruel?'

'But young men are easily led astray, daughter, as you should know. Besides, did he not tell you of his lapse himself, as you had asked?' Oliver Simpson could not remember when he had last seen his daughter so distressed.

'That is quibbling, Father. Two days after he had pledged himself to me! Before you, too – that was not well done, was it?

'He says it will remain a secret. Ha! The Banburys have servants – soon the whole town will gossip of this secret, and cheated Lucy Simpson will be the laughing stock of all Holborn. Only yesterday you crowed to Mistress Biddle how I had secured the affections of Gentleman Verney. Secured! Oh!'

Torn by the pain of humiliation and heartbreak, Lucy was unable to go on. She laid her head on her father's shoulder and wept without restraint. 'Never,' she gasped between sobs, 'never will I permit him to pay court to me again.'

The tailor's tired face crumpled with anxiety and regret. Tenderly stroking his daughter's hair, he said softly, 'We will see, my dearest. Time will heal all.'

'Will it? Maybe. But it will not bring Master heartless, pompous, shifty Verney back to this house.'

'Shhh! You are too upset to know what you are saying.'

'I do know what I am saying.' She stood up, brushing away her tears with the back of her hand. 'And I am not upset, Father. I am angry.' She stamped her foot. 'Yes, Father, I am angry. Angry at that weak man. Angry at myself for allowing him into my heart. And, though it pains me to confess it, angry even with you for encouraging his importuning advances.'

'I am sorry, Lucy. Truly I am. Yet I did not think him wicked, and still do not. I am certain he cares for you. At this moment I do not expect he is any happier than yourself.'

Oliver Simpson was right. During the three hours that Tom had spent with Lady Banbury, whose raw passion and shameless, good-humoured quest for pleasure had left him with scarcely enough energy to climb into Princess's saddle, current fascination had totally blotted out future complications. But back in his chambers, after he had re-read his letters from home and mused on his lover's remarkable athleticism and ingenuity, he had grown increasingly agitated about what, if anything, he should say to Lucy. In the end, determined to honour his pledge and clear his conscience, he had called round at her house and, finding her alone, had confessed his misdemeanour immediately. Even as he had begun, laughing and trying to make light of the incident, he had realised, with an unpleasant sick feeling in his stomach, that she had not seen the matter as he did.

Five minutes later he had been back in the street, a string of bitter, recriminating epithets ringing in his ears. He had not tried to justify his behaviour, even to himself, and as he had walked back to the Inn he had been overwhelmed by a feeling of total despondency. Almost everything he encountered, he told himself, was either rotten before he touched it or fell to pieces at his clumsy, insensitive hands.

Depression, like night, crept inexorably forward as the pale afternoon light faded into shadows. 'God's blood, Bird,' he sighed when House Martin came in to see if there was anything for him to do, 'was there ever a creature more wretched, more unfortunate than myself?'

'Eh, sir?'

'Do you not think me a miserable fellow, a puffin?'

'No, sir, I do not. I know as you're a gentleman. And a very good-hearted one. But ...'

'Go on.'

'You can be a squeak wild, sir. But that's the doing of Mr Williams and Mr Corbet, isn't it, sir?'

'I do not like those ruffians, and have played the last of their loaded games.'

'I am pleased to hear that, sir, 'cause on the way to your chambers I heard them saying as they was coming to call on you.'

'Heart and hell!! I thank you, sweet Bird, for that timely chirrup. If I meet with them now I fear I will kill them both. Quick, my cloak!' Without further ado, Tom slammed the door of his chambers, ran downstairs out into the courtyard and slipped through the main gates just as Callow was closing them for the night.

In the street he paused, unsure whether to call on Lucy to try to effect a reconciliation or to wander off on his own. Surmising that she would probably throw him out as abruptly as she had done that afternoon, he chose to shield his self-esteem from further hurt and walked disconsolately along Fleet Street, across the bridge spanning the clogged stream from which it took its name, up Ludgate Hill and so into the dark alleys of the walled city.

ii

For three hours Tom walked the shadowed streets of the capital. Preoccupied with his own thoughts and scarcely conscious of where he was going, he wandered in a broad circle along Thames Street, up Dowgate and Wallbrook, left past the lighted windows of the Old Barge into Bucklesbury and so west again along the broad avenue of West Cheap. By the spire of Eleanor Cross he paused and, finding a dry spot on the stone plinth, sat down to rest and take stock. Unlike St Paul, he had received no blinding revelation on the road. If anything, he was more confused now than when he had set out. There were just too many pieces, too many contradictions for him to make sense of them. He knew full well what he ought to do – that was easy. He should study hard, lead a temperate and thrifty life according to the teachings of the church, be charitable to all men and write long, regular and informative letters home to his doting parents. No drinking bouts or whoremongering with the closet papists, no frolics with Lady Banbury and no, not even sweet dalliance with dear Lucy, for they all threatened the fragile fabric of ordered society.

Huh! Tom spat at his feet and put on his spectacles to see what was going on around him. It was a dangerous time of night for a man to venture abroad unaccompanied, particularly when he carried so fat a purse. Even as he looked, he saw a haggard creature watching him closely from beneath the eves of Goldsmith Row. He stood up and placing his hand on the hilt of his sword called out, 'Yes, slave? You wish to speak with me?' The vagabond shuffled off in search of easier prey and Tom resumed his seat.

So, he sighed, if I live a life of virtue, what do I become? A milksop? A bore? A monk? Or even a saint? God forbid that Tom Verney should ever join that castrated quartet! No, he must begin by being true to himself, for that in a way was being true to God, in whose image he had been made. But what if being true to himself meant trugging his figs off with Bessie Banbury? Or falling in love with Lucy? Were those the actions of someone made in the image of God, or were they the work of the devil?

The devil – there's another pretty proposition, he reflected, eyeing a pair of footpads stalking towards him from Guthrun's Lane. Was the devil part of God's creation? If so, it was a pretty poor joke. Then if he was not, was God truly almighty?

'Fie! I do not understand!' he howled at the top of his voice, leaping to his feet and drawing his sword. 'Sweet Jesus Christ, why in the name of thunder did You build this poxy maze and place me in the crossbitten midst of it?'

His shouts echoed off the buildings all around. 'Would I were a dumb-headed goat that I could eat my way out!'

Alarmed by the sudden commotion, a dog ran whimpering from the porch of St Peter's church and the pair of foisters noiselessly slipped back into the obscurity from which they had emerged.

A watchman hurried up. 'All well, sir?'

'All well, muttonbrain?' Tom sneered. 'God's life! Here we crawl, maggots on a stinking orange, and you ask if all is well! Take these, Bartimaeus, and see for yourself!' He wrenched off his spectacles and proffered them to the officer.

'It would be as well, sir, for you to return home,' shrugged the man, assuming Tom to be drunk and walking off in the direction of St Paul's.

'Ha! Happier blind, eh?' called Tom after him. 'Wise fellow!' He donned his spectacles again and stood watching the man as he withdrew into the gloom. At that moment, the clouds parted for an instant, allowing a flood of clear moonlight to fall on the city. In the distance the bulk of the ancient cathedral rose like a silvery phantom out of the darkness. Tom gazed in silence till the breeze drew the curtain once more and the picture dissolved into the night as swiftly as it had arisen.

'Well,' he whispered to the empty street, 'is that a sign? An image to hold fast to? Light shining through the darkness – or was it darkness triumphing over light? Who knows? Who cares!'

Tired of trying to comprehend the incomprehensible, and feeling the need for food and company, he directed his steps along Newgate towards the hearty fires of the George by Holborn Bridge. As the inn was a popular terminus for coaches from the northern towns of Buckinghamshire and Oxfordshire, he hoped he might pick up some gossip about his native county. On his way, partly to stop thinking about Lucy, he tried with little success to conjure up a mental picture of Anne Hutchinson. No matter, he told himself, there was just a chance that he might meet someone at the George who knew her family and then he could steer the conversation round to the girl whose letter had cheered him so unexpectedly. The idea gave fresh purpose to his visit, and, lengthening his pace, he strode rapidly towards his destination.

Some two weeks previously, the landlord of the George, Seth Carter, had rented out a room at the top of his inn to a large, bearded man who had said that he needed to stay there while recuperating from a serious illness. The nature of the illness had not been specified and although since his arrival the stranger had received an odd collection of visitors, ranging from well-spoken men in dark cloaks, who slipped in and out like wraiths, to others who appeared little more than vagabonds, the tenant himself was such a genial fellow that for the time being the host overcame his natural suspicion and accepted the man's presence with little more than the occasional quizzical look.

On the night in question the mysterious lodger had asked Carter to bring to his room a large jug of ale and 'a meal as large as a hill for two hungry men – the best you have, by the mass!'

'Six o clock, Mr Shakespeare?' enquired the landlord.

'But no, good host. We will eat late, when the candles are gnawing at their holders like the fires of hell at the legs of the ungodly. Eight.'

'Very good, sir.' Carter paused. 'A friend from the country, sir?' he asked tentatively, keen to find out a little more about this flamboyant but puzzling Mr Shakespeare.

'The country? Oh aye.' The reply was uncustomarily hesitant. 'Oxfordshire, I believe. That's where he dwelt a while back.'

'In any particular place, sir?'

'My most excellent host, did you in a previous incarnation find employment with the Spanish Inquisition? What is it to you if my friend hails from Bicester or Bombay, eh? Be off with you. I am not well and have need of rest.' The smile on his face told that he was not as angry as he sounded.

Odd creature, Carter thought as he descended the stairs. Very odd. Fancy him being named Shakespeare! I don't credit it for a wink. And why does he wear his hair so unkempt when all the rest of him is set up so gentlemanly? Something's awry, sure as birds have wings.

True to his word, at the hour appointed, the landlord reappeared bearing three large dishes laden with roast meats and vegetables. When he went down to collect the ale, he returned with Shakespeare's guest.

'Your friend, sir. From Bicester,' he announced as he laid a brimming jug on the table.

'From where, sirrah? Oh aye! From Bicester.' Shakespeare stood up and greeted the new arrival warmly. 'Well met, Malvolio! Welcome to London!' His guest stared at him blankly. 'Come, Malvolio' – he pronounced the name with careful precision – 'sit and eat. Thank you, landlord.'

After closing the door, Carter stood and listened for a moment. Not a sound came to his ears. 'Too wise a dog for that trick, aren't you, my fine jester!' he muttered, turning and walking downstairs with a deliberately heavy tread. 'First Shakespeare, then Malvolio – you'll have Julius poxy Caesar up there next! But Carter will winkle you out, my strutting actor, just you see if he doesn't.'

The prying host's opportunity came sooner than he had expected. Shortly after he had returned to the tap room, a tall, handsome, well-dressed young man wearing spectacles entered the inn and began asking customers if they were from the vicinity of Bicester. Here's a fine piece of fortune, thought Carter.

'I believe I can be of assistance, sir,' he called over to the gentleman.

'You can? I am most grateful to you, landlord.'

'If you would follow me, sir, upstairs ...'

He led the way to Shakespeare's room and, with the most cursory of knocks, threw open the door.

'Excuse me, Mr Shakespeare, but here's a gentleman as would like to exchange a few words with your friend on the subject of Bicester ...' Before he could finish what he was saying, Tom had pushed past him into the room.

'Clifford!' he exploded, drawing his sword. Chicken leg in hand, the supper guest rose from the table and backed towards the wall.

'And wait! Zounds, if I am not mistaken it is Great John, too! Oh, what a nest of villainy have we here!'

'You know these men, sir?' enquired Carter, confused by what was going on but delighted that his suspicions had not been without foundation.

'Know them! They would have killed me, landlord! Go, find a constable this instant!' Carter scuttled off to do as he was bidden.

Keeping the tip of his sword pointing directly towards their throats, Tom scowled at his two captives. 'Sit down, Clifford!' he barked, his heart beating furiously against his ribs. 'And place your hands on the table before you. You likewise, ruffian.'

Great John, for it was indeed he, had not moved a muscle since Tom had burst in. But now, ignoring his captor's command, he rose painfully to his feet.

'Do as the gentleman instructs you, Sloper,' he ordered in deep, authoritative tones. His broad, bearded face turned towards Tom. 'Master Verney – I recall your name correctly, do I not, sir? – Sloper he was christened, not Clifford, and Sloper he shall stay. Francis Sloper, nothing but a foolish rogue.' A chuckle bubbled in his throat like an irrepressible spring. 'And a thief, too, I have heard men say?'

'Sit, slave, and place your hands before you!' shouted Tom, wondering whether he was brave enough to run someone through in cold blood. He was uneasy at the way John's cool, almost avuncular manner was dousing his fiery confidence.

'As valiant now, I warrant, as in the woods above Stokenchurch,' smiled John with an unctuous calm that bordered on the insolent. He still refused to do as he was told. 'Come, soldier Verney, I will sit if it will calm your temper.'

Tom snorted his refusal.

'Very well,' the giant said, 'but I pray you at least put up your sword, sir gallant – surely you would not hole me a second time before the first wound has healed?'

Aware that in this battle of wills he was likely to be driven from the field with hardly a fight, Tom remained silent. He had no wish to reveal still more of his position to the enemy.

'See here,' John went on in a more serious tone, taking a silver crucifix from a pocket in his breeches, 'I swear by the Holy Virgin Mother of Our Lord Jesus Christ that I will neither harm you, nor seek to flee. And if Sloper here tries either, I will beat his body to a mess of pepper and jam with my own hands!'

'Oaths will not shield you, thief. The constable will be here shortly,' Tom said hopefully, praying that assistance would appear before it was too late.

'He will, by the mass! And I have little time and much

to explain.' John rubbed his huge hands together. 'Come, Master Verney, if you will listen closely, I believe you will see we have no need of a constable.'

By God! thought Tom, noticing a twinkle in the man's eyes, it is almost as if the rogue is enjoying himself.

'Speak on, all you wish,' he scoffed. 'It will be of no avail.' Yet even as he spoke he felt held in the same inexplicable thrall of the man as had overwhelmed him at their last meeting. He lowered his sword a little.

Holding his side, John carefully eased his massive frame into his chair, took a deep draught of ale and, without once taking his eyes from Tom's face, began his defence in a rolling voice of honey and thunder.

'There was once a gentleman, Master Verney, neither a saint nor a rogue, just a gentleman like yourself,' he nodded in Tom's direction, 'who, for reasons which need not concern us, spent long years roving the seas and lands like an errant knight in the days when all Christendom knelt in a single faith before the feet of Our Lord Jesus Christ.' A ham-like fist waved an easy sign of the cross over his embroidered shirt.

'In his wanderings our hero survived such a multitude of hardships and temptations that he foolishly came to believe an angel of God walked at his side. Alas! Therein lay the seeds of his undoing. Proud as a tiger, he felt himself clothed in such adamantine armour of body and mind that nothing – no dart of affection, no spear of avarice or stab of covetousness – could ever find him out.'

The point of Tom's sword had drooped to the floor. 'Continue,' he said with as much disinterest as he could muster. The thunder rumbled on.

'Pride, Master Verney, is a terrible sin. Like the gnawing beetle in the beam, it works wonderfully silent through the entire body, consuming its strength hour by hour, day by day. Then – Ah! – with one puny blow the whole oak of being crumbles to dust.

'So it was with our knight. And the elfin cut that pierced him to the heart? It was love, Master Verney. A passionate, consuming, burning, roaring furnace of love. Love for a young and very beautiful maid named Sarah, whose brightness outshone the very sun itself.'

Tom's sword fell to the ground with a clatter. As neither of his captives moved, he smiled weakly, stooped and picked it up. The power of John's words and the bass music of his voice, whose strange interbreeding of accents he still could not place, had disarmed him more effectively than a regiment of robbers.

'Young sir, I see that you know the power I speak of. The love of man for woman, created by God to run like a thread of pleasure through the tangled skein of His creation, is a pale image of the Almighty's own love for us. And so it was that in their brief hours together the knight and the maid Sarah tasted the milk of Paradise.'

Tom noticed a dark shadow descend over John's face. If this man is a player, he thought, he should be acting before the court, not spinning yarns in an inn.

'But as the fairest summer, this brief passage of joy had but a little time to run.' John's hands began to shake and he spoke more quickly. 'One day Sarah's father, a jealous, narrow man whose heart had long since shrivelled like an old apple in the desert, by chance came upon his daughter with her lover. Bitter fury seized him. He locked the maid within doors and beat her cruelly. Misusing the authority entrusted in him by the King, he incarcerated her sweetheart and agreed to his release only after he had burned him with this!'

With a sweep of his broad hand, he lifted the hair from

his forehead. There, as clear as it had been when Tom first set eyes on it, was the raised, livid red brand of the vagrant.

'Aye, Master Verney,' said John in a low whisper, 'I was that knight. And if I am not mistaken you know by whose command this cruel injustice was performed.' He tapped a large finger on the indelible scar.

Tom winced. Surely no man could feign the truth so convincingly? 'Justice Fuller,' he said quietly, remembering how much he had disliked the puritanical magistrate whom he had met at the Green Man. 'He caused that to be done to you because you loved his daughter?'

'He did.'

'And you are a papist?'

'Is that a sin? Was not the Roman faith espoused by the great Richard Lionheart and all our mighty kings before the time of the last King Henry?'

Recalling what else Fuller had told him, Tom ignored the question. 'This Sarah, the justice's daughter, you know she is with child?'

John nodded. Before he could say anything further, he was interrupted by the sound of footsteps.

'The constable,' said Tom awkwardly, not knowing quite what to do. 'You have told a goodly story, John, and I am sorry for you. But highway robbery? And what of this man Clifford, or Sloper as you say he is called? For sure he must hang for a varlet and a cozening knave!' The warmth he felt towards John did not extend towards his silent, frozen partner.

'The quality of mercy is not strained, Master Verney. Trust me. Tell the constable you were mistaken, and I will explain further and make amends for the wrong you have suffered. Trust me.' The plea was steeped in sincerity.

As the heavy tread of the constable approached, John

raised his voice, ' ... and now, Master Verney, we must tell the good constable the nature of this confusion.' The door opened. 'Ah! Here he is! Welcome, constable. I fear we have brought you here on a false scent, eh, Master Verney?'

Staff in hand, the constable paused on the threshold. Behind him, standing on tiptoe to see what was going on, Seth Carter peered into the room. To his right he saw Tom carefully returning his sword to its scabbard. John was sitting back easily, lowering a slice of beef into his mouth from the point of a knife, while Sloper, who had not moved for the last ten minutes, was still bolt upright with his hands before him on the table.

'I am summoned by the landlord to make an arrest,' said the officer in formal tones. 'Who is the accused party here? This him?' He took a step towards Clifford.

For a second Tom was tempted to let the rogue be seized, but as he opened his mouth to speak he met John's gaze and instead of an affirmation he found himself saying, 'No, constable. I fear it is you who are the wronged party.'

'Me?'

'Yes. My eyes are not what they ought to be,' said Tom with a shake of the head, 'and when I entered the room I mistook these men for two others, two villains who had robbed me on the road. Now I see I am mistaken. Pray take this for your pains' – he gave the man twopence – 'and trouble us no further.'

The constable turned on his heel and left, leaving Carter gaping open-mouthed in the doorway.

'Yes, landlord?' enquired John with a grin.

'Oh, it is no matter, Mr – Shakespeare. No great matter. It was just that the young gentleman seemed so certain.'

'I was in error, landlord. Are you never confused yourself?'

'I am, sir. Never more so than now.'

'Well, sirrah,' said Tom briskly as soon as Carter had gone, 'that was but a stay of execution. I am a quarter convinced. If you do not present a good reason why I should perjure myself further in protection of two men who have used me most vilely, I will send for another constable. And there will be no mercy.' His demand was motivated as much by inquisitiveness as moral indignation, for he knew that he would not find it easy to persuade the bemused Carter to summon the law a second time.

To his surprise, however, John did not try to excuse the way Sloper had tricked him into parting with his clothes and money. Instead, upbraiding his guest for an ungrateful fool and a blackguard, he made him pay back all he had taken, together with a handsome recompense for the stolen garments and two shillings extra, 'as a mark of gratitude to Master Verney for saving you from the law and to remind you never again to cloy an honest gentleman.'

Confident that his safety was not threatened and feeling John's spell once more winding about him, Tom found his pose as impromptu gaoler rather ridiculous, and was relieved to be invited to sit at the table and listen to the rest of the singular tale. He heard that after his release by Justice Fuller (who at that time had not known of his daughter's pregnancy), John had found himself both destitute and a social outcast. In desperation, he had taken up with a band of robbers, whose kindness to him in his hour of need he had found as touching as it was surprising. The experience of the next few weeks, he said, had taught him more about Man's contradictory nature than all his past travels and occupations. Like himself, his three companions had not chosen to put themselves outside the law but had been forced to do so by a society which ordained that all without work were idle. Clifford, Tom was assured, really did come from a family ruined by recusancy. Pym, the cowardly, weasel-faced man who had sworn at Tom so colourfully during the attempted robbery, was an orphan who had no idea in which parish he had been born and so was unable to claim relief, while the fourth member of the gang, Harry, was too simple to hold down a job and had been found by the others wandering the highroad delirious with starvation. For what they had done before he joined them, John explained, he accepted no responsibility. But once in charge, his dominating personality had transformed both their behaviour and tactics.

The band had thrived, building up a store of money and valuables. John confessed with a grin that he had even come to enjoy the work. 'There I was, Master Verney, like Robin Hood in the greenwood, taking from the rich and giving to the poor — I saw to it that the poor boxes in the neighbouring parishes were well filled with our takings.'

Tom now realised why his reception by the villagers who had gathered in the Green Man to hear his story had been so contradictory — presumably, without being able to ask him straight, they had been trying to find out whether he had identified one of their folk heroes. At the same time, John's mention of the poor reminded him of Blind Jane, and her warning that a man had been killed where the London road crossed the Chilterns.

'You make thieving sound like a child's romance,' he scoffed. 'By God, I do not regard killing an innocent traveller as noble! You are murderers!' As he thought how close he too had come to being done to death that September evening, once again righteous anger smouldered within him.

'Murderers? No, Master Verney, not us. Not when I was their captain. Obliged to play at thieving, my mission was to reform the trade, to turn robbery into a branch of justice. I would countenance no hellish villainy.'

'It was so,' agreed Sloper. Tom's look showed he was not convinced.

'Ah! So you know of the unhappy fellow who was slain on the highway?' John asked. 'By Mary, that was not our doing, though we have a fair idea whose it was!' He looked at Sloper, who again concurred.

John related how when they spied a likely quarry approaching his gang hid in the woods where the path was narrowest. Then John, being the strongest of them, would jump out without a word and seize the person from behind, covering the victim's eyes lest he recognise his assailants. He was deprived of his wealth and left bound, gagged and blindfolded to be rescued by whoever happened to pass by. 'In this amusing and rewarding fashion,' said John, 'Great Robin of the Chilterns and his merry men passed their days, outside the law of men, but maybe not so far from those of God.' He waited for the meaning of his words to sink in.

'Yet in time, as will always happen, we grew careless. Along came this sharp-eyed young gentleman on a fine horse and – the rest of that stanza is known to you, I believe?'

'It is,' said Tom, unable to resist smiling at the flattery. 'But that is not the end of the tale.'

'No. Your shooting cleared my head, Master Verney, like a plunge in a winter stream, though no ice ever hurt like your ball. Yet I thank God for your skill.'

'You do?'

'When I was hit Harry fled I know not where and Pym, always a villain at heart, I fear, went his own way. For certain, he will hang one day soon. Sloper here saved my life. He tended me and brought me to London to lie low and recover my strength. Now that his share of our treasure is sorely depleted he has to fill his purse as best he can – I cannot say I am pleased by the means he has chosen.' He turned and punched Sloper playfully on the arm. 'You'll swing, you rogue, won't you?'

'Never! Unless you dangle beside me, John.'

'Hang Great John! Ha! I have done with all thieving and breaking of laws.' Sloper eyed him suspiciously. 'Besides, there is no rope in all London stout enough to hold me.'

As he watched the ill-assorted couple and listened to their macabre banter, fresh doubts grew in Tom's mind. John's story was so extraordinary and had been so convincingly delivered that it could be true, but too much remained unexplained. Why, he did not even know the man's surname! Moreover, however romantic their motives and light-handed their methods, these men had lived by robbery. Against his better judgement he had been persuaded to receive Sloper's money and on two separate occasions he had taken the law into his own hands by failing to denounce a man who by his own admission was – or had been – a common criminal.

Afraid that he had heard too much and frightened that the situation was becoming more dangerous by the minute, he wished to get away as quickly as possible. Taking up his hat, he delivered a curt farewell and left the inn. Never more, he told himself, would he have anything to do with those men. And if either of them crossed his path again, they would find they had drunk his well of pity bone-dry.

After Tom's departure, John and Sloper sat in silence for a long time. 'Well, John,' said the latter eventually, 'the finest performance as ever you gave!'

'Performance? By Christ! I do not perform, Sloper, you leatherhead! I spoke the golden truth.'

'Some of it. Gold-plated.' He took a drink. 'Will he blab?'

'Master Verney? I think not, Sloper; there is more charity in his fingernail than in all your poxy body. Should you live to be as old as Methuselah, which God forbid, you would never understand such a man. He is what they call a gentleman, Sloper.'

'Do they? Well, I know a gentleman whose precious charity has led him into deep water, up to the neck. Should he go to the law, he'll not find it comfortable explaining himself, will he?'

iii

Tom spent the last fortnight in November dawdling about the Inn in a preoccupied daze. Whenever he tried to settle to his studies, other matters jostled to command his attention so effectively that, try as he might, he was unable to concentrate for more than a few minutes. Lucy was constantly in his thoughts. No matter how hard he sought to convince himself that there was little point in mooning over a mere tailor's daughter, he knew that her rejection had bruised more than just his pride. Now that the humble Simpson household was no longer open to him, he realised how much his visits there had meant to him. He urgently needed to confide in Lucy about that extraordinary night at the George and hear her say that he had acted as a true Christian. Above all, he longed to take her in his arms once more and feel her rounded body pressed to his in a tantalising suggestion of what might one day happen between them.

When not dreaming of Lucy, Tom was turning John's story over and over in his mind, going through each detail, looking for flaws and inconsistencies. Anxious about his equivocal involvement with the plausible thief, he asked George about the standing of those who failed to hand over a known law-breaker. There was no problem, George had replied: those who aided and abetted criminals, in whatever way, were as culpable as the villains themselves.

The verdict sent a shiver down Tom's spine. How ironic, he thought, to be studying and flouting the same law! And how unfair that he should be suffering as a result of both his selfishness and his kindness. If he had kept his sympathy for Lucy and not wasted it on a pair of robbers, he would not be in such an unhappy predicament. But perhaps, unable to resist being well regarded, whether as a lover by Lady Banbury or as a charitable gentleman by the two robbers, he had received his just deserts in both cases? 'Flattery and Vanity', he scrawled in large letters across the back page of his commonplace book – 'twin worms of the devil. Beware!'

Gilbert Marshall, tall, lean, beak-nosed and bald, was now in the middle of one of his brief periods of residence in the capital. Although his company eased Tom's loneliness a little, he was an uncommunicative man who appeared to regard the student merely as a useful means of sharing the cost of his chambers. Busy all day in the courts or meeting clients, he sat up most of the night at his desk poring over legal books and papers. Only once, when they met in the vestibule common to both their apartments, did he share more than a few words with Tom.

'Verney,' he said in a sharp tenor voice, peering down at him from the cobwebs that festooned the panelling beyond House Martin's reach, 'seen a hanging?'

'No, sir.'

'You must. Great sport. Law in action. Purging the kingdom.' With a sudden display of animation he began to wave a long arm by his side like a pendulum. 'Swing, swing! Swing to hell!'

Tom stared in amazement. Swallowing hard to stop himself laughing, he asked, 'Do you often attend the hangings, sir?'

'Whenever in London. Never miss them. Accompany me, before I depart?'

'Certainly, sir.' Although he would have chosen company more his own age, Tom welcomed the opportunity of experiencing the macabre fascination of public executions.

'Splendid! Now to court. Case to master.' With this abrupt explanation, he strode from the chambers.

Gingerly fingering his neck and wondering whether, if he were given the choice, he would prefer to be hanged or beheaded, Tom went slowly to his room. As he did every week now, he composed a long letter to his father and mother. Next he wrote to his sister Elizabeth, enclosing a note to Anne Hutchinson. The latter, his second letter to Anne, was a short and rather hesitant communication, reflecting his uncertain feelings towards the girl. He confessed that he missed her company, which was true following his rift with Lucy, and announced proudly that to his great relief he had managed to 'break the damnable habit of squandering his life in taverns'.

At the opposite side of the Inn, in the chambers at the

top of staircase twelve, Williams and Corbet were also commenting on Tom's withdrawal from raucous society, though with rather less approval.

'Poxy country mushroom believes he can drop us like a plague corpse,' Williams muttered. 'God's foot! He has too much of the puritan in him for my comfort.'

Corbet grunted. 'Gentlemen of Verney's ilk, wound about the heretical church of their king like ivy, are the very rigging of the Commonwealth. They may dance a little in their cups, yet in the sober morning they return to their old ways soon enough. Change? Why, they would not change a Tuesday to a Wednesday if it did not hasten the collection of their rents.'

'He has mocked us, Silas, rejected us. Shall we test his faith?'

'The test? It is a dangerous game, Leo. Remember Cropley.'

'We will be as discreet as snakes, and twice as deadly. Verney is too puffed up. We must bring him down, Silas. Listen closely...'

Tom was surprised when, two days later, Williams sauntered into his room with a cheery look on his dark, oval face. He was even more surprised at what the Welshman had to say.

'Tom, Silas and I have been talking together. We understand that a great cloud of seriousness has come over you and that now you wish to study the law rather than the ale pot. It is a noble ambition, and if I were blessed with your steadfastness I would ride the same horse myself. But alas! I am weak.'

'It is not easy for me, Leo, but I am trying.'

'You will succeed, Tom. I feel it in my bones. An iron-will hides behind your sweet visage, does it not?' Tom smiled, wondering what Williams was leading up to.

'Silas and I miss your company, Tom.'

'And I yours,' Tom lied.

'Well then, we wondered if you could make time to walk out with us one last time? To bid farewell to your old ways and your old friends.'

Tom hesitated. His first reaction was to refuse the invitation. But thinking it better to remain on good terms with his old cronies, who were quite capable of making trouble for him if he fell out with them openly, he eventually agreed to meet them by the Inn gate at four o'clock for a final evening of merriment. 'It will be like old times,' he smiled, resolving to remain sober so that it certainly would not be.

'Old times, Tom?' laughed Williams. 'No, it will be even better. Just wait and see.'

By the time Tom realised that Williams and Corbet had planned the evening as a round of humiliation rather than the promised farewell festivity, he was incapable of doing anything about it. Having taken a boat to the Paris Garden Stairs on the south bank of the river, the trio had sat drinking in the Falcon for two hours. Upon their arrival Corbet presented Tom with a tankard of old Canary wine, heavily spiced, which he said was a 'gift to a man leaving the world of pleasure'. Tom later recalled the phrase with a groan, cursing himself for not catching its grim double meaning. At first he drank slowly and carefully, noting with satisfaction that while his companions refilled their beakers time and again, he was content to sip cautiously at his single, sweet measure. But honest caution was useless against the potency of his spiked concoction, and before long he grew garrulous and light-headed. A second bumper was brought. By the time he had finished it and Williams suggested it was time to try their luck at the cock-pit, Tom could hardly stand.

'Here,' he called to Corbet as he fumbled to unbuckle his purse, 'manage my wagers, good fellow. Tom's not – altogether – sober.'

Corbet was annoyed to find that the purse contained only a few coins, as Tom had left the bulk of his money hidden in his chambers. It proved a wise precaution. While their charge stood swaying in the torchlight beside the rail at the side of the pit, gazing in drugged stupidity at the bloody conflicts before him, under the pretence of managing his bets Williams and Corbet speedily ran through his small supply of crowns and nobles. The man who ran the cock-pit soon saw what was going on and, with a wink at Corbet, joined in the cruel cozening with evident amusement.

'The red or the blue, sir?' he called derisively when a fight was about to begin. 'The red's a fine cock, sir. True fighter. Try a few shillings?'

Colours meant nothing to Tom. The torches flamed green. The yellow sand shifted from pink and purple before his glazed eyes and the cocks, sometimes eagles, sometimes dragons, lost all individual identity. 'The indigo!' he slurred. 'No, the black! Look, Leo! A black dragon! A Welsh dragon – that will overcome all! Leo, place a sovereign on the dragon. I will be a rich man.'

'Shall we wager your sword too, Thomas?'

'Why yes,' cried Tom, delighted at the novelty. 'And my jerkin!'

Twenty minutes later, after Tom had been deprived of his money, his spectacles and all his clothes apart from his shirt, breeches and stockings, Williams tossed the empty purse into the ring with a laugh and said it was time for another drink. Taking his barefooted ward firmly by the arm, he led the way down a narrow alley to a small, seedy-looking wooden tavern. There, in a hot, smoky room behind the kitchens, they joined a sweaty throng of drinkers, mostly well-dressed young men with loud, haughty voices. As Tom stumbled through the door, Williams cried, 'Behold! Gentlemen of the jury, the accused is brought before you!' A loud cheer went up.

Tom gazed blankly about him at the circle of leering faces. Through the din he recognised Cranfield's arrogant drawl. 'The Oxfordshire cony – and all undressed!' he sneered. 'Come to take the test, Verney?'

The word 'test' stirred a note of alarm somewhere at the back of Tom's befuddled mind. 'Test?' he muttered. 'Test – is – not – wholesome.' The countenances of the crowd swayed before him like an array of multi-coloured gargoyles.

'Prig Verney!' snarled Williams in a tone Tom had never heard before. 'You will do as we bid, see?' Several hands grasped Tom by the arms and turned him roughly around.

When the room had stopped spinning, Tom saw before him a frayed white curtain hanging from a pole. On it the rough outline of two churches had been drawn in charcoal. Cranfield lurched into view.

'What's this, Verney?' he demanded, pointing to the picture on the left. The mob grew silent.

'House – of – God.'

'Oh! Brilliant, turnip-head! But which one?' Tom tried to focus on the crude image.

'St Paul's?' he ventured. There was a burst of sarcastic applause.

'So clever, clod. And this one?' Tom stared at rows of pillars and a huge dome.

'Do – not – know. Seems – popish.' Someone slapped

his face, making his eyes water.

'That,' Cranfield's oily voice announced, 'is the great cathedral of St Peter, in Rome.'

'Said – popish!' grunted Tom defiantly. A second blow made his nose bleed. 'Let – me – go!'

'No. Test time, turd-face.'

The crowd began to chant: 'Test! Test! Test!' Tom licked his lips, tasting the bitter-sweet mix of sweat and blood.

'Now, Verney, you have two buildings.' The chanting subsided. 'Which will you enter? Left, St Paul's, or right, St Peter's?' Tom hesitated. He thought he saw the curtain on the right move.

'Someone's – there!' he said.

'God's wounds! You are stupid!' replied Cranfield. 'Choose, Verney. Do not keep the gentlemen waiting. They may turn cruel.' As if to support the remark, one of Tom's arms was twisted painfully towards his shoulder blades. He groaned. 'One or the other, Verney. Which do you choose to – go into?'

The room was completely still.

'St – Paul's!' Tom stuttered.

As the crowd erupted into a chorus of laughter and cheering, Cranfield stepped forward and drew back the curtain.

'Master Verney? Thomas Verney of Stratton Audley?' The voice, vaguely familiar, seemed to Tom to come from out of the clouds. 'By the mass! Wake up, Master Verney!' He felt a strong hand pulling at his shoulder. 'Wake up! It is not seemly that a gentleman lie like a bursted sack in the street. You will be prey to all kinds of villainy.'

Tom rolled over in the mud and lay on his back gazing at the stars. 'I am in – heaven,' he murmured. 'Look!

Coloured like the starling – the kingfisher – gold and blue, blue and gold ...' As his voice trailed away and he lay staring into the night sky, the passer-by knelt beside him and peered into his unblinking eyes.

'So, so,' he said quietly to himself, getting to his feet, 'it was not the vine, nor the grain. You have not been keeping wise company, have you, Master Thomas?' He glanced down at Tom's breeches lying around his ankles, dirty and torn. 'Mary Mother of Jesus! This is evil work.' He turned to a man standing behind him. 'Here, cover this fellow and stay by him until I return with a carriage.'

While Tom was being hauled into the vehicle, his head cleared a little. He looked blearily about him. 'Where are you taking me?' he asked. 'No more test I pray, Mr Cranfield!'

'Do not fear, Master Verney,' soothed his rescuer. 'You are in safe hands. The parable of the Samaritan acted again, in London this time. By Jesus! Me a Samaritan! There's a pretty turn about!'

'Heaven be praised! I thank you, sir.'

'Praise heaven indeed, young man,' came the pointed reply. Then, handing over a substantial sum of money, the anonymous rescuer instructed the driver to take his passenger back to Clement's Inn and put him to bed. Lulled by the rolling motion of the carriage, Tom was soon asleep again.

When he awoke late the next day he found the events of the previous night so tangled together in a confused nightmare of horror and shame that he could remember almost nothing about the stranger who had saved him. All he could recall was a deep, poetic voice and the image of a great bearded face staring in at him through the carriage window. He knew he had seen that face somewhere before, but not until later that evening did he manage to place it.

'Bird!' he called. 'Quick, bring me paper! I am writing to one John, at the George, Holborn. I believe he calls himself Mr Shakespeare. You must find him. He has just repaid a great debt.'

iv

Tom's letter of thanks to Great John was never delivered. House Martin returned with it the next day, saying the landlord of the George had told him that Mr John Shakespeare had gone away without leaving an address where he might be contacted. While disappointed at not being able to tell John how grateful he was for his ministrations that fateful night, Tom was nevertheless relieved that he was not obliged to renew the thief's acquaintance. John's act of Christian charity might have confirmed his basic kindliness in Tom's eyes, but it did nothing to remove the fact that in the eyes of the law he was still a criminal, the sort of man Tom was well advised to stay clear of.

Williams and Corbet were two others whom Tom determined to stay away from. At first he had contemplated revenge, either personally in the form of a duel or through the courts. But having talked the matter over with George, he decided that since he had no witnesses and neither of his persecutors could be trusted to fight fair in single combat, the wisest course would be to let the matter rest for the moment. One day, he hoped, he would get his own back; but for the moment he chose to ignore them. As they obviously did not wish to have any further dealings with him, he had no difficulty upholding his resolution. The only time he allowed himself a little leeway was when he heard that Corbet had fallen ill and he sent House Martin to the invalid's chambers with the message that his master hoped the sickness would be prolonged, painful and even terminal. His wish was not granted, however, and Corbet was soon sauntering about the Inn, his customary scowl growing even blacker whenever his path chanced to cross Tom's.

The shoes, sword and spectacles which Tom had lost at the cock-pit were soon replaced, although it hurt him to add still further to the cost of that wretched evening in the Paris Garden. It was not strictly necessary to replace the jerkin, as he still had the suit made for him by Oliver Simpson. Yet, try as he might, he could not reconcile himself to absence from Lucy, and seizing an excuse to visit the tailor's again, he called round one morning to see whether she would receive him. She would not. On answering his knock and finding her former suitor standing before her, she said briskly that neither she nor her father were at home, and closed the door.

Undaunted by the rebuttal, Tom tried again a week later, with the same result. At the third attempt he was met by the tailor, who welcomed him warmly and took him through to the workshop. As he measured and pinned and sorted through materials, Simpson chatted away in his usual pleasant, rambling manner. But neither he nor Tom brought up the subject of his daughter. When the business was finished, however, and Tom was pulling on his cloak, he heard the sound of the front door closing. A few seconds later Lucy walked briskly into the room.

'Ah, daughter,' said Oliver Simpson. 'Mr Verney has come about a new jerkin. I have taken the measurements. Would you – ahem! – care to show him out, my dear?' Tom felt that the old man was as anxious as himself to hear his daughter's reply. There was a long pause.

'Very well,' said Lucy with a resigned sigh. What did that mean? Tom wondered as he followed the girl's familiar form into the house. An unwilling obedience to her father, or a reluctant acceptance that, for all Tom's faults, she still cared for him? By the front door he found out.

'Farewell, Lucy. I have missed you, sorely.'

'And I you, Tom.' As she stared up at him with large, uncertain eyes, he felt an overwhelming surge of relief.

'I am truly sorry.'

'And you should be. I was deeply wounded.'

'Wounds heal, Lucy,' he said, wishing with all his heart that he had never hurt so innocent a creature.

'But they leave scars, don't they?'

'Not always.'

'We shall see, Tom, in time.' He took her hand and squeezed it. 'Will you return in person for your jerkin, Tom, or will you send your Bird for it?'

'What would you wish?'

A tiny smile brightened her face. 'That you come, Tom.'

'Then I will.'

From that time forward, slowly and sometimes hesitantly, Tom and Lucy rebuilt their friendship. By the time November had passed into December and each morning the rutted streets were glazed with ice, the period of separation had become a faded memory, leaving, as Tom had hoped, no visible scar.

It was after a happy afternoon spent before the Simpsons' parlour fire – when he was at peace with himself and all the world – that, returning to his chambers, Tom bumped into Gilbert Marshall for the first time for almost a week.

'Home Wednesday,' explained the lawyer in his customary staccato.

'Is it so, sir? I am sorry to hear that,' Tom replied, more

out of politeness than honesty. He saw the man so infrequently that it made little difference to him whether he was in London or not.

'Hanging then?'

The invitation of several weeks ago had quite slipped Tom's mind. 'I beg your pardon, sir?' he asked.

'Hanging. Tomorrow. Tyburn. You will accompany me?'

'Why yes!' said Tom eagerly. Whatever he might feel about the spectacle, a few hours in Marshall's company would give him a good opportunity to create a favourable impression on the man. He would be certain to report back to Justice Verney when he returned home, and Tom was keen that his father be given impartial confirmation of his son's reformation.

Unhappily, events did not turn out as Tom planned. The Tyburn executions provided unimpeachable evidence that the repercussions of Tom's previous folly would continue to haunt him for a long while yet.

SIX

TYBURN

i

The morning of Tuesday 5th December dawned cold and foggy. By half past ten, well wrapped up against the chill, Tom and Marshall were guiding their horses carefully along the frozen ruts of Holborn High Street, past St Giles in the Field and out into the still, grey countryside along the Tyburn Road. As they neared the place of execution, some half a mile south of St Mary le Bon, the road was so thronged with citizens of every class and calling eager to witness the last hanging before Christmas that they were obliged to leave their frightened mounts in the care of a cottager and complete their journey on foot.

Marshall was unusually animated. He had not stopped talking since they left the Inn, and as they pushed their way through the packed crowd towards the gallows he grew even more excited.

'Not like the axe, of course,' he called to Tom over his shoulder as he barged aside a large woman selling chestnuts, spilling her tray of wares onto the hard ground. 'No blood. Shame. Yet fine sounds. The snapping bones, creaking timbers, throttled cries!' He kicked aside a weeping child which had inadvertently wandered into his path. 'Better than the chase, Master Verney. Much. Follow me!'

He veered to the right and began haggling with the owner of a cart who had drawn up his vehicle as a makeshift grandstand. A price was soon agreed, and Tom clambered onto the platform, pulled on his spectacles and gazed at the astonishing scene around him.

About a dozen yards away, beside a broad stream which served as a partial moat against the encroachment of the crowd, stood the gallows themselves. A massive triangle of oak lintels was suspended about fifteen feet from the ground by stout wooden pillars, one at each corner. From the cross-pieces fifteen ropes, five to a beam, dangled motionless in the still air. The ropes terminated in fifteen carefully tied nooses. In a wide circle round the grizzly apparatus — the 'tree' Marshall euphemistically called it — men armed with pikes and swords held back the spectators and kept clear a narrow path for the criminals' cart to enter the arena. An agitated officer walked briskly along the line, calling his men to attention when they leaned on their weapons or exchanged ribald comments with the heaving multitude behind them. Vigilance and strict discipline were essential. The London mob was notoriously capricious, and it was not unknown for public executions to deteriorate into riots.

Tom had never in his life seen anything like the vast lake of humanity which lapped and pushed around the gallows in a babbling surge of hats, faces and limbs. Above, the breath from many thousand throats rose like morning mist over the waters. Even as he watched, fed from the river of bodies pouring out from the capital, the throng continued to grow until every conceivable vantage point had been taken up. As well as numerous carts like the one Tom and Marshall had requisitioned, some reserved exclusively for women, spectators were perched upon clumps and hummocks, ingenious makeshift stands, stilts, ladders and trees. Most of the latter growing within sight of the scaffold had been broken down long ago and were now just barren stumps, as bleak as the gibbet itself. The handful of elms and beeches strong enough to survive the periodic vandalism of the crowd were completely hidden beneath a swaying foliage of onlookers.

The whole city must be here, thought Tom, catching sight of the Three Tradesmen on the opposite side of the burn. What a strange creature he is that flocks in such numbers and so eagerly to watch his fellows die! Nevertheless, despite his fleeting attempt at philosophising, Tom found himself unavoidably caught up in the excitement of an occasion which promised better drama than any theatre or bear garden. The noise and bustling enthusiasm of the mob were contagious. Tingling with anticipation, he looked towards the grim machinery of execution where skeletal Death sat astride the beam, patiently waiting to welcome new subjects to his grisly kingdom.

Fifteen criminals were to be hung that day, in three batches of five. The arrival of the first cartload was heralded by a swelling murmur from the crowd, rising to a prolonged chorus of shouts, groans, screams and cries. By the time the cart creaked into view Marshall had worked himself into a frenzy of excitation. Nudging Tom and wrapping his long arms around himself, he hopped up and down like an agitated stork, muttering, 'Ah! Death where is your swing? Look, Master Verney! That fellow's eyes — what fear! Why, the knave is blubbering! O rapture!'

Sweet Jesus! laughed Tom to himself, the man has taken Suffering for a mistress and will be spent before her if he does not control his passion! He was still wondering at the sexual nature of Marshall's ecstasy, when a commotion at the gallows diverted his attention.

The two-wheeled prison wagon, pulled by a mangy piebald mare, had drawn up beneath one of the crossbeams. A large man with a hard, immobile face and dressed in a leather apron had climbed onto the tailboard and was now passing along the row of bound criminals, slipping a noose over each of their heads. The first two stood upright and allowed the knots to be drawn tight about their necks without complaint. But the third, a small man, more tidily dressed than the others, was ducking and weaving so energetically that it was impossible for the hangman to get the rope over him.

'See, Master Verney!' screamed Marshall. 'A fighter! What is it? Ah! He will not be hanged next to a woman. That is it! Such scruple only minutes from hell!' He burst into peals of manic laughter.

The lawyer had appraised the situation correctly. The fourth of the sorry unfortunates was indeed a woman, a thin, shivering, wispy-haired creature who stared blankly at the crowd, oblivious of the struggle beside her.

The interruption was ended when a second man jumped up onto the cart and seized the trouble-maker by the wrists. The executioner then laid into him with his fists, punching him in the face, stomach and groin. The crowd howled with delight at this unexpected side-show, greeting each vicious blow with a scream of rapture. Marshall was rigid with pleasure. The female prisoner continued to gaze into the distance, her lips moving in silent prayer.

When the mischief-maker had been knocked senseless to the floor, the assistant kicked away a tooth dislodged in the beating and hauled him upright. Laughing at a comment made by his partner, the executioner put the noose in place, pulled it tight and moved on to complete his task.

The unconscious man hung limply from the rope, his arms swinging forward like a doll's and a deep gurgling sound emerging from his throat. Blood dripped from his nose and mouth onto the rough planks of the cart. The woman beside him continued to pray.

'Now the climax!' cried Marshall as an official began to read out the names and crimes of those who were about to die. An overweight chaplain hauled himself into the cart to utter a short prayer. A reverent hush descended on the crowd. Men removed their hats. Some bowed their heads. The words of Christian comfort carried far through the winter stillness. 'Dear God, Father of Our Lord Jesus Christ ... have mercy we pray you on the souls of these miserable offenders ... the law of Man wrought to uphold Your own law ... look kindly on them ... we beseech you ... they lie not too long in the furnace of hell ... Amen.'

'Amen!' growled the mob. A girl kneeling near the edge of the stream began to weep hysterically. Someone shouted. Having helped the priest down from the cart, the hangman walked slowly to the horse's head. He took hold of the animal's bridle and looked round. The muttering of the crowd faded to silence.

As the chimes of distant St Giles struck twelve, the officer in charge dropped his hand.

'For-ward!' called the hangman, and led the horse quickly away from the gallows.

'Mercy!' screamed one of the wretches, jumping

frantically along the floor of the cart as it slipped swiftly away. The feet of the unconscious man grated along the rough boards beside him. The woman was still praying when she fell into the air.

The ropes hummed as they received their sudden burdens. The beam creaked. The bodies jerked and danced like puppets for a few seconds, before locking into postures of death. As they swung gently backwards and forwards in the icy air, trickles of involuntary excretion dripped onto the grass below. The mob sighed with delight.

Tom surveyed the second batch of criminals with a mixture of pity and expectation. The atmosphere of the execution field was far more dramatic than he had expected and he found something inexplicably fascinating in watching others die, particularly when they were strangers whom he knew to have done great wrong. But as he glanced down the fresh line of wretches huddled together on the cart only a few yards before him, he was seized with a sudden horror. By Jesus! That man on the left – he would recognise that Weasel-face anywhere! It was – yes, he was certain – it was the fellow John had named Pym, the coward who had taken so precipitously to his heels after Tom had beaten off the ambush in the Stokenchurch woods. God knows what he will say if he recognises me, Tom thought, looking for a clear space so that he could jump from the cart.

Marshall noticed Tom's agitation. 'Verney,' he asked, 'need to water the grass?'

'Yes, Mr Marshall. I must climb down for a moment.'

'But you shan't! Miss the hanging. Better to soil yourself, eh? Hold fast. Will not be long.' He put an arm round Tom's shoulder, making it impossible for him to escape.

Pym was peering round at the crowd. As he turned in Marshall's direction, Tom glanced away. When he looked up again, he saw to his dread that the man was still staring towards him. He stared back, showing no sign of recognition, hoping that the prospect of imminent death would either dull the villain's memory, or at least instil in him a charitable taciturnity.

As he watched, however, he saw Pym's mouth break into a grin. The man was desperate, prepared to try anything, however fanciful, to save himself. 'Sir!' he cried out. 'You was Christian enough not to turn one of us in 'afore. Will you help a poor wretch again, sir?'

Feeling a thousand pairs of eyes turning in his direction, Tom looked innocently about him, as if trying to ascertain who was being addressed.

'Yes, you, sir,' Pym went on, 'the gentleman in spectacles. You were a saviour once. Will you not be so again?' Tom felt the blood rushing to his cheeks.

Marshall turned and looked at him. 'Know the knave, Verney? Says you helped him. Help a villain, eh?'

'No I did not!' said Tom angrily.

The voice from the gallows called again. 'Mr Spectacles! 'Elp me! I never done it! By God's blood I never done it! 'Ave mercy on me! Use your good influences, I beg of you!'

The crowd began to murmur angrily. 'Here,' shouted a man standing beside Tom's cart, 'you a friend of murderers, are you?'

'Never!' Tom screamed back at him. The situation was getting more ugly by the second. He could taste fear in his mouth.

'Then why does that sharping son of the devil say you are?'

'He lies! He is a villain!'

'And you aren't? Seize him!' The words came from a broad-shouldered bald man in a greasy worsted doublet. He made a grab at Tom's ankles.

Tom turned to Marshall for help. 'Mr Marshall, sir, tell these people ...' He did not finish the sentence. The lawyer had vanished. Sensing trouble, he had leaped from the cart and was already moving off through the crowd.

While Tom's head was turned, a hand took hold of his leg and pulled him to the ground. As he landed, his muscular assailant trod his spectacles into the mud and kicked him hard in the stomach, driving the wind from his body. Struggling for breath, Tom staggered to his feet to find himself surrounded by a hostile mob. 'This supposed gentleman,' roared the bald-head man provocatively, 'is an accomplice of murderers! You heard the knave at the gallows, didn't you?' Growls of assent ran round the onlookers. 'God's holy hair! Do we care for flick-pimps such as this arrant whelp?'

'No!' yelled the crowd. 'Take him! Beat him!'

Tom glanced around. There was no escape.

'By God's light!' bellowed the rabble-rouser. 'Leave the poxy nigget to me!' He lurched towards Tom, swinging his great fists like windmill sails. 'Come, dab-chick, take your sentence!'

Tom was no coward, nor was he a weakling, but still suffering from the effects of the kick, he realised it would be foolish to stand and face the vicious onslaught of a far stronger man. Stepping painfully to one side, he slipped behind the lumbering aggressor. 'Here slave!' he panted. 'Are you as slow as you are stupid?'

Instead of making another charge, the bully stood and harangued the crowd once more. 'Friends! See what a slippery snake this accomplice is! He will not fight like a man, but runs like a cur. Throw him to me that

I may break his murdering bones!'

The speech had the desired effect. The crowd closed in behind Tom, pushing him towards his opponent. When he tried to side-step, unseen arms held him fast. His persecutor drew closer. Tom could smell the drink on his breath. 'Now, my pretty canting gull,' he snarled, 'shall we play?' He aimed a blow at Tom's head.

Tom ducked, but as he did so he was pushed forward to his knees. The brute fell on him with a savage cry, mercilessly kicking him on the thigh and landing a hammer blow on the side of his head. In desperation Tom tried to roll away, but succeeded only in turning onto his back, leaving his face fully exposed to the fists waving furiously above him.

All of a sudden there was a tremendous crack. A shudder ran through the assailant's body. His eyes closed and he fell forward onto the grass.

Tom looked up to see a large, familiar figure standing over him. Passing the staff with which he had laid out the bully into his left hand, the man pulled Tom to his feet and turned to speak to the crowd, some of whom were muttering against his intervention.

'Good people, was this right?' The deep, strangely accented voice was resonant with authority. 'Would you stand by to see an honest son of a justice cruelly set upon by this ... this drunken ape? By the mass! Master Verney is a virtuous Christian gentleman. But if there is one here as would take issue with me over that particular,' he challenged, glowering about him, 'let him step forward and try me.' Cowed by the giant's massive frame and furious aspect, the crowd took him at his word and turned again to watch the spectacle which they had originally come to see.

'Now, Tom,' said his rescuer grimly when he was sure

that the incident was over, 'come away from this evil place before you fall into further snares.'

As a watery sun finally broke through the mist and the chaplain's complacent tones began again to invoke God's mercy for the condemned souls standing in the shadow of the gallows, Tom took John's arm and allowed himself to be led through the bareheaded and silent crowd towards the open road beyond.

ii

'And now, John, I know I can trust you,' said Tom. So that they could converse more easily, he was returning to the city on foot, leading Princess by the bridle. The painful bruise on his leg caused him to walk with a slight limp.

'By the veil of the Virgin, Tom Verney! Will you never learn? Trust no man. We are all fallen creatures.'

'But you saved me, John. By some miracle, God has twice now directed you to a position where you might help me; and twice you have chosen to do so. Is that not the mark of a man to be trusted?'

'No, my credulous young Verney. Consider. The matter in the woods gave you an iron hold over me. Then, in the George, to save myself I was obliged to open the window into my past still further. Strengthened by what you saw, your grip was screwed yet tighter.

'Zounds! Do you not see? It was my own restless anxiety, not God, which ordained that I should appear like a guardian angel when you were troubled.'

'How was that?'

'It costs little to hire a fellow with sharp eyes.'

Tom felt his gratitude ebbing away. 'You had me watched?'

'Too grand a phrase, Verney. I trusted you, but could not be certain. Lest I needed to flee the city in haste, I had to know whether you called on a magistrate. When I was informed you had gone in the direction of the Paris Gardens, I went thither too, more to take a little pleasure myself than to spy on yours. It was mostly chance I came across you lying in the street. So it was today. I had planned to witness the end of sorry Pym and when told that you had left for Tyburn in the company of a lawyer, it suited me to keep close to see what kind of fellow he was. Not a true friend, I gather?'

'No, indeed,' replied Tom, wondering what to make of yet another of John's remarkable explanations. He limped on a few steps before observing, 'Yet you did come to my assistance.'

'I suppose it was to help myself that I helped you, young sir,' John explained. 'Are you not more valuable to me as friend than foe? If you had a mind to, with scarcely a nod you could set me swinging beside the wretched Pym back there!' He waved behind him and added with a grin, 'Though first you would need to persuade the magistrate of your own innocence.'

Tom did not appreciate being reminded of this uncomfortable fact. 'I know I am an accessory to your villainy, John,' he retorted. 'But I am well connected. My father would stand by me and see you hanged. Perhaps I should turn you in now, before I am compromised further?'

John stood still and placed a hand on Tom's shoulder. 'Should I not have left you senseless in the street? Or watched you broken to sawdust by the Tyburn mob? Maybe I should kill you here, on this lonely road, and cast your body into the ditch, so ending my fears of betrayal?'

For a full minute the two men stood face to face in a trial of strength and credibility, each searching the other's expression for clues as to what they were thinking. Like wrestlers locked together on the edge of a cliff, they had to decide whether to continue the struggle in the hope that their hold would prove the more effective, or to end the contest and so avoid the possibility of their both falling to their deaths.

Without taking his eyes from John's, Tom spoke first. 'Well, you have not killed me, John.'

'And you have not surrendered me to the law, Tom.'

'Is that not trust?'

'Or fear. Both are sturdy bonds.'

'Then here we stand,' Tom said with a laugh, 'fastened together by links of trust – or fear – which neither cares to break!'

'Like marriage,' John grinned.

Alone on the highway in the pale winter sunshine, the incongruous pair threw their arms about each other in an embrace of mutual respect and growing affection.

Over a long and ample dinner taken on the first floor of an ordinary in Duck Lane, near St Bartholomew's Hospital, John opened what he had called the 'window in his past' a little wider. But the more Tom peered in, the more he realised how little he could see. John readily supplied more details of his time as a robber, most of which tied in with his previous account. But try as he might, Tom could not get the secretive giant to talk about his life before he met Sarah Fuller.

'So you appeared on this earth fully grown and fashioned?' he asked in despair after one of John's more evasive responses.

'God's light, Tom! You are as eager as host Carter to overturn stones to see what lies beneath! I am what you see. You know what you see. Pray do not squeeze me further, for a man cannot live without some juice in his bones!'

'But what do I see, John? A great bearded fellow with a brand that he hides beneath a hedge of hair and a low hat; a garrulous giant of a sometime thief with a twinkle in his eye; a mystery-voiced actor of some thirty years with a magical command of words; a well-mannered outcast with a propensity for oaths, spying and popery; and a ready commentator on all matters, burdened with a deep suspicion of the world and its people. All of those, and yet none of them. Why, in faith, I do not even know your name!'

'John will suffice. You seem to have the rest of me catalogued well enough.'

'Fie! Must I must make you drunk before you babble out your past?' Tom laughed, refilling John's beaker with wine.

'You may try, Tom. But I assure you I will sit here with a head as clear as water long after you are snoring beneath the table!' Casting an eye over John's ox-like form, Tom knew it was no idle boast. He sighed.

'Have patience, Tom. I am no Madam Suppository ready to strip herself naked before "Well met!" has passed her lips. In time you may discover more, although I fear you will not care for what you find. Friendships are best made in the dark, when hands feel the softness, not the wrinkles, and the eye conjures up a beauty which light would soon dispel.'

He leaned back in his chair, tugging his hat further down over his forehead with an instinctive movement. 'But enough of me. What of Tom Verney? Who is he, and what sorry course of events, pray, brought him to lie in the mud with his mind spinning like a child's top?'

As if to show John that, unlike himself, he had nothing

to hide, Tom launched forth into a lengthy description of his family and childhood, his life at the Inn, his affection for Lucy Simpson and his exploit with Lady Banbury. His period of friendship with Williams and Corbet he left until last. 'As for the evening when you played the Samaritan,' he said solemnly, 'that is not an episode I wish to recall.'

'I take it you had been carousing and whoring?' enquired John, knowing full well that was not the whole story.

'No,' snapped Tom. John waited for him to continue. 'Very well, you wheedling Goliath!' the younger man said eventually. 'Listen.' As well as he was able, he pieced together the story of the drugged possets, the way he had been swindled out of his money and clothes at the cockpit, and the humiliation of the so-called test.

'This test, Tom – tell me. I believe I have heard it talked of,' John said, showing greater interest than he had in the rest of Tom's unexceptional tale.

'You know of it? How?'

'That is part of my mystery, Tom. Pray continue.'

Tom described what he remembered of the two drawings on the sheet and how he had been compelled to choose which he would enter. When he had chosen St Paul's, he explained, the curtain had been drawn back to reveal a boy – the fellow Sodda, whom he had met before – behind the Anglican place of worship, and the whore Lettie behind St Peter's.

'They said I had sworn to go into the one I had chosen,' Tom muttered quietly. 'You may imagine what that meant.'

'Alas! Readily, Tom.'

'It was foul and cruel. Not just that, but the whole stratagem. There was treason in the air, too, not simple lechery.' He lowered his voice further and glanced about him to see that they were not overheard. 'The king was cursed and condemned as a heretical sodomite – that is why the boy had been chosen to represent his church. And the church of Rome – the girl – was hailed as the true home for all men. That little drab, a mere child, did not know what she had agreed to. They used her most wickedly, John. Even now I can hear her screams.'

Tom sat in silence for a long time. 'Despite the depths of my own distress, I felt pity for her, John. Pity for a silly, low-born trug. Why?'

Inspired by what he had heard, John sat forward with the brim of his hat almost touching Tom's. 'Give ear, Tom Verney. You wished to know the workings of John's clock? Well, harken and I will show a wheel or two. Yet if I venture upon ground too uncertain for you, stop me and I will proceed no further.

'I am a papist, as you know, but not such a one as you might readily understand. We come in many guises. There are earnest men and women who hold fast to the ancient church because their hearts will let them serve no other, but who are, even so, loyal to King James. They are no threat to the state. Then there are those hot-blooded fellows whose Roman Catholicism desires an end to the Protestant House of Stuart. Such men laid the Gunpowder Plot. They preach a return to Rome on a horse of fire and blood, even if the same saddle carries a king more tyrannous than he whom now we serve. It is a heady philosophy which attracts young and rebellious hearts. Those who used you so vilely – that Cranfield in particular – are most likely a twisted and ill-thinking battalion of that small army. For most it is a passing game – truly a dangerous one – but none the less a game which they will tire of when they are older.'

'And you, John, in which of these camps do you stand?' Tom asked.

'Both and neither. My life has taught me that I am for the people of this land, all the people. I have seen them, Tom, I have lived among them: the poor, the ill-gotten, the ill-used, the ill-favoured, the ill-endowed.' Beads of sweat broke out on his face. 'Is this not their land as much as ours? Are they not as precious in the eyes of our Heavenly Father as the justices, the bishops and the merchants of this great city?'

Tom listened intently. He had never heard such thoughts before, not even when eavesdropping on the grumbles of his father's labourers, and he was transfixed. He realised with alarm that the man opposite him was no longer Great John the jester, the player, but a dangerous prophet of strange doctrines, any one of whose sentences might take him to the rack. For a second Tom thought of calling a halt to the speech lest he be infected with its rebellious sentiments. But the words struck a chord within him that would not be muted.

'Who sat with sinners, Tom?' John went on, fire dancing on every word. 'Who took dinner with the whores? Who rejected the hallowed laws? By God, Tom! Who? Answer me!'

'Our Lord Jesus Christ.'

'Just so, Tom. Even He. Now do you see the faith I hold, the church to which I belong? It is the universal church, not that of England but of the world and of all its folk, humble and great alike. That church of yours, King James's church, is a prison, like your precious law. When the language of the law is not that of the common man, how is it to be his shield? He cannot even lift it! The law and the church both serve alike to hold matters as they are, not as God would have them be, by the mass!'

Tom thought for a moment. 'And you know how God would have the world he created, do you, John? You know more than kings and councillors, doctors and – well – lawyers?'

He was shocked to see the question hit John like an arrow. His furrowed brow crumpled, his great shoulders folded forward and tears came into his deep, brown eyes. 'Oh Tom!' he said with an air of almost tangible sadness. 'You are right. I do not know. No one knows. It is arrogance to say otherwise. Mine is like all faiths – I believe it to be true. I feel it here—' he placed a broad hand over his heart. 'If you had lived as I had lived, Tom, you might feel it too. I have seen how men, men born good and true, are trodden into the earth like snails.

'Tom, do you – raised to the fat of the land – understand what I am saying?'

'Maybe, John. Maybe a little.' He stared into his glass. 'I can still hear poor Lettie crying.'

iii

John's seditious words unsettled Tom profoundly. Hitherto, like his father and virtually everyone else with whom he had held serious conversation, he had accepted without question that the nature of government and society was divinely ordered and immutable: each individual was born to a certain station in life, thereby forming a link in the chain of being which bound all living things. There was movement, of course, as some rose and others fell, yet the rules and framework remained the same: the poor and, by definition, morally and mentally inferior bulk of the population had few privileges and few responsibilities – their reward for living according to the light of the Gospel brought to them by the church lay in heaven, a prospect which gleamed far more brightly than any earthly prize; the rich and privileged, whose status stemmed from an innate superiority, were obliged to bear burdens commensurate with their position, and they would be judged hereafter according to their own exalted lights. God's punishment for those who abused their privileges would be truly terrible – what were a few years of earthly pleasure, the story of Dr Faustus taught, compared with an eternity of torment? The king, God's lieutenant on earth, his church and the law were triple pillars upholding this natural order of things – to shake them was to risk bringing in chaos and anarchy, under which no one, neither rich nor poor, would benefit.

All this, John had challenged as falsehood: 'a stockade of logic reinforced by stakes of religion to protect the few from the plundering of the many,' he said. Tom felt like a man gazing on a window of coloured glass who has been told that if he changes his focus he can see through it to a different scene. Is the new vision mirage or reality? he wondered. His logic and upbringing told him it was mirage. His heart was less sure.

Two days after the Tyburn hangings he had accompanied John to a performance of *Troilus and Cressida*, where Ulysses had proclaimed: 'Take but degree away, untune that string, And hark what discord follows.' Hearing the words, Tom had nudged his friend and whispered, 'There! That's the answer to your treacherous teachings!'

'Nay,' John had replied, 'there is a counter to every fine phrase. You recall the words of Father John Ball when the poor folk rose up in the reign of the second King Richard? "When Adam delved and Eve span, who was then the gentleman?" Read your Gospel more closely,

Tom. There is more of God's design in that than Mr Shakespeare's plays.'

On another occasion they had engaged in a heated discussion about criminality. Tom argued that everyone was responsible for their own actions – if they turned to a life of crime, that was their decision and they had to accept the consequences.

'Fine words, Tom!' John retorted. 'But God will judge, not man. "Let he who is without sin cast the first stone" – remember? You should, for they are the English words of your king's new gospel.'

'So we are to live without law, are we, John?'

'No, there must be law. Yet it must be fair and merciful. There are times when those who break the law have small choice in the matter.'

'Never! An example?'

'Your sister Elizabeth – she is not a whore, I trust?'

Tom flushed with anger. 'By the church, John, at times you try me sorely! No. She is a sweet, virtuous creature who would rather die than stoop to such sin.'

'I trust so. Yet what if your father lost his fortune and the plague carried off him and all the others of your family, leaving Elizabeth and her child – she was married but her husband died – alone and destitute in this wicked city? If she dies, the babe she has loved and nursed dies too. Then up comes a gentleman and offers her a goodly sum, sufficient for a month's bread, for the use of her body for an hour. Now, Tom virtuous Verney, what does she choose?'

'To die of starvation rather than lose her honour.'

'And the child dies too?'

'Sadly, yes.'

'Many would take that road. But should she have surrendered her honour that her child might live, would that have been so wicked? Would God have condemned her for loving the fruit of her womb more than herself?'

'Zounds! I do not know, word-monger!'

'It is not easy, you see, Tom. I pray you think before you condemn over-hastily those who fall foul of your wonderful law. That strumpet Lettie who was so mistreated by Mr Cranfield and his mob – did she choose the way of wantonness or was it pressed upon her? You said you pitied her, Tom. Good. It is likely she needs your pity more than your approbation.'

John made no attempt to proselytise Tom to his angry creed. He was, he admitted, too aware of his own shortcomings and the fallibility of human understanding to be a prophet. Besides, his blend of conservative Catholicism and radical politics was his own child, conceived of misfortune and folly, and no messiah sent to lead mankind to the promised land. 'God's death!' he warned Tom. 'Neither am I a princely Bohemian saint that you will find comfort walking in my foot marks. Consider well, Tom, before you place your easy shoes in prints which may lead to damnation by both God and man!'

Despite such honest words of caution, Tom had to admit to himself that although he had no time for John's popery, some of his social comments agreed with half-formed opinions of his own. He found it hard to believe, for example, that a loving and just God endorsed an order in which revolting figures like Lord Banbury stood higher than his dear Lucy, or even the sprightly little House Martin. And the more he saw of the law, with its blatant corruption and obscure proceedings in an outmoded French, the more he felt that it was indeed partly an elaborate fortress erected for the benefit of those with property to protect.

But it was the question of individual responsibility

which teased him most. And whenever he considered it, the alluring, wan figure of Lettie drifted before his eyes. His feelings towards the child-whore were complex. On one level she was the ideal figure on whom to test John's thesis – he wanted to seek her out and discover why she had turned to a life of sinful crime. If, as John suggested, she had been forced into her present situation, Tom would help her escape. Yet the eagerness with which he contemplated this charitable course did not stem entirely from virtuous motives, for his pity was inextricably bound up with a fixation for the girl as a sexual being. He was undeniably aroused by the memory of her pitiable striptease the first time he met her, by the rough physical gratification he had taken from her later that evening, and even by the image of the continuous, cruel assault on her splayed body in the Paris Gardens.

Thus, one rainy afternoon, fired by a paradoxical confluence of missionary zeal and unspoken prurient lust, Tom determined to find Lettie and discover just what it was that drew him to her. Placing two sovereigns and some other small coins in his purse, he left the Inn and took a boat to Old Swan Stairs.

From the tavern in Ebgate Lane he was directed across the river to a sizeable, tidy-looking dwelling surrounded by a high wall near Winchester House. A heavily painted woman lolling in the shelter of a tiled porch left no doubt as to the occupation of the house's inmates. Told by a hefty gatekeeper that this was where Lettie 'had her bed', Tom was led through a lawned garden set with apple trees to a large, brightly painted front room from which a heavy oak staircase led to the floor above. A coal fire burned pleasantly in the stone-flanked hearth. The air was heavy with the scent of perfume and spice. Half a dozen bare-breasted whores lolled in padded chairs scattered about the room.

As he entered, a short, blotchy-faced woman, whose ill looks required her to tout harder for custom than her more prepossessing workmates, sidled up to him and began running her fingers up his thigh.

'Seeking a party-bawd, handsome? Come with me and turn your fantasies to flesh, sweetheart.'

'No. Do not finger me, I pray,' he retorted sharply, unable to disguise his repulsion for the creature's crude advances.

'Oh! See how lordy lank-pizzle shuns a little nun!'

'I would speak with one Lettie.'

'Speak with her! Oh, there's modesty for you! Waggle your tongue at her you mean!' The woman wandered away and sat down.

Tom stood about awkwardly for a few minutes before one of the other bawds called over to him, 'Lettie? She's working.'

'I will wait.'

The speaker rose languidly to her feet. 'Waiting's lonely, dearest. Come over 'ere and sit by me. I'll find a pennyworth of conversation for you myself.'

As Tom approached to look at her more closely, wondering what fancy he could buy for a penny, he heard an upstairs door close and a few seconds later watched as a portly middle-aged man walked hurriedly down the stairs and disappeared through the front door without saying a word.

'Lettie!' called out the woman who had offered Tom cheap comfort. 'Gentleman here says as he wishes to speak with you.'

'Mary's hot mine!' came the reply. 'I'll be tupped to a frazzle 'afore nightfall if they come on like this. Send 'im up, Eve. Door's open.'

The woman pointed to the stairs. 'Mount, sir. Shame we never fell a-talking.'

Tom climbed to the first-floor landing, found the open door and closed it behind him. He could not have imagined a place less conducive to intimacy than the cold, narrow chamber in which he found himself. Every wall, every fixture bore sordid testimony to vulgarity and tawdry poverty. Such light as found its way through the grimy panes of the window was further filtered by a torn brown curtain hanging askew from a broken pole. The thin fabric fluttered in the draught from a cracked pane. From a meagre grate the cold ashes of last night's fire, tragically adorned with the faded blooms of a long-discarded posy of winter violets, spilled onto the bare boards of the floor. A plain pine coffer and a low bed, strewn with coarse, yellowing sheets, were the only furniture. The damp air reeked of cheap scent and still cheaper sex.

In one corner, dressed only in an underskirt, which she had gathered clumsily about her waist, Lettie squatted over a bowl of cold water washing herself. She did not look up as her visitor came in.

'Lettie,' Tom called quietly, gratefully disappointed at finding her so unalluring.

'Wait a minute. You wants me fresh, don't you?' She still did not look up.

'Lettie, I wish to talk with you.'

Lowering her skirt, the girl turned towards him. Her thin, painted face was tired, her eyes expressionless. 'You?' she said slowly as she recognised Tom. 'Seen what I does and come for more?' Her mouth formed the shape of a smile, but she spoke without emotion, like a bad actress content simply to get her words right. Already the fragile, appealing uncertainty of two months previously had been overlain or even replaced by a shell of crude insensitivity, making it easy for Tom to convince himself that he had made the visit solely out of charity. Clearing a space on the bed, he sat down with his hands clasped before him and began a premeditated apology.

'I am sorry for what happened in that tavern, Lettie. All those men ...'

She looked at him suspiciously and shrugged. 'Paid handsome.'

It was hardly the answer he had been expecting. 'Ah, good.' He smiled, as if acknowledging a tacit understanding between them. Then he leaned forward and enquired earnestly, 'Why do you do this, Lettie?'

'You as well?' she asked with a look of relief. 'That's what they all want to know, duckling.' A trace of laboured animation came into her voice and she walked slowly towards him, running her hands down her narrow hips. 'And why do you think I does it, young sir?'

Ignoring her presence only inches in front of him, Tom ventured, 'Because you had no choice? You were forced to take up this vile trade ...'

Lettie cut him short. '"Vile trade", says he! By the lap of the Virgin! You don't think this a vile trade no more than I do, sir.' Stooping down so that her small, pointed breasts brushed against his face, she continued huskily, 'I plays my game 'cause I chooses to.' Tom felt her hands on his knees. 'Listen, sweetheart: when I lies back on my bed and I feels a great pestle –' her fingers began easing their way up Tom's thighs – 'slipping into my little mortar, I says to myself, "God's apples, Lettie! You're a fortunate one!"'

'But Lettie,' implored Tom, frustrated by her lies, 'is this the girl who wept at Cranfield's scorn? Who cried out in the Paris Gardens? Think.' He ambushed her wandering hands before they succeeded in distracting him. 'Speak the truth: do you take true pleasure from the life of a ... a strumpet?'

'True pleasure, Mr Puritan?' she scoffed, sitting beside him and hanging her thin arms about his neck. In vain he searched her rain-grey eyes for a hint of former vulnerability. 'You ride a horse?' she asked.

'Of course,' Tom replied, surprised at the question.

'When you was learning, you fell, taking bruises and pain, didn't you? But you went on. You knew what fun you'd have when you'd learned.' Lowering her arms, she began mechanically to unbutton Tom's jerkin. 'That's us nuns too, see? Apprenticeship's hard. But it don't last long. Master craftsmen gets great joy from their work.' Tom gently took hold of her wrists to prevent her from undressing him further. He had not expected to find her so unappealing. Undaunted, she leant forward to kiss him. 'Don't be shy, young sir. I'm a master craftsman now – surely you would sample my skills?'

Tom turned his head to one side. 'Lettie, I wish to speak with you. Truly. Is that forbidden in this place? You are not a creature in the market for me to buy. I wish to help you.'

Her look of disbelief was replaced by an enigmatic smile. 'Cost you just the same,' she muttered, freeing her hands and resting them over his purse for a second before sliding round to the front of his breeches. 'But you're a man with coin enough to satisfy a woman, aren't you, my cocky!'

'Very well.' He reached down for his money, intending to buy off her pathetic advances.

'In good time, sir. I earn according as what you receive.'

Unused to the ways of the stews, Tom thought nothing

of the remark. Nor was he surprised when Lettie went to the door and called equivocally downstairs, 'Eve! No callers! This fine gentleman has sufficient to fill the hours till nightfall!'

Bolting the door, she discarded her skirt and sidled towards the bed. 'Now, preacher,' she smirked, standing before Tom with her legs astride and her bony hips thrust forward, 'there's a little ear-hole as would appreciate your sermon. Let your tongue get wagging.'

Sweet Jesus Christ! thought Tom, has this girl's heart been so hardened in so short a time that she thinks all men driven by nothing but lust? He stood up and put his hands on her frozen shoulders. 'Do you hate us?'

'Hate you, sirrah? Does the milk-maid hate the cow what gives her a living?' She nestled against him, shivering. 'But come, why do you refuse me? Am I such an ugly creature?' She fingered the front of his shirt. 'Please, sir.' For the first time since entering the room Tom noticed an edge of sorrow in her voice, and with pity came involuntary desire.

'I do not reject you, Lettie.' He ran his hands down her back to her bottom.

'Show me.'

He closed his eyes, thinking of Lucy and how frustrated he was by her unwillingness to be carried away by their embraces. 'Damn you and bless you, Lettie!' he whispered. 'There is one who would not wish me here.'

'What will she know? Besides, I warrant she boils the pot without getting down to the cooking, don't she?'

Tom smiled and moved his hands round the inside of Lettie's thighs. 'She does. There is much steam to be let out.'

'Then we knows a place where it can go, don't we, sir?' She moved her legs together, trapping his hand.

'Maybe you should remove my clothes?' he said hoarsely, finally admitting defeat. 'We can talk afterwards.'

'Anything you wish, sir.'

A couple of minutes later, as Tom stood naked in the middle of the room with his clothes strewn untidily about him and Lettie was running her tongue down his stomach, they were interrupted by a fearful hammering at the door. 'Open!' yelled a rough male voice. 'Open for the law!'

Tom pulled away. 'Zounds!' he cried, 'What in the name of God is that?'

'Mary's sainted pails! The trugging constables!' Lettie jumped to her feet and began drawing on a gown.

'Constables? Do they seek a master craftsman too?'

'Don't jest, sirrah. They're come to search this house for the likes of you.' Watching Tom closely, she tied her laces with quick, nimble fingers. The noise outside began again.

'Open the door, strumpet, or I will beat it down!'

In a trice Tom realised the seriousness of the situation. Brothels, for all their abundance, were illegal and therefore at the mercy of raids by capricious magistrates. If he were discovered, he would have to appear before a justice, to the detriment of his purse, his reputation and his hopes with Lucy.

'What am I to do?' he groaned, anxiously stooping for his clothes and wondering why every conceivable misfortune selected his head as a target.

'Make haste! By Jesus, you must hide – no, fond fool, I'll put your things beneath the bed. Climb in here—' She pulled open the lid of the large chest which stood against the wall and he jumped inside.

Crouching stark naked in his dark, cramped refuge, he

heard Lettie turn the key of the chest, move quickly across the room and unbolt the door. Heavy feet entered.

'A pox on you, callet!' barked a rough voice. 'Where's the tupping knave?'

'God's light, constable!' came her indignant retort. 'There's no man here. I am taking my rest like any honest woman when you comes bursting in like a bull. Shame on you, sirrah!'

'Where have you hidden him, traffic? God's eyes, I will uncover the varlet!' Tom heard the muffled noise of the foul-mouthed officer searching around the room. Footsteps approached the chest and the lid moved as the man tried to lift it. 'Ah, pox-vendor! That's your game, is it! The key, strumpet!'

Tom held his breath, praying that Lettie would not betray him. In his anxiety he wondered that any magistrate should employ so uncouth a fellow; certainly his father would never countenance such hectoring behaviour in his parish. But then, he reminded himself, this is London, where all things were possible.

'Alas! The chest is not mine, constable. It belongs to the master of the house – he is away at present and always has the key about him.'

Hearing the man snort and move off to a different part of the room, Tom exhaled slowly. Lettie might be a common callet, he told himself, vulgar beyond redemption, but she retained some code of honour, thank God! She was not to be overawed, either. His silent vote of thanks was interrupted by the muffled sound of the constable's voice.

'And these? Whose clothes are these, slut?' Tom froze.

'My brother's, sirrah. And why not? He stays here of nights and needs them for a change.'

Tom was amazed at Lettie's quick-wittedness. 'Lord

bless you, Lettie,' he whispered into the stuffy darkness of the chest.

'Leave off this hunt, collier,' the girl went on crossly. 'Will you never be satisfied?'

'Satisfied? I tell you, whore, you are the one whose hunt satisfies! Where is the knave?'

'Let go, blockhead! Must I repeat like a church clock? By my bloody troth, there's no man here.'

'Very well. If you will not surrender your paymaster, I will remove his pay.' Sweat broke out on Tom's brow. His purse! He wanted to call out, but deciding that to reveal himself would only make matters worse and might endanger Lettie, he bit his lip and kept quiet.

The spirited whore tried to save him from further misfortune. 'Varlet, those are my brother's clothes – and his money! You may not take them, pox-face!'

'I may and I will. Apply to the magistrate if you would seek redress.' Laughing at his own wit, the constable left the room.

Fortunately for Tom, it was dark when he left the brothel. Wrapped only in a threadbare blanket which Lettie had reluctantly given him, he stood shivering on the jetty before Winchester House and hailed a boatman out of the gloom.

'And where would you be going at this time of night, woman?' called the man, peering up at Tom from the stern of his craft.

'Temple steps. And I am a man, sirrah. A knave has stolen my true apparel.'

'Purse too?' smiled the ferryman.

'Yes,' Tom confessed, adding quickly, 'but I am not poor. I will bring you twice the fee tomorrow.' The man looked unsympathetic. 'I need your help, by God. I am

Thomas Verney of Clement's Inn — come look me out if I do not reward you handsomely.'

'Been in a trugging house?'

Tom nodded, pleased to find some understanding in the man.

'Said the constable was come?' continued the ferryman, his grin growing broader.

'Yes, an officer made a search.' Tom was somewhat taken aback that the fellow had guessed so accurately. 'He removed my garments and my purse,' he explained with a sheepish smile.

The fellow burst into guffaws of laughter. 'Then you are the whitest gull that ever flew! You have been cozened, sir!'

'I have not!'

'Oh, but you have, young sir! That trick is as old as King Cole. That weren't no officer, just a strumpet's cove play-acting to lift your valuables.' Tom folded inwardly with embarrassment. 'Come, I will take you across 'afore you die of cold, young quodling. But for a promise of two shilling. Paid tonight. I will follow you to the Inn.'

Tom had no choice but to accept.

Curse you, Lettie, he muttered to himself, stepping gingerly into the rocking boat and feeling the icy wind blowing about his bare legs. And curse you too, John, for all your theory. In future he would take people as he found them — king, cottager or callet — and not waste time wondering what train of circumstances had made them as they were. The world was as it was — only fools wished it otherwise.

Half an hour later, barefoot, mud-splattered and frozen, with the smirking boatman sidling along behind him, he crept past Callow's lodge and up the staircase to his chambers. Thanking God that he had not been recognised in this humiliating condition, he pushed open the outer door and let himself in.

His relief was premature. Walking along the passage he noticed with alarm a light showing beneath the door to his room. Who could possibly be behaving so familiarly with his property? 'Hello!' he called anxiously. 'Who's there?'

The reply made him wish he were dead.

'Well met, Thomas! Been at your studies all this while? I have sat here these two hours waiting for your return. Come!'

Tom bade his escort wait where he was. Pulling his blanket closer about him and brushing back a wisp of damp hair from his forehead, he stepped into the room and turned to face his astonished father.

iv

'Well, wife, do you believe it?' growled John Verney, pausing to refill his glass from the bottle beside him on the table. 'My money! Tipped down that sink of a son that he might cavort with whores and make himself the greatest fool in London!'

Travel-stained and tired, the justice had returned from London late that afternoon. The minute she had seen her husband's scowling face, Mary Verney knew that his meeting with Tom had not passed off smoothly. Ignoring his family's eager requests for news, he had gone straight to his study and remained there until supper, which he sat through in furious taciturnity, drinking heavily. As soon as the children and servants had departed, he had burst into an incoherent stream of invective against his son.

As the tirade wore on, not even the softening candlelight could hide the look of concern deepening on

Mary's handsome, furrowed face. Twisting her hands together, she opened her mouth as if to speak, then thought better of it. Twenty-two years of marriage had taught her that it was unwise to stand in the way of her husband's anger. She took some comfort from the knowledge that, like a conflagration started by lightning, it would burn itself out soon enough, although the ensuing cold embers of misery were often harder to endure than the fire itself.

John scowled indignantly down the table, his eyes glowing angrily behind his spectacles. 'Picture it, wife! In comes this nigget — my son, if you please — wound about with a mangy shroud and looking for all the world as if he had been fished from the Thames. And if that was not enough, behind him stood some gawping boatman asking for two shillings! Two shillings! By God, Mary, there are men in this land who would work a week for such a sum!'

'And what did he say?' Mary asked, judging it safe to speak at last. 'Did he excuse himself?'

'Excuse himself! Why, the shivering knave muttered about his ill-fortune and said he could explain all.'

'And could he?'

'When I had paid his debt and sent the thieving ferry fellow packing, he did weave together some sorry story.' John drained his glass at one gulp. 'Little sense it made, though. Said he had sought to save a fallen strumpet. Took pity on — a whore! Such sanctimonious cow's water I never heard!'

'Tom has a good heart, husband, for all his proud vanity.'

'Codpieces, woman! Do you not see that while he was writing sweet words to us of his studies and Christian behaviour he was dallying in brothels and congregating with cutpurses. You recall what Gilbert Marshall said, eh?'

'I do.'

'Tom recognised by a fellow on the gallows! God's life!' he thundered, hammering his fist so hard on the table that wine spilled into glistening pools of garnet around the stem of his glass. 'I warrant he'll finish there himself one day if I do not bring him home.'

Distressed at her husband's gloomy prognosis, which she knew owed more to drink and humiliation than reason, Mary instinctively came to her son's defence. 'The villain may have been mistaken, John – Marshall did not know the end of the tale. What did Tom tell you of the matter?'

'Zounds! What worth are his words? He spreads them like a false scent to lead us from his track.'

'But what did he say?' Mary persevered.

'He said – and I admit he spoke trippingly enough – the rogue had been among those who assailed him on the highway – by Stokenchurch, you remember – and being on the point of death had tried to draw our son down with him, for revenge.'

'There, John. I knew Tom would set us right. And Marshall did report that he passed long hours with his books.'

She looked imploringly towards her husband. 'I pray you, John, do not be too harsh on the lad.'

'Harsh! Pish woman! One cannot be too harsh on a deceiving scoundrel.'

'He is your son, John. Your first born. Should you not love him even as the Gospel father loved his prodigal?'

John Verney's face fell. 'Do not cast texts at me, Mary,' he said, suddenly deflated. 'Indeed I love him, as well you know. That is why I am so tormented.'

He emptied the bottle into his glass and for a long time stared at the heavy, dark liquid in silence. Eventually, without raising his eyes, he went on, 'I believed a time at the Inn would be best for him. I trusted him, as he was always asking me to do.'

Mary suggested quietly, 'Then should you not allow him to err?'

'I should. But it hurts me so.' He leaned forward and cradled his face in his hands, pushing his spectacles onto his forehead. 'I travelled to London to see if all was well after what Marshall had said. I went to tell Tom with my own lips that Banbury had at last arranged an introduction at court for him. I went out of concern, bearing good news for the son I loved.'

Caught up by cross-currents of sentimental self-pity and paternal care, both swollen by heavy drinking, he began to weep. 'And what did I find? A wastrel! A liar! Oh, Mary!' he cried. 'What sort of son have I created?'

'A good, honest one, John. I promise you that. You will see one day.'

'One day may be too late,' he sniffed, lifting bloodshot eyes towards his wife.

'All is in God's hands, husband. You have done what you can.'

'I have. Truly I have. And, perhaps foolishly, I gave him yet more money.'

'That was kind. And necessary for what lies ahead.'

Tempers and depressions breezed like clouds across the canopy of the ageing justice's restless mind; and now, as his melancholy lifted, a roguish star twinkled in his watery eye. 'Ah yes! What lies ahead. Ha! We would not wish the rogue presented at court in a blanket, would we, eh?' Mary smiled, more in relief at his recovered equilibrium than at the quip itself.

John's face brightened still further. 'The king, Mary! Think of it!'

'I do. Often.'

'My son to meet with King James! Surely not even Tom can squander such a chance?'

Mary sighed. 'I trust not, John. Yet we shall see. Only God can tell.'

SEVEN

HAMPTON COURT

i

The news that Lord Banbury had finally undertaken to introduce Tom at court went a long way towards ameliorating the young man's bitterness at the way he had been treated by both Lettie and his father. Having made clear what he thought of his son's explanations for the Tyburn and brothel incidents, the justice had lectured his son for several hours before retiring to Marshall's room for the night. When Tom awoke, he found his father had already departed, leaving behind a packet and a brief note. The former contained money, the latter reminded Tom that in four days' time he had to present himself at Pickering House at nine o'clock in the morning. It concluded with a pitiful plea:

> I beg you, Thomas, remember the Verneys of Stratton Audley have waited a hundred years for this moment. It is now time for you to make amends for your former foolishness. We pray

constantly for your good fortune. Come home swiftly and tell us all that passes between the king and yourself. Your mother and I will watch constantly at the window for the happy sight of Princess riding through the gates.

God bless you, son, and may He watch over you in your coming undertaking.

Your affectionate father,

John Verney

(Tom – no more folly, I beseech you.)

'Well,' said Tom, addressing the letter as if it were its author, 'What a contrary man you are that you chastise me all night then wheedle at me in the morning! If you had but listened with unstopped ears, you would not have found me so perplexing. Yet I will not fail you now, Father, you will see! But first I must attire myself as becomes a gentleman of court.'

So saying, he left for the Simpsons' house to tell them his good news and seek their advice on what he should wear for a royal audience.

The tailor and his daughter lived halfway down Blackmore Street, near Drury Lane. As Tom approached the point where the alley issued forth into the broader road, he became vaguely aware of a crowd milling about the junction. When he reached the spot, out of curiosity he asked the onlookers what was going on. 'Man been hit,' said a stout woman without raising her eyes from the scene before her.

'By whom?' asked Tom.

'No person – a carriage. Didn't stop, just galloped away. Fellow's all broken and bloody. Dead, I reckon.'

Such accidents were common enough in the busy streets and not particularly interested in seeing the victim's mangled remains, Tom was just about to resume his journey when he heard a cry that made him spin round in anguish.

'Father! Oh, Father! Open your eyes! Do not die! Dear God, let not my father die!'

Immediately, he began pushing frantically towards the direction of the sound. 'Lucy!' he cried. 'Lucy, my dearest, what is it?'

As he brushed through the inner ring of spectators, he was confronted by a scene that made him choke with horror. Lucy, tears streaming down her cheeks and her untied hair falling heavily about her shoulders and breast, was kneeling in the muddy road. In her lap she cradled the pale, broken head of her father. His eyes were closed, his thin hair matted with dirt. From his mouth and an ugly gash below his ear blood trickled into a congealing crimson pool on the white linen of his daughter's dress. She was trying unsuccessfully to stem the flow with her sleeve. One of Oliver Simpson's legs was twisted unnaturally beneath him. The other stretched out straight as a rod into a brown puddle. The quivering calf sent tiny ripples across the surface of the water. From his right arm a pointed shaft of bone, as clean as a spring shoot, projected through the torn sleeve. His breathing was slow and laboured.

God be praised! thought Tom, he is still alive! Calling loudly for water, bandages and a hurdle, he knelt beside Lucy. He tried to comfort her as a woman washed her father's wounds and four men carefully placed his shattered body on the wattle stretcher and carried it home. Here it was lowered onto a makeshift bed laid out on the parlour floor. The bearers departed, muttering among themselves about 'murdering carriage drivers who took no heed for common folk'. Shortly afterwards a coarse-faced man who called himself a surgeon appeared, carrying wooden splints and a bag of iron tools which clattered ominously as he dropped it on the stone floor beside his patient. Tom gave him money and, as the physician began cutting away Simpson's clothing to ascertain the extent of his injuries, led Lucy gently from the room.

He stayed with her the whole day. He knelt in prayer beside her. He placed his hands over her ears so she would not hear the patient's heart-rending groans as his fractured limbs were set. Later, he stood beside her when she stroked her father's head and whispered words of comfort in his ear. And that evening, when the last of the kindly neighbours had left and Simpson lay sleeping uneasily on his bloody pallet, he finally talked to her of the future.

'The double pity is that this morning I was coming to you with good news, Lucy,' he said sadly.

'Good news?' Her face was blanched and haggard, her eyes red with weeping.

'I am to have an audience with the king on Thursday. My father brought the message himself. I was to ask ...' He stopped, unsure whether he should explain why he had wanted to see Oliver Simpson so urgently.

'I know, Tom. You wanted my father to dress you for court.' She made a sound that lay somewhere between a sob and a laugh. 'I fear you were too late, Tom. He will never work again.'

'Lucy, how can you be so sure? He has a strong heart. Soon enough he will be at his table making me the finest suit in town, just as he used to.' He spoke more in hope than with conviction.

'No, Tom. You know you do not believe that.' Fresh tears rolled down her face. 'He is dying, Tom. He is an old man who has taken more wounding than such a frail body can endure. He may live on for several weeks, but he is dying nonetheless.'

She sat up and took a deep breath. 'Yet I am alive, and strong.' A fierce resolution came into her voice, as if she had been toughened, not broken, by the day's tragic events. 'With God's help I will do what my father would wish. Jack and Peter are still our apprentices – they will continue to work for me and I will manage our affairs.'

Tom was taken aback. 'But Lucy, you are a woman.'

'Was not the late Queen Elizabeth a woman? If she could rule a kingdom, I can rule a tailor's shop! I have watched my father often enough to know what is to be done.' She hesitated. 'We shall take in work for ladies, of course – but you will have your courtly finery, Tom, just you see if you don't!'

And so it was. Between caring for her invalid father, who recovered consciousness but was too feeble to do more than take a few sips of broth, and visiting homes where there were orders to complete, Lucy hectored and bribed the apprentices into completing Tom's apparel on time.

He saw much of her during those difficult days, marvelling at her strength and determination. With his previous affection thus reinforced by a new admiration, as he kissed her good night on the evening before he was due at court he could not help whispering in her ear, 'Lucy Simpson, I believe I love you.'

'Do you, Tom Verney?' she replied, holding his face in her hands. 'Yes, I believe you do. And here's a thought for you, Tom. Tomorrow, when you are in the midst of all those grand ladies and gentlemen, remember humble Lucy Simpson loves you too.'

ii

The king lay at Hampton Court, the russet–brick, riverside palace presented as a peace offering to his great-great-uncle Henry by the desperate Cardinal Wolsey almost a century before. As Lord Banbury's coach rattled and heaved its way thither through the winter-black villages of Hammersmith, Turnham Green and Twickenham, Tom was subjected to a self-opinionated and bewilderingly inaccurate homily on politics and etiquette. Though his garrulous patron told him little that he did not already know about courtly conduct, Banbury did reveal why he had suddenly decided to bring his handsome protégé before the king.

'I will arrange my lesson under three heads, Master Verney,' his lordship had begun as they rumbled down the Strand towards Westminster. 'That way you can fathom it more readily. We scholars understand that everything worth the knowing is in three parts, don't we?' Tom nodded. 'It was always so since Julian Caesar found that – what was the place? – was so divided.'

'Gaul, my lord?' Tom suggested.

'Eh? Oh yes, Gaul. Just testing your knowledge, Verney. We courtiers have to have such illusions on the tips of our tongues to impress our learned king.'

Wondering how King James could possibly be impressed by a man who failed to recall correctly the name of the most famous Roman of all, Tom guessed, quite correctly, that it was not for social or aesthetic reasons that His Majesty tolerated Banbury's graceless presence.

'Head one: manners. French is all the rage. French deportment, French wines, French horsemanship, French dances, French fashions, French everything – even French Welcomes! Ha! Ha!' Tom smiled politely. 'You get my meaning, Master Verney, do you? French Welcome is what the wags call the pox!'

'Thank you, sir.' He knew the expression, but felt it tactful not to admit as much.

'Don't mention it, Verney. I have travelled to France many times myself and am – how do they say? – oh-fay with such matters. Not the pox, of course. Who needs to risk cont-agion when their beds are warmed by such a one as my Bessie, eh?' He smirked and nudged Tom heavily in the ribs.

'Who indeed, sir. You are a fortunate man.'

'I am. Now, to my discourse. I see you are tidily attired, though not quite in the French fashion – your breeches are a trifle narrow, if I may say so. Yet it will do.' Tom felt a lump rise in his throat when he heard Lucy's hours of labour dismissed so casually, but he said nothing.

For the next quarter of an hour Banbury rambled on about how to make a bow, when to speak and the necessity of appearing humble and grateful at all times in the presence of the king. 'I am by nature a humble man myself,' he confessed, 'so it comes easy to me, Verney. You, on the other hand, being less finely bred, may find some difficulty in restraining your natural incline-ation to say what you think. Yet sit on that incline-ation, Master Verney. Sit on it tight.'

Sorely tempted to point out that he had been sitting on his inclination to say what he thought ever since the conversation had begun, Tom merely thanked his lordship for his advice and tried to change the subject. 'And your second head, sir?'

'Eh? Two heads? Even the French have only one head!'

'I meant the second head of your lesson, my lord. You said it came in three parts, like Gaul.'

'So I did! You are eager to learn, aren't you, sir? Well, the second head, as you so aptly put it, is the king himself.' He leaned forward and put a chubby finger to his lips. 'Speak low. Not one word of what you are about to hear must be repeated, Master Verney. It is highly confident.'

At this moment the coach swerved sharply to avoid a pedestrian, throwing the bulky peer against the door. 'Ben!' he screamed up at the driver without a chance of making himself heard. 'Run the vermin down rather than do that to me, do you hear?'

Thinking of poor Oliver Simpson lying broken on his parlour floor, Tom looked at his companion in contemptuous disbelief.

'By God!' Banbury exclaimed, recoiling into the cushions. 'That is not a pretty gaze, Master Verney. What do you mean by it?'

'I was thinking, sir,' said Tom slowly, 'that if the jolt had been more violent you would have been thrown into the road. You might have been killed.'

Banbury looked at him suspiciously. 'Of course. That would have been a terrible tragedy, would it not?'

'Truly, sir.'

'Lady Banbury would never have been the same again, would she, Verney?'

'I very much doubt it, sir.' Tom forced himself to smile. 'But there was no accident, thank God. Pray continue, my lord, with what you were on the point of telling me about the king.'

'I will. But remember those manners, Verney. A look like that to someone who knows you less well than myself might be taken for disapproval. At court it would never do – ruin everything.'

Having apologised, Tom lay back in his seat and

listened to Banbury's disjointed character sketch of King James. He learned nothing new about the only son of Mary Queen of Scots – the whole country was already well aware that he was a bawdy intellectual with a penchant for the company of good-looking young men. But hearing the way the baronet dwelt on the king's emotional weakness, it gradually dawned on Tom why he had been invited to attend his lordship. By Jesus! he realised, the scheming, slippery Toad hopes to use me as a lubricant to ease his way into royal favour! A screen behind which this unprepossessing creature may waddle unnoticed into the halls of power! His opinion of the man sank to new depths and he wished he had cuckolded him not once but a thousand times. He even considered stopping the coach and taking a boat back to London, bidding farewell to the swaggering nincompoop and his devious conceit for ever. Then he remembered his family. A vision of his mother and father watching anxiously at the window for his return arose before his eyes. No, he must not act precipitously, if only for their sakes, for he had caused them enough pain.

As his initial anger subsided, he decided to go along with the Toad's game, doing everything in his power to gain the king's attention. But he vowed that if he ever succeeded in climbing the ladder of favour and found Banbury clinging to his back, he would shrug the reptile down with no compunction whatsoever.

So when the baronet paused to drink from a small bottle he had secreted in a panel beside him, Tom asked coyly, 'Surely you cannot think, my lord, that the king will find anything that pleases him in a country lad such as myself?'

'You are rough, I warrant, Master Verney. You lack the French polish of those, such as myself, with whom His

Majesty is pleased to spend his daylight hours. And yet, after sunset, when his sensitations have been somewhat dulled by much wine, he has been known to incline himself towards what I might call less celestial temptations.'

'Really?'

'Well, you do have a shapely leg, Master Verney. And a certain freshness about the vis-age.'

Tom prodded him further. 'And if the king approves of me — which is most unlikely, of course — would that be of assistance to you, my lord?'

Banbury waited a moment before answering. 'Maybe, Verney,' he said with uncustomary caution. 'You see, there are plans afoot.' He went on to outline the issue that was exercising every mind in the royal council. Troops in Spanish pay had recently overrun the Palatinate, driving out Elector Frederick and his wife Elizabeth, James's daughter. Those of a fiercely anti-Catholic persuasion, who had found much support in the House of Commons the previous year, were urging the king to help his son-in-law win back his inheritance by force. But such action was expensive and contrary to James's peace-loving nature. As a self-styled 'Rex Pacificus', he saw himself not as a knight in the lists of faith, but as a mediator between Catholic and Protestant Europe. Rather than be drawn into the religious-dynastic war which had been raging for the last four years, he sought to marry his son Charles to the Spanish Infanta, thereby bringing together Britain and Spain as the first step towards healing the continent-wide division. With Princess Maria as his daughter-in-law, James reasoned, it would be easy for him to persuade her father, Philip IV, to restore the Palatinate.

Knowing most of this already, Tom put on his spectacles and gazed out of the coach window. Beyond the meadows, the swollen grey Thames slipped silently along between bare willows, and as he looked, a single oarsman came into view, struggling in vain to propel his frail craft against the flood. The sight induced in Tom a teasing flippancy.

When the tedious history lesson was over he turned to the peer and asked with scarecely veiled irony, 'Pray, sir, where does the significant figure of Baronet Banbury fit into this mighty scheme?'

'Ah! Perceptible question, Master Verney. He is a key player in the game. A castle beside the king. You see, I have a little money to spare. No, why should I be modest? I have a considerable fortune which I am prepared to put at the dispersal of Treasurer Cranfield, lately created Earl of Middlesex. In return, I hope for a little consider-ation. Cranfield, who I think I may call a close friend of mine, has been charged with equipping a costly exhibition to carry His Highness Prince Charles to Spain, that he may see the Inflanta for himself. The prince is, I gather, much taken with her picture and burns with desire to cast eyes on her fair flesh.

'Today, God willing, I will meet with His Majesty and Treasurer Cranfield – in your company – and put to them the terms for making my money available. You see how delicately the matter stands, Thomas? There are others with funds before the treasurer. I will strike a hard bargain, of course, but wish to be considered above them.'

'I understand, my lord.'

'You do? Zounds! Then we will take the court by storm, Thomas! My brains, your looks! The Beauty and the Beast, eh? What a combine-ation!' Banbury passed Tom his bottle. 'Here, Thomas, drink to our success!'

'The Beauty and the Beast!' toasted Tom with a laugh.

As he drank, he heard the carriage wheels roll onto firm cobbles and grind to a halt.

'Welcome to Hampton Court, Thomas Verney,' announced Banbury, grabbing back his bottle. 'Now, remove your spectacles – they do not become a young gallant – and follow me. Mind you do not forget what you have learned.'

Before withdrawing into his world of clouded myopia, Tom turned and looked straight into Banbury's small, oyster eyes. 'No, my lord, I will forget nothing. Nothing at all.'

iii

From the Great Gatehouse a bored-looking usher led Banbury and Tom across the rain-swept Base Court, under Anne Boleyn's Gateway with its remarkable astronomical clock, left over a second courtyard, and through the broad doorway leading to the state rooms north-east of Henry VIII's Great Hall. The blank look with which Banbury had been received at the gate and the perfunctory manner with which they were deposited in the Great Watching Chamber with the words 'His Majesty may call for you in due course', suggested that for all his boasting of how familiar he was at court, his lordship was in fact a very small star in this brilliant firmament. Noticing his companion's surprise, Banbury explained that as he was accustomed to arrive by water, he was less well known to the servants responsible for the palace's landward approaches. He would, he assured Tom, 'place a word in the ear of the Master of the Household and see the fellows rebuked for their insolence'. Tom dismissed the remark as another piece of Banbury bluster.

To his unfocused eyes the huge chamber, with its

sprawling Flanders tapestries and panelled ceiling emblazoned with the arms of Tudor and Seymour, was little more than a colourful blur. Neither could he make much of the groups of hopeful supplicants talking in hushed tones. He was obliged, therefore, to stand beside Banbury and endure still more of his witless persiflage. Every now and again a door at the far end of the room was thrown open and a liveried messenger called the names of those summoned to the royal presence. Minutes slipped by. Banbury became visibly agitated as men who had arrived after him were called forward. From time to time a page came into the room with a question for one of those waiting. Once a richly dressed man accompanied by a bevy of clerks sauntered by on his way to the royal apartments.

'Middlesex,' hissed Banbury in Tom's ear. 'What good fortune!' He stepped forward which a clumsy bow and cried out, 'My lord of Middlesex! How my humble heart leaps up when I behold his lordship looking so well!'

The treasurer paused and cast a sharp look in the speaker's direction. 'Banbury, is it not?'

'Aye, my lord. And may I be so bold as to say that your cloak is the finest I have had the pleasure to—'

'Indeed. You have business with His Majesty?'

'Quite so, my lord. Among the many and weighty matters pressing upon your lordship's mind at present,' Banbury grovelled, almost falling over in exaggerated obeisance, 'you may recall my little pro-posal?'

'Ah yes! The loan.'

'Even so, my lord. I would be only too pleased to be of assurance at this trying time—'

'I am sure you would. I will speak to the king and you will be called forward shortly. Good day to you, my lord of Banbury.' Offering a slight nod in the baronet's direction, Middlesex resumed his conversation with those about him and left the room.

'Oh, Verney,' said Banbury, dripping with perspiration, 'what it is to be well connected!'

'So I see,' replied Tom, wondering whether it would have been wiser not to come to court at all rather than be seen there in the company of such a buffoon.

Nevertheless, embarrassing though Banbury's performance might have been, it seemed to have had the desired effect. Fifteen minutes later his name was called and having adjusted his belt with nervous fingers and muttered one final reminder of the importance of manners, he waddled towards the door with Tom following eagerly in his wake.

They were taken down a long gallery lined with innumerable sets of antlers — tokens, Tom was later told, of royal prowess in the chase — to a lobby lined with guards. Here they waited for a further couple of minutes before a heavily panelled door was thrown open and they were shown through into the audience chamber itself.

Before he entered, Tom had visions of a massive, brilliantly lit hall rising in steps to a golden throne set on a marble dais. He imagined throngs of courtiers, a company of musicians, jugglers and dancers, trumpeters and all the glorious paraphernalia of a fairy-tale court. The reality was quite different. James had selected this modest-sized, rectangular room for his audiences because it was easy to keep warm and had a homely, almost cosy feel to it. At the far end, driving rain beat against the leaded panes of a single oriel window. To the left, taking up almost half the wall, was a fireplace of Portland stone with the arms of the House of Stuart carved in deep relief above it. Huge logs hissed and snapped in the grate, constantly attended by a boy with a face baked to a brown crust by the heat. The folded panelling on either side of the fire was hung with hunting scenes, which were also the subject of the inevitable tapestries covering the wall opposite. Treasurer Middlesex, flanked by clerks, was flicking through papers at a heavy table in the middle of the room; nearby, lolling with easy grace in a high-backed chair, sat a tall, sumptuously attired man in his early thirties.

'Sir Julius Pickering, Lord Banbury!' announced the footman. Oh well, thought Tom, as the door closed behind him, since this is his lordship's party it is only to be expected that I should not feature in it. He stood with his back to the entrance, trying to make out the main features of the scene before him. Middlesex was the first to speak.

'Banbury, I have talked with His Majesty on the question of finance for the Spanish expedition. First, I trust that you understand that the matter is of the utmost secrecy. It is to be spoken of with no one.'

Banbury shuffled a few steps towards him. 'Oh, my lord,' he simpered, 'I am a man noted for his discretion. My lips are sewn.'

'Good. Now to business. You can, I believe, furnish us with twenty thousand pounds?'

'Well, I had believed that it was to be fifteen thousand' – Middlesex looked up quickly – 'but I must have been mistaken. I will ensure in future that my clerk writes these matters down. He is such a scatterbrain of a fellow—'

'My lord, the attributes of your clerk are no concern of ours. Servants have a habit, I believe, of taking after their masters.' Although the treasurer's face remained impassive, the man in the chair smiled and sat up. 'Is it twenty thousand pounds, Banbury?' Middlesex demanded.

The baronet looked crestfallen. 'It is, my lord.'

'Very well. And we will pay you at fifteen per cent per annum, with the whole capital to be returned within ten years?'

'Fifteen per cent?' Banbury repeated breathlessly.

'That is what I said.'

'My Lord Treasurer, although no man is more eager than I to assist in this great matter, I must intimate that those are not generous terms.'

'You wish for more?'

'No. Well, yes,' he stammered. 'I did hope that twenty-five might be agreed. It is a business of much risk, and I have a young wife whose spending is, well, incontinent.'

'Ha!' cried a thin tenor voice from below the window. 'By Jesus, Banbury, are ye married to a wife both young and incontinent?' Tom recognised a soft Scots accent. 'There's tragedy for ye!'

The elderly speaker, who had been sitting on the window seat, rose and came forward into the centre of the room. He wore a plain cap, which had slipped to a rakish angle over one ear, and his sagging face, adorned with thin grey beard, was undistinguished. But from his confident bearing, magnificent ermine-trimmed gown and the reactions of those present it was abundantly clear who he was. Middlesex half rose and bowed. The figure in the chair got easily to his feet and offered his arm, which was gratefully received. Banbury sank heavily to his knees. Tom did likewise, lowering his head and staring at the floor.

'Your Majesty!' mumbled Banbury. 'I was not aware of your gracious presence, Your Majesty. Had I but known, I would have—'

'Aye, and what would ye have done, my lord?' asked the king, stretching out a pale, plump hand for Banbury to kiss.

'I would have admitted Your Majesty sooner.' Tom was aware of his patron shaking as he spoke.

'Admitted?' the king frowned. 'Are we a sin that ye needs confess us, Banbury?'

'Oh no, Your Majesty!' His quivering became so violent that Tom feared he might capsize onto the floor. 'It is I, Your Majesty, who are the sinner. Overcome by Your Majesty's gracious presence, I forgot my termination—'

'Hell's teeth, Banbury!' James interrupted, his stern expression collapsing into a grin which revealed wide gaps in his discoloured teeth. 'Your termination is entirely in our hands. Do not forget it.' He smiled up at the tall figure on whose arm he was still leaning and squeezed his hand. 'His Majesty and the Marquis of Buckingham,' he went on, adopting a more formal, mocking tone, 'note with pleasure that ye have taken the advice proffered at our last meeting, my lord, and availed yourself of grammar lessons in the English tongue. Is that not so, Steenie?'

'It is, sire.' Buckingham's voice, like his deportment, was elegant, graceful and immensely attractive.

'Eh?' Banbury grunted, placing a hand on the floor to steady his quaking frame.

'No matter,' cut in James, bored with shooting at so easy a target. 'Stand up, ye lexicon of misprints. By God, we cannot abide crawlers!' As Banbury struggled to his feet, James's round, wet eyes alighted on Tom, still on his knees. 'And who's this, Banbury? A young man? There may be some good in ye after all that ye come so prettily accompanied.'

The next quarter of an hour was the most temulent Tom had ever known. Sitting in the chair previously occupied by the Marquis of Buckingham and calling Tom 'Banbury's wee bait', James peppered him with questions about his family, his education and the purpose of his stay in London. He had not heard of Stratton Audley, though Justice Verney was known to him – 'an irascible fellow, we believe, though true enough'. For Clement's Inn he had little liking, and asked Tom why he had not chosen to study at Oxford.

'It was my father's decision, Your Majesty,' Tom replied, casting what he knew to be a winsome grin in James's direction. 'He wished to put a goodly distance between us.'

'Fancy choosing to be apart from so comely a son, Steenie!' the king retorted, taking Buckingham's hand. He sighed. 'We die afresh each minute we are parted from our dear son and his loving companion.'

Tom's thoughts sped like a racehorse through the streets of his mind as he strove to fathom his strange inquisitor and create a favourable impression with him. The man was quick-witted and learned, but also crude, almost childishly sentimental and easily bored. He was impatiently critical, too, as he had showed by the way he had treated the wretched Banbury and now left him fidgeting and grinning in inane isolation in the middle of the room. The aspect of the king Tom found most difficult to come to terms with was the way he could swing in an instant from easy, almost affectionate familiarity to an icy formality, as if he sometimes forgot his station, or chose to ignore it, and then had to bring himself up sharply when he found those about him overstepping the boundary which circled the throne. Although this prevented Tom from ever feeling comfortable throughout the interview, he could not dislike James. Rather, he gained the impression of an intensely lonely old man, a sorry figure who leaned both physically and metaphorically on the splendid young Buckingham for companionship and affection.

To his surprise, the king made no secret of his need for young male company. His feelings for Buckingham were quite evident and by describing Tom as 'bait' he revealed that he had seen through Banbury's tawdry little device the moment he set eyes on the baronet's young accomplice. Once, when Banbury tried clumsily to introduce himself into the conversation, the king cut him dead, telling Tom he believed God had created Yorkshire to save his native kingdom from southern conquest, 'for which Englishman, Master Verney, however eager he might be to get his hands on fair Scotland, would relish a journey through a county peopled by such boneheaded, bloated barbarians, eh?'

Sir Julius burst into peals of sycophantic laughter. The king turned to Buckingham. 'Tell us, Steenie,' he asked, 'does not the ancient family of Pickering come from Yorkshire?' The baronet's mouth flopped open like a damp cave, and he took no further part in the conversation.

For all his apparent lack of sophistication, Tom reflected, this king is not a man to be underestimated; deep currents run beneath that disconcertingly straightforward surface.

Only once, when the king ventured upon the subject of marriage, did Tom let his guard slip.

'Tell us, Master Verney, so bonny a young fellow as yourself, though not promised in wedlock, must have a sweetheart, must he not?'

'Indeed, Your Majesty.' Even as he spoke, he knew it was the wrong reply.

'A-ha! Ye hear that, Steenie?' said the king delightedly. 'Wee Verney's heart is taken. Tell us more, young Thomas. Who is the maid? She is a maid, is she not?' he chuckled.

'Yes, Your Majesty. Yet – I am not sure that – well, perhaps ...'

'Come, Master Verney. Would ye have secrets from your king? He is the loving father to all his people and would know what they do.'

'I understand, Your Majesty. It is only that ... I do not know what to say.' He felt himself blushing deeply. 'I have not told Justice Verney – yet.'

'Well then, it is a match he would not consent to?' Tom nodded, noting with relief that Banbury was too preoccupied with trying to work out fifteen per cent of twenty thousand to pay much attention to James's interrogation. 'That is not wise. Do not give your heart to one of a lower station than yourself, Master Thomas. The Commonwealth stands upon ordered degree. Do not seek to upset it. The head must rule the heart, must it not?'

'It must, Your Majesty.'

Noticing Tom's embarrassed expression, James's tone became more kindly. 'It will pass in time, as all things must. Pray do not withdraw from us, Thomas, for we take pleasure in your company.' His voice softened still further and for the first time he abandoned the formal plural. 'I may be God's lieutenant upon earth, yet I am also a fond old man. Here I sit a wee god, but hereafter I shall be judged by the Great God Himself. Dear Jesus! My piles, like clappers on the bells of hell, serve well enough to remind me of the torment that awaits me for my sins!'

The silence which followed this unusual admission was broken by Treasurer Cranfield. 'Your Majesty, if I may intervene, we have the matter of Lord Banbury's loan to settle before dinner.'

James looked up wearily. 'If you say so, my lord.' He turned to Banbury. 'If we recall correctly, it was fifteen per cent, was it not, baronet?' Sir Julius hesitated. 'Come, Yorkshire Jew, would you haggle with your king? Ye have your way. We will see Master Verney again, and we will see ye recompensed for troubling to introduce him to us. That was what ye sought, was it not?'

Flustered by the King's perception, Banbury concurred. Five minutes later, when the door of the audience chamber had been closed behind them, he threw his arms around Tom. 'By God, Master Verney!' he cried in a voice hoarse with relief and self-satisfied delight. 'Just as I predicted – the Beauty and the Beast have triumphed!'

iv

During the week following his audience Tom behaved as if he were perpetually intoxicated. He ran up stairs, whistled down corridors and lay in bed until dinner time. On returning from Pickering House on the day of his audience, where he had sat chatting with his patron like an old friend, he had roared into George's chambers, clapped him on the back and insisted that he leave his books at once and accompany him for a celebratory meal. The next morning he hugged the startled House Martin, called him the most fortunate boy in London and tipped him a month's wages. He even engaged in amiable, one-sided conversations with Callow and, now that the Michaelmas term was over, rewarded him handsomely whenever he opened the Inn gates. Study and careful management of his allowance went by the board, dismissed as tedious requirements of a life that was gone for ever. Their place was taken by open-handed hospitality and such polishing and preening as would have made his straightforward father burst with contempt. Never before had his fingernails and hair received such attention, and he examined himself so closely and so often that if looking-glasses could be worn out by use, his would have been quite blank within thirty-six hours.

In a sense he was indeed drunk, though with a concoction infinitely more heady than any he had yet tasted. Not even the potion prepared for him on the evening of Cranfield's test had deprived him of his sense of reality so completely as the exhilarating double draught of love and royal favour.

To the Simpsons' depressed household, where the tailor still lay semi-comatose on his lowly bed, he brought a welcome breath of optimism. As soon as they were alone together he took Lucy's hand and, with child-like enthusiasm, went through his interview with the king word by word, repeating the most flattering phrases and glancing at her anxiously for approval. When she expressed concern at James's cautionary advice about forming attachments outside one's social circle, he dismissed the remark with a laugh, saying that when he knew His Majesty better – which he surely would – then he was certain of winning royal approval for his irregular passion. 'And armed with that, Lucy, my love,' he smiled, drawing her to him, 'we can tell my father of our affection without fear of rebuke.' Won over by his irrepressible optimism, she kissed him fondly.

From that time forward, recklessly ignoring the neighbours' mounting disapproval, he took to staying with her long after the apprentices had departed. Alone, unchaperoned and emotionally vulnerable, she gradually allowed her ardour a longer and longer rein until only the sobering proximity of her dying father and fear of pregnancy prevented consummation of the dangerous, intense love flaring between the confident young courtier and the lonely tailor's daughter.

The mood in Stratton Audley Manor was scarcely less elated. News of what had occurred at Hampton Court arrived almost simultaneously in letters from Lord Banbury and Tom. Needless to say, the baronet dwelt on his part in Tom's favourable reception. 'So it was', he had written, 'that on the ladder so generously errected by myself – I speak metaphysically – your son Thomas climed to favour etc with His Majesty. There were moments (particlarly when he spoke of his unworthy attachments etc) when I feared he might throw away all that I had handed to him but they passed and now I expect we will be called to court again before long.'

At first the words 'unworthy attachments' worried Mary Verney, but when her husband assured her that they were just another of Banbury's inaccuracies, she agreed to overlook them. Tom's long, somewhat disjointed letter, full of studied modesty, made no mention of the king's awkward questioning. Justice Verney proudly read it again and again, sometimes to himself, sometimes out loud at meal times, with the result that within a few days the document became so dog-eared that Mary had to lock it away in a drawer to prevent it from disintegrating completely. But by this time the family were sufficiently familiar with its contents to recite whole paragraphs by heart. The magistrate's recitations, delivered at the slightest excuse, soon became a neighbourhood joke, earning him the nickname among his friends of 'Justice Courtierson'. It was an epithet coined as much in envy as mockery.

Two disappointments prevented Tom's good fortune from bringing unalloyed joy to his parents' household. The first was his announcement that, since he might be called to court again at any moment, he had no immediate plans to return home. The second was John Verney's health. For a year or two now the volatile justice had been troubled by occasional pains in the chest, and since the arrival of his son's letter, probably owing to the excitement it had engendered, these had become more frequent and more debilitating. It was with deep regret, therefore, that he wrote to Tom saying that for the time being he would be unable to come to London to share his son's obvious delight at the way his career had so unexpectedly taken a turn for the better. As Tom still had no intention of telling his family about Lucy, on whom he was calling almost every day, he received the decision with as much relief as disappointment.

Tom had not seen Great John, who was now resident at the other end of the city in the Saracen's Head by Aldgate, since his dismal escapade with the whore Lettie, and knowing what he did of the man's radical outlook he was not sure that he would be impressed by the tale of his royal audience. Late one morning, however, when no message had come from court and there was no one left in the Inn to tell his story to, he thought he would pass the day by calling on John for an hour or so before returning to take supper with Lucy.

The bearded giant seemed pleased enough to see him, particularly when Tom declared that he wished to order a large dinner to celebrate a recent stroke of good fortune. As they sat together near the fire, on either side of a table loaded with the best fare the inn could provide, Tom began by telling his friend how he had been robbed of his clothes and purse. He spoke quickly, full of anger and scorn for the bawd and her accomplices and her sordid accommodation.

When he had finished, John looked at him carefully. 'Master Thomas,' he observed sadly, 'what has taken hold of you? The last time we met lines of rich charity marbled your young heart. Where are they fled? What are a few coins and a suit of fine clothes to you? You were humiliated, to be sure, not an easy cut for one as proud as yourself to bear. Yet does it warrant such bitterness?'

Tom made light of the accusation. 'I am changed, John, that is all. I admit that for a while I was seduced by your talk of Christian kindness to all men, by the contempt in which you held the established order. But now I see a different world. It was not merely the trick of that vicious strumpet which brought this about, though I confess it did little to buttress your crumbling thesis. You must accept that I now understand life as it really is.'

John looked surprised. 'Life as it really is, Tom? Was the Winchester goose not real enough?'

'Perhaps. But she represents only one part of reality. The corrupt, sinful, lower part, inhabited by those who have fallen through their own fault and weakness. We must each make our own way, John.' His tone was harsh and arrogant.

John sat back and gazed into his glass. 'Tom, I do not like this new vision you speak of.' With a wave of the hand he bade his visitor continue.

'Maybe not. But I have set eyes on another scene, John. A scene of love and civility. Of noble people and worthy sentiments. A scene which welcomes me and offers me high hopes.' He proceeded to outline what had happened at court, dwelling on the king's kindness towards him and on the obvious, competent nobility of Buckingham and Middlesex. He explained next how things stood between Lucy and himself. 'You see, John,' he concluded, 'how two lamps have shown me the true way. At court I met great men, majestic arts. In Lucy I recognise sincere affection and worthiness. Beside these, what are your sorry masses with their tawdry, backbiting deceits? You can dress them in ermine if you wish, send them all to Oxford, instruct them in good manners, do what you will to hide their nature – but it will out, John. You cannot gild a dunghill!'

Grinning at his eloquence, he resumed his meal with exaggerated indifference, for deep in his heart he knew what he had said to be both illogical and deeply wounding to his friend.

At the beginning of Tom's speech John had grown agitated. Several times he had made as if to intervene, restraining himself only with difficulty. As the youth ploughed callously on, however, his mood had altered, first to resignation, then to despair, and when the conceited address finished he covered his face with his hands and moaned.

'Oh, Tom, Tom, Tom! What are you saying? I will not challenge you now, for you are in no mood for contradiction. Yet when your head stops spinning, I beseech you think on this: do these two lamps you speak of give the same beam? Can courtly life and honesty ever share the same bed? Never! And you know it to be so. They are sinner and saint, salt and honey.'

Lifting his head, he heaved a great sigh, as if every ounce of breath had been knocked from his body by an invisible fist. Through his unkempt hair the scar of his ugly brand showed livid red on his furrowed brow. 'Tom,' he said with the deliberate solemnity of a judge passing sentence, 'you may well be in love, as you say, for you are blind enough. Remind me, I beg, who is the object of your affections?'

Tom frowned with irritation. 'Have you forgotten so

soon? She is called Lucy Simpson.'

'No, Tom,' John replied, folding his hands together as if in prayer. 'You are not in love with Lucy Simpson. You are in love with someone else.'

An eerie quiet had fallen on the room. No noise came from the street outside; even the fire burned in silence.

'And who is this someone else, pray?'

'A person well known to you, whom you meet every day.' Not for an instant did John lift his eyes from the proud face opposite.

'The name?'

'The name, sir, is Thomas Verney.'

PART II

THE TAILOR'S DAUGHTER

FOOL When every case in law is right,
No squire in debt nor no poor knight;
When slanders do not live in tongues
Nor cutpurses come not to the throngs;
When usurers tell their gold i' th' field,
And bawds and whores do churches build,
Then shall the great realm of Albion
Come to great confusion.

KING LEAR, Act III, scene ii

EIGHT

MILK STREET

i

That winter the Thames first froze over one night early in the new year, and Londoners awoke the next morning to find their familiar heavy black snake of water transformed into a ribbon of silvery beauty. But not until the frosty afternoon of 4th February did the first adult, a ruddy-faced butcher's apprentice from Cheapside balancing a long pole to facilitate his rescue if the surface gave way, attempt to walk between Worcester Place and Bankside, where the river was narrowest.

From his vantage point high in Princess's saddle, Tom watched the exploit from a jetty at the end of Three Cranes Lane. A smile of amused admiration lit up what was visible of his handsome features as he peered out between heavy hat and upturned collar. At his side a gloved hand hung ready to pull off his spectacles the moment he was recognised by anyone with courtly connections.

The intrepid pioneer had almost reached the middle of

the stream. The crowds of spectators gathering on either bank had fallen quiet, listening for the ominous, reverberating crack that would herald imminent disaster – while ponds and smaller rivers had become noisy playgrounds long ago, the swift-flowing, tidal waters of the city's principal artery kept the ice-sheet treacherously unpredictable. Half a dozen children had already fallen to their deaths in the dark depths below. Sometimes slipping to his knees on the frosty surface, sometimes clambering over jagged blocks grasped in the floe's bitter vice, the adventurer moved slowly on across the unpredictable bridge towards glory as transitory as the path he was treading. Fame was not his only spur, however, for several proprietors of Bankside places of entertainment, eager to attract new custom as soon as the river could be crossed without payment, had recently clubbed together to offer a substantial reward to whoever first blazed the precarious trail.

Behind Tom, scarved, hatted and cloaked against the cold, half a dozen doleful boatmen sat like smoking bales round a driftwood fire, grumbling uncharitably at the way the river's gradual solidification was throttling their trade. The scores of solitary rowers, normally able to scrape a laborious living by plying back and forth across the current, had been out of work for the last fortnight. Even when their craft had managed to break through the ice thickening near the banks, they risked being holed by the mace-spiked floes of ice drifting down the clear water. More recently, even the stout eight-oared wherries, which in warmer weather splashed incessantly from shore to shore like heavy black beetles, had given up the struggle and lay wedged alongside the jetties or pulled up among the steely white furrows of the shoreline.

The apprentice was nearing his destination, and some

of the braver onlookers had ventured onto the ice to help him ashore. Already a second man had set out from the north bank a few yards upstream. Soon the whole surface of the waterway would be alive with Londoners eager to experience the thrill of temporary mastery over their sleeping mistress.

As Tom turned to leave, he paused to listen to the jeers of the watching ferrymen, now certain to be out of business until the thaw. The voice of a middle-aged man with hands gnarled to claws by years at the oar caught Tom's attention. 'Shag-visaged knave!' he cursed. 'The river should've swallowed him for seeking to filch the work of honest fellows!'

Although illogical, it suited the man to find a mortal scapegoat for his unemployment — to have blamed a heavenly architect for his misfortunes would have implied supernatural punishment for past misdeeds which he and his colleagues, though not their overcharged customers, were loath to recognise.

Having repeated his colleague's imprecation, an aged ferry-owner added in a more despondent, philosophical tone, 'Lately the stinking world's clogged with whoreson young monkeys like him, Abe, clambering over their betters for a peck of glory and fortune.' He spat into the fire. 'But they're all trotting on ice, Abe. Mark my words. They'll tumble to their graves soon enough, by Jesus. If not in our water, then elsewhere. Vaulting fools always do.'

'Aye, Jacob,' replied his companion, 'fools always do. Stick to the place God gave you, I say.'

The foolhardy exploit on the ice and the overheard snatch of conversation awoke half-formed doubts, first raised by Great John and growing during the events of the past few weeks, which had lain at the back of Tom's mind for some time. During the slow ride back to the Inn through the darkening streets, he pondered the events of the past two months and tried to work out precisely what it was that was troubling him.

ii

Superficially, Tom's success with the king had exceeded his wildest fancies.

As promised, His Majesty had eventually summoned 'Banbury's bonny bait' to court for a second audience. When he arrived, decked out in yet another new suit of clothes which included a pair of breeches so voluminous that House Martin had cheekily asked if he could hide in them and come to meet the king too, he found James in an excellent mood and clearly delighted to see his handsome young protégé again. The royal bonhomie soared still higher when Tom, straining his knowledge of theology to its limits, managed to steer the conversation round to the topic of witchcraft. In this matter, as the whole country was well aware, the learned monarch considered himself – with some justification – an expert, and for about thirty minutes he delivered an almost unbroken monologue on the subject, embroidering his speech with colourful threads of learned argument, biblical references – often slightly irreverent – and startlingly earthy examples. Seated on a cushion at his master's feet, Tom followed the speaker's academic logic with difficulty. His concentration was not helped by the way James absent-mindedly stroked his hair as he spoke, nor by the knowing, sideways looks this behaviour drew from the Lords of Middlesex and Buckingham, both in perspicacious attendance as they had been during his previous interview. The hour-long colloquy concluded with James pressing a copy of his book *Demonology* into Tom's hands and insisting that he come to a performance of a court masque five days' hence.

'A masque!' Tom gasped, making the most of his delighted surprise. 'I have never seen a masque, Your Majesty.' He gave the old man what he knew was a winning grin.

'Then ye shall!' James insisted, much taken with the youth's innocent enthusiasm. He raised a soft hand affectionately to Tom's shoulder. 'Oh, what pleasures await ye!'

Pleasure was the last thing Tom experienced when he arrived at Hampton Court on the appointed day. His reception taught him just how precarious, even dangerous, was the voyage he had embarked on. When he turned up on horseback, the grooms treated him as if he were little better than themselves. For the early part of the evening the King appeared totally unaware of his presence among the scores of other courtiers fawning and jostling for attention.

At the banquet which preceded the performance, Tom found himself seated far from the high table, amid a group of aloof young aristocrats and gentlemen-in-waiting who took great pleasure in mocking his crude country manners and ignorance of high society, seizing on his accent to call him 'Tom-arse' and taunting him with demands for a detailed description of his father's non-existent deer park. Resisting a powerful urge to punch their supercilious faces, he defended himself verbally as best he could, but was so frustrated by the end of the meal that as the throng began to troop towards the Great Hall, he considered slipping quietly away. Staring rather awkwardly about him, he tried to decide which door would offer him the swiftest escape route. He had just selected one to the right of the screen and was starting to make his way towards it, when a hand grasped him urgently by the elbow.

'Master Verney,' said a light, familiar voice, 'may I say what a pleasure it is that we meet again in such – ahem! – elevated circumstances? A true pleasure.'

Tom looked round. 'Canon Chillingworth!' he exclaimed, taking the pale clergyman warmly by the hands. 'I am indeed happy to see you again. Particularly at this moment.'

Initially Chillingworth was taken aback by the warmth of his former travelling companion's greeting. But looking into the young man's anxious brown eyes, he immediately guessed the reason for it. 'The first time that God has been gracious enough to guide your young feet to such magnificence, eh, Thomas?'

'Yes. And I cannot say, Canon, that I am much taken with what I have seen. Most of those present seem arrogant, ill-mannered reptiles!'

White fingers pinched his arm. 'Hush, Master Verney! In times past men have fallen more precipitously than the Gadarine swine for uttering such a remark. It is not wise to speak your mind too openly. Not wise.' He relaxed his grip. 'Besides, you know not what you say, eh? Which man with true vision cannot help but delight in the King's court, seeing as it is the earthly mirror of the court of the King Eternal? An earthly mirror, Master Verney.'

What a queer fish you are! Tom thought with a smile. What cynicism lurks beneath your piously scriptured surface? Do you mean anything you say?

Despite his reservations, Tom was glad to see the man and, abandoning the idea of retreat, he allowed himself to be led from the room with the rest of the chattering throng.

As Tom had hoped, for all his ironic oddity, Chillingworth proved a knowledgeable and kindly companion. A figure of some consequence at court, he had heard that Tom had found favour with the king and explained that jealousy was undoubtedly the reason for his ill-treatment at table. 'You are already talked of Master Verney,' he said, surreptitiously looking about him. 'There are no secrets in this glass house. No secrets.'

The observation was confirmed when, during the short walk to the hall, several strangers came up to Tom and introduced themselves. Most did so out of curiosity, examining him like a prize calf at market for a minute or so before sauntering off with the weakest of excuses. More flattering was the approach of an anxious, elderly man who begged Tom to use his good offices with His Majesty to raise the question of some obscure suit or other. Tom was so impressed that someone should consider making such a request, that he forgot the unfortunate fellow's name and the details of his case as soon as they were given.

During the course of the long masque Chillingworth talked incessantly, pointing out the important figures in the audience, relaying titbits of scandal and bringing Tom up to date with the latest political gossip. It was certain, he said, that a party – perhaps including both Prince Charles and the Marquis of Buckingham – was about to leave for Spain to woo the Infanta in person. It was a reckless enterprise, the canon reckoned, for it would give Buckingham's potential opponents – 'among whom may appear Bishop John Williams of Lincoln, the Lord Keeper, and perhaps even Treasurer Middlesex' – an opportunity to work behind the favourite's back in his absence. And if the marriage party failed to reach an acceptable accord with Spain, relations between the two countries would certainly deteriorate, maybe to the point of open war. 'Then we shall witness a performance round the council table!' Chillingworth concluded with a chuckle. 'A scrap far surpassing the drama of this merry show. Far exceeding.' As he spoke, a half-naked, cherubic young boy, suspended from a wire and armed with Cupid's bow, was winched on stage to loud applause.

'I pray I will be well placed to watch this council theatre,' Tom replied eagerly.

The canon leant towards him. 'Watch it, Master Verney? Why, by the Lord, do you not grasp what I say? Your looks may give you a place on the very stage itself.'

Tom was taken aback by such an audacious suggestion. Excited and at the same time frightened, he asked Chillingworth what he meant. The clergyman explained that if the king continued to favour him, he might acquire a modicum of political influence. Of course, he would never be much more than a pawn in the game of political chess — Buckingham would see to that — but he would be on the board. And that was what mattered. Members of the council would find it wise to court him. It was a situation which, if he handled it carefully, might bring him rewards far richer than any he had ever dreamed of.

The words went to Tom's head like a drug. He imagined riding about the city in his own coach, the king arriving to stay at a rebuilt Stratton Audley Manor, his parents kneeling on the gravelled forecourt, their faces glowing with pride. Why, he would even be able to set up house with Lucy... A cloud slipped over the sun of his dream. Lucy. A tailor's daughter. Could she really have a place in the wonderful career he saw lying before him? On the other hand, could he conceive of a future without her? With his mind tossing backwards and forwards in contradictory gusts of love, ambition, pride and loyalty, he tried in vain to concentrate on the hazy swirl of brilliant colour before him.

To Tom's delight, Chillingworth's prophesy began to unfold later the same evening. Unknown to his young friend, towards the end of the performance the canon sent a page with a message to the king, as a result of which Tom was summoned to attend His Majesty after the show had ended. For the first time he was directed to the royal family's private apartments where, together with a dozen or so members of the household, he witnessed all but the most intimate stages of the ritual by which James was prepared for bed. The king, who had clearly drunk a good deal during the course of the evening, declared himself to be 'mightily relieved to be beyond the sight of the goggle-eyed court magpies' and was pleasantly relaxed. While being divested of his robes, he chatted and joked about the spectacle they had just witnessed, saying – with a piercing look towards Tom – how fortunate he was to be surrounded by such beauty. Interrupting the laboured and unnecessarily flamboyant reply of a fair-haired gentleman of the bedchamber, Tom suggested that beauty could be found only in the presence of those with sufficient sensitivity and intelligence to appreciate it. The king clapped his hands in approval. 'Excellent, Master Verney!' he chortled. 'The sage of Stratton Audley, eh?'

Before retiring, he clasped Tom warmly round the waist and bade a chamberlain find him accommodation within the palace. 'I would never sleep if I thought his dear flesh was being gnawed by fleas in a common inn,' he confessed. 'Moreover, I wish to lay my old head down in the comfort of knowing that my comely wee lawyer friend rests nearby, and will be here to greet me on the morrow.'

Tom's face burned as he knelt to kiss his benefactor's dry, puffy hand with sincere gratitude. Delighted, James ruffled his hair like a fond lover and shuffled away to bed.

Tom remained at court for the next two days. As well as spending several hours in the king's company, during which he was subjected to further flattery and innocent fondling, he received separate visits from a pair of influential private secretaries. The first came from Treasurer Middlesex. His message was as blunt as it was welcome. Seeing that Tom was likely to be spending some time in attendance on His Majesty and would therefore be obliged to meet a number of expenses, the marquis had arranged, with royal approval, for Tom to be given the post of Deputy Receiver of Customs for the Cornish port of Helford. Although the position carried only the nominal salary of twenty pounds a year, it involved no actual work. If Tom agreed — and the emissary made it quite clear that he was expected to do so — the treasurer would arrange for the job to be farmed out to local businessmen who would pay Tom one hundred pounds a year (via the treasury) for the profitable opportunity of collecting the revenues on his behalf. He accepted the offer at once and was immediately presented with a pouch containing fifteen pounds, being an advance on the larger sums he would receive shortly. Nothing was said about what he was to do in return, but from the manner in which the secretary continually referred to his master as Tom's 'patron', it was clear that henceforth the rising star was expected to follow an orbit mapped out for him by the ambitious treasurer.

The second envoy came from the Marquis of Buckingham. Although superficially more genial, his subtle approach was also considerably more threatening. After a few sentences of introduction, he remarked that the favourite had noted with pleasure the happiness the king found in Tom's company. Therefore, the man explained, in order that Tom be properly equipped to play a full part in court life, Buckingham was thinking of sending him to France for a while, at considerable cost to his lordship.

Tom's heart sank. He realised at once that the plan was not in any way intended to further his education, but to get him out of the way. If the marquis was going to Spain, he wished to ensure that possible adversaries at court were left nothing with which to undermine his unique position. The secretary's oblique reference to 'certain Cornish benefits' showed that Buckingham already suspected his fellow councillor's designs, and was determined to thwart them.

Nevertheless, the caller continued, maintaining his easy, friendly manner in the face of Tom's obvious disappointment, his master had not finally made up his mind. He was loath to see so becoming a young man leave the court unnecessarily – particularly as both king and favourite took such pleasure in his company – and in the light of this he had decided to furnish Tom with a little money to enable him to take such lessons as he needed in England. The secretary placed an embroidered purse on the table. 'If my lord of Buckingham discovers that by this means you are able to learn what is expected of a courtier,' he concluded, 'he will continue to patronise your refinement. If, on the other hand, he finds you slow to learn from native masters, surely he will spare neither effort nor expense to find alternatives in France.

'I have heard there is a minor post vacant at our embassy in Paris. It would become you well for a year or so. Pray, Master Verney, do not forget that the marquis is concerned only for your welfare, sir.'

With an unctuous smile, he bowed and left the room.

Inside the purse Tom found twenty-five pounds in gold.

Tom returned to Hampton Court twice more, each time residing there for several days. He became familiar with the corridors and chambers of the great palace and made friends with some of the younger gentlemen in waiting, with whom he gambled heavily, losing a great deal of money. That and the cost of many new articles of clothing, boat trips, tips to servants and other expenses expected of one in regular attendance on the king quickly ate away at the money he had been given. James continued to treat him kindly and despite the old man's embarrassing vulgarities and public petting, Tom grew quite fond of him. As conversation between them became easier, though never familiar on his part, he learned how to pander to James's vanities and cheer him when he was depressed by his numerous ailments. Politics was never broached in Tom's presence, however, and he had enough sense never to raise matters of state himself. Throughout his time at court, he was aware of the twin presences of the brooding treasurer and the urbane favourite, studying his progress, watching over his shoulder and waiting to see how skilfully he played the attractive hand Fate had dealt him.

They were heady days. Except in the king's presence, Tom carried himself with all the grand hauteur of one who genuinely believed himself on the threshold of a magnificent career. Only many months later, when he was able to look back objectively on his time at Hampton Court, did he come to understand his true position. James's affection was real enough. Nevertheless, though racked by the illnesses and loneliness of old age, he was too wise to regard Tom as anything but a pleasant distraction from the profound anxieties – financial, political and diplomatic – that beset him. And Tom was far too young and inexperienced to know how to turn transient royal favour into enduring power, as Buckingham had done.

To make matters more difficult for himself, Tom refused to acknowledge the weaknesses of his position, so leaving himself a hostage to fortune. He did not, for example, tell the king of his short-sightedness. Once, when James appeared at the far end of the room holding a jewelled ring which he announced was 'a wee gift for Banbury's fond bait', and Tom screwed up his eyes to see what his benefactor was holding, his myopic frown was mistaken for ingratitude. Even then vanity prevented him from admitting to his disability, and it was a while before the king was mollified. For a while thereafter, with an edge to his voice that betokened disapproval as well as humour, he made numerous references to 'Master Verney's angry glances'.

Tom's lack of courtly graces was another handicap. The only occasion that James insisted he dance before him ended in confusion after a few halting steps. 'Nay, Thomas,' interrupted the disappointed king, 'that may be how ye caper about the barns of Stratton Audley at harvest time, but it is not the manner at court.'

Buckingham smiled. Cranfield frowned. The rest of the small audience of courtiers tittered politely.

Tom turned scarlet with anger and shame. 'I was never taught, sire,' he explained.

'That is quite clear, bumpkin Verney,' James laughed. 'But ye are well enough proportioned and will learn soon enough, we dare say.'

He spoke with kindly reassurance and did not refer to the matter again. But the damage had been done. More than once Tom overheard himself disparagingly referred to as 'bumpkin Verney' by servants and jealous fellow courtiers.

It should have come as no great surprise to Tom, therefore, when in response to a further royal summons in the middle of January, he arrived at Hampton Court to find the place strangely deserted. He made his way past the guards straight to the royal apartments and asked a chamberlain what was going on.

'Ah! Master Verney, sir. His Majesty asked me to give you his compliments and explain that the court has moved to the palace at Theobalds. It was at my lord of Buckingham's suggestion, I believe.'

'To Theobalds?' stammered Tom, completely nonplussed.

'Theobalds, sir. But some fifteen miles north of London, in the county of Hertfordshire. It is one of His Majesty's favourite residences and he often repairs thither at this time of the year.'

'And did His Majesty not bid me follow him there?'

'I believe the king did play with the idea. But the Marquis of Buckingham suggested that since you had your studies to attend to, it were better you remained in London. His Majesty concurred. He said he hoped he might see you again on his return – or on some other occasion.'

Feeling his world crumbling about him, Tom muttered reproachfully, 'How thoughtful of his lordship!' and turned to leave. The servant called him back.

'I beg your pardon, Master Verney, but His Majesty bade me give you this.' He produced a miniature portrait of the king. On the back was written, 'To Thomas Verney with gratitude for cheering an old man on winter days – James R.'

Slipping the gift into his pocket, Tom walked slowly

from the room. He did not know what to think. But as the guard closed the door behind him he heard, or believed he heard, the chamberlain explaining to a colleague who had just come in, 'Only bumpkin Verney. Returning to his barn.'

iii

The Verney household followed Tom's adventures at court with eager anticipation, although throughout the severe winter the justice's precarious health compelled them to do so from a distance. His son's long and dutiful letters, embellishing his successes and glossing over his slip-ups, kept them more than adequately informed. And like the account of his first meeting with the king, they were read and re-read countless times, then relayed to neighbours with further exaggeration. It was not long before the small community felt they knew Hampton Court and its inmates as well as their own village, and every day they expected a post to arrive with the news that Customs Receiver Verney had been raised still further – to a post in the royal household, or even the council itself. The Verneys were treated with uncustomary civility. Folk took to giving them unsolicited presents and calling to ask whether Tom might consider taking up such-and-such a matter with the king. In the new year, to his wife's concern, the justice began holding a miniature court in his chamber, where three times a week locals were permitted to approach with their humble requests. There was nothing they believed Tom could not do, from repairing the parish church to preventing ambitious farmers from enclosing common land.

Farcical though some aspects of this sudden glory

might have been, it also held the seeds of a bitter double tragedy. The hopes of the Verneys and those close to them were raised to a point where they could not possibly be fulfilled. Each day fresh palaces were erected upon foundations of fine words. Disappointment and disillusionment were bound to follow, and when they did, human nature being what it is, it was Tom who was certain to be blamed.

The many letters of love and admiration passing from Oxfordshire to London served only to feed Tom's conceit and reinforce his misguided belief that he was on the point of becoming a figure of genuine importance. Of the many messages he received, however, one from Anne Hutchinson stood apart from the rest on account of its sanguine frankness. Having begun with the usual congratulations, she adopted a more solicitous tone than the other correspondents. While Mary Verney had offered practical warnings against the type of people – men and women – who would try to take advantage of her son at court, the younger woman was more direct. It was not others she worried about, she said, but Tom himself. In phrases so tactful that he had to re-read them before he was sure of their meaning, she pointed out that 'since no harvest was gathered until safe in the barn', she hoped Tom would not set too much store by the current attentions of a solitary old man, 'no matter how so high he stands in the eyes of the world'. More irritating, as far as Tom was concerned, was the observation that 'the greatest beauty is quickest drawn to the glass'. She trusted that so much adulation would not turn Tom's head, for she knew him at heart to be 'an honest, true and worthy man, who knows at the final count what is and what is not of true worth in this world.'

Arriving two days before he discovered that the king

had left for Theobalds, the letter made Tom feel awkward for reasons he did not wish to face up to. Dismissing it as simply an effort by Anne to maintain some sort of relationship with him at a time when she feared he was being drawn into more exalted circles, he threw it aside and did not reply. But when he returned to his chambers after watching the apprentice cross the frozen Thames, he took it out and read through it again. And when he had finished, he folded it carefully and placed it under his pillow.

Lucy showed none of Anne's reservation at Tom's good fortune, for in the last dark days of 1622 it was just about her only source of happiness and hope. Her father died two days after Christmas and was interred three days later in St Clement's burial ground behind the Inn. It was a wretched service, conducted in the pouring rain by a bored parson before a bedraggled congregation. Lucy had no relations still living in London, and many neighbours who had been close friends during her father's lifetime stayed away in cruel protest at what they regarded as the immoral way she was conducting her relationship with Tom. She did not weep as the coffin was lowered into the sodden ground, but afterwards, when everyone but Tom and she had departed and they stood watching the sexton impassively shovelling clods of heavy earth into her father's muddy grave, she broke down for the first time since the day of the accident.

'Oh, Tom,' she sobbed, clinging to his arm, 'whatever will become of me now? Even when dear Father lay dying, he was something I could hold fast to. He was the chain which tied me to the shore. Now I am alone, I am afraid I shall drift God only knows where. What shall I do?'

Tom had never seen her so miserable, and his heart swelled with pity at her vulnerability. Images of court, with its blazing fires and lavish consumption flashed through his mind. 'You have me, Lucy,' he said quietly. 'You know that. And you always will.'

'But you are becoming so great, Tom. With all your talking with the king and such like, what do you want with the orphaned daughter of a poor tailor?'

He was not sure whether this was a genuine question or a plea for reassurance. 'You know what I want, Lucy. I love you. I will protect you and care for you' – he slipped his hand round her waist – 'always.' The fast-moving events of the past few weeks had made him wary of all absolutes, but he meant what he said. 'And if I am not enough,' he smiled, trying to cheer her, 'you have your father's business to maintain, my love. That will give you a new life.'

But without his steady hand to guide it, Oliver Simpson's business did not flourish. Men did not like ordering their clothes from a young girl – indeed, some of them sought Lucy's services only because they assumed she was a traffic masquerading as a gentleman's tailor, and they cancelled their orders when they discovered otherwise. To make matters worse, it was soon evident that neither the apprentices nor Lucy had her father's skill with the needle. Within a few weeks some of Oliver Simpson's oldest clients had taken their custom elsewhere and there were precious few new ones to take their place. By the beginning of February Lucy had been obliged to dismiss Peter, and only generous subsidies from her sweetheart enabled her to keep on Jack.

When Tom called round at about five o'clock on the afternoon of the Thames crossing, and found Jack idly chewing his nails before the meagre workshop fire, he sent the apprentice home early without consulting Lucy. As soon as she found out what he had done, she was furious with him for interfering with her business. He had no idea when a customer might appear needing some item of apparel at short notice, she scolded. 'Why, you meddler, only yesterday a lady from Fleet Lane said she might call before nightfall to order a new gown to be sewn by Sunday. That is but two days. I wanted Jack here so we might start tonight. Now you have ruined everything.' She stood before Tom, hands on hips, scowling up at him.

He glared back, surprised by her sudden flare of temper but in no way prepared to accept it. 'Oh yes?' he asked scornfully. 'I have ruined everything, have I? And who is it, pray, as pays for Master Jack to remain here?' Lucy's eyes narrowed. 'A lady will come today will she? Well, she is not here. Remember, Lucy Simpson, that no harvest is gathered until safe in the barn.' Only after he had spoken did he realise where the phrase had come from and what it implied, and then he regretted uttering it.

Fixing him with a steady look, Lucy said slowly, 'Tom, that is too cruel and too proud. I can live without your silver, haughty boy. And you are not a harvest that I would gather, nor a fruit that I would pluck.' Her face softened as she realised the equivocation in what she had said. She folded her arms across her chest. 'And I am not a fruit for you to pluck, either.'

Tom's anger melted as swiftly as it had arisen. 'I am truly sorry, Lucy,' he grinned, 'I spoke without thinking.' He approached and laid a hand on her breast. 'No plucking? May I at least feel the fruit while I wait for it to fall?'

They both laughed, and in the fevered fondling that

followed they forgot the sharpness of the squall that had momentarily divided them. But later, when his desire had been satisfied by Lucy's careful caresses, he recalled Anne's words and wondered why they had made such an impression on him.

iv

Tom saw nothing of Lord Banbury for several weeks after their Hampton Court triumph. As he did not meet his lordship at court, where he gathered that the king had granted the baronet some long-awaited sinecure as a reward for introducing Tom to him, he assumed that with his loan accepted and his favour granted, Banbury had no further use for a magistrate's son. For his own part, Tom felt he could manage perfectly well without the man's devious assistance, and he was not sure that he wanted his fidelity to Lucy tested by Lady Elizabeth's considerable charms. So he conducted his correspondence with his parents without recourse to the Banbury's conditional mailbag, and when her ladyship wrote a second time seeking his consolation in her husband's absence, he politely – though somewhat reluctantly – declined the loaded invitation.

The day after the court's departure for Hertfordshire, however, when Tom pulled out from beneath his bed the iron chest in which he kept his money, he found himself compelled to direct his thoughts towards the opulent Toad once again. Since his coffer had been filled by money from his father and the lords of Middlesex and Buckingham, before he got up in the morning Tom had been in the habit of leaning over the side of his bed, unlocking his box and helping himself to a handful of coins. Assuming that his fortune would last almost indefinitely, he had not bothered keeping any account of his spending. Now he found to his horror that he was down to his last five pounds. At first he thought he must have been robbed. But when he jotted down the huge sums he had frittered away at court, particularly on gambling, and the money he had spent on clothes, presents and other aspects of his new life, together with the subsidies given to Lucy, he realised that his position was entirely of his own making. He dared not approach his father for more, and after what he had been told of Buckingham's desire to part him from the king, he was afraid to travel to Theobalds to draw from the royal purse. In the end, he decided on a double course of action. First he wrote to Treasurer Middlesex, asking whether any progress had been made in securing the profits of the Helford customs farm; then he sent House Martin round to Pickering House with the message that he would like to call on his lordship to discuss matters of mutual interest. The boy returned an hour later with the news that the baronet would be only too pleased to receive Tom at ten o'clock the following morning.

'Welcome, young Verney,' whispered the Toad, as a timid servant showed Tom into a chamber known as 'his lordship's Crimson Closet' and retired without a sound. It was a small room with a single high, narrow window, walls covered with dark red flock-paper and a ceiling decorated with a painting of fleshy ladies, partly covered by diaphanous veils resembling threadbare curtains, bathing in a clear lake. There was no fireplace, and in the gloom Tom could only just make out the hazy figure of his host, wrapped in a voluminous gown and with a towel wound turban-fashion round his head, slumped on a padded couch.

'Ah! Your lordship,' said Tom briskly, eager to create a good impression at the start of his delicate mission, 'may I say what a pleasure it is to see you again?'

Banbury feebly raised a pale fat hand. 'Pray do not bellow, Verney,' he begged. 'You do not find me well.'

'I am sorry to hear that,' replied Tom quietly. The nature of the drunkard's malady was not hard to guess. Trying to sound sincere, he asked solicitously, 'Not a dangerous complaint, I trust, sir?'

'I am poisoned, Verney.' The voice was thick and hoarse. 'I have par-taken of poisoned wine.'

'Ah!'

'Last night some friends and I enjoyed a little bacciferous feast. I drank sparingly, as is my custom, you know.' Tom nodded. 'But this morning I am stricken. For certain it was an inflected barrel we tasted.'

'For certain,' Tom agreed. 'But I hope you are well enough to offer me advice, sir?'

'We nobles never permit personal in-con-veniences to stand in the way of our duty to lesser mortalities, Master Verney,' Banbury sighed, taking a sip of water from the glass at his side. 'I am all ears. Speak – but gently, I pray, for my head is beating like a regiment drum.'

Carefully Tom explained how the sudden withdrawal of the court had left him temporarily short of money. He concluded with what he thought was an obvious, though tactfully expressed hint: 'And so, sir, knowing that your lordship has experience in lending money, I have come here this morning to ask what I should do.'

There was a long pause. The Toad lay back and gazed at the ladies above him through heavy-lidded, half-closed, bloodshot eyes. As he watched him, Tom knew that he was trying to decide whether the new favourite was worth investing in. Tom regretted having mentioned the king's departure for Theobalds without him, for it weakened his position considerably.

Banbury must have been thinking along the same lines. He lowered his gaze to the young supplicant and said with a sly smile, 'I believe I can help, Verney.' A look of relief came over Tom's face. The baronet watched it dissolve as he went on, 'There is a man living in Milk Street – by the name of Abraham Kettle – who I have heard is delighted to assist courtiers awaiting what we might call expectorations.' Tom's heart sank. 'Large house, on the left, with a sprig of mint carved on the door. Nice touch that, don't you think, Verney? It's a play on mint, being both a plant and a place where coin is fashioned.'

Tom's disappointment turned to anger. 'Very comic,' he snapped. Forcing himself to maintain a veneer of politeness, without further ado he thanked Banbury for his advice and left the room, slamming the door behind him as hard as he could.

'Poxy serpent!' he muttered as he stood in the corridor trying to remember which way to turn for the entrance.

'My sentiments precisely,' dovetailed a familiar voice.

Turning, Tom saw the speaker leaning languidly against the doorway to the left of the Crimson Chamber. She smiled at him with sparkling green eyes.

'I did not intend my remark for public ears, Lady Elizabeth,' Tom began, 'but I am glad that you heard, for I really do think him the most vile Toad that ever laid his slimy trail upon the surface of this globe!'

'Need I repeat myself, Apollo? My sentiments precisely, much of the time.'

Tom was seeing his lover in full daylight for the first time, and was unnerved by her alluring appearance. Tall, with a strong lithe figure and handsome face beneath what seemed to be armfuls of fiery red hair, he realised with a mixture of disappointment and eagerness that her raw animal attraction was altogether more powerful than that of homely Lucy Simpson. Wafts of exotic perfume filled the corridor.

'Why have you been staying away, Tom?' she asked, extending her hand towards him.

'I was not sure, Lady Elizabeth—'

'Not a lady now — just Elizabeth—'

'I was not sure, Elizabeth, that I had the will to resist you.' As he was speaking, she drew him into the room and closed the door with her foot.

'And do you have the will?' Her supple hands ran down his back to his buttocks.

'I might have,' he teased, pushing himself against her and gathering her skirts up the back of her legs. 'If I wanted to.' The skin of her thighs was smooth and firm.

She nibbled playfully at his ear. 'Do you want to?'

A warm hand slipped down the front of his breeches and grasped him tightly. 'Not at all.'

'Then we must be quick, and quiet.'

While their mouths remained locked together in a tongue-tied kiss, they urgently pulled aside their lower garments. Soon both were naked from the navel to the knee. She broke away and leaned back against the wall, her long legs apart and her hips thrust forward. With one hand she held up her gown, with the other she guided Tom towards her. Pausing, he placed his fingers gently over her warm, moist opening and caressed back its folds of soft flesh. As he eased a finger inside, he felt her shudder with delight. She closed her eyes. Bending slightly at the knees, he pushed himself into her.

At that moment a soft tapping sounded on the wall behind them.

'Hell!' she whispered, pulling away and smoothing

down the front of her gown. 'I am summoned by the frigging Toad.' She tapped back, then, seeing Tom still exposed before her, bent down and kissed him with an open mouth. 'Do not worry, my fine friend,' she smiled. 'We'll meet again.'

Straightening her hair as she went, she opened the door, pointed Tom in the direction of the front entrance, blew him a kiss and went to join her husband. Tom tiptoed down the corridor and made his own way out.

v

Tom had no difficulty finding Abraham Kettle's house. It was a large brick and timber building standing behind a high wall halfway up Milk Street, between the church of St Mary Magdalen and the public pump at the cross-roads at the eastern end of Lad Lane. He was admitted immediately and shown into a heavily aromatic room lined with books. Kettle, a round-faced, fleshy man of middle height with a wide mouth that turned down at the edges, was sitting at a table strewn with papers. He puffed furiously at a huge pipe clasped between brown teeth. Clouds of smoke hung about his bald head, so that when he stood up he looked to Tom like a sinister genie emerging from a bottle.

'Welcome to the Mint, sir.' The voice was deep and tarry. 'I trust I may be able to help you? Pray be seated.'

Lowering himself into a chair and putting on his spectacles to give the appearance of sincerity and trustworthiness, Tom introduced himself and began to outline his story. At first Kettle seemed to take no notice of what he was saying, and busied himself with amendments to a document before him. But when Tom mentioned Treasurer Cranfield and the Helford farm, he put down his pen and asked through a screen of smog, 'How much, Mr Verney?'

'I believe the position will bring me one hundred pounds per annum.'

'No, sir. How much do you require?' He spoke without removing his pipe from his mouth and his teeth clacked like castanets against the clay stem.

Surprised at the directness of the question, Tom waited a moment before replying, 'Fifty pounds.'

Kettle temporarily disappeared from view behind a vast cloud of smoke. 'Very well.' He lifted a paper from his desk. 'Here is the bond for you to sign. I will advance to Mr Thomas Verney, Deputy Receiver of His Majesty's Customs for Helford, the sum of fifty pounds.' Another cloud billowed towards the blackened ceiling. 'In return the aforementioned Mr Verney will promise to return to Abraham Kettle of Mint House, Milk Street, the sum of one hundred pounds in gold one year hence.'

Tom could not believe his ears. 'One hundred pounds!' he cried. 'That is impossible.'

'Then so, sir, is my fifty,' growled Kettle, emerging from within another brown pall.

'Is not seventy-five more reasonable?'

'I do not haggle, sir,' Kettle stated firmly, skilfully blowing out a huge monochrome rainbow.

Although he needed the money desperately, Tom could not bring himself to accept such furacious terms. 'I do not haggle either, Kettle,' he retorted, getting to his feet. 'I shall find assistance elsewhere.'

'You shall? I wish you well, sir. In the meantime, I trust you will be able to maintain yourself in a becoming manner. And remember, the doors of the Mint are always open ...'

Tom heard no more. He was already passing through

the front door and breathing deeply to clear his lungs of the money lender's vile pollution.

vi

Lord Middlesex's reply to Tom's letter arrived on 6th February. Couched in formal, though friendly terms, it explained that Tom could expect further funds before the end of the month, and ended with a suggestion that it might be wise for Tom to pay a visit to court – now moved to Royston – at about that time, 'when things may not stand quite as they do now'. Guessing that the Treasurer referred to the likelihood of Buckingham's departure for Spain, Tom was considerably cheered by the news and determined to make do for three weeks without borrowing. It was not a difficult task, and with only a week to go he was congratulating himself on how smoothly things were progressing, when Maurice Green returned to Clement's Inn.

To save money Tom had taken to dining in commons every day, and since the court's withdrawal to the country he had even spent a little time furthering his study of the law. But it was now many months since Ancient Green had advised him to brush up his Latin and the supervisor's suggestion had quite slipped his mind. He thought nothing, therefore, when, glancing up at the high table during dinner one Tuesday towards the end of February, he saw Green's lean, agitated figure sitting with the Principal and others of the Inn's governing Pension. He did became a little concerned, however, when at the close of the meal Principal Edwards announced that in place of the customary discussion of a case or a writ, Mr Maurice Green wished to conduct a little examination. A stir of excited conversation ran through the hall as the venerable lawyer rose unsteadily to his feet and stood peering over his spectacles at the assembled Companions.

'Hurrah for Ancient Green!' called out a young solicitor from Coventry who had already emptied two bottles of wine and was making swift progress through a third. The cry was taken up by others, and for a couple of minutes the proceedings were held up by a prolonged burst of unruly clapping, stamping, shouting and banging on the tables. Green stood leaning impassively on the back of his chair, one hand raised in a gesture of acknowledgement. If the members of Clement's Inn were determined to enjoy themselves, he was not going to stand in their way.

'Mr Principal, fellow Ancients, Companions and others,' Green began in his high, wavering voice, 'today is the feast of, er, St Matthias' – a loud 'hurrah' from the Coventry inebriate – 'the disciple of Our Lord chosen to replace the traitor, Judas Iscariot.' Boos from all around the hall. 'I hope we Ancients are not, er, Judases' – more cheers – 'but some of us are indeed, well, ancient' – laughter and whistling – 'and will ere long need to be replaced.'

'For shame!' yelled the Coventry man, now lying on a bench and signalling frantically for a servant to bring him a fourth bottle.

Green looked towards him. 'I thank you, recumbent sir,' he said, earning a fresh round of laughter and applause. 'We are not immortal. Not at all. But this Inn must continue' – further cheering – 'and to that end we need to educate learned lawyers to take our places. And the foundation, sirs, the very root of education is' – he paused and peered about him, as if trying to seek someone out – 'the Latin language.' To prevent further interruption he held up both hands in a saintly gesture worthy of St Matthias himself.

Tom felt sweat breaking out on his forehead. He was sure that Green was going to select him to perform some piece of Latin, but could think of no way out. If he tried to leave, he would almost certainly be ordered back and compelled to pay a fine he could not afford. On the other hand, failure in the examination would lead either to a further fine or even to ejection from the Inn. He was caught. As Green wittered on about the virtues of Classical learning, he decided to face out the ordeal, trusting that the good-humoured mood of the Companions would prevent his being too severely reprimanded. To boost his confidence he drained three large bumpers of wine before Green finished his long-winded introduction.

'And now,' the Ancient finally concluded, 'I call upon the first of my students to stand erect before us and utter a few words in the language of true law and learning.'

The hall went quiet. All heads turned towards the table at the bottom end of the hall where the students were seated. Green fumbled theatrically with the piece of paper he held in his hand. Adjusting his spectacles, he pretended to read, 'Master Thomas ... Ah yes! Verney!'

Tom stood up to an explosion of noise. 'Good luck!' said George as his friend climbed over the bench and made towards the dais at the further end of the hall. There was no corresponding goodwill in the mind of Leoline Williams. As Tom passed he stuck out a foot and tripped him to his knees. Assuming the examinee to be drunk, which was not so very wide of the mark, the company howled with delight, anticipating further amusement. Tom picked himself up, threw a curse in the direction of his enemy and took his place beside the top table.

The public examination in Latin for the students of

Clement's Inn was not the daunting test it had once been. In times past they had been required to converse with the Principal in that tongue for a quarter of an hour. But since the time of Principal Hubbert, whose Classical learning had extended no further than a nodding acquaintance with obscenely illustrated translations of Catullus's love poems, all the examinees were required to do was recite about two hundred lines of prepared prose or verse, taken from any source they wished. Tom had intended to offer something from Caesar's *Gallic Wars*, which he had already committed to memory at school. Given an hour or so of revision and a clear head, he could have passed Green's examination with no difficulty. But now, not having opened his Caesar for months, with his brain fuddled by wine and confronted by an audience of almost a hundred critical, jeering lawyers, his mind went completely blank.

'Master Verney,' asked Green, turning to Tom standing beside him, 'pray inform the Inn what it is you wish to recite.'

Tom decided to play for time. 'Principal Edwards, Ancient Green, other Ancients, Companions of Clement's Inn, hewers of wood and drawers of water,' he began, looking about him and grinning, 'I bid you all good afternoon.' During the whistles and catcalls occasioned by this bizarre opening sentence, he racked his brain for a phrase, even a word, which might trigger his memory. Try as he might, nothing came.

'Come, Master Verney,' said Green, a trace of irritation in his voice, 'what is your chosen text?'

Tom coughed. 'My passage, dearly esteemed Principal, Ancients and Companions, will come when it is ready, which I hope will be soon, from Julius Caesar—'

'Fifty-five BC!' interrupted the man on the bench.

'—that most celebrated of Roman generals and authors, whose name is known even to the most meagre—'

Principal Edwards banged on the table. 'Master Verney,' he warned, 'you are bringing the Inn into disrepute. Do you mock us, sir? Pray commence your recitation forthwith.'

Having decided to run through the tenses of amo, Tom took a deep breath and opened his mouth. But before he could say anything, another voice cried out, 'Oh, Verney! Do you play with us as you play with the mighty at court?' Williams' mocking Welsh lilt was unmistakable. 'Fiddle, fiddle, fiddle! Are you now so fondly tickled with Scottish fingers that you will not deign speak with common men?'

The scandalous accusation changed the mood of the hall in an instant. The Companions divided. Some hooted and clapped, others cried 'shame' and craned their necks to see who was responsible for the intervention. Arguments broke out between the two parties. Again Edwards banged the table, calling for silence. But it was too late. The place was in uproar.

Tom glared down the hall, his face red with fury. 'Williams!' he bellowed. 'You are nothing but a traitorous papist swine. I will not be mocked.' He turned to the astonished Principal. 'Mr Edwards, sir, I demand that Williams be brought to account for his foul innuendo.'

Several men stood up, gesticulating wildly and shouting in support of Tom. Through the hubbub Edwards cried, 'Hold your tongue, Verney! You have turned an examination into a bear garden!'

Tom marched over and seized him by the shoulder. 'No, sir! It is not I who have brought on this riot. By Christ, I will not hold my tongue until that poxy Welsh slave is made to answer for his slander!'

'Unhand me, sir!' Edwards screamed. 'Get off! Get off!'

As servants hurried forward to protect their Principal, Tom threw him back into his chair and stormed to the front of the dais. The commons had deteriorated into chaos. The noise was deafening. Everyone, apart from the Coventry inebriate, who was approaching the bottom of his fourth bottle, was on their feet, waving their arms about and yelling. A fight was raging near the students' table. Dishes, candlesticks and bottles crashed to the floor in a carpet of shards and wax.

'Gentlemen!' yelled Tom, trying in vain to make himself heard above the tumult. 'You call this a place of justice? God's eyes! There is more justice in the stews of Shoreditch than in this sanctimonious den of idlers! I denounce you all. You will not see me again!'

So saying, he jumped from the platform and barged his way angrily through the throng towards the door. By the students' table he singled out Williams, who was arguing furiously with George, and punched him as hard as he could in the stomach. Pausing only to savour momentarily the sight of the foul-mouthed Welshman groaning on the floor, he threw off his gown and strode from the hall.

'You saw what he did, Ancient Green? You heard what he said?' screamed Edwards, who had resumed his fruitless hammering on the table.

'I did, Principal. The man's mad!'

'Maybe. But he's dangerous, too. We will not allow him to enter our Inn again. Never. No, not though he offer a fine of one thousand pounds. Never again! Never! Never! Never!'

Beating upon the table each time he repeated the word, he continued until he collapsed from exhaustion and had to be carried unconscious to his chambers.

NINE

NEWMARKET

i

The deserted interior of St Clement Danes was cold and dark and smelled of damp. Tom shivered as he shut the heavy door behind him. Buttoning his doublet, he hunched his shoulders and walked slowly up the stone flags of the nave towards the single candle burning on the Lord's Table. More than once, alarmed by the reverberating echo of his footsteps, he glanced around to see if he was being followed. He saw no one. Before the chancel he turned right into a small side chapel dedicated to St Thomas. Here, choosing a shadowy corner where he was sure he would not be seen, he fell on his knees, clasped his hands before him and prayed in silence.

Instinctively he chose the words of the general confession, written by Archbishop Cranmer for the Protestant communion service almost seventy-five years before. Having first learned them as a child, on many occasions since he had turned to them for comfort and solace. 'Almighty God,' he began, 'Father of our Lord Jesus Christ, maker of all things, Judge of all men, we knowledge and bewail our manifold sins and wickedness, which we from time to time most grievously have committed, by thought, word and deed, against Thy divine Majesty: provoking most justly Thy wrath and indignation against us ...' He stopped, unable to concentrate. Had his behaviour in the hall been so wicked? It had been about the first positive thing he had done since arriving in London, and he could not help feeling proud of it. He was tired of fawning and indecision, of apologies and guilt. Perhaps he should not have hit Williams, but the man did deserve it.

His meditation was interrupted by the sound of slow, shuffling footsteps making their way down the adjacent aisle. Glancing up and putting on his spectacles, he saw a dark, shapeless form pause at the entrance to the chapel. As he watched, the creature shambled in and threw itself on the floor with a hideous groan. Motionless in the shadows, Tom saw it raise a bedraggled head and heard it mumble in a congealed whisper, 'Sweet Jesus, let me die! I am unclean. I beg you take my life and that of the poor child within me. Let me die.'

Tom felt dishonest at being an unseen witness to such terrible personal grief. He coughed and stood up.

'Who's there?' screamed the woman, rolling onto her side to get a look at the intruder.

'No one who wishes you harm,' said Tom, taking a couple of steps towards her. In the darkness he could just make out her thin face. Open sores pocked the dirt-encrusted skin around her mouth and eyes. Her uncovered hair hung like rotted hay about her cheeks.

'No harm?' she asked. 'By God, is there anyone in this

devilish city who does not wish me harm? Even myself?' When she spoke, her mouth became a small, black, toothless gash.

Tom turned aside and felt inside his purse. 'Here,' he said, taking out one of his last two remaining sovereigns and placing it in her hand. 'You are no worse a creature than I, whatever you have done.'

'Bless you, sir!' cried the woman as he stepped round her into the main body of the church. 'But your name, sir? I must thank God, sir, for sending you. And I must tell Him your name.'

By one of the soaring columns Tom stopped and looked back. 'Thomas,' he called. 'But not the saint. Just plain Thomas.'

ii

From St Clement's Tom made his way through the dreary lanes to Blackmore Street. Lucy opened the door almost before he had knocked.

'Tom,' she said, kissing him fondly, 'what has held you? You said you would be here shortly after dinner.' She stood back and looked at him. 'And no cloak, too, in this inclement weather.'

'It is an inclement day, Lucy,' said Tom, taking her hand with a smile and leading her through to the parlour. 'Inclement and out of Clement.'

'No riddles, Tom,' she frowned playfully. 'You know I am a simple girl.'

Sitting by the fire with Lucy kneeling beside him, he went through the events of the afternoon. When she asked who Williams was – previously he had made no more than a passing reference to the man – he explained to her about the humiliation of the test, though he omitted the part played by Great John, about whom he had told no one. At the end of his story he turned and asked, 'So, Lucy, did I do right? Speak honestly.'

She thought for a while. 'Well, Tom,' she said eventually, choosing her words with great care, 'you did right and you did wrong. Right not to accept the slanders of that foul Welshman, but maybe wrong to act so hotly. You say you can never return to the Inn?'

'Never.'

'That may be for the good. I did not think highly of those penny-thieving lawyers and their pompous foreign tongue. It was not your stage was it?'

'Perhaps not.'

'Your stage is the royal court, not the law court. Why, you told me that even His Majesty had little good to say for Clement's Inn. He will be pleased with you for what you have done.'

Tom took her hands and lifted her onto his knees. 'I hope so. For sure my father will not like it.'

Placing her arms round his neck and kissing him tenderly on the lips between each phrase, she answered, 'Your father will follow the king, won't he, my sweetheart?' She held him playfully by the ears. 'When do you leave for Royston?'

'Ow! As soon as possible.'

'Not now, surely, Tom?' Her lips formed a slight pout.

He cupped her cheeks in his hands. 'No, not now.' His brown eyes gleamed like topaz in the firelight. 'Yet what shall I do now? I have nowhere to stay.'

Lucy bent forward and whispered in his ear.

'Here?' he asked huskily. 'What, you and I, as husband and wife?'

'As husband and wife.'

He moved his hands slowly down to her waist. 'Lucy

Simpson, you know what husbands and wives do, don't you?'

With her mouth still touching his ear, she replied quietly, 'I have heard people talk of it, Mr Verney. You will have to teach me, won't you?'

Without another word they rose and, with arms entwined about each other, slowly climbed the stairs to Lucy's small bedroom. There, in the darkness, she carefully helped Tom to undress her. When she stood naked before him, and he began kissing her over and over again, intoxicated with the scent of her body and the sweetness of her skin, she felt the cares and anxieties of recent weeks fall away, as if her lover's strong, deft fingers were divesting her of a cloak of lead. She held tightly to him, unsure whether she would float into the air or melt into the floor if she let go. 'Oh, Tom!' she repeated softly, locking her fingers together behind his neck and staring up at the obscure silhouette of his face, 'Oh, Tom! We are together. Husband and wife.' Her body and mind were caught up in the same unyielding clasp of love.

After a few minutes she became aware of a rather more mundane sensation. The unheated room was bitterly cold. An involuntary shiver ran through her body. 'Tom, sweetheart?'

'Yes?' As he looked up, she could just make out the whites of his eyes. She stood on tiptoe and kissed them.

'Tom, Lucy's cold. Brrr! Is it customary for lovers to remove their ladies' clothes and oblige them to stand freezing in the dark? I don't think it stokes the fires of passion.' She took his hands and placed them against the goosepimpled skin on her stomach.

'Lucy, you are frozen! I am sorry, dearest.' Holding her by the hand, he threw back the bedcovers. 'Come, sweet love. Make a warm nest for us. I will be with you before you can say "Clement's Inn".'

She dived into the bed and sat with the blankets pulled up around her neck. 'Tom?' she called, listening to him struggling out of his clothes.

'Yes?'

'I can't see you.'

'Do you want to?'

'I am curious. I have never seen an unclothed man before. At least not one sticking up.'

'Sticking up?'

'You know, my love,' she giggled. 'Your pizzle.'

'Then wait. Where are the flint and candle?'

'On the chest.'

A few seconds later Tom stood in the middle of the room holding the lighted candle in his hand. His clothing lay scattered on the floor around him. She stared at the unfamiliar shadows and contours. 'Well?' he laughed, placing the candle on the chest and leaping onto the bed. 'What do you think?'

'Odd,' she said, raising her hand and touching him. 'Ugh! And not very beautiful.' She gave a slight shudder.

Tom pretended to be upset, curling his lips down at the edges. 'Not beautiful? Do you want me without him?' He made the shape of scissors with his fingers and snipped at himself. 'Here, shall I cut him off, like a wart?'

Laughing, she grasped his hands. 'No, Tom. I think he's very clever, standing up with no one to help him. I will learn to love him, as I love his owner. Come, climb in with me and show me what he can do.'

For a while, entwined together, they waited for the heat from their bodies to warm the bed around them. Then, lying quietly by his side, she felt him stroking her body again. The unreal floating sensation returned. Her skin tingled. 'Dear Tom,' she whispered. 'That's wonderful. I love being your wife.'

'Are you happy, Lucy?' he asked, kissing her softly on the neck.

'Oh yes! Don't stop now, Tom. Please.'

'Are you sure?' There was a new eagerness in his tone.

As he raised himself onto an elbow to look at her, with one finger she traced a line from the bridge of his nose, over his mouth and chin, down to his chest, stomach and below. 'You are a lovely man, Tom Verney,' she sighed. 'You know that, don't you?'

'Sometimes, maybe.'

'It is true.' She lay back and stared at him. 'Now I'm yours, lovely Tom Verney.' Her eyes closed. 'For ever.'

When passion replaced love as his master, at first she was unsure how to respond. Hurt, proud, ashamed and yet quietly triumphant, she listened to his sighs and felt his movements as if they were something apart from her, taking place in an isolated world where she could not follow. 'I do so love you, Lucy!' he soliloquised. 'Oh! I do! I do!'

Beneath him, she lay smiling up into the flickering shadows and clinging steadfastly to his muscular body. 'Tom, darling,' she asked when he had stopped shuddering, 'was that right?'

He stroked the hair away from her face and kissed her. 'Right?'

'I did not disappoint you?'

'Oh, Lucy! How could you disappoint me? You carried me to the threshold of heaven.' Her mouth spread into a broad grin. 'Did you follow me there?'

Snuggling against his smooth, hard chest, she answered quietly, 'Dearest Tom, of course I followed you. And I always will follow you, my love, in everything you do. You know that.'

iii

There was a strange atmosphere in the Simpson house early the following morning. For a while neither lover was quite certain that what had taken place the previous night was really what they had intended. Lucy reacted by getting out of bed as soon as she awoke – laughing off Tom's suggestion that they spend the day in an impromptu orgy – and busying herself about the house. She took out some washing, brushed Tom's clothes, swept the floor and tidied the workshop in a bustling hurricane of domesticity. Her doubts evaporated as she worked. By half past nine, when Jack arrived having collected a dress that required alteration, she felt wholly justified and in complete control of herself.

Tom could find no such peace of mind. He stayed in bed late, at first pretending to sulk at the rejection of his advances, then considering what he should do next. As he lay there, listening to Lucy singing at her work and chatting with Jack, a feeling of being old before his time came over him. Here he was, not yet nineteen, set up in a house in London with a woman who looked upon him as her husband. He loved Lucy and wished to marry her – one day. Yet he was not sure that he had wanted their relationship to move in this direction so swiftly. Circumstances – her bereavement and his recent expulsion – had conspired against him, leaving too many unanswered questions and loose ends. Somehow he had to explain his position to the king and his father; if he failed to do so convincingly, now that he had been thrown out of the Inn his future would be bleak indeed. And what of Lucy herself? It was not simply the social gulf between them that worried him. However much he might have wanted to, he could not ignore the fact that he had been slightly disappointed by their first night together. He felt a nagging anxiety that her attitude in bed, and this morning, too, had verged on the proprietorial. It was almost as if she were going through a kind of subconscious ritual, binding him to her with strands of love which he would not have the heart to break. Even her singing sounded like a triumphant secular Te Deum, giving thanks for victory. So, as the chimes of a nearby church struck ten, he jumped out of bed, pulled on his clothes and went downstairs to tell Lucy that he could not possibly stay with her another night for fear of what the neighbours might say.

As he entered the parlour, he found her cleaning his shoes. 'Ah! There you are, sleepy one,' she laughed quietly, getting up and giving him a pert kiss on the nose. 'There's beer and a loaf of bread in the pantry. I will bring you breakfast as soon as I have finished with your shoes.' She flashed him an impudent smile. 'All that work last night must have made you as hungry as an ox. But hush!' – she raised a finger to her lips – 'Jack does not know you are here. You must feign arrival.'

Having given her a hug, he moved to the front door, opened it and closed it again with a bang. 'There,' he said laughing, 'I have arrived!'

Grinning, she handed him his shoes. 'Quick! Put these on. Surely you did not come here in stockinged feet, sir?'

'Thank you.' He lowered his voice. 'But, Lucy, all my possessions are at the Inn.' He wanted to break the news of his decision gently.

'Have no worry, dearest Tom. While you were lying abed, your little Lucy has been arranging your affairs for you.'

'How?' he asked, disconcerted by her business-like manner.

'Your Bird called round early this morning to see if you

were here. You were dozing. He is a most worthy fellow, isn't he, my love?' Tom nodded. 'He was worried for you after what happened yesterday. Anyway,' she went on with a chuckle, 'I assured him that you were safe and well, and that a bed has been found for you here.'

'He will guess.'

'Let him. He will discover the truth soon enough. I asked him whether he wished to remain your boy, and when he said he did, I bade him bring all your belongings round to this house forthwith and arrange for Princess to be stabled at the Angel Inn, by Clare Market. I have done well, have I not?'

He felt as if another bolt had been drawn across the door to his future. But he did not have the heart to rebuke her. 'You are wonderful, Lucy, my love.'

She detected the hesitancy in his voice. 'Tom, what is the matter?'

'Nothing. It is just that it has all moved so fast.'

'It had to, didn't it, my darling? But do not worry. I will make you happy. I did last night, didn't I?'

'You know you did.'

'And when we are married ...'

The phrase clanged through Tom's mind like the closing of a vault. 'When we are married?'

'We will marry soon, won't we, Tom?' She laid her head on his chest and held him tight. 'It is God's wish, not to mention the neighbours'.'

He determined to be fenced in no closer for the moment, however sincere and well-meaning his pursuer. 'Darling, in God's eyes we are married already. And the wishes of the king and my father are far more important than those of the busybodies of Blackmore Street. We must bide our time, Lucy, love. It would not be wise to act in too great haste.'

She lifted her face to his. 'Very well, Tom. But it would not be wise to wait too long, either.' She placed a hand on her stomach and chuckled, 'All that sticking up of yours could make me swell with pride.'

The phrase rekindled his desire. 'And your pretty body makes me swell, too, Lucy.' He drew her to him. 'Come upstairs.'

'Oh, Tom! What about Jack?'

He kissed the back of her neck and ran his fingers down her spine. 'The boy's at work, is he not?'

'He is,' Lucy replied, closing her eyes.

'Then so should we be,' he said, leading her from the room. She did not object.

iv

When after a hard day's ride Tom arrived at Royston late the following afternoon, he was told by the palace's permanent staff that the court had moved on to Newmarket almost a fortnight previously. They also confirmed what the whole of London had been gossiping about before Tom's departure – that, disguised as Thomas and John Smith, Prince Charles and the Marquis of Buckingham, accompanied by only Richard Graham, Buckingham's Scottish master of horse, had left on 18th February to travel overland to Spain. Fortunately, Middlesex had left instructions at Royston that Tom be accommodated at the palace for the night and set on the road for Newmarket the next day. So he enjoyed a good night's rest and a hearty breakfast at the king's expense, and shortly after nine o'clock in the morning on the penultimate day of the shortest month of the year, he climbed into Princess's saddle and headed north-east towards his new destination.

Although the chilly damp weather did not make riding pleasant, he took his time. Newmarket lay only some twenty-five miles distant and the road, maintained at the king's personal expense, was in excellent order. Besides, Princess was tired after the previous day's long journey, and he had no wish to exhaust her further. He was content to jog along, wondering at the rich, rolling farmland of Cambridgeshire and doing his best not to think about the worrying situation he had left behind him in London. In the course of his journey three royal posts galloped past him, making for the capital, and once, as he was crossing the River Granta near Sawston Hall, he was overtaken by one moving in the opposite direction. The horse's sides were flecked with foam and the rider's face fixed firmly on the road ahead. 'Oh, Princess!' said Tom, stretching forward to pat the animal's neck as the sound of hoofs receded into the distance. 'What power these kings have that we fly about the countryside at their beck and call!'

He was looking forward to seeing James again. Despite the man's pitiable gropings, which he was coming to realise were more requests for affection than homosexual advances, he quite liked the strange Scotsman. He was amused by his sharp, no-nonsense wit and admired his considerable perception. And, so far, he had never found him anything but kindly. But before he had ridden much further he was shown another side of the king's nature, one which threw a rather less attractive light on a man who claimed, in his own words, to exercise a 'resemblance of divine power upon earth'.

Tom recognised the sound as soon as he heard it. It was familiar to every man, woman and child in the country – the harsh blare of hunting horns. As soon as the noise reached him, he instinctively sat up and grasped the reins more firmly. Princess knew what it meant, too. She pricked up her ears and snorted. Her breath billowed into the air in damp clouds.

Soon the baying of dogs was audible away to Tom's left, where a knoll of bare beeches stood like impaled hedgehogs on the summit of a low hill. Putting on his spectacles just in time, he saw a large stag come bounding through the trees and down the open grassy slope towards the road. A pack of fine limer hounds, each one red-eyed, loll-tongued and covered in mud from nose to tail, bounded along hard on the creature's heels. Surmising correctly that in these parts only the king could own such a number of splendid beasts, Tom turned to the huntsmen following a short distance behind. First came the liveried professionals, their faces furrowed with concentration, crying and hooting at their dogs to drive the prey to a place where it could be brought to bay; then came the gentlemen, some of whom Tom recognised, shouting and laughing, galloping recklessly in pursuit of the pack, their long hair blowing out behind them. Of the king himself there was no sign. He rarely rode out now and Tom guessed that the weather had been considered too unrelenting for one of James's rare winter sorties.

Tom loved the chase. He loved the excitement, the physical challenge, the teamwork and the sense of achievement that followed a successful outing. He loved, too, the feeling of warm contentment at the close of the day, when the horses had been safely stabled and darkness was closing in and he sat with friends resting his weary body by the fire, chatting over the adventures they had shared. Now, as the cavalcade of stag, hounds and steaming horses thundered over the road only yards in front of him, and the scent of sweat and fear thrilled his nostrils, he longed to join in. But he knew it would be foolish to do so. He was keen to get to Newmarket in good time and unsure whether so noble a group of huntsmen would take kindly to finding a mere student in their midst.

Yet he had hardly set his heels to Princess's sides and begun to move off, before the air was rent by a fresh fanfare. He looked up. A strange procession was riding across the brow of the hill, following slowly in the footsteps of the main body of the hunt. To the front and rear rode posses of armed soldiers. A circling phalanx of bowmen, about a hundred yards from the centre of the group, scouted about among copses and bushes. A dozen brightly clad buglers, constantly blowing their horns in exhortation of non-existent hounds, cantered in a zigzag path between the soldiers and the scouts. Round the centre of the party horsemen galloped in frantic circles, calling to one another and waving their hats in the air as if at any moment they were about to move in for the kill. Mud from their horses' hoofs flew far into the grey sky. Tom could not remember ever seeing such an extraordinary simulation. All the noise and atmosphere of a hunt, without any of the speed or danger.

The sole purpose of the charade, he realised, was to entertain the king, who rode on a grey mare in the centre of the creeping cavalcade. Obsessed with hunting but unable any longer to keep up with the quarry, whenever his health permitted James insisted on going out under escort to play his part in the chase. No one could have mistaken him. Dressed in an absurdly oversized blue hunting outfit, including a gigantic hat decorated with a long ostrich feather, which had caught in an overhanging branch and broken in two, he was perched on a broad saddle, clinging to the pommel and staring about him. His sagging florid face, pinched by the cold, streamed with glistening brooks flowing from his eyes and nose. The reins of his horse were held by a groom riding in front, while a number of anxious-looking gentlemen rode alongside, poised to grab him if he looked like losing his balance. James ignored them. From time to time he waved a voluminous arm and let out an old Scots hunting cry. He had not enjoyed himself so much for weeks.

'Halt!' cried the king as his horse reached the road. 'Who goes there?' He pointed to Tom. 'Who is yonder highwayman with a mask over his eyes? Does he wish us ill? Bowmen! Prepare to shoot him down!' Never quite sure of James's quirky sense of humour, one or two archers fitted arrows to their strings.

A gentleman on the king's left explained, 'It is Master Verney, sire. It appears he is on the road to visit Your Majesty at Newmarket.'

'Verney, eh? Banbury's bumpkin bait. Then why is he disguised as a highwayman in a mask of spectacles? He is no scholar, surely? Come hither, Verney.'

Whipping off his spectacles, Tom eased Princess through the press of courtiers and attendants towards the king. He bowed in the saddle and smiled. 'It was even as explained, Your Majesty. I am travelling to Newmarket.'

'Then this is a happy meeting, Thomas.' James leaned precariously over and tapped him on the elbow. 'You see us at our bravest. This is the life we love.'

At that moment sound of distant horns announced that the stag was at bay and about to be slain. James leaped up as if struck by lightning. 'Ho, ho! We have him! Onward, fellow huntsmen! To the kill! Follow, Master Verney, follow! To the kill! To the kill!' Breaking into something approaching a trot, the retinue set off in the direction of the horns. Tom tagged along behind, eager to see what would happen.

When they reached the stag, brought down by the hounds in open ground, the creature was already dead. It lay on its side, torn and ragged from the savage attack of the dogs. These had now been leashed and pulled to one side, where they stood howling and straining to return to their quarry. A light drizzle had started to fall. Hoofs, pads and feet had churned the ground around the steaming body to a porridge of mud and blood. Dismounted, the hunt stood in a circle around the kill, waiting for the king to perform his customary ritual.

James's horse was led to the middle of the ring and its rider helped from the saddle. A huntsman handed him a large knife. 'Now watch!' the king called, waving his weapon in the air. 'Beloved subjects, see your father huntsman bring down the mightiest creature of the field!' A ripple of applause ran round the circle of onlookers.

He made heavy weather of the short walk to the dead beast, slipping on the greasy surface and tripping over the hem of his gown. But when a groom stepped forward to help him, he burst with sudden anger, 'God's blood, ye fawning, obsequious spawn of a butter-brained whore! Are we so frail that we cannot walk i' the field? Get back, cur!'

Reaching his destination, the king moved round behind the stag's neck, grasped its antlers, raised his knife and paused. It was a scene Tom would never forget.

'See here!' the old man cried, standing in the fading light with the rain dripping off his ridiculous hat. 'We slay this beast in memory of our beloved son Charles and his companion, our other son, George, Marquis of Buckingham.' His thin voice did not carry far through the damp air. 'Even now this noble pair are risking their dear lives on an enterprise to bring sweet peace to the world.'

His eyes filled with tears. 'For them I kill! I kill! I kill!' With remarkable force for one of his years, he swung the knife into the beast's throat, simultaneously pulling back its head. From the wide gash, red-black blood oozed into the mud.

Leaning forward and placing his hand in the wound, James cried, 'Come forward, ye merry hunters, that we may baptise ye with the blood of the beast. Master Verney! Ye have never hunted with us afore – come hither that we may lay the mark of our approval on ye.'

Tom had been bloodied as a child. It was a common ceremony, part of everyday country life, and he accepted it without question. But James seemed to turn it into something else, a more sinister, almost pagan ritual of unnecessary barbarity. Tom was made to kneel on the ground and raise his face to the king, who thrust his hands into the stag's neck again and drew forth great gouts of congealing blood. He wiped these first on his own face, then on Tom's. Not just smears but hot, sweet-smelling handfuls that clung to his hair and trickled down his neck onto his chest, staining his shirt scarlet. As the king scooped and smeared, he giggled quietly to himself, like a child playing in the dirt.

The rite did not end there. When he had baptised all those he wanted to, the king moved round to the creature's belly and sliced it open, allowing the entrails to spill forth onto the ground. Stepping right inside the carcass, he pulled up armfuls of foul-smelling guts and proffered them to the dogs one by one, laughing and talking all the while. By the time the last hound had been fed, it was almost dark. Torches were lit to illuminate the scene. In their flaring light, covered in blood from head to toe, the man who called himself Rex Pacificus – the

King of Peace – wiped his gory blade on the sleeve of his gown and smiled down at the mutilated remains of his kill.

V

Tom remained at Newmarket for ten days. He spent many hours with the king, reading to him, joining in card games with a select group of close attendants and accompanying the royal party to horse races at one of the several courses James had established on the heath near the town. His Majesty obviously enjoyed the young man's company and continued to show him favour. Nevertheless, Tom could not help feeling that on both sides a subtle change had come over their relationship. On his part, he could never clear his mind of the image of James the barbarous huntsman, revelling in bloodshed, while the king himself was preoccupied with the absence of his son and of his favourite. He wrote to them frequently and waited anxiously for return news of their adventures. Buckingham's communications, in particular, sent him reeling with delight, driving all other business from his mind and leaving those in attendance feeling abandoned and insignificant.

It was during one of these periods of distraction, following the arrival of a letter from the marquis, which announced that the prince and he were making good progress through southern France towards the Spanish border, that Tom plucked up courage to return obliquely to the question of his own eventual marriage. When James observed that God was clearly smiling on his son's mission, Tom expressed the hope that He would continue to do so until the time when Charles and the Infanta were united in holy wedlock. 'For,' he concluded, 'is it not a fact, Your Majesty, that all true marriages are made in heaven?'

'Eh? Oh aye, Master Tom. Aye,' the King replied absent-mindedly, gazing at Buckingham's letter and trying to imagine the hand that had written it.

'Then, sire, God will arrange my marriage, will He not?'

James held the scented paper to his nose and sniffed. 'Just so.'

'God will show me in His own way the bride He has chosen – be she plain or beautiful, high or low – and I am to accept?'

James kissed the letter and laid it down. Looking at Tom with a gaze focused seven hundred miles away, he answered, 'Aye. Ye are to accept. High or low, the Almighty will make it clear.' His face broke into a wan smile. 'We pray, young lover, that ye will have your old dad at the ceremony?'

Tom, who without his spectacles had not noticed James's distracted look, was delighted. 'It would not be worthy of Your Majesty's presence, sire.'

The king seemed hardly to hear. 'Ah, well! Be happy, Verney, be happy. And never part from him.'

'Her, Your Majesty.'

'Quite so.'

'With your blessing I shall never be parted from her, Your Majesty. Thank you.' Taking the king's hand, he kissed it fervently, believing that without losing face by saying so openly, the old man had reversed his previous warning and consented to his courtier marrying whomsoever he wished.

But he had heard only what he had wanted to hear. Had he thought more carefully about James's replies and the context in which they had been made, or even observed the man's expression as he was making them, he might have saved himself and others a great deal of pain.

Middlesex, too, was pleased to see Tom at Newmarket. Well satisfied by the cordial manner in which James was responding to the company of the young Deputy Receiver, the Treasurer gave his client a further twenty-five pounds from the Helford farm and a letter embossed with a treasury seal allowing him to draw the remainder of the money from a Lombard Street merchant when he returned to London. The transaction took place at a large house in the centre of Newmarket which became the makeshift treasury whenever the court translated to Cambridgeshire. When the formalities were over, to Tom's surprise Middlesex bade him come through to a small room at the rear of the building to take a glass of wine. He was even more surprised at the incongruous couple he found already there.

'Canon Chillingworth, whom I believe you know well, Master Verney,' introduced the Treasurer, dismissing the servants with an imperious wave, 'and my lord the Bishop of Lincoln, Lord Keeper of the Great Seal.' Tom bowed in acknowledgement to both men, though more easily to the former than the latter. He had met Bishop-Keeper John Williams at court and was not sure what to make of the man. He was clever and witty, which was why James appreciated him. But Tom was instinctively put off by the man's Welsh background and accent, his surname and his darting dark eyes, similar to those of his namesake at Clement's Inn. Moreover, like Chillingworth, he seemed to regard religious scruple as a political matter, to be fashioned like soft clay into whatever form was currently in vogue. He abhorred all absolutes, whether Romish or puritan, and all certainties apart from death. For him the middle path was the only one worth taking. Since it had no existence before others had set out their positions, it was a highway of delightful practicality and infinite flexibility. His only principle, therefore, was that there was no principle. Compromise was all. Armed with this supremely pragmatic philosophy, the very epitome of Anglicanism, the gifted, largely self-made cleric had been duly rewarded with rich benefices, including the deanery of Westminster and the bishopric of Lincoln. Both he and Middlesex were fiercely ambitious, and both owed their elevation in good part to Buckingham's patronage.

'Canon and Master Verney,' began the treasurer, taking a seat, 'I have asked you here in the company of the lord keeper so that we may ensure that we are all doing everything in our power to assist His Majesty at this, well, exacting time.' Pointing to some bottles on the sideboard, he asked Tom to pour them all a drink. 'Now,' he went on when Tom had finished and sat down, 'it is only prudent for me to remind you all' – he looked at Chillingworth and Tom – 'that this little meeting is entirely confidential.'

'In fact,' interrupted the bishop, 'I believe it is not happening at all. You take the drift of my remark, Verney?' Tom nodded. He disliked being patronised, particularly in a Welsh accent.

Middlesex continued. 'His Majesty is an unhappy and lonely man. He is also elderly and of frail health. The absence of his only son and the dear Marquis of Buckingham on a dangerous and, some say, ill-advised mission to Spain, leaves him vulnerable to approaches and insinuations from some who may not have the best interests of the kingdom at heart. Furthermore, should Prince Charles and his noble companion be thwarted in their quest, or should the Spaniards drive a bargain unacceptable to true Protestant hearts, then upon the return of the intrepid pair His Majesty will be in need of much trustworthy support and succour, much learned counsel and advice. We, gentlemen, are assembled here to agree how best to proffer that assistance.'

Well, Tom thought, it is just as Chillingworth said it would be. Buckingham is no sooner out of the country than the wolves begin to gather, led by two who owe most to the absent favourite. What price loyalty in this court? he asked himself, looking towards the canon for some hint as to why he was present at the meeting. Chillingworth's face, frozen in an attentive smile, revealed nothing.

Lord Keeper Williams took up the explanation. His voice was soft, almost humorous, and beneath a fair, greying moustache his mouth was ever flickering towards a grin. 'You may wonder, Master Verney and Canon Chillingworth, what a royal chaplain and his young Oxfordshire friend can do to assist a pair whose offices sit upon them as heavy as the world on the shoulders of Hercules? Well, listen now. His ancient Majesty is, it seems, much taken with the fair company of Thomas here. We – the lord treasurer and myself – would welcome it if Thomas saw fit, while in His Majesty's presence, to speak fair of the king's true friends – some of whom he may notice even within this room – and pour a corresponding scorn on the heads of those whose advice is not to be trusted.

'Who are such knaves, you ask? Well, it is not fit that a prince of the church speak ill of anyone. I will not name names. Let it suffice for me to say that these vipers are everywhere, near and far. Why, it is even rumoured that some are overseas, in countries as distant as France and

Spain! Fie, Master Verney, what a world we live in!'

What a world, indeed! thought Tom.

'Ahem!' coughed Chillingworth. 'By the Lord's sweet grace, I see, I see.' His manner was even more eccentric than usual. 'My lord bishop, you would wish me, by God's grace, to, er, supervise Master Verney in a little discreet verbal attack on the papists of France and Rome, eh? A little attack.'

Middlesex grew rather irritated. 'Those who might undermine the kingdom are not all papists, canon, though they may visit papist lands ...'

'Hush, my lord treasurer!' cut in Bishop Williams. 'I believe Canon Chillingworth understands full well my meaning. He may sound like an old clock, full of strange ticks and odd chimes, but he keeps time well enough. Don't you, Canon?'

'Eh? With the Lord's help I know what hour of the day it is, my lord. Yes, I know the hour.' He smiled sheepishly beneath the rim of his black hat.

'You surely do, Canon,' the bishop replied. 'You have been much attached to the Marquis of Buckingham, as have we all. We owe God great thanks for sending him to comfort King James. Yet now he is absent there is a void. As a loyal clergyman, you would not wish the Church of England exploited by any low, furious spider that had climbed upon the Villiers coat, would you, Canon?'

'Low, furious spider?' Chillingworth's pale eyes narrowed.

'I have heard Bishop William Laud described thus. You suffered under his harsh deanship at Gloucester, I believe.' There was not much about the Church of England that Bishop Williams did not know.

'Ah! I recall it. Yes, truly, his rule was not altogether to my, er, liking. Not at all.'

Cranfield was unwilling to be left out of the conversation for long. 'By assisting, Master Verney,' he interrupted bluntly, 'you may prevent the further ascent of fiery Laud.'

'And even bring blessings upon your own head, Canon,' the bishop continued, smiling. 'Forgive me, but you are a canon, not yet a dean, I believe?'

'I forget. Ah yes! A canon. A simple canon.'

One by one, Williams placed his fingertips together. 'A canon, yes. Simple, no.' He turned to Tom. 'That, Master Verney, is all we have to say. It has been a pleasure making your acquaintance and I would regard it as an honour if you would accept this small token of my thanks for what you have undertaken to do on my behalf.' He handed Tom a small box. 'Only a ring, Verney. A trifle. Do not feel you have to keep it. It will fetch a fair price in London.'

Tom tried to look Williams straight in the eyes, but found his target shifting each time he took aim. 'Thank you, my lord.'

'A trifle, as I said. You students need help, don't you? I have a nephew who is of Clement's Inn. He is for ever begging of me.'

'Leoline Williams?' Tom blurted.

'The very same! You are not of Clement's Inn are you, Master Verney?'

'I am. Well, I used ... I am surprised, my lord, that you did not know.'

For the first time since the meeting began, the bishop appeared a little flustered. He slid his fingers together and wound them in a knot. 'I did not know. Nephew Leoline did not mention Thomas Verney to me.'

Once again, he refused to meet Tom's glance.

vi

Before his departure, Tom attempted to fulfil his tacit bargain with Middlesex and the Bishop of Lincoln. Now and again, when he felt the moment propitious, he made flattering references about them to the king. James deliberately ignored these remarks until the day before Tom's return to London. Finding himself momentarily alone with the king, Tom had commented casually how wise and witty he found Bishop Williams, when James suddenly turned towards him and held him by the shoulders. Embarrassed, Tom gazed into his melancholy, wet eyes, and listened with a racing heart.

'God's breeches, Thomas! D'ye take your king for a fool that he needs a wee snip of a student to remind him of his ministers' qualities? Williams is a sharp Welsh wizard with a bellyful of wit, I know. Cranfield is a crafty old fox standing on a box of business, I know. They pay ye, no doubt, to speak honey words of them while my darling boys are away, for they are men of politics. But if they believe there's a tunnel of love from the old king's wrinkled crab apples to his heart, they're terrible mistaken. Cruel age has closed the passage of lust. Beneath my belt all hangs down now, my piles as far as my pitch fork. By the lashed body of St Andrew, Thomas! Understand that your old dad takes ye for a sweet child, an innocent amid the corruption in which we kings must stand.' He clasped Tom to him. 'If ye become tainted, Thomas, that is the end and my heart will be sore wounded. Never seek to raise one finger betwixt my Steenie and myself. Remember that. Be honest, kind and true to your old father.'

At the time Tom was too taken aback to do anything but mumble an apology and make a mental note not to mention his backers in the king's presence for a while. But when the next day Chillingworth appeared and announced that he too was travelling to London, Tom was pleased to ride along with him in the hope of talking through his position.

Moving at the canon's leisurely pace, the journey took three days. As before, the cleric was fascinating company, regaling Tom with anecdotes of church and court, full of gossip, saucy equivocation and fleeting insights into his private life. In contrast to their first journey together, Tom was not eager to bare his heart, and he mentioned neither his expulsion from the Inn, nor his love for Lucy Simpson. At supper on the second day, taken at the Bell in Hertford where they were staying, Chillingworth remarked on Tom's new-found reticence. 'I see, Master Verney, that six months have, er, changed you. Somewhat.'

'Is that so?' asked Tom, hoping for a flattering answer.

'It is. You are no longer, if I may be so bold as to remark, the open book in which the world may stand and read the history of Thomas Verney as they would stand to read the history of the people of Israel in the Holy Bible on the church lectern. No longer. I must take care with you, must I not?'

'Never. Maybe I have built a low wall about myself, but that is to keep out villains, not friends.'

Chillingworth muttered, 'Very good,' and wiped chicken grease from his lips with a white handkerchief.

'Now, Canon. I would approach the subject we have both stepped round like a snake on the road since we left Newmarket ...'

His companion lifted his hand. 'It is wiser, Master Verney, to avoid the adder in the dust than tread on it. They bite, eh? But this I will say. Listen close. It is best expressed, I venture to suggest, by turning one of Our Lord's sayings onto its head, though it might be blasphemous to do so: "Where your heart is, there will your treasure be also".'

Tom thought for a moment. 'My heart or the king's?'

'Of whom were you about to ask?'

'The king. I see. His heart is in Spain and fixed there. So you believe Middlesex and the Bishop of Lincoln are sure to fail?'

'Hey-ho, Master Verney! Who spoke of Middlesex or Lincoln or any other part of this pleasant isle, eh? Come, more wine? Let us be merry, for tomorrow we part, you to your Inn, me to – ahem! – York House.'

Tom lifted his head from his plate and stared at Chillingworth. York House! Why, that was one of the Marquis of Buckingham's London residences. Well, well, he said to himself, there is more than one adder on this road.

vii

After a short stop at Theobalds for Chillingworth to collect some papers, Tom arrived home on the afternoon of 14th March. The longer he had been away, the more he had missed Lucy, not just her physical presence, but her kindness, her practicality and her loving companionship. He was longing to see her face light up when he produced the money and ring he had been given, and told her what the king had said about his marrying. It was with a happy heart, therefore, that he stabled Princess and walked down Blackmore Street to the house. But when he arrived, his mood changed. Something had happened to the door. When he left, it had been dark brown. Now, for some reason, it had a large, untidy white stain across it. Fearing this might be a warning mark for some disease, even the plague, he put his key in the lock, threw open the door and rushed inside.

'Lucy!' he cried. 'Lucy, I am returned! Where are you? Are you well?'

He found her in the parlour. She rose to greet him, her eyes red with weeping. 'Oh, Tom, my love!' she cried, breaking into fresh sobs as soon as he put his arms round her. 'You must go!'

He laughed. 'Go! But I am only just arrived. Tell me, what is the matter? What is the meaning of that mark on the door?'

'Tom, it has been like hell. I am afraid to go out. They throw stones at me. That mark on the door. They wrote "whore" in red paint, and I had to scrub it clean as best I could. I did not do very well, did I?' She sniffed and managed a weak smile.

Tom's anger boiled within him. 'Who is this?' he asked, moving towards the street entrance. 'Tell me who dares to persecute you, and I will break their bones! Who is it, Lucy?'

'No, Tom, no!' She held fast to his arm. 'It is not one or two. But the whole street. Even you cannot fight a hundred.'

'Then I will go to the magistrates.'

'And say what, Tom? We have sinned. The men and women of this street are good people. I have known them all my life. They are worried lest this become a bawdy house and so attract wickedness of every sort. Do you not see that?' She paused. 'I feel it is our punishment. You must go.'

He turned and stood with his back to the street and took a deep breath. Lucy gazed up at him, her round, sincere face wet and blotchy. Her arms hung down by her sides. The harsh soap she had used to clean the door had left her hands red and chapped. Her gown was crumpled, her hair had partly fallen down.

Looking at her, Tom thought his heart would break in two. He could not believe there was a single dot of artifice in her whole being. She was so honest, so kind, so brave – and so mistreated. Who could not love her?

'Yes, Lucy. You are right. I must go.' He saw her swallow. Her lip quivered. 'But I will be back, my love. Tomorrow.'

'Perhaps it is not wise to return so soon, Tom.' She started to weep again. 'Think of me.'

'I can think of nothing else, Lucy.' He stepped forward and took her hands. 'Lucy Simpson,' he asked, his voice shaking, 'I have spoken with the king. Will you marry me?'

'Oh! You need not ask, Tom Verney.' Her tears turned to those of joy. 'I married you in my heart two weeks ago. Yes, my sweetheart. Yes. Yes.'

For a long time, together yet separated by private thoughts, they stood clasped in each other's arms. Slowly, as the blurred cloud of emotions began to settle, Tom was aware that the familiar words of the marriage service were clanging through his mind like a tocsin, *Holy matrimony ... instituted of God in Paradise ... is not to be ... taken in hand unadvisedly, lightly, or wantonly ...*

Dear God, he asked himself, what have we undertaken? Even if we find a corrupt priest to conduct the ceremony without bans or parental consent, the marriage will still be illegal. A breach of Man's laws as well as God's. Staring over Lucy's shoulder, he saw the anguished faces of his family projected onto the whitewashed wall behind. Silently, from deep in his heart, he begged their forgiveness.

TEN

ST ANDREW UNDERSHAFT

i

Situated near the river-bank in a broad garden stretching from the Thames to the Charing Cross end of the Strand, York House had been the official London residence of the archbishops of York for as long as anyone could remember. Yet no ecclesiastic had resided there since the reign of Queen Elizabeth's Roman Catholic elder sister Mary – 'Bloody Mary' Londoners still liked to call her. Between then and 1622 the increasingly dilapidated and outmoded house had been occupied by a succession of lord keepers and lord chancellors, the last of whom, Sir Francis Bacon, had been forced by debt and dishonour to sell the remaining five years of his lease to the Marquis of Buckingham for one thousand and three hundred pounds. Now, assisted by grants and gifts from the king, the favourite was determined to transform the dwelling into one of the finest residences in the capital. Under the supervision of

Balthazar Gerbier, the marquis's Huguenot-born artistic mentor, the place was in the process of being reroofed, redesigned, refurbished. Ceilings came down, floors came up, walls were moved, fireplaces altered, staircases replaced, brickwork plastered, pictures hung, façades erected and gardens relaid. 'We do not suppose,' commented the king wryly on a visit of inspection during Buckingham's continental absence, 'that even the golden Croesus could have effected so swift and glorious a transformation.' Nor, thought Chillingworth, standing at James's side, so costly a one.

The anaemic-looking canon-chaplain was thoroughly enjoying his stay at York House. Buckingham had invited him to live there for a while ostensibly to keep on eye on Gerbier's remodelling of the chapel. The favourite's hardening religious views had of late become a major talking point in court circles, particularly now that he had gone to Spain to assist the prince in his Catholic match. It was well known that Buckingham's wife had been a Catholic before their marriage, changing her faith, it was rumoured, only after a prenuptial night with the most handsome man in England had whetted her appetite for more Protestant love-making. His mother was hovering on the brink of conversion to Rome and he himself had begun openly to favour those of an Arminian, antipuritan persuasion. The most aggressive of these high church zealots was Bishop Williams's *bête noire*, William Laud, Bishop of St David's and another royal chaplain. Fearing that his architect – whose parents had fled France to escape persecution for their Protestant faith – might produce a building too austere for his increasingly flamboyant tastes, Buckingham had instructed Chillingworth to make sure that he did not return from Spain to pray in a whitewashed box.

It was not solely the canon's theological correctness that had attracted Buckingham. Chillingworth had also been charged with keeping an eye on Tom and sending regular reports to Spain about how the young man was getting on at court, especially with regard to his relations with Treasurer Middlesex and Lord Keeper Williams. On returning to London from Newmarket, therefore, Chillingworth had duly put pen to paper and composed a full yet veiled account of the meeting in the makeshift treasury. He concluded with the non-committal remark, 'At present I know not whether the Stratton Audley dab has taken the Lincoln bait – if he has nibbled, for certain he is not yet hooked.'

Chillingworth's next meeting with the 'dab' came sooner than he had expected. Having spent his first morning back in the capital trying to explain to Gerbier, who was working on the chapel ceiling, why his patron might not appreciate sitting beneath a representation of the Last Supper in which a diminutive, hunchbacked St Peter was relegated with Judas Iscariot to a side-table, Chillingworth had retired to dinner in his rooms. He was amused by the accommodation put at his disposal, for it included the bedroom – and the very bed – previously occupied by successive archbishops, and he liked to lie there at night hearing the imaginary confessions of the chamber's former incumbents. But now, as he pecked at a huge plate of cold beef and tried to decide between Archbishop Thomas Wolsey and Archbishop Richard Scrope as the candidate for the night's confession, he was disturbed by Gerbier suddenly bursting into his dining room waving a piece of paper.

'By God, Shillingverth!' he cried. 'See 'ere! *Une lettre* from Buckingham. He command me go to *Espagne* now. *Maintenant!* Is that not *magnifique*?'

Chillingworth sometimes found Gerbier's artistic volatility difficult to handle, yet he admired the exile's ingenuity and creative energy, and would be sorry to see him go. 'Good heavens, Balthazar!' he said, putting down his knife. 'To Spain? Why are you commanded thither?'

'The marquis vishes me to paint the Infanta for that King James to see how she is beautiful. It is a *belle* commission, is it not?'

'It is indeed. Bell. I wish you well and God's blessing on your mission. Yes, God's blessing.'

'I thank you, Canon. You are *gentil*. Now I go to prepare for the voyage.' He halted by the door. 'By God! I am forgetting! There is a young man who is asking see you. I told him *attendez*!'

'Young man, eh? Thank you, Balthazar. Be so good as to send him in.'

'*Vraiment. Au revoir*, Canon! To *Espagne*! Ho, ho!' Gerbier swept out, calling, '*Entrez, monsieur!*' to the stranger who was waiting just outside the door.

'Master Verney!' cried Chillingworth, rising to his feet when Tom appeared. 'This is a happy occasion, indeed. Come in and partake of a little, er, dinner.'

Tom declined the invitation to eat but accepted wine. 'Excellent,' said the canon, filling his visitor's glass. 'Now, Thomas Verney, what happy breeze brings you to York House?' His face was as pale and inscrutable as ever. Only a slight gleam in his eyes betrayed his eagerness to discover what had brought Tom to see him so soon after their return from Newmarket. Did the lad want money? Was he in trouble with the church courts for immoral acts? Perhaps he was anxious about being beholden to both Buckingham and Middlesex? These and half a dozen other possibilities flashed through Chillingworth's mind. But all landed wide of the mark. And when he heard the real reason for Tom's visit, for once in his life the canon was lost for words.

'Ahem!' he spluttered. 'Mr, er, Master Verney, would you be so kind as to, ah, repeat what you said?'

'Canon Chillingworth, you are the only man to whom I can turn. I wish to be married. As soon as is possible. Today!' Tom's face glowed with enthusiasm.

'Eh? Today?' Chillingworth gradually regained his composure. 'This is irregular, Master Verney. Quite irregular.'

'But it can be done?'

The reply was non-committal. 'I have heard of some cases of, er, well – what shall we say? – holy matrimony arranged with convenient celerity.'

'Then listen, sir,' said Tom, leaning forward in his chair and laying his hands flat on the table, 'and I will explain all.'

He proceeded to outline the full story of his relationship with Lucy and of his expulsion from the Inn, which had been confirmed in a letter awaiting him on his return from Newmarket. Chillingworth listened without interruption, his sparkling black eyes standing out on his face like currants on unbaked pastry. His mind raced ahead. Was the young man telling the truth, or springing some Cranfield-inspired trap to trick him into acting illegally? Tom's patent enthusiasm led him to dismiss this possibility. Nevertheless, it was still not prudent for him to become involved. He cared for Tom – if he cared for anyone – but could not believe that the king really had blessed the fellow's marriage to a tailor's daughter. There must be some misunderstanding. If that was so and the young man still insisted on going ahead with the foolish act, perhaps it might be put to good use on behalf of the master of York House ...? He needed to know more.

So when Tom had finished, he asked, 'Well, Thomas, has love sunk her talons so deep into your heart that you cannot shake them off? So deep, eh?'

Tom looked straight at him. 'I do not want them removed. My Lucy is true and honest and good. I will not desert her.'

'"Till death do you depart"?' the canon tested.

Tom hesitated. 'That may be many years.'

'Truly. God willing.'

'Then, "Till death do us depart".'

'Even though the king and your father may renounce you for what you do, eh?'

Tom's face flushed. 'I told you, Canon, the king has given his consent.'

Chillingworth clasped his hands together as if in prayer. Hunching his shoulders, he sat forward and spoke in a soft, conciliatory voice, 'Of course, of course. And yet, young sir, there is no possibility that you might have been, er, mistaken? I could not help but notice when we were at Newmarket how distracted His Majesty had become by ill-health and the absence of the prince and the marquis. He did not always attend to what was being said to him. Perhaps there was a, um, misunderstanding between you?'

This was as far as the wily cleric was prepared to go in giving Tom a lifeline. He had cast it near enough to be grasped, but would not haul it in and try a second time. He was prepared to give his young acquaintance just one chance.

Tom was a little unsettled by the canon's perceptive comment. Yes, he thought, James had been rather off-hand. But had he been truly unaware of what Tom had been asking? Impossible! After all, he had even asked to be invited to the wedding. The situation was quite straightforward. Besides, Tom could not betray Lucy now, after all her kindnesses and the trouble he had caused her.

He spoke directly and firmly. 'No, sir, there was no misunderstanding. With your help I would be married directly.'

Listening to Tom, Chillingworth watched the line sink beneath the surface of the water and disappear from view. With a sigh, he reeled it in. 'Very well. Very well. He is a foolish man who believes himself powerful enough to stem a raging torrent. Better to float with it, eh?'

'Thank you.'

'Pray do not thank me, Master Verney. I will play no part in this matter, no part at all. But I know a man who, with the Lord's blessing, may be of assistance. Two days hence you must call at St Andrew Undershaft in Aldgate Street and ask for Mr St John Pillar. You have that?'

'I have. I will always be obliged to you, good Canon ...'

Chillingworth raised a pale hand. 'No! No! Master Verney. Recall my words correctly, I pray. I have done nothing. Nothing at all.'

As soon as Tom had gone, the canon went over to a shelf at the side of the room and took down a large leather-bound book fastened with locked clasp. Drawing forth a key, he unlocked it and found a clean page. There, in his tiny, neat hand, he wrote, 'Mstr Verney. Love-struck — Lucy Simpson. Pillar to marry? An ace to play vsus Crfld & Lncln?' He chewed the tip of his quill for a moment before adding, 'Poor boy!'

Closing the book, he sent a servant to ask Mr Pillar, rector of St Andrew Undershaft, to call on him at his earliest convenience.

Although Chillingworth had met St John Pillar on several previous occasions, when he walked into the York House library at about four o'clock that afternoon, the canon could not help but be struck by the man's unrelieved ugliness. His round and protruding belly gave him the appearance of having swallowed an inflated pig's bladder. His misshapen head was too big for his body. His brown hair, stuck in a flat sheaf across a protruding left ear, was thin and undistinguished. His lips were fat, his skin sallow and his leather sack of a chin hung and wobbled like a goitre. The sorry picture was completed by eyes set so deep that unless one met the fellow head-on he appeared to have none at all. It was, mused Chillingworth, as if Our Lord and Maker had suffered from a touch of cramp when assembling the fellow, so that he looked more like a child's clay figure come to life than a creature fashioned in the image of God. Nor had the Almighty compensated for his lack of dexterity by endowing Pillar with more than his fair share of other qualities. He was large, loud and weak.

'Canon!' he cried, roaring into the room. 'Well met!'

Chillingworth neither rose nor extended his hand. 'No, sir. I believe it is not well met. Not at all.'

Pillar froze in his tracks, his hands extended before him. A look of fear came into his cavernous eyes. 'How so, Canon?' he asked, thawing and looking about for a chair.

'Pray remain standing, sir. I will be brief. At the request of my lord the Bishop of London, I have been examining the, well, proclivities of some of the clergy within his diocese.' Pillar visibly wilted. His knees sagged, his head sank to his shoulders and his arms hung loose by his sides. 'And the Lord has revealed to me some behaviour on the part of the rector of St Andrew Undershaft that is not quite – ahem! – seemly?'

'Lord have mercy on me,' muttered Pillar.

'So drunken at the Lord's Table that he spewed forth into the communion chalice?'

'Scurrilous folk spread that story. I was sick ...'

'Taking young maidens – and even, on occasion, young boys – into the vestry to instruct them in their catechism, when all that took place there was, well, not instruction in the catechism, eh? Not at all.'

'I am a frail vessel. On occasion the temptations of the flesh have been too great for me, I confess. The devil took child's form and led me astray.' Pillar's tone grew desperate. 'But I am a reformed man, Canon. Never again—'

'Really? So I am not to recommend that you be dismissed?'

'In the name of Jesus, no! I beg you!'

'We shall see.' Chillingworth's voice was as hard as his face. 'In the meantime you will do as I request?'

A look of anxious relief came into Pillar's well-like eyes. 'I will.'

'I have heard a colleague say that there is a young fellow named Verney who seeks some, er, ecclesiastical assistance. You will provide it.'

'I will. I thank you, Canon,' Pillar simpered. 'May the Lord bless you and keep you!'

'Thank me, sir? I have done nothing. Nothing. It is you who must, er, perform, is it not?'

'It is.'

'Then do so. I bid you good day.'

As the door closed, Chillingworth once again took down his secret volume and penned a few carefully chosen words. Smiling to himself, he replaced the book, pulled on his hat and cloak and went out to inspect the chapel.

ii

The marriage of Thomas Verney, bachelor of the parish of Stratton Audley, Oxfordshire, and Lucy Simpson, spinster of the parish of St Clement Danes, London, took place in the crypt of St Andrew Undershaft on Thursday, 20th March 1623 at eight o'clock in the evening. An irregular place, an irregular time, and a distinctly irregular ceremony.

No bans had been read beforehand. The service was conducted by candlelight in the presence of House Martin and Jack the apprentice, both of whom had been sworn to secrecy until such time as the wedding could be made public. The officiating priest, St John Pillar, swayed gently as he struggled to read out the order of service, which he pronounced in a flamboyant and slurred singsong manner reminiscent of that used for the Romish mass. Tom, wearing the first clothes his bride's late father had ever made for him, was stern-faced and quiet throughout. Lucy, prettily attired in a tight-fitting, silver-green gown and matching cap made specially for the occasion, entered the church smiling and full of joy. But when House Martin led her down the slippery steps into the ill-lit, chill and mildewed crypt, where she met the drunken Pillar, who leered at her through red sunken eyes all the time she was there, her happiness evaporated into the damp shadows. At first she stood as solemnly as the groom. But when Pillar forgot her name and turned over two pages in the prayer book at the same time, so that he would have missed out the marriage altogether had he not been corrected, her bottom lip began to tremble. This was the ceremony she had longed for all her life, yet now it had come she wished it over as quickly as possible. There was nothing to savour, nothing to remember. Even the beautiful ring Tom gave her, fashioned from that given him by Bishop Williams, appeared heavy and ominously out of place on her small finger. As the candles spluttered and smoked, and Pillar intoned his faltering way from line to line with all the enthusiasm of a boatman reciting his fares, she had no thought but to leave that dismal place and its hideous, foul-breathed priest, and return home with her husband. To prevent herself crying, she bit her quivering lip until it bled. A trickle of blood ran down her chin onto the front of her dress.

When they had returned to Blackmore street, Tom did his best to cheer his forlorn bride. After a small celebratory supper and a good deal of wine, he danced about the parlour floor, waving the marriage certificate in the air. He announced that this was the best day of their lives and roared with laughter at the thought of the looks on the faces of their censorious neighbours when he showed them the paper in the morning. He spoke of the future, of the king, of his family and how things could only get better from now on. All the while, Lucy sat watching him, a broad smile on her pretty face. She loved him in this mood. She loved his enthusiasm, his confidence and his youth.

But his revelry did not stop there. In time, as he strove to shut out the doubts and anxieties which cried from the back of his mind, it acquired a new, almost frantic edge. He drank still more, urging her to do the same. His eyes became glazed, his speech slurred, until he was not sure what he was saying. 'Well, Lucy, my wife, my lovely little rabbit,' he cried, fondly pressing her back against the table, 'what will the poxy world say now? Eh? By God! We have defied them all! Even Great John!'

'Take care, my love,' she replied, gently pushing him away. 'And who's that, Tom? Who's this Great John?'

'Ah! Just a man I met ... once.' He moved unsteadily towards her again, smiling and extending his arms.

Taking hold of his wrists, she asked, 'A secret, Tom love?'

'Of a kind, but of no importance. At least, no great importance. Not now.' He sat down awkwardly in a chair and gazed into the fire. 'This John, Lucy dearest – he saved my life.'

'I am glad. Yet you had not told me before.' Her apprehension sparked towards anger. 'Why not? Is that the way between husband and wife?'

He turned his unfocused gaze towards her. His face was flushed, his eyes bloodshot. Wishing he had not drunk so much, she realised it was pointless getting cross with him. 'I asked, Tom love, whether that was the way between husband and wife?'

'What way?'

'Secrets. We should tell each other everything. Listen, I have a secret too ...'

'Secrets, secrets,' he interrupted, half turning towards her and smiling. 'You have secrets. We all have secrets. But come, what is yours? Tell me now ...' The sentence remained unfinished. His voice faded away and his body relaxed into sleep. His breathing became slow and rhythmical.

Lucy shook him, but he did not stir. 'Oh, Tom!' she whispered. 'This night of all nights you choose to sleep apart from me. And before I could tell you, too.' She kissed his forehead, fetched a blanket to cover him and went upstairs to bed. Before getting under the covers, she knelt in prayer for ten minutes.

Two hours later she was still awake when her husband joined her, bumping up the stairs and crashing into bed beside her fully dressed. When one of his arms fell like a beam across her body, she raised it gently and placed it by his side. Then she lay still, gazing at his face in the moonlight streaming through the unshuttered casement.

She sighed. He was such a handsome man. But so young. So very, very young. If he found it difficult to manage his own life, how would he cope with the added responsibility of a wife and child?

iii

Tom and Lucy's first week of married life was a happy oasis of tranquillity amid long months of turmoil. All smiles and charm and parading his marriage certificate, he called on the houses of those suspected of having led the attacks on Lucy, apologised for any offence their past conduct might have caused and explained that they were now legally man and wife. One or two households, notably an elderly woman and her daughter who made a living by carving horn buttons, were delighted at the news, wishing them well with a present of a box of buttons exquisitely fashioned into tiny apples. But the majority of the street remained aloof. One man even insisted on examining the certificate line by line, holding it up to the light and declaring that he had heard 'in some parts of town counterfeit papers may be bought by whores for a penny'. For Lucy's sake, Tom did not respond. She had told him that she suspected she was with child, and he did not want to make things more difficult for her. By the end of his mission, the street was convinced of the legality of their liaison and whatever they thought privately of the way in which it had been established, they left the young couple alone.

On 22nd March the Verneys invited George Cowley round to celebrate Tom's nineteenth birthday. The button-carvers, Faith and Ruth Paye, happened to call in, Jack was summoned from the workshop and a cheerful little party ensued. George gave a short speech, followed by one from Mrs Paye and then, unsolicited and unannounced, by a few hesitant – and rather tipsy – words from House Martin, who declared that no lad in the whole of London had such a kind master and mistress as those he called 'the new Mr and Mrs Verney'. Standing in the middle of the parlour floor, with one arm tightly round Lucy's waist, Tom thanked them all warmly. 'I have been fortunate of late,' he beamed, 'to meet with some of the mightiest in the land. But I have been more fortunate to meet with some of the kindest.' He looked around him, and down at Lucy, whose face was wreathed in smiles of utter contentment. 'And I say this: if I were obliged to chose between Blackmore Street and Newmarket, I would choose here – this place of good, honest, kindly people.'

With clapping and cheering ringing in his ears, he turned and gazed at Lucy. 'Is this not a good moment, my sweetheart?' he asked.

'It is, Tom! Oh, it is! Let us remember it. Always.'

As the likelihood of Lucy's pregnancy grew with each day that passed, so did Tom's unease. Whatever he now said about his motives for marrying, no one would believe that it was not because Lucy was expecting his child. Although he was a little anxious about how and when he was to approach the king with the news, he was far more concerned about how he should tackle his family. He hated deceiving them, and the longer he delayed breaking the news to them, the worse he felt. Lucy urged him to ride home and confess all to his parents, but he knew that was impossible. If, before he had royal blessing, he revealed that he had been thrown out of the Inn, had married beneath himself without consent and that his wife was expecting a child, they would almost certainly renounce him for ever. He considered writing to Anne Hutchinson, seeking the advice of someone in daily contact with his family and therefore able to suggest how best he might proceed. But when he tried to put on paper his feelings for Lucy and the news of his marriage, for some reason the figure of his correspondent, dressed in the gown she had worn when they had met in the orchard the previous summer, floated before him, and he could not find the right words. He screwed up the letter half finished and burned it.

He was fortunate in two respects, however. House Martin discovered from his grandfather that Gilbert Marshall had not returned to his chambers since Christmas, and the riot occasioned by Tom's examination had so shaken Ancient Green that he had retired to the country without writing to Justice Verney of the decision to expel his son from the Inn. These twin strokes of good fortune gave Tom time. He used it to slip into his correspondence home one or two disparaging comments about Clement's Inn, such as King James's remark that it was 'an old Inn for lawyers who never had any brains or, if they did once possess them, had so allowed them to rust that they lay like blunt old scythes in a barn'. He also paved the way for further revelations by mentioning the 'comely, sweet daughter of my tailor, whose fine taste is in no little way responsible for the favourable manner in which I have been received by His Majesty'.

Anxious to hear how these hints had been received, each day Tom sent House Martin scuttling round to Clement's Inn to see if his father had written. For several days the boy returned empty-handed. Then, on the last

Saturday of the month, he finally came home with news from Oxfordshire. But it came in no letter, packet or parcel. Nor was it on the subject Tom had been expecting. It was brought by word of mouth, and it related not to himself but to someone he had come to believe he would probably never hear of again – Great John.

iv

Justice Fuller, the magistrate to whom Tom had told the story of his fight in the woods above Stokenchurch, had never been a popular figure in his locality. Mean-spirited, strict and puritanical, for a long time he had prided himself on overseeing the best ordered district for fifty miles around. It was with mixed feelings, therefore, that those dwelling on the Chilterns had followed the struggle between this sour, self-satisfied justice and Great John. The lower orders, particularly when it was confirmed that the murders on the Oxford road had not been the work of John's gang, had sided secretly with the thief. Those of Fuller's own class, who had suffered heavily at John's hands, had tended to find themselves the magistrate's allies, however much they might have disliked him personally. John's mysterious disappearance in early September had increased rather than diminished his popularity, turning him into something of a folk hero. His fame had spread far and wide, and although admirers did not know where he had gone, or even whether he was still alive, they believed that one day he would return to resume his brave struggle against injustice.

Blind Jane of Potscombe had benefited more than once from John's anonymous donations to the village poorbox. Consequently, she had been considerably alarmed to overhear travellers saying that Justice Fuller planned to search for John in the capital, where he had recently been told the rogue was hiding. Fired by a powerful feeling of solidarity with her mysterious benefactor, she had undertaken to travel to London to warn him what was afoot. Having little idea where John might be found, she had decided to begin by seeking out Tom Verney, the proud young man she had met the previous September. Rumour held that he had spared John's life in the woods. If this was correct, she reasoned, there was just a chance that the grateful thief had contacted his saviour at Clement's Inn to thank him. She knew it was a remote possibility, but to begin with it was all she had to go on.

The journey was far tougher than she had anticipated. In Potscombe she had been known and understood; on the highway she was no more than a cantankerous blind beggar woman, for whom few felt much sympathy. Sometimes she fell in with other walkers, struggling along with them until her feet and joints grew too painful for her to continue. Twice she was given a ride on a cart. She slept in barns and beneath trees. She was molested, bullied and mocked. Her clothes wore to rags. Her health deteriorated to the point where she found it difficult to place one foot in front of the other without wincing, and her nights became long nightmares of painful, bloody coughing. By the time she reached Tyburn, she realised that this journey was almost certainly the last she would ever make in this life. Yet still she went on, driven by an almost religious fervour to save the man whose deeds had made him a legend in her part of the country. From the city gallows the disciple tapped and stumbled to Clement's Inn. Here she happened to meet House Martin, who led her to Blackmore Street.

'By God, Bird!' cried Lucy when he appeared at the

door supporting the bundle of filthy rags that Jane had become. 'What have you there?'

'Old woman from the country,' replied the boy anxiously. 'Says she needs to speak with Mr Verney. Urgent.'

Lucy wrinkled her nose at the woman's stench. 'Well, you had better bring her in and fetch my husband. Though the Lord knows what foul diseases she brings with her.'

While House Martin summoned Tom from the workshop, Lucy sat Jane before the fire and offered her a mug of ale and some bread. Although clearly starving, the wretch seemed little interested in nourishment. She sat with her head cocked to one side, waiting for the sound of Tom's footsteps. When he entered she extended a shaking, claw-like hand towards him and croaked, 'This be him? Master Verney – Thomas vain Verney of Stratton Audley?'

Tom allowed himself to be grasped by the sleeve and pulled towards her. 'Yes. It is Thomas Verney. And, if I recall correctly, you are Blind Jane of Potscombe, though in a more sorry state than when I saw you last.' The memory of that scorching afternoon in late summer came flooding back. It seemed so long ago now. 'If I recall correctly, you warned me of rogues on the London road, Jane. What now brings you to London?' He spoke kindly, but with his head turned away from her, for the smell of her unwashed body and soiled clothing was quite overpowering.

'Those same men i'the woods as what I spoke of'afore brings me here. Or one of them does,' Jane replied, her voice thin and hoarse.

'You are come to warn me again, Jane?'

'Nay, good sir! Come close and listen, I pray.' Tom and

Lucy pulled up chairs and sat as close to her as they could bear, casting quizzical looks at each other as they did so. 'Blind Jane knows as there is little Christian goodness in this world,' the woman began speaking with difficulty, 'yet once she thought she knew of a good man. It was one of those what set upon you on the road, Master Verney.' Tom stiffened. 'That is the man I now seek. To warn him. His name is Great John.'

Simultaneously, Lucy and Tom lifted their heads and looked at each other. Before Lucy could speak, however, Tom placed a finger over his lips and said, 'Pray continue, Jane. Why should you wish to warn this Great John?'

And so Jane told her story. Tom listened carefully, interrupting only when he was unsure of her meaning or needed clarification of some detail. When she had finished and slumped back exhausted into her chair, Tom stood up and began pacing about the room.

'So this Great John helped you, Jane,' he summarised, checking what he was and what he was not supposed to know, as well as giving himself time to decide on a response. 'Now you wish to help the, well, good-hearted thief by warning him that Fuller has picked up his scent and followed it here to London.' Jane croaked assent.

'The justice is staying with Lord Banbury, accompanied by his daughter — how did you say she was named, Sarah? — whom he will not let out of his sight. You say she has recently given birth to a child, whose father is this same John. And you have come here because it was said that John was beholden to me for some good turn, and you believe he may have tried to contact me here, in the city.' Again, with a scarcely audible grunt, Jane confirmed that he had understood correctly.

Tom paused by the door. He looked down at his feet and clicked his tongue. The only other noises were the crackle of the fire and the shallow rasp of Jane's breath, straining through her throat like steam from a furred kettle. At a gesture from Tom, House Martin had left the room as soon as Jane had begun her tale. Lucy sat in silence, looking anxiously from her husband to the pitiable old crone who sought his assistance. Her brow was furrowed in puzzlement. Jane herself, now recovered slightly from the exhaustion of her story-telling, sat gripping the arm of her chair, waiting nervously to hear what Tom would say next.

He was tempted to deny ever having seen John after their encounter in the woods. It was true that he had mentioned the man to Lucy on their wedding night, but he had already explained that away as drunken confusion. The simplest course of action was to continue that line. 'Well, Jane,' he began, without raising his eyes, 'I am sorry to say that this John did not contact me when he came to London.'

The words smote Jane like a blow. Uttering a thin shriek, she tried to stand. 'Then all is vain!' she cried, falling back into the chair. 'I have given my life for nothing.'

Lucy bent over and pressed the mug of ale to her lips. Tom remained where he was. The story of St Peter denying Christ flitted somewhere through the back of his mind. Looking up at last, he spoke.

'Jane. Listen carefully.' The words came slowly, as if he had to force them from his mouth, one by one. 'John did not come to me. Yet we did meet. Frequently. I believe I can find him.'

Two heads turned in Tom's direction. One, normally young and pretty, was distorted by a look of amazed disbelief and disillusionment. The other, scarcely more than a sightless and shrunken skull, was radiant with the inner joy of martyrdom. Lasting no more than a second or two, the image of surreal contrast burned itself indelibly into Tom's memory.

The spell was broken by Lucy jumping to her feet and approaching her husband. 'Tom,' she scowled, 'what have you not told me? What sort of man have I married? I shall tell you: one that consorts with thieves and tells me nothing. A cheat! How can I believe anything you say?'

Before Tom could reply, they were interrupted by a movement behind them. Jane was clutching at her chest, a thick gurgling sound coming from her throat. Before either Tom or Lucy could move, she rolled slowly forward from her chair towards the fire. The mug of ale slipped to the floor and smashed. Her head struck the hearth with a crack and a thick red worm of blood eased silently from the corner of her mouth. Her left hand, thrown forward in a desperate attempt to break her fall, pushed slowly into the burning embers of the grate. There it twitched momentarily, then lay still. The fingers blackened and a foul-sweet smell rose into the room.

Blind Jane was dead.

v

The rest of the day passed like a nightmare. Between explaining to the authorities the awkward presence of a dead body in their house, and making arrangements for Jane to be given as swift a funeral as possible, Tom and Lucy snarled and snapped at each other like dogs. Both were too shocked by the nature of Jane's revelation and the horrible manner of her death to think very clearly. Lucy alternated between handwringing despair, declaring that Death itself had taken up residence with her since she first met Tom, and bitter recrimination against him for not telling her about his shady past. Tom either ignored his wife's accusations, which, he said, were grossly unjust since all he had tried to do was shelter her from unpleasantness, or he complained that she was turning their marriage into a branch of the Inquisition. The fact that he knew the retort to be unfair only made him more stubborn. Not even their naked proximity in bed that night served to bring them together, and early the following morning, leaving Lucy sitting by the privy door feeling sick, Tom threw on his clothes and stomped out of the house. Closing the door, he shouted that he was going to visit the Banburys. 'Yes, Lucy,' he called over his shoulder, 'the house of Lady Banbury. You remember her? When I return, do you wish me to write a report of what has happened?' He regretted the unworthy taunt, so ill-considered and uncharacteristically cruel, even as he was making it.

Still furious – though now more with himself than anyone else – he collected Princess and galloped north for several miles until he reached the village of Kentishtown. Finding a pleasant-looking inn, he entered and ordered a hearty breakfast of kidneys, bacon and ale. With the meal inside him, he felt much relieved and a good deal calmer. He sat back and reflected.

For the moment, at least, far from the narrow cloying atmosphere of Blackmore Street, he was free, and he enjoyed the sensation. It was like plunging into a cool river on a hot summer's day. With a smile on his lips and a new confidence in his deportment, he paid his bill and walked outside into the world he knew. He closed his eyes and breathed deeply. The spring air was warm and perfumed with the natural scent of damp grass and early flowers. On every side he was serenaded by the familiar, siren noises of his beloved countryside – the barking and bleating, birdsong, lowing and crowing that had greeted him every morning for the first eighteen years of his life. Turning and looking south, where only a smudge of smoke marked the presence of the city, he realised where his heart really lay. One day, he resolved, one day I will return. But when and how only God can tell. For the moment, he had other matters to attend to.

Untying Princess, he climbed into the saddle and turned her head back the way he had come. Now we'll see if Blind Jane was correct, he said to himself as he trotted along between sprouting hedgerows alive with nesting birds. A visit to the Banburys – it was not such an unpleasant task after all. In fact, he was rather looking forward to it.

As Tom was shown into the room hung with the tapestry of the *Sabine Women*, Lord Banbury welcomed him with his usual flamboyant insincerity, demanding to know how he was getting on at court and how his studies were progressing. Tom avoided giving direct responses by asking after his lordship's and Lady Banbury's health, reminding the baronet that the last time they had met he had thought himself poisoned.

'And that I was, Master Verney. I was most forceful with the merchant that sold me the tinted barrel, most forceful. I obliged him to make amends by supplying me with two further tuns. Gratis, if you take my meaning?'

'I do, sir. Without payment?'

'Pre-cisely, Master Verney. But that is, as they say, water under the bridge. Or maybe in my case it should be wine ...'

'Wine is more apt, sir,' cut in Tom, trying not to sound too sarcastic.

Banbury flashed him a suspicious look. 'Well, water or

wine, it has flowed past. Now we have another matter on our hands. A matter of considerable excitement. A chase, no less.'

So Blind Jane was right, thought Tom, realising that before long he was going to have another difficult decision to make. 'A chase? In London?' he enquired innocently. 'Are there deer still in the streets, your lordship?'

'Oh, Master Verney!' laughed Banbury, his fat jowls wobbling like saddle-bags. 'What a one you are! At times I think you the most simple man in town. We do not hunt beasts, but a man. A rogue, a villain, a thief, a seducer and a murderer!'

The last epithet sent a shiver down Tom's spine. So that was another label of criminality that Fuller was pinning to John, was it? Realising that the man was in serious, immediate danger, he tried to find out more. 'What a fellow, my lord! All those crimes from one pair of hands?'

'Yes, Verney,' replied a harsh voice from near the door. 'All those crimes. And for all of them, with God's help, he shall die!' Fuller had silently let himself into the room and was now moving towards Tom with the unpleasant grace of an angular black cat.

'I bid you good morning, Justice,' said Tom, straining to raise a smile.

The puritanical magistrate made no corresponding effort. 'We meet again, young man,' he said coldly. 'Lord Banbury tells me you have been welcome at court. I am not surprised.'

'Thank you, sir.'

'There is nothing to thank me for, Master Verney. I have not complimented you.'

Even Banbury sensed the uneasy atmosphere between the two men. 'Now, Justice,' he interpolated, 'I was telling Master Verney here about the multiplude of crimes for which you seek to apprehend this varlet John.'

Fuller's mouth cracked into an obsequious smile. 'I am grateful to your lordship. But I believe Master Verney knows him well.'

'Know him? I do not know him, sir,' interjected Tom. 'Yet I suppose I might have shot him,' he added, keen to keep on the right side of Banbury.

The baronet slapped his thigh. 'So you might!' he remembered. 'In the woods.'

'But you did not kill him,' capped Fuller.

Tom made no reply, allowing his lordship to continue. 'Well, maybe you can be of assistance to us, Verney. Justice Fuller has discovered, by – well – screwing the thumbs of a thief he seized, that this John came to London and resided at the George in Holborn. From there he has vanished.'

Keeping his tight black eyes fixed on Tom all the time Banbury was speaking, when he had finished Fuller added, 'But the landlord of the George was able to assist us, Master Verney. He gave us much information. He said, for example, we should watch for a young man from Oxfordshire wearing spectacles.'

Before Tom could say anything, Banbury blurted out, 'Ho! That is of little help, eh, Thomas? Why, even you wear spectacles on occasion, do you not?'

'Never in public,' spluttered Tom.

'How strange!' muttered Fuller. 'I recollect Master Verney saying, the last time we met, that he saw well enough without mechanical assistance.'

'He is a vain lad, Fuller, very vain.' The baronet's unwitting defence went no further, for at that point the door opened and two women entered. The first Tom recognised at once. Lady Banbury, as redolent with seasonal stirrings as the morning itself, walked gracefully up to him and offered her hand. As Tom stooped to kiss it, out of the corner of his eye he saw Fuller spring forward.

'I pray you excuse me, my lord and lady,' he hissed, striding across the room to the figure who had entered behind her ladyship. She was a short, pale girl, about Tom's age, with vivid bright blue eyes and delicate features. She might have been pretty if she had taken care with her appearance and not dressed in a plain, ill-fitting gown of grey wool.

'Father, I would ...' she pleaded as Fuller approached. The remark was never finished. As he reached her, the furious magistrate brought down the flat of his hand across her cheek with a slap that made the others gasp.

'Strumpet!' he screamed between his teeth. 'Shameless hussy! Did I not command you to keep to your room when there were others present?'

Tears were streaming down her face and a livid bruise was starting to appear on her left cheek. But she refused to weep. Keeping her head erect, Sarah Fuller looked straight at her father, her blue eyes gleaming like steel. 'I am sorry, Father. I was not aware that there were others here. I will return to my room at once.'

Lifting a hand to her damaged face, with heart-rending dignity she turned on her heel and left the room. If he had not been certain before that moment, Tom now knew precisely what he had to do.

Before leaving Pickering House and setting out for Aldgate, Tom had learned of another example of Fuller's furious vindictiveness. A few months previously Sarah had given birth to her child by John. Immediately, the baby girl had been taken from her mother and given to a wet nurse, with the instructions that neither she nor the child were ever to approach near Sarah again. Tom also learned a good deal about the plan to capture Great John. Not that these had been voluntarily released — most had been let slip by the garrulous Banbury in the course of conversation. The operation was far more extensive than Tom had realised. Because Lord Banbury's steward had been one of John's victims and, although not harmed, had been deprived of a considerable sum of his master's gold, Fuller had shrewdly approached the baronet — by no means a natural ally of his — and asked him to fund a trawl of the capital. The combination of Fuller's ruthless efficiency and Banbury's money was making the normally hopeless task of finding a wanted man in London's maze of streets and alleys quite promising. John was distinctive-looking; the baronet had offered a substantial reward for anyone coming forward with information leading to his capture; Fuller had half a dozen hired spies systematically going round the inns, ordinaries and taverns, making enquiries, eavesdropping on conversations and keeping notes on what they discovered; all local magistrates and constables had been alerted; and most well-known Roman Catholic households were kept under occasional surveillance.

'We have only to wait,' Fuller had said, his black eyes burning with confidence, 'and, God willing, the rotten fruit will drop into our net. Then we can crush it. Or, better still, burn it!' And while he waited for his moment of revenge, he remained at Pickering House, supervising the search for John and watching over his fallen daughter like a gaoler.

Tom had not seen Great John since the acrimonious dinner-time quarrel in late December, when the giant had poured scorn on his friend's declaration of love. Since that time Tom had often thought of him, though not always charitably. When he had felt well favoured at court, or certain in his relationship with Lucy, the thief-hero became an embittered rogue whom he had no wish ever to see again. But at other times, such as the royal blood-letting outside Newmarket or when he had doubts about the wisdom of marrying, he had very much wished to see John again. He missed his unusual, irreverent outlook and his humour. And now, having seen Sarah Fuller and the way in which her father was treating her, and having witnessed the devotion which John's behaviour had engendered in the heart of poor Blind Jane, Tom was convinced that he knew which side God was on in this battle.

And yet, he mused as he rode east by St Swithin's church in Candlewick Street, he still wished John would be more open with him. It was not easy risking serious trouble to help a man who would not reveal his surname, who kept his past a closed book and who even had one watched by spies ...

Spies! By God! thought Tom, what if Fuller is having me watched? He has never trusted me since we first spoke about my fight with John, and after what he has been told by the landlord of the George, he is probably even more suspicious. If I am being followed, I will lead them straight to John, to his certain death and to my, well ... It did not bear thinking about. He could not be certain that his father, or even the king, would be prepared to side with him if he were accused, however unjustly, of harbouring a murderer.

A thrill of horror and excitement surged through him. He could not help feeling that however dangerous this business was, it was vastly more enjoyable, and perhaps even more worthwhile, than playing the role of husband-tailor in Blackmore Street. Or even that of courtier in Newmarket.

Striving to appear as natural as possible, he put on his spectacles and glanced over his shoulder, pretending to be looking at the clock on the tower of St Mary Abchurch to his left.

The street seemed normal enough. Three or four carts, hawkers, a milk-girl, children playing in the gutter, numerous pedestrians going about their business – and a small, solitary figure on a pony, riding in the same direction as himself. Nothing unusual in that, he thought. But just to be sure, he turned right before the Boar's Head, into St Michael's Lane. Just past the church he turned left again, down a narrow passage known as Crooked Lane.

Ten yards into the alley he pulled hard on Princess's rein, swinging her round so that they were going back the way they had just come. No sooner had he completed the manoeuvre, than the figure on the pony appeared in front of him at the entrance to Crooked Lane, making as if to enter it. But seeing Tom bearing down rapidly upon him, he veered to the right and trotted in the direction of the river.

Tom let out a quiet, low whistle. So that is Fuller's game, is it? he said to himself. Well, let us see who will win, shall we? He pulled Princess to a halt and wheeled her about a second time. 'Now, my lovely,' he whispered, bending forward and patting her neck, 'can you outrun a pony?' As if she understood what her rider had said, the mare neighed and broke into a swift trot, the sound of her hoofs echoing off the overhanging houses.

At the eastern end of the lane he turned north, heading for Bishopsgate along Grass Church Street. He drove Princess as fast as the thronged highway would allow, weaving between carts, leaping piles of rubbish and throwing up clods of mud behind them. By Leaden Hall he glanced over his shoulder. His pursuer was nowhere to be seen. Nevertheless, he determined to press on, taking no chances.

Along Bishopsgate Street the traffic thinned and he urged Princess into a gallop. Soon he was thundering through the narrow stone arch of the gateway and up to the Dolphin, where he had to swerve sharply to avoid a carriage turning into the inn. Five hundred yards further on he veered suddenly right into the lane that ran behind Artillery Yard. Careering south again at breakneck speed, he soon came to the Whitechapel bars and so back to Aldgate.

Barely quarter of an hour since first realising he was being followed, Tom had handed over Princess to an ostler at the Saracen's Head and was climbing the stairs to John's room, certain that no one knew where he was.

ELEVEN

BLACKMORE STREET

i

Spreading his cloak on the yielding mattress of the meadow, Tom lay down and gazed about him. Above domed the blue and grey-white wash of the spring sky, around swayed a woven wall of grasses and flowers. Like a wild creature in his lair, secure, sheltered from the wind and warmed by the spring sunshine, he relaxed and tried to recall the names which had once been as familiar to him as schoolfellows. He had no trouble with the stately brushes of Fox Tail and Cat's Tail, the delicate Sweet Vernal, the Buttercups, Dandelions, Cowslips, Hawkweed and Hawksbeard, all of which grew in shameless profusion across the field. But what was that strange, lean lady, dancing before him on her stalk like a puppet? He racked his brain. Why – Shepherd's Purse, of course! Smiling to himself, he lifted his head and listened: cutting through the sad wailing of the lapwings and the chattering of common hedgerow gossips, he was sure he could make out the unfamiliar, onomatopoetic cry of a corncrake.

As he sat up, wondering if he could catch sight of the buff plumage of the secretive bird, a loud bellowing brought his nature study to a sudden end.

'Blood of the Holy Virgin!' roared John, similarly concealed in a grassy hollow to Tom's left. 'What a pair of egg-brained explorers we are, Thomas! Stepping out so bold without charts or maps into lands we scarce recognise, then quaking with worry and perturbation when we find the ways do not lead as we wish.' He threw back his head to allow the April sun to play upon his broad, lined face.

Still trapped in a rare moment of perfect tranquillity, Tom had been only half listening. The renewal of his friendship with the bewitching Bear, giving him a much needed opportunity to unburden himself, and the reassuring presence of the country sights, sounds and smells that meant so much, had combined to lift him quite beyond the anxieties which had recently closed so tight about him.

'Your courtly ambition and love-struck heart have led you to such a clockwork of confusion,' John continued, his deep voice burring through the grass like the wings of a giant insect, 'that I fear you will not be free of it until the whole tower falls. And it may bring you down too.

'And what of me? Ha, ha!' As his laughter drummed into the air, a single startled magpie flew off to join its mate. 'My affliction, drawing me to dream of building the commonwealth of heaven on earth, will surely lead only to the gallows.' Smiling, he placed his hands behind his head and closed his eyes. 'Well, Tom, have I not set out our position as clear as any doctor of philosophy?'

There was no reply. 'What? Quiet at last – have the ants bitten off your tongue?'

Gazing up at the gallery of cloud faces forming and

re-forming against the clear backdrop of the sky, Tom still did not reply.

The reconciliation between the two men had needed no longer than it took Tom to apologise for his arrogance at their previous meeting and John to admit that he had spoken with unnecessary clumsiness. Tom had suggested that they take advantage of the brightness of the day and walk out into the countryside. The proposition, he said, had the double appeal of removing them from city squalor and allowing freedom to talk where they would be neither interrupted nor overheard. When he added that he believed someone had tried to follow him that morning, John had readily agreed to the plan. Furnishing themselves with a large duck pie and a bottle of Canary wine, to which John was particularly partial, they had struck out at a brisk pace along the main Colchester road. Soon they had left White Chapel behind them and turned right to Stepney and the hamlet of World's End. Here they had left the road and found the pleasant meadow in which they were now resting.

During the journey Tom had done most of the talking, telling John about his extraordinary adventures of the last three months. As far as possible, he had offered a purely factual account. But at certain points in the story his hesitant or overconfident tone and cautious choice of epithets had made it quite clear that real worries lay only just beneath the surface of his brittle enthusiasm. For a long time John had made no direct comment, greeting the news of his friend's expulsion from the Inn and subsequent marriage with no more than grunts. His simile comparing the two of them to incompetent explorers had been his first direct, coherent reaction to Tom's revelations.

Now, having still evoked no response, he pushed aside

the grass and poked Tom in the ribs with his fingers, trying once more to stir him from his daydream. 'Thomas,' he asked, 'why did you seek me out again?'

The younger man finally surfaced. 'Oh, I do not know, John.' He rolled onto his side and propped himself up on his elbow. 'When I am with you I do not know anything,' he smiled.

'Maybe, like the contortion man at the fair, you find yourself wrapped in such knots as you cannot untie without assistance?'

Tom chuckled. Then his face grew more sombre and, drawing a deep breath, he rose to his knees. 'Come, John,' he said, 'let us take dinner upon the grass like rabbits. And while we are eating I will tell you more. It is true that I am here to seek advice. But that is not all — I am not so taken with my own reflection that I cannot be a true friend. Listen close, and you shall hear something which will convince you that there is good in me yet.'

'Good in you? Never!' Once again the rumbling laugh rose like smoke in the wind.

'You may recall my saying I was followed this morning?'

John sat up. 'I do. I was waiting for you to return to that sweetmeat.' He broke the pie in half and offered the larger part to Tom.

'The meat I talk of is not sweet, John,' he replied, leaning over and taking the smaller piece of pie, 'nor is it meet for jest. I believe the spy was in the pay of Justice Fuller, who is even now in London.' John's huge frame stiffened, and he laid down his crumbling pie on the cloak beside him. 'He knows you are in the city and is combing for you, aided by money from Toad Banbury. He thinks I may know of your whereabouts. And John—'

'Yes?'

'The justice has his daughter Sarah with him. At Pickering House. I have seen her.'

John ripped up great handfuls of grass and hurled them into the air. 'Holy Mother of God!' he cried, rising to his feet. 'Why do you come to me with such news, Tom?' Pushing back his hair, he ran his fingers across the scar on his forehead. 'I was learning to live alone. The wound was healing. Now you have ripped it open once more, and it hurts, Tom! By the screaming suffering of Our Lord on the cross, it hurts!' With a burst of surprising energy he went bounding through the grass, waving his arms and howling like a wolf. Tom sat and stared in amazement.

After a few minutes John quietened down. For a while he stood many yards off, staring up at the sky, his hands locked together behind his neck. Then he walked slowly back to where he had started, sat down, took a long pull at the wine and said, 'Tom Verney, I pray forgiveness. You are a better friend than I deserve. Here, drink.' He offered Tom the bottle. 'Now, I beg you, tell me all you know. How is sweet Sarah? Is her father so cruel to her?'

When Tom had finished giving John all the information in his possession, he expected him to announce that he was leaving the city at once. Instead, to his surprise, the Bear asked for further assistance.

Tom could smell rain in the wind. 'In what way, John?' he enquired, watching a heavy cloud blowing up from the west.

'Soon I will leave London. But I will not do so alone.'

'Sarah?'

'Aye, Sarah. We will rescue her from Pickering House and she will come with me.'

Tom shivered as the cloud obscured the sun and the

wind began to shake the hedgerow behind them. 'We?' he asked.

John stood up and wrapped his cloak about him. 'Come. We must bend our steps homeward. The better part of the day is gone.' He pulled Tom to his feet. 'I hoped you might assist me, Tom.'

A few raindrops blew against Tom's face. 'Help you? How?'

'You know the Banburys, do you not?'

'Yes.'

'Could you not help Sarah escape?'

Hearing again in his mind the sound of the vicious blow against the girl's cheek and seeing her brave, defiant face, Tom could not deny his friend. 'What would you have me do, John?'

The rain was now falling quite hard. The two men linked arms and, pulling their hats firmly down over their heads, began the long trudge back to the city. As they walked, they planned the rescue.

The idea was simple enough. To avoid the chance of detection by Fuller's men, John would leave the Saracen's Head and reside outside the city boundaries, never staying more than one night in the same place. He would send a daily message to Tom saying where he might be found each evening. Meanwhile, under the pretence of meeting with Lady Banbury, an aspect of the arrangements which John tactfully passed over with no more than a squeeze of his friend's elbow, Tom would go to Pickering House when Banbury and Fuller were absent and somehow let his friend in. John would meet with Sarah, whom Tom would try to warn in advance, and lead her away. With luck, it would be several hours before the baronet and the justice returned, by which time John and his love would be on the way to Mosley Hall, near Wolverhampton, where he had friends who he knew would harbour them both.

Tom undertook to find where Sarah's room was and provide her lover with a sketch of the interior of Pickering House. He also suggested that it might be wise if at the time of the rescue someone could be found to keep watch in the street, in case Fuller returned earlier than expected. John said he had just the fellow.

Detecting an uncustomary hesitancy in the man's voice, Tom asked, 'Surely not Limper – I mean Clifford, or Sloper, as you call him?'

'You do not trust him, Tom?'

'It was you yourself who told me to trust no man. How could I trust a man who has robbed me? He is a rogue.'

John laughed. 'Rogue he was. But so was I. We are both turned angels now.'

'No. Not Sloper,' Tom insisted.

'Very well. I will see if I can find another,' smiled John, adding, 'You are a stronger man nowadays, are you not, Master Verney?'

Tom stopped. The rain dripped off his hat and down onto his chin. 'Not stronger,' he replied, blowing a droplet off the end of his nose, 'but more cautious. Where are you leading me, John?'

The Bear placed a heavy hand on the young man's shoulder. 'Home,' he rumbled.

'I hope so, John,' Tom replied. 'I truly hope so.'

Before he arrived at Blackmore Street, in an effort to heal the rift which Blind Jane's revelations had opened up, Tom had decided to be as honest as possible with Lucy about what he had undertaken to do. She, on the other hand, aware of her vulnerable position, had decided that it would be wiser to let her husband have a life of his own rather than risk driving him away by making his marriage an unwonted constriction. As a result, their reunion early that evening verged on the farcical. Jane's corpse had been removed early in the afternoon, making the atmosphere in the house much easier, both literally and metaphorically. After he had apologised for his unkind remarks and hasty departure that morning, Tom tried to tell his wife where he had been all day and what he had arranged. But she refused to listen, saying that his life was his own affair and it was not meet for her to pry into it. In the end, they both looked at each other and burst into fits of laughter. The rest of the evening was spent in happy harmony. Although disappointed that there was still no letter from Tom's parents, they agreed that he should return to court as soon as John had left London. Then, armed with royal approbation, he could finally return to Stratton Audley in triumph, bringing his bride with him.

ii

The following morning, having told Lucy where he was going and what he was planning to do, but tactfully stopping short of revealing the part in the operation assigned to Lady Banbury, Tom called round at Pickering House. Fuller was out on business, and he had no trouble in getting Banbury to reveal that he and the justice were dining alone with friends on the afternoon of Monday 4th April. With the baronet's attention momentarily diverted by a servant, Tom mouthed to Lady Elizabeth that he would call on Monday as soon as her husband had left. Narrowing her eyes, she indicated her approval with a lascivious lick of the lips.

During this illicit exchange, Tom reflected on the propriety of continuing such games now that he was married. From behind her husband's back, Elizabeth winked and waggled her tongue at him. There was his answer. Wedded he might be, but he was not yet ready for canonisation. Besides, as there already was a Saint Thomas, it was unlikely there would be space in the halls of heavenly delight for another of that name. He would have to make do with earthly pleasures, thank goodness. With a final grin towards the irresistible Lady Elizabeth, he forced his attention back to her ridiculous Banby.

Two parts of Tom's mission remained. He had to find where Sarah was accommodated, and he had to make sure an outside door would be left open for John on the day of the planned escape. Both were easily accomplished. Revealing to Lord Banbury that he had never seen the full extent of the improvements and refurbishments which his lordship had made to Pickering House, his host afforded him a room-by-room guided tour. From this he learned that Sarah had been given a large first-floor room at the south-west corner of the house. It remained locked from the outside whenever Fuller was absent and he kept the key about his person.

It was well past noon by the time the tour had finished, and Banbury was clearly desperate for a drink. Politely declining to join him, Tom said he would see himself out. Instead of passing through the hall to the outer vestibule and the front door, however, he slipped right into the servants' quarters. Here, as luck would have it, he met Peter, Lord Banbury's butler, seated at his desk and making entries in a large ledger.

'Peter,' he called, trying to sound nonchalant, 'I believe your master takes his dinner elsewhere on Monday?'

The butler laid down his quill and rose slowly to his feet. 'I believe it to be so, sir,' he purred. His dignified expression and egg-bald head contrasted sharply with the garish stockings and jacket which Banbury insisted he wore.

Tom walked up to the desk. Laying a silver coin upon the open page of the ledger, he said quietly, 'I wish to enter Pickering House unawares when his lordship is absent.'

Peter neither blinked nor looked down. 'Is that so, sir?'

'It is,' said Tom, wondering why the fellow would not react. He placed a second coin beside the first. Peter's eyes dipped for an instant but he remained unyielding. A third coin clinked down beside the others.

As if he were coin-operated, Peter finally moved. 'Would you be so good as to repeat your question, sir?' he asked, deftly gathering up the bribe with long, white fingers.

'On Monday, when his lordship is away to dinner, I wish to enter this house unobserved,' Tom repeated.

'Would her ladyship know of this, sir?'

Tom wondered whether he detected a wisp of irony in the question. 'Her ladyship? Well, I will be seeing Lady Banbury...'

'Very good, sir. I understand your requirements. May I suggest the servants' garden door, sir? If you will follow me, I will show you out that way, after which you will be able to employ it as you see fit. Sir.' He glided off towards the rear of the house.

'It is not locked, Peter?'

'Never, sir. I am generally responsible for keeping it safe. But on Monday I will have urgent business elsewhere, sir. You will enter unseen.'

With these words, he opened a small door at the end of a long passage strewn with cobwebs, trugs, hoes and other small implements of cultivation, and let Tom out into the garden. 'The path to the west of the house, sir, leads directly to the stables and the Strand. I believe a stable boy will assist you if his purse is weighted a little, sir.'

Blinking in the bright light, Tom thanked the butler and put on his spectacles to look about him. He was standing on a gravel path at a rear corner of the house. Before him, across gardens and orchards, he could make out the glistening river. As he turned and looked up at the house, he realised with a quickening heart that he was directly below one of the windows of Sarah's room. He stepped back a few paces and looked up. A large creeper ran up the brickwork to an open casement. He called quietly, 'Sarah! Sarah Fuller!'

After a few seconds, the girl's pale face appeared above him. 'I have no time,' he whispered, cupping his hands together to help the sound travel further. 'Monday. About noon. John will come here to take you away.'

When, much later, he tried to explain to John the look on Sarah's face when she heard these words, he could not do so. It was, he said, a wonderful confusion of relief, love and delight, overlain with a veil of apprehension.

'Who are you?' she called down.

Before replying, Tom glanced along the row of ground floor windows to make sure he was not observed. From the leaded and barred lancet beside the garden door, Peter's pale face was staring out at him.

Damn the man! cursed Tom. Without looking up, he turned swiftly and followed the path towards the stables. Once there, he paid a boy to leave open the street gate after his arrival on Monday, collected Princess and rode home. So far, he reflected, all had gone without a hitch. Except for the face at the window.

'God's teeth!' he muttered as he pulled up outside his

stables. 'I would I knew what that unctuous Peter had been about. What did he see? More important, what did he hear?'

Had Tom been present in Lord Banbury's private smoking room that evening he would have been given at least part of the answer to his questions. Having enjoyed a hearty meal, the baronet and his guest were chatting about how Fuller's search was going, when Peter slipped into the room.

'Yes, Peter?' barked Banbury. 'What brings you creeping in here like an Arabian in the sand?'

'May I speak, sir?' The candlelight gleamed on his bald head.

'May you speak?' retorted the flushed peer. 'What sort of talk is that, Justice? The man's mad!'

Fuller raised his hand. 'Maybe, my lord. But he may have something to tell us. If he does not, you may punish him for insolence.' Banbury grunted in agreement. 'Very well, butler,' the justice continued, 'speak!'

'I have had a dream, sirs,' he began. 'A warning ...'

'What did I say?' chortled Banbury. 'Mad, quite mad!'

Fuller intervened. 'I pray you be patient, my lord. Remember dreams are used in the Holy Bible to pass God's word from heaven to earth.'

Banbury blushed and buried his nose in his cup.

Peter resumed his announcement. 'I dreamed a warning, sirs. It concerns Monday, when you propose to dine abroad.' Fuller tensed and stared hard at the speaker. Banbury put down his drink. 'I dreamed terrible creatures came into your house while you were out. They took off your possessions.' While he was speaking, he stared directly into the eyes of the justice. The two men understood each other perfectly.

'That is all, butler,' said Fuller when Peter had finished. 'Leave us now.'

As soon as the door had closed, Banbury announced, 'I think it were better for us if we dined at home on Monday, Fuller. That fellow Peter is full of strange informations. They are often correct.'

'Indeed, we could remain here, your lordship. That way all would be safe. But we would have no prisoners. If I may be so bold, sir, might I propose another plan?'

iii

Lucy listened to her husband's account of his morning's work with mixed feelings. She was happy that he had something to do, rather than hang about the house waiting to hear from his father or one of his courtly patrons, and she admired the generous way he had agreed to help his friend John. However odd the man sounded and however dubious some of his past conduct, she agreed that Fuller's treatment of him had been grossly unjust. Furthermore, she sympathised wholeheartedly with the unfortunate Sarah, with whom she automatically sided against her tyrannical father. She even allowed herself to get caught up in the dangerous thrill of the plot. On Friday morning, since Tom was out attending to some matter at the stables, it was she rather than her husband who received John's messenger and gave him the letter containing the plan of Pickering House and the details of the rescue operation proposed for the following Monday.

Nevertheless, exciting though all this was, it was not what she really wanted. She wanted security, not adventure. To that end, she needed John out of the way as quickly and painlessly as possible — which was one reason why she went along with the Pickering House plot – so that her marriage could be formally recognised long before the birth of her child. Since, from what Tom had told her, she gathered that he had become embroiled in the tricky world of factional infighting, his courtly escapades now interested her only as a means to an end. She no longer dreamed of belonging at court – she would be happy to belong anywhere. Blackmore Street tolerated her, but little more. Among tailors her business was regarded as inferior and its proprietress as an upstart outsider. Her only known living relative was an Aunt Mary, a younger sister of her father's who long ago had moved to Rochester with her husband. All her hopes, therefore, were pinned on the Verneys of Stratton Audley, the family which she had never met but already felt she knew quite well. She longed for the day when she would be able to regard them as her own. Understandably, the appearance of House Martin on Saturday morning with a letter from Justice Verney sent her heart racing with expectation.

'Tom!' she called. 'Tom, here's a letter from your father come at last.'

Her husband came in from the workshop, where he had been chatting to Jack about the previous night's street fight in the Paris Gardens, and took the letter from his servant. 'Well, Lucy, my love,' he said, breaking the document's seal and unfolding it, 'we will discover soon enough whether the old pike has swallowed his son's hints.'

He sat at the table and laid the letter flat before him. Lucy stood behind him, looking over his shoulder and resting her hand on his. Absent-mindedly, he placed his other hand on her knee. Thus posed, the very picture of domestic harmony, they read the fateful letter together.

Son Thomas —

Lawyer Marshall returned from London two days ago bearing tidings that at first I did not understand. He says that you were required to leave Clement's Inn some while ago, and he brought a document to that effect from the Principal. It spoke of riotous behaviour and ungentlemanly conduct.

Your mother and I near died with shame. I did not inform Marshall that this was news to us, but pretended I knew it already. I fear he did not believe me.

Now I understand why you wrote of the Inn with such mocking words. It was to prepare me, so to speak, for your thunderbolt.

What, pray, is the thunderbolt for which you are smoothing the path by writing so fondly of a tailor's wench? Pray God, for your sake and ours, your mother's fears are unfounded, for not while I live will I ever see a Verney tied beneath himself. I speak openly, Thomas, for that is, I fear, the only way you will listen. Bastards can be lost, paid for, forgiven even. But not so other follies.

Are we to believe you when you brag of your courtly visits and conquests? We do not know where we are with you now.

As your father, therefore, I command that you return home this very day to stand before us and explain your conduct. I will accept no delay, no excuse. No, not even though the king himself do send for you. Remember, Thomas, it is commanded of God, 'Honour thy father and mother'.

You will receive this letter by Monday 4th April. We expect to see you ride up on Princess at the

latest on Wednesday 6th April.
   Your affectionate father,
   John Verney

The young couple read through the letter three or four times before either of them spoke. 'Throw scripture at me, would you, Father?' said Tom eventually, leaning back and firmly pushing the letter from him so that it fell off the other side of the table and floated backwards and forwards to the floor. 'Have you forgotten charity and loving your neighbour as yourself and the parable of the Samaritan and of the prodigal son and of – oh, God blast you, Father!' he expostulated suddenly. Feeling tears come into his eyes, he rose quickly to his feet and strode round the parlour like a caged beast. House Martin slipped discreetly from the room.

Although she tried hard not to show it, Lucy was, if anything, even more distressed by the contents of the letter than her husband. 'Fury will not help us, Tom darling,' she suggested, picking up the offending document and glancing through it again in the hope of finding a redeeming paragraph she had overlooked.

'Help, Lucy? I do not need his help. He will need mine when he finds he has spoken contrary to the king's wishes.'

She came over to him and put her arms round his waist. 'You are sure, Tom, aren't you?' she asked.

'Sure?'

'Sure of the king's approval. You did take his meaning correct, did you not, my love?' The arrival of Justice Verney's letter had made royal consent for their match a solitary spring in the desert of Lucy's future. She could not bear to think that it might turn out to be a mirage.

Tom had often asked himself the same question,

particularly since Chillingworth's sceptical remarks about the king's preoccupied behaviour at Newmarket. He wished there was some way of going back over the crucial conversation, of dispelling the shadowy doubts that lingered at the edge of his mind. In the absence of any such relief, like a pilot whose navigation was challenged, he could only hold his course and insist that his bearings were correct.

'I heard him aright, my love,' he laughed. 'Wait and see. When John and Sarah are safely packed off to the country, I will to the king, and before the summer is come you will be home with me in Oxfordshire. I cannot wait for my mother to meet with you. My sisters, too. And your smile will surely win over my surly father, for all his grumbling letters!'

His certainty and enthusiasm were so infectious that Lucy laughed too. Pushing aside her doubts, she clung to him like a limpet in a storm.

Lucy did not feel well that evening. Tired and emotionally drained after the trauma of the summons from Tom's father, she went to bed early. Tom remained downstairs, sitting at the table with quill and paper, composing a firm yet tactful rejection of his father's command. He could not come home directly, he explained, because he was required to attend His Majesty, but he would return as soon as time allowed, which he hoped would be before the end of the month. As for the business at Clement's Inn, he would explain that when they met. It was not, he suggested, an issue of great importance, certainly not compared with other developments in his life. That was the closest he came to mentioning his marriage.

The rest of the letter was taken up with city gossip and requests for news from home. The tone of the whole communication was polite, almost deferential. Perhaps only in the final sentences did he reveal his true feelings. 'Dearest Father,' he wrote, 'I remain, whatever small troubles may have arisen between us, your devoted and loving son. I miss you, my dear mother and all my family and friends. Be assured that if I were not so tied here, I would be on Princess's back and among you again even tomorrow.'

He signed and sealed the letter and set it on one side. But instead of retiring for the night, he brought fresh paper and began a second communication.

My Dearest Friend Anne,
   I have news to relate which I do not know how to express.
   In a phrase, I am married.
   There, it is out. You are one of the few people to whom I can entrust this information because the step has been taken in haste and without the due formality of bans and consent etc. My family remain ignorant of what I have done, although I fear they are beginning to suspect.
   I should be glad to be writing thus. Indeed I am. Yet something nags at my happiness, spoiling its pleasure, like a sore tooth at a banquet.

Once he had begun in this tone, he could not stop. He wrote on and on, far into the night, telling the full story of his meeting with Lucy, their love for one another, the circumstances of their marriage and how feelings of guilt at betraying his family and friends fought against his deep affection for his wife. 'But with His Majesty's assistance', he announced, 'all will soon be reconciled, and I will be home again.' He paused and looked up. Before him the dying embers of the fire glowed dark red in the gloom.

His candle had almost burned itself out. He fetched his cloak and wrapped it round his shoulders to keep out the cold. There was one more paragraph to write, he knew, but he was not sure what it would contain. He dipped his pen into the ink and wrote.

> I suppose, dear Anne, this is a farewell. I do not wish to say that, for there is some part of me – whether heart or mind, I know not – which had hoped one day ... Well, you know what it is without my saying. Now we will never discover what might have been. Sometimes, when I think on you in moments of quiet, I believe I have not done right, and then I look inside my heart and find the smallest speck of hope hidden away in a corner where no one can see it. Except me, and now you. And I want to weep.
> Your friend, who but for his folly might have been more,
> Tom Verney

iv

The morning of 4th April dawned wet and blustery. Justice Christopher Fuller rose at six o'clock, knelt in prayer, gave himself half a dozen lashes about the legs with a leather thong, dressed and went to see his daughter. After taking her through morning prayers, he informed her that he was going out to dine and she must therefore remain in her room. Suggesting that the Book of Job would make suitable reading for such a disagreeable day, he told her that breakfast would be brought soon, and left, locking the door securely behind him. As soon as he was gone, Sarah did her best to make herself look as becoming as possible with the minimal resources available to her, drew up a chair by the window and sat gazing out through the rain towards the grey streak of the distant river.

In another part of the house, Elizabeth Banbury was taking similar care over her appearance, although the range of aids at her disposal was infinitely greater and the eventual result, completed by eleven o'clock, was quite ravishing.

Her husband, meanwhile, having poked his head into her dressing room before breakfast for a quick exchange of banalities, had joined Fuller at the table.

'I readily admit, Justice,' confided Banbury, 'that I'm all a-quiver waiting for our little adventure.' He dismissed the servants with a wave.

Fuller looked up from his plate with an expression as hard and cold as a frozen pond. 'Are you, my lord? I am quite calm, for which I thank God. I believe it is the result of constant prayer.' He sniffed. 'And yet, like you, my lord, I am eager to lay my hands on these scoundrels. Something tells me that our bearded murderer will be among them.' His hands began to shake. 'Did I not say that he was certain to walk into a trap baited with my daughter's tainted flesh?'

'Aye, you did, Justice. Most preceptive of you.'

'But if this knave does truly know of my daughter's presence here, my lord, do you not wonder how he came by such knowledge? Strange, is it not?'

'Aye, Fuller, most strange. But come, remind me of our stations once more, I pray.'

Fuller gave an imperceptible sigh. 'We will leave Pickering House at half past eleven, accompanied by your gardeners, Ned and Perkin. We will proceed to Charing Cross, where we will turn and trace our steps back here.

Then we will divide, your lordship with Ned to the rear entrances, myself and Perkin to the front door. You and I, furnished with the pistols and small arquebuses I have procured, will guard the doorways. The servants will scour the house, driving the prey towards the guns. Like any hunt in the field, my lord.'

'I like it, Fuller. I do indeed. I consider myself something of a crack with the guns.'

Leaving his chair, he crouched below the table and took aim at the magistrate with a candlestick. 'Death, thief!' he giggled, shaking so much that if he had been holding a real weapon he would have missed his target by a furlong. 'No prisoners! All who enter Pickering House without the consult of Sir Julius must meet their maker – now!' With a crash he brought the candlestick down on a plate, smashing it to a thousand fragments.

The noise brought Peter hurrying back into the room. 'Is all well, sir?' he enquired.

'Yes, Peter,' Banbury replied, rising to his feet and brushing fragments of china from his clothing. 'I was just shooting Justice Fuller. Ho, ho!'

'Very amusing, your lordship,' said Fuller, who had remained unmoved throughout the performance. 'I hope your aim will be as sharp for the real target.'

John had barely slept at all that night. He rose before dawn and went for a long walk through the countryside around Hampstead, where he had been staying, before returning for an early breakfast. By seven o'clock, well hidden beneath a heavy cloak and a broad hat, he was walking at a brisk pace towards the capital. Two hours later he entered a tavern behind St Bartholomew the Great and sat near the door, watching those who came in. He did not have long to wait.

'Sloper,' he hissed, as the familiar figure limped through the door, 'over here.' He stood up and walked through to a back room. Sloper halted after him.

'Well, I will be brief,' said John when they were alone. 'You know what it is I would have you do?'

'Simple. Watch the door of Pickering House from the Strand. Come in and bellow my head off if I sees his lordship returning.' His lips split into a thin grin. 'For which I will earn handsome.'

John opened his purse and pushed two coins across the table. 'Francis,' he asked, covering the money with his hands, 'you may be trusted, may you not?'

A startled look came into Sloper's face. 'You know me, John.'

'Truly, I do.' John lifted his hand and Sloper whisked away his reward. 'Take care, Francis. And may the Lord bless you. I may well never set eyes on you again.'

With these words, he held Sloper's face between his hands for a second, then left the room.

A minute later, another man entered. 'Yeah?' he asked, looking about him suspiciously. 'What is it, pox-head?'

'Jarking. Pickering House. Strand. Half after eleven. Easy in, easy out. You watch, I do it. Split the garbage?'

'Fifty–fifty?'

'Thirty–seventy, Phil.'

'Scurvy dell-donger! Thirty-five–sixty-five, or no deal. You avaricious bone crusher!'

Sloper thought for a moment and put out his hand. 'You have a flicking bargain.' They shook hands warily. 'Now, shog off, Phil. Eleven and a half, Pickering House, Strand.'

'Christ's seeds, Francis! Am I dung-brained? I'll be there.'

★

To make sure there was no room for error, Tom left Blackmore Street in plenty of time. Fondly kissing Lucy and telling her not to worry, he closed the door behind him at about a quarter to eleven and strolled towards Drury Lane and the Strand. By the time he had reached Pickering House it had stopped raining and a stiff breeze had sprung up from the south-west. He loitered in a side alley until shortly after half past eleven, when he watched Lord Banbury and Justice Fuller emerging from the stable yard in a coach and turn left towards Charing Cross and Westminster.

His heart pounding, Tom crossed the road and tried the gates. To his relief, they swung open at his touch, allowing him to enter. Leaving them ajar, he walked quickly round the side of the house and in through the garden door. He had not seen a soul.

Seconds later, he was upstairs and tapping at Lady Elizabeth's door. It opened an inch or two.

'Who is there?'

'A poor lawyer, your ladyship.'

Elizabeth threw the door wide open. 'Why, Tom,' she exclaimed, grabbing him by the hand and pulling him into the room, 'how did you get into the house?' She was wearing a tight-fitting, silken gown which did little to hide the contours of her body.

Tom placed his hands on her hips and leaned against her. The thrill of the plot coupled with sexual adventure had wound him to a pitch of fervour he had not previously experienced. He felt his breeches would burst with desire. 'How did I get in, Elizabeth?' he panted. 'I know secret ways in.' He slipped her gown from her shoulders.

'You do? Perhaps my lovely boy will show me the secret entrances?' She stepped away from the crumpled silk at her feet and started to unfasten his shirt.

'I think,' he muttered slowly, sliding his hand down her stomach, 'that there is a secret passage – here?'

Elizabeth Banbury sighed with pleasure.

Shortly after Tom had disappeared through the stable gates, John sauntered up and slipped in the same way. Two minutes later, the front door opened and he signalled to Sloper to begin his watch. He then went back inside and shut the door.

After allowing sufficient time for John to climb the stairs to Sarah's room, Sloper abandoned his vantage point opposite, strode across the street, up the steps and let himself in. He was carrying a folded sack. Once inside, he looked about him. No one was about.

His eyes alighted on a large coffer in the hallway. Kneeling beside it, he tried the lid. Locked! From his pocket he drew a blunt chisel and levered away at the fastening. The mechanism soon broke. He lifted the lid and peered inside.

Leaning against the public pump about fifty yards further up the Strand in the direction of Ludgate Hill, Sloper's accomplice Phil drank idly from a bottle and kept a wary eye on the traffic passing before him. Easy as picking your nose, he said to himself, glancing casually in the direction of Westminster.

He looked again. Faith! Some slave is driving like a man from Bedlam, he thought. A large coach was approaching at great speed down the middle of the road. He narrowed his eyes. God's light! It was Banbury's vehicle! He made to cross the street, but it was too late. The coach would get there before him.

As it floundered to a halt in a welter of mud and puddle

water, four men carrying an assortment of heavy weapons jumped from the doors. Phil shrugged, spat into the road, took another swig from his bottle and wandered off towards the city.

v

Sloper was the first to die.

Pushing open the front door, Fuller caught him kneeling beside the coffer, pushing a silver goblet into his sack. He jumped up as soon as he was discovered but, by chance, as he did so the sleeve of his coat caught in the broken mechanism of the lock, preventing him from running away.

'We have him, sir,' said Perkin, brandishing his club and advancing towards the trapped thief.

'Stand back, you fool!' cried Fuller. 'He will kill you if you move too close!' While he was speaking, he was setting up his arquebus on the banisters. When Sloper saw what was intended, he danced about even more furiously, trying to free himself, and screaming for mercy.

Suddenly there was a loud explosion. The glass in the windows shook and the hall filled with black, acrid smoke. As it cleared, the remains of Sloper's broken body could be seen beside the coffer. Hit at almost point-blank range, the force of the shot had thrown him back against the wall. Now he lay slumped against the panelling like a rag doll, with a gaping, bloody hole in the middle of his chest. His right hand was still fastened about the stem of the silver-gilt goblet.

Perkin sat on the stairs and vomited between his legs. Ignoring him, Fuller went up to the body. 'Slave!' he muttered. 'Now you have learned not to stand in the way of the law.' As he bent down to recover the goblet, he added quietly, 'But I wish you had been another.'

Without warning, he spun round. 'Get up, bantam!' he yelled at Perkin. 'Search the house! Drive the murderer down here that I may slay him!'

While Perkin dragged himself upstairs, wiping his mouth on his sleeve, Fuller took up his pistols and stood guard beside the bleeding corpse.

Startled by the thief's cries and the subsequent noise of the gun, Tom and Elizabeth had been obliged to break off their love-making with uncomfortable haste. As Elizabeth slipped into a gown, Tom threw on his clothes and opened the dressing-room door a fraction. He heard the sound of Perkin's footsteps mounting the stairs.

'God's eyes!' he cursed, closing the door and wondering what on earth had gone wrong with John's plan. 'The house is gone mad! How can I escape?'

Moving over to a door on the other side of the room, Elizabeth said, 'Just as you know secret passages, my handsome lover, so do I. Here, this goes to the servants' stairway.' She pulled open the door. 'Descend to the passage and climb through the window at the end. I have been told it can be done.'

Tom kissed her once more and fled. The window, screened by a hedge, gave onto the garden at the back of the house. Peering round the bushes, he saw Lord Banbury standing in a flower bed waving a gun. As he watched, the window of Sarah's room slid open and Great John appeared on the sill with Sarah standing beside him.

Reaching for the creeper, John began to climb down towards the ground. He was a sitting target. Lord Banbury shouted something, there was a loud bang and he fell backwards among the flowers. John tumbled to the ground. To Tom's intense relief, he struggled to his feet and ran off towards the river, leaving the prostrate Banbury shaking his fist at him in impotent fury.

Tom had seen enough. Keeping behind the hedge, he too headed south. Scaling an orchard wall, he caught sight of John ahead of him. He thought of calling out, but afraid his voice would be recognised, he decided to save his breath for flight.

Five minutes later, panting heavily, he lowered himself over the perimeter wall and came to the Thames. Fortunately, it was low tide, and he was able to wade upstream through the mud and rushes for half a mile, then cut back north towards Westminster. By late afternoon, filthy dirty and thoroughly exhausted, he arrived home. It was only when he sat trying to explain to Lucy what had happened, that he realised he had lost his hat in the garden of Pickering House.

As it happened, at that moment the discovery of a stray felt hat in the long grass of his orchard was the least of Lord Banbury's worries. Lying in the rose bed where he had been thrown by the recoil of his arquebus, he had been distressed by two sights. The first was John making off into the distance. The second was Justice Fuller leaning out of the window of his daughter's room.

'Whoreson villain!' the peer screamed at the back of the fleeing giant. Wondering anxiously whether he was expected to set off in pursuit, he looked at the window and confessed, 'I missed, Fuller.'

'Not entirely, my lord,' the magistrate replied, his face rigidly inscrutable. 'You have just killed my daughter.'

TWELVE

ROYSTON

i

Lady Elizabeth Banbury, twenty-eight years old, second and most attractive daughter of Sir Henry Weston of Caliborne Hall, Northamptonshire, was both confused and unhappy. Ever since her childhood, when a mean-minded governess had insisted the whole day be set aside for needlework, an occupation which Elizabeth found indescribably boring, she had disliked Mondays. And this Monday was turning out worse than most.

It had begun promisingly enough. Her ridiculous husband, apparently preoccupied with some little scheme concocted by his nasty new magistrate friend, Justice Christopher Fuller, had left her alone. And she had spent a pleasant morning looking forward to shedding some of her passionate frustration in the company of her charming and well-connected young friend, Thomas Verney. But unfortunately Verney's arrival had proved the day's high point. Shortly afterwards things had begun to move rapidly and disastrously downhill.

First, roused to fever pitch by Tom's caresses, she had been abandoned on the threshold of Paradise when the sound of shouting, shooting and other commotion had necessitated his hasty withdrawal. Having directed him to a passage infinitely less welcoming – but perhaps rather safer – than that which he had just left, she had emerged from her room and ventured downstairs in the direction of the noise. In the entrance hall she had found Fuller gloating over the body of a thief he had just shot. Judging by the mutilated state of the corpse, which had most of its chest blown away, the poor fellow had stood little chance. Before they had exchanged more than a couple of sentences, the sound of a second shot had come from the back of the house. On hearing the sound, Fuller had immediately pushed her aside without explanation or apology and dashed upstairs to the room of his daughter Sarah. Keen to see what was going on, Elizabeth had followed the magistrate at a safe distance, reaching the broken door of Sarah's room just in time to see Fuller emerging. For a second, as he paused on the threshold, she thought that he too had been shot. His lower lip was jerking nervously, there was a glazed stare in his eyes and a strange, insincere smile on his twitching mouth. Then, muttering incoherently about fornication, popery, wages, sin and death, he had walked straight past Lady Elizabeth without seeming to notice her and retired to his room.

Elizabeth had immediately entered Sarah's room, where she had found the girl's dead body, shot neatly through the head. In a state of partial shock, she had summoned the servants and gone to the open window to ascertain the cause of the din coming from the garden.

She had seen her unprepossessing, middle-aged husband sober and she had seen him drunk; she had seen him in sickness and in health; she had seen him depressed and she had seen him joyous. In fact, after eleven years of marriage she had become so accustomed to his moods and eccentricities that she had thought there was nothing he could do to surprise or shock her further.

She had been wrong.

On first looking out of the window, she had thought a giant hedgehog had somehow got into the garden and was snuffling about the flower bed directly below her. But closer inspection had revealed that the creature was not a hedgehog, but her husband, curled up into a ball and rolling wildly about among the roses, blubbering and uttering low wailing noises. His clothing was torn, filthy dirty and covered in broken pieces of stem, giving the effect of spines. A couple of gardeners stood around staring at the apparition, unsure what to do. Peter the butler, the only one present who had appeared to be in command of his senses, was shouting orders to a kitchen boy and pointing towards the distant river.

Confused and still numb with the shock of Sarah's death, with the greatest difficulty Elizabeth had forced herself to go down into the garden, pick her husband out of the dirt and escort him gibbering back to the house. Having ascertained from Ned the cause of his master's distress, she had seen him to his rooms and ordered that he be cleaned up and well plied with drink. She then left, tears streaming down her face. To most observers these were the outward manifestation of wifely pity for her husband at this time of great misfortune. In reality they were tears of mourning and despair.

Now, back in her private sitting room, as she looked out at the sun setting over the distant towers and spires of Westminster, Elizabeth tried to come to terms with what had gone on. Although Fuller's jealousy had allowed them little time alone together, over the past few days she had become attached to Sarah Fuller. She had enjoyed having another woman of her own generation in the house and found they had much in common. The more she had heard of Sarah's story, the more she had come to admire the girl's fortitude. As a consequence, her sudden and horrible accidental death was deeply distressing to the young baroness. She was further upset that the tragic killing should have been caused by the incompetence of her own husband. Nor had his hysterical display in the rose garden made it any easier to feel sympathy for him.

Gradually, however, as Elizabeth thought more carefully about what her husband had been doing, she realised that there remained several rather important unanswered questions. She now knew that at about noon three things had been happening simultaneously in Pickering House – an attempt to rescue the unfortunate Sarah, a theft and her own little dalliance with Tom. What she did not know, yet dearly wished to, was how they related to each other, if at all. Had her lover used his affair with her to allow others access to the house? Where did the thief fit in? Furthermore, if, as seemed to be the case, her husband and Fuller had received warning of what was afoot, did they also know that Tom had been in the house? There were too many mysteries for Elizabeth's liking.

Telling herself that Sarah would have approved of what she was doing, she tidied herself and went downstairs to see if she could find out more.

Lady Elizabeth found that while she had been in her room Fuller and her husband had come downstairs and repaired to the Crimson Closet, the room his lordship reserved for times of great emotional or physical crisis. Normally, as when Tom had met him there, that meant those mornings when his hangover was more than usually debilitating. But today, as Elizabeth noticed the moment she entered, the situation was completely different. Though Banbury had adopted his pose customary for times of despair – lying prostrate, belly-up on the couch – his pale face, marked with the cuts and scratches of rose thorns, was more than usually animated. Opposite him Fuller was sitting bolt upright in a hard-backed chair, his knees pressed together, only the toes of his shoes resting on the floor. His elbows were tucked tightly to his sides, his hands clasped rigidly before him. Just as it had done when she saw him leaving Sarah's room, his lower lip was twitching violently. Both men were staring fixedly at a hat resting on a low table between them. Elizabeth recognised it at once.

Tiptoeing across to the couch, she knelt before her husband and cooed, 'Oh, my poor Banby! Is my little sweetie otter-baby in better spirits now? Should he be sitting here in this nasty dark room?' She laid a hand gently on his arm. 'Come now! It was not the fault of the valiant soldier that the poor girl stood in the path of his ball.'

'Poor girl?' asked Fuller sharply. 'Which poor girl, pray, my lady?'

Elizabeth spoke without turning round. She was afraid her intense dislike of the man would show on her face. 'Why, sir, the poor girl your daughter. Who is most unhappily slain.'

'"The wages of sin is death" – St Paul's epistle to the Romans.' Fuller's voice was remote and icy cold. 'She was a whore and had to die. God decreed it thus.'

'She died through my husband's ill aim, not the hand of God.' Elizabeth felt anger rising within her.

'The hand of God directed the arquebus,' replied Fuller.

'That is correct, my tripping vole,' interjected Banbury before his wife could reply. 'Fuller has explained to me that for a second I was an agent of the Almighty. I felt His power! Hallelujah!'

Elizabeth could not believe her ears – where was the jabbering, semi-atheistic nincompoop of a husband whom she had dragged indoors a few hours previously? She looked up to see his face transfixed with an idiotic, far-off grin. Under his breath he continued to mutter, 'agent of the Almighty, agent of the Almighty', over and over again.

She stood up. 'Justice Fuller,' she said, her voice uncompromisingly hard, 'what is the meaning of this?'

'Meaning, my lady?'

'What is my husband saying?' She tried hard not to stare at the contorting spasms playing like lightning across the magistrate's lean face.

'Lady Banbury, do you not see? Today has been a day of holy wonder. God has shown Himself to us. We are marked men. He warned us the idolaters would be here, and He permitted me to slay one. When the other fled, He chose to put an end to the serpent in our midst—'

Elizabeth could restrain herself no longer. 'In the name of pity, Justice! That girl was no serpent but your only daughter! The fruit of the womb of your departed wife! If not for your own sake, then for that of her dear soul, I pray you speak not so unkindly of Sarah! She is dead, sir! Dead!' She sat down in a chair, trying hard to regain control of herself.

Fuller scarcely moved. His eyes became blacker, his twitch more pronounced. 'Look at your husband, Lady Banbury.' Through the tears welling in her eyes, she glanced at the Toad's inane, bloated face, all scratched and torn. 'Do you not see the marks of the crown of thorns?

It is a sure sign that he was the agent of Almighty God.'

'He rolled in the rose bushes,' she protested.

Banbury himself joined in. 'I know, my petal. That is pre-cisely what I said. But Fuller asked me why, why did I do it? I said I did not know, I just fell. He explicated the meaning of it all. The sound, the flash, the mighty force of God pushing my arquebus into the air and casting me to the ground.' He gingerly felt the cuts around his scalp. 'I have looked in the glass – I am just like Jesus.' His voice sank to a whisper. 'Sir Julius Pickering, baronet, like Jesus Christ! Fuller says so, too.'

Elizabeth had had enough. She rose and walked towards the door. 'Before you take your leave, Lady Banbury,' Fuller asked when she reached the door, 'may I ask whether you recognise this hat?'

She opened the door and looked back. 'I do.' She felt angry and reckless, eager to wound any way she could.

'Bessie, my angel,' Banbury said, 'would you be so kind as to tell the justice and myself whose it is?'

'I will.'

'And to whom does it belong, Lady Banbury?'

'It is the hat of Thomas Verney. A man whom I understand to be quite sane.' She closed the door quietly behind her, muttering, 'Which is more than I can say for two others I know.'

'There, my lord,' said Fuller as soon as she had gone, 'what did I say? It is the hat of that young fellow. The consort of thieves and friend of papists. I am sure of it.'

Banbury stared. 'Why was he in my garden? I will call my wife again and ask her.'

'No, my lord. Do not trouble her, I pray. We must discover the truth, as they say, from the horse's mouth. You must summon Verney himself. In the name of God and the true religion, it is our heavenly duty to find the truth.'

ii

Although wilful, Lady Elizabeth was neither callous nor unintelligent. At the age of seventeen she had married Lord Banbury partly because, in her innocence, she had found him amusing, partly because she had been attracted by his wealth, and partly because her father, whom she loved dearly as long as he was not telling her what to do, had advised against the match. She had realised her mistake six hours after Lord Banbury's large and vulgar ring had been slipped over her finger, and six minutes after his similarly large and vulgar body had slipped into bed beside her that evening. The following morning, still very much a virgin, she had made three resolutions. One – never again, if she could help it, would she make a lifelong commitment to anyone or anything. Two – she would resist the almost overwhelming temptation to humiliate her husband in public, and strive to maintain a façade of domestic harmony as long as he continued to dote on her and treat her well. Three – her marriage notwithstanding, she would enjoy life to the full.

For almost eleven years she had kept her word. With consummate skill and no little pleasure, she had led a fulfilling double life. In public she was Banbury's 'sweet Bessie'; in private she was many other things, none of them Banbury's. He still worshipped the very ground she stood upon; she still spent his money and revelled in the luxurious lifestyle which it provided. Although any vestige of respect she might once have felt for him had long since evaporated, she had never told him to his face what she thought of him. It would have served no purpose. She would be lost without his money. Besides, she was essentially kind-hearted and feared, possibly correctly, that the truth might deal his already shrivelled inner confidence a blow from which it would never recover.

But as she walked slowly back to her rooms after meeting with Fuller and her husband in the Crimson Closet, she was aware that things were starting to change. For a while now, almost without realising it, she had become increasingly dissatisfied with the superficiality of her existence. It was not the silly game she played with her husband that worried her so much as what she did with the rest of her time, which she regarded as her real life. Talking with Sarah Fuller had brought this home to her – for all the girl's hardship and suffering, or even because of it, she had appeared to have had a purpose to her life. This had increased Elizabeth's feeling of worthlessness. She too wanted a cause, a reason for her being. Her conventional Anglicanism was founded on little more than social necessity and a vague fear of death. She had never become pregnant and was beginning to think she never would. So what else was there? She thought of the mysterious events of the past twelve hours, of the twitching puritan and the worrying religious mania which had come over her husband. Although she did not like Sir Julius any more than she had done, she found that she had an almost proprietorial concern that he should not come to harm, particularly at the hand of the sinister, exploitive Fuller. It was almost as if her Banby was becoming the child she had never borne.

More as a mark of respect for the dead Sarah than for herself, with a toss of the head and a resolute grin to herself in the mirror, she made up her mind to get to the bottom of what was going on. That, she decided, was reason enough for her existence. For the time being, anyway.

Tom was requested to call on Lord Banbury on the morning of 7th April. Two days previously he had ascertained from officials at St James's that the court had now moved back to Royston and he had planned to be out of town on the day of Banbury's invitation. But wishing to clear up the matter of his hat before he left, he chose to remain in London a while longer and so presented himself at Pickering House at ten in the morning on the day appointed.

The moment he entered the house, he realised something was wrong. The footman, normally an exhibition of colourful gaiety, was dressed in a black coat and matching hose. Around the plaster breasts and loins of the statue of a naked nymph which adorned the inner vestibule, someone had draped a modest shawl. Tom was taken to the principal reception room, where he found that a similar exercise in censorship had been performed on the *Sabine Women*, which now sported leafy tunics. Banbury, dressed in a robe-like garment of shimmering black silk, sat beside Justice Fuller, wearing his customary old-fashioned jerkin and breeches of sombre hue.

Taking the mood from his hosts, Tom offered muted greetings, sat down and enquired after the reason for the mourning. The explanation for this and the reason why he had been asked to call at this difficult time, were given by Fuller. He spoke in short, clipped sentences. Tom noticed that in the interval since he had last seen him, he had developed a nervous twitch in his lower lip. Banbury sat in silence, glowing like a gross luminous totem.

The news of the death of the thief and the shooting of Sarah sent Tom's mind reeling. Poor, poor John! he thought. He could not bear to think what he would do now. And who was this thief? Surely John had not reverted to his old ways at such a time? But he scarcely had time to take in what Fuller had said and start to ponder what it meant before the magistrate stood up and walked towards him.

'Now, Master Verney,' he said, staring down with burning black eyes, 'have you lost an item of apparel?'

'Yes. I have mislaid a hat.' He had prepared his answers carefully. Despite the rapidity with which the topic had been raised and the confusion engendered in him by the news of Sarah's death, he was able to reply quickly and with confidence. 'I believe it may have been left here.'

Fuller leaned forward eagerly. 'You were here? When, pray?'

'On the very same Monday, when all those terrible things happened.' He met Fuller's gaze unflinching.

The magistrate turned and walked slowly back to his seat. 'I pray you excuse my prying, Master Verney, but his lordship and I believe you may have seen something which could be of help to us.'

'I am eager to please, of course.'

'I see. Would you – kindly – tell us when – precisely – you were here?' The words rapped at him like gunshots.

'In the morning, shortly after eleven o'clock.' The inquiry was drawing too close for Tom's comfort. He needed to bring it to a close, now. 'Really, my lord,' he expostulated indignantly to Banbury, 'I have called here out of courtesy and find my self on a rack!'

The baronet opened his mouth to reply, but Fuller cut him short. Ignoring Tom's complaint, he continued, 'I was here at that hour. Lord Banbury was here at that hour. We did not see you, sir.'

Tom thought fast. He had not expected such detailed, penetrating questions. 'No. I entered through the stable gate and came to the gardens.' He decided to gamble. 'There I chanced to meet with Lady Banbury. She said the gentlemen – yourself and Lord Banbury – were shortly to leave for dinner, so we walked together for a few minutes. Then I departed.' He turned to the baronet and tried again to end the inquiry. 'My lord, you have such a modest, dutiful wife!'

For a second time Fuller got in before Banbury could speak, 'Indeed. You saw no one else?'

Tom smiled. 'I saw no one else.'

Finally, Banbury managed to say something. 'Well, Justice,' he said, speaking as if waking from a dream, 'now let me call my Bessie. I am always burning to set eyes on her' – he paused and glanced at Fuller – 'with due, holy purity, of course. She will uphold what Master Verney has said, and that will be an end to the matter.' Such was his eagerness to see his wife, radiant in her mourning, that for once he managed to override Fuller when the magistrate suggested it might be wiser if they spoke to Lady Banbury alone. Rising, the baronet walked to the servants' door and called for a housemaid to send Lady Banbury his compliments, but would she be so good as to attend on his lordship for a minute? The three stood in silence, waiting anxiously for the vital witness to appear.

As soon as her footsteps sounded in the hallway, Fuller stood up. But Tom was too fast for him. Springing from his chair, he crossed the room with a few quick strides and placed himself between the magistrate and the door. Thus positioned, he was the first person Elizabeth saw as she entered.

Both men began addressing her loudly the moment she came in. Although neither could be heard clearly, it was only a second before she had worked out what was happening.

'Good sirs,' she said, raising her hands in mock horror, 'what is this?' Needing time to think, she went over to her husband and asked, 'Now, my sweet Banby darling, would you tell your poor little Bessie what these quarrelling gentlemen are about?' She kissed him on the cheek.

'My wife, my one earthly treasure! It is the affair of the hat again. Justice Fuller wishes to know whether you met Master Verney, as he says, in the garden of this house after ten o'clock—'

'—eleven,' corrected Fuller.

'—after eleven o'clock on the day that the Lord God took it upon Himself to act through my hands.'

'Monday,' Fuller explained, in case Elizabeth's secular mind had not grasped her husband's meaning.

Her response remained printed on Tom's mind for many years. Drawing back her shoulders and walking slowly over to Fuller, she stood only inches away from him and stared into his eyes. For well nigh half a minute she stood there, breathing deeply but not saying a word. It was a truly magnificent performance, and one which Fuller had no answer to. Eventually, he coughed and turned away, his face blazing with shame and hatred, his lower lip working like a weaver's bobbin. Elizabeth then turned to Tom and did the same. He did not move. But neither, with Fuller staring straight at him, did he dare to make any sign that might betray Elizabeth or himself. Instead, he opened his eyes wide and prayed that 'yes' was written upon them.

He need not have worried. Elizabeth was enjoying herself. She had remembered being asked about the hat in the Crimson Closet on the day of the shootings, and now that her husband had clumsily told her Tom's version of events, it was easy for her to endorse that story, for her own sake as well as his. But in due course, she told herself, by way of recompense she would expect him to tell her everything else he knew of the events of that sorry day.

'Yes,' she said eventually, speaking with supreme innocence but somehow contriving to let the word slip from her lips like a kiss. Turning and going to stand behind her husband, she continued, 'I do recall speaking with Master Verney. In the storm that followed I clean forgot the meeting, though I remember the justice asking me about a hat afterwards. I thought the matter of no consequence.'

She smiled as a mischievous embellishment came to mind. 'Master Verney was in high spirits that day. Saying he had grown tired of his hat, which was not of the latest fashion, he cast it into the grass, saying he would leave it to adorn some badger, or toad.'

'Precisely!' added Tom, feeling as if he had just been let out of prison. 'I did not say what my lady has just told you for fear you would think me foolish. But now you know.' For a second his eyes met Elizabeth's in a glance of profound gratitude.

'I trust we do,' replied Fuller, looking darkly down at his feet.

The gathering lasted only a few minutes longer. Elizabeth left first, followed a few minutes later by Tom, who was eager to get home. As soon as he had gone, Fuller ran to the servants' door and called harshly for a fellow named Spid.

'Go, Spid,' he commanded, as soon as the man appeared, 'follow Master Verney as before. This time do not lose him. I wish to know where he goes, whom he meets, what he does.'

By the time Spid had reached the front of the house,

Tom was already several yards down the Strand. As a result, the spy had not seen a window swing open above Tom's head as he walked out of the building, nor had he heard a female voice call softly down, 'Thomas Verney, you rogue! Your guardian angel bids you farewell, trusting that one day soon you will repay her with the true story.'

Tom was so relieved at having escaped from Pickering House without serious difficulty that the possibility of his being followed did not cross his mind. Consequently, Spid had no trouble trailing him to Blackmore Street. Then, having sat on his pony outside the house for a further two hours and seen no one leave or enter, he returned to his master. To his surprise, his report was received by Fuller with delight and by Lord Banbury with incredulity. It was only when the magistrate explained that this meant Tom was leading a duplicitous life, that the peer understood the significance of the discovery.

'Think what this means, my lord,' Fuller urged.

'I believed him to be residenced at Clement's Inn,' Banbury mumbled, 'but now I learn he is not. His lies have deceived me.' His face assumed a pious expression. 'I suppose he has broken a commandment.'

'More, my lord! More!' Fuller cried. 'Why is he there? Who is he with? God be praised for leading us to a nest of papist vipers. I will have a warrant drawn up on the morrow and the house searched. Let us kneel in grateful prayer to the Almighty.'

As Banbury lowered himself painfully to his knees, he could not help wondering why Fuller was so certain that Tom was a papist. It did not make sense to him at all. But since God had clearly singled out Sir Julius Pickering, Lord Banbury, to play a vital part in the fight against sin and Romanism, the peer decided it would be best for him to keep quiet and let himself be led by the crusading magistrate.

In the middle of the following morning, Spid and two local constables known for their anti-Catholic views arrived at Blackmore Street and hammered on Lucy's front door. The presence of an armed troop – the constables boasted cumbersome halberds and their commander a brace of finely decorated German matchlock pistols – attracted a small crowd of passers-by, eager to see what new scandal the tailor's house had to offer.

House Martin opened the door. The searchers burst in, pushing him aside and spreading out through the house. The lad's cries and sound of heavy feet on the stairs brought Lucy hurrying from the workshop.

'How now!' she cried, backing towards the door she had just come through. 'Help! Thieves! Help, help!' Eager to see what the noise was about, some of the crowd approached closer and peered in through the street door.

'Nay,' interrupted Spid, whose squeaky voice matched his diminutive, jockey-like figure, 'stifle your squealing, lady.' To the disappointment of the crowd, he closed the front door. 'We are no thieves, but true Christian officers of the law, come to seek out the papist vermin sheltering in this kennel of sin. See here—' He held out the warrant provided for him by a London magistrate sympathetic to Fuller's cause.

Glancing down at the paper, Lucy retorted, 'Kennel of sin? Papists in this house? What in the name of St Peter do you mean by all this, you blockhead?'

Spid stayed where he was. Only his eyes moved, flickering round the room and beyond into the workshop, looking for signs of danger. At his side his thin fingers shifted uneasily around the triggers of his smouldering matchlocks.

From the bedroom came the rough grating noise of furniture being moved. Throwing down the warrant, Lucy made a dash for the stairs.

'Stand!' screamed Spid, raising his weapons. 'I am loath to shoot a woman. But I have done so before and will do so again, if God wills it. Here you shall remain until we have found what we came for.'

For a second Lucy thought of testing his resolution, but abandoned the idea after a single glance at her warder. There was more pity in the eyes of a snake than in the whole of that cold, pinched and pock-marked visage.

Flushed and breathing heavily, she stood at the foot of the stairs and listened in impotent fury to the sound of destruction going on about her. After a further minute, she could stand it no longer. 'Just wait, sir, till my husband hears of this,' she fumed. 'Mr Verney left for court this very morning. He has friends in the highest places and will not hesitate to see you whipped for this insolence.'

She noticed with pleasure that her words had found a chink in Spid's armour. An uneasy look entered his eyes. 'Mr Verney is your husband? And he has gone to the royal court?' he asked, trying unsuccessfully to sound sarcastic. He thought for a moment. Then, without taking his eyes off Lucy, he called, 'Here, Moses! Ben! Come here!'

Moses lumped heavily downstairs. Ben came in from the workshop, preceded by House Martin, whom he had been using as a shield in case of ambush.

'Well?' barked Spid.

'Nothing,' Moses growled.

'Only cloth,' said Ben angrily, 'and this damned wriggling, biting boy!' He cuffed House Martin across the ear, knocking him to his knees.

Spid pressed further. 'No holes, no passages, no covert hiding places?'

'Maybe,' Ben explained, 'but we need time. And levers to pull up the floor. And poles to push into the roof—'

Lucy's anger boiled over. 'Never!' she screamed at Moses, going right up to him. 'You slave!' She spun round. 'Leave this house, the three of you! There are no papists here, just a defenceless boy and a woman with child. Are they fit meat for pursuivant folly?' She singled out Spid. 'You heard, sir! Get you gone, dwarf! Now! Or you will have yet more cause to regret what you have done.'

Glancing at each other, the intruders turned and started to slope off towards the front door. Lucy pursued them all the way, nipping at their heels like a terrier. 'I will write this day to Mr Verney and ask him to speak with the king. Return to your Justice Webb and tell him that! This is an honest household of true Christian people. It is no place for prying, ant-brained serpents such as yourselves. Avaunt, ignorant spies! Woodworms!'

Shouting the last word at the top of her voice, she slammed the door shut, bolted it and went to make a written record of the damage the interlopers had left behind.

Spid had not looked forward to announcing to Fuller and Banbury that his search had come up with nothing. He eked out his account of the morning's work for a full fifteen minutes, trying to put off what he was sure would be a furious response from his master. Yet when he had finally finished and stood there writhing and glancing about as if the ceiling were about to fall, he was surprised to see Fuller's lean face contorted into something approaching a smile.

'Repeat!' he commanded, his lip twitching furiously. 'Whom did you meet with?'

'A boy, sir. And his mistress.'

'I know, I know. Her name?'

'Mistress Verney, sir.'

'You are certain she is the wife of Mr Verney, whom you followed thither but yesterday?'

'The very same, sir. She told me so herself. To be certain, when we left I asked a neighbour if it were so. She said she had seen the marriage paper.'

Fuller gave what could only be described as a whoop of delight. 'Whoa-ho! We have him now. You may go.'

Turning to Banbury the moment Spid had left, he clasped him by the hand and cried, 'Manna from heaven, my lord! All that was required!'

Suddenly he stiffened. He stood bolt upright, his hands clenched before him, his eyes screwed shut. 'Almighty God,' he prayed rapidly and with more passion in his voice than Banbury had ever heard before, 'I beseech you accept the thanks of thine unworthy servant Christopher for providing him with a rod for the beating of his enemies. Teach him to use it aright, I pray. Show him that it has not been provided solely for chastising Master Verney. Reveal to him its purpose as a heavenly lever with which to force the cover from John Beelzebub himself!'

Ah! thought Banbury. Now I understand. So the game is holy blackmail, is it? Standing beside Fuller, he too shut his eyes and joined in the prayer — though with not quite so much enthusiasm — for further success in their battle with the evil one.

iii

Tom arrived at Royston later the same day. The journey,

a dismal trudge along muddy roads through ceaseless squally rain, had been one of the most unpleasant he had endured, and it was with considerable relief that within an hour of his arrival he found himself accommodated in spacious chambers within the palace and given an opportunity to wash, change his clothes and dine. The reception proved deceptive. Over the course of the next twenty-four hours he learned that his unpleasant ride, not his initial welcome, was the more accurate omen for the way the visit was to develop.

As always, James seemed pleased to see him. But he was more preoccupied than ever with the fates of his son and favourite, who had now arrived in Spain but were, by all reports, finding it difficult to make much headway in the marriage negotiations. At the oddest times and in the most awkward situations the king would suddenly remember his absent 'sweet boys' and lose all concentration on the matter in hand. The slightest thing could trigger him off. On one occasion, while being introduced to an ambassador from the United Provinces, the unfortunate man happened to mention that he had brought His Majesty a gift of some prints.

'Prints?' James had sighed, rolling his eyes and gazing up at the ceiling. 'Or prince? Oh! We would ye had brought us the latter, sir! Not paper, but flesh. What similar words do separate such dissimilar substances. Fie! We are come over quite faint when we think how our darling wee laddies do suffer in the heat and grease of a papist land. Are no letters come today? Ah! We will retire to await them.'

Nonplussed, the Dutch diplomat was ushered from the room.

A week later, on hearing a group of musicians performing one of Buckingham's favourite airs, James was so overcome that his howling drowned out the sound of the music, obliging the players to stop and begin another, less affecting tune.

Tom's position was further complicated by his not knowing exactly where he stood. The king had found a new nickname for him – 'Tom o' the wisp' – because, he said, he never knew where or when he would appear. 'Are ye a courtier, or a lawyer, or just a young gallant, eh, Verney?' he had quipped shortly after Tom's arrival, forcing him to admit that he did not rightly know.

'Well,' James had replied, somewhat petulantly, 'ye needs decide. How can your fond old dad place his affections on a head that is always a-bobbing in and out of his sight like a cork in the ocean?'

Remarks like this, and James's failure to make any reference to what he had previously said about marriage, made it very difficult for Tom to judge when it might be appropriate for him to mention Lucy. Once or twice he had dropped what he thought were heavy hints, but none was taken up. In the end, growing desperate, he decided to raise the issue unequivocally. He chose his moment carefully. Accompanied by only a handful of courtiers, Tom among them, early one sunny afternoon James had decided to inspect the gardens which were being relaid to the west of the palace. Having that morning received an encouraging letter from Buckingham, he was in good spirits.

'Your Majesty,' began Tom, walking by the king's side along the gravel drive leading to the gardens from the front entrance to the palace, 'may I crave Your Majesty's humble blessing on a venture of mine?'

James took his arm. 'Oh, a venture, eh? The blessing of a king is balm indeed. Speak on, Tom o' the wisp. For what would ye be blessed?'

Tom took a deep breath. 'Sire, when first I came to London from the country—'

'Stratton Whore-dilly, was it not?'

'Ha-ha! Even so, Your Majesty, though I neither dillied nor dallied with whores there.' Tom was pleased with the way he was learning to respond to the king's crude humour.

'Come, this blessing, Verney,' urged James with a smile. He was never happier than when feeling needed. 'What is it for?'

'In London I met this sweet young maid, sire, whom I wished to marry.'

'Aye?' The ears of everyone present burned to catch Tom's response. Whatever it was, scandalous or otherwise, it would make a good story.

'But she is not of my station, sire. She is but the daughter of a tailor. Yet I love her—'

'It will pass, Verney.' Tom felt James's fingers fix upon his arm like claws. 'Ye have sidled upon us with this subject before, but we have chosen to look aside, hoping that ye would take heed and leave off. Now we understand your country bluntness will not be parried. Listen, Thomas. We will be brief, for we had rather contemplate the newly fashioned statue of the darling boy set in the lavender garden than your rash heart and loins.'

Those about the king chuckled politely. Tom blushed, aware that news of his rejection would be all over Royston by nightfall. While he held his head to one side as if listening attentively to what the king had to say, he heard only the rumble and crash of falling masonry, as stone by stone, brick by brick, the future he had constructed so optimistically crumbled to the ground in a useless pile of dust and rubble. He felt hot and sick, and like a stricken animal, longed to run away and hide.

'Consider all God's great universe, Thomas. What is it that binds it together? Why, order, degree, custom, law and office are the mortars of every life, the foundations of all enterprises. Does Mars fly off to the sun because his heart is smitten with her warmth? Does the tide stay in flood because it loves the land? Do squirrels mate with rats? Do kings marry milk-maids? No, Thomas! In His infinite wisdom God has decreed that all have their places, all have their courses. When Man defies that which God has ordained, he brings ruin, destruction, plague, famine and death. Remember what followed the first great disobedience in the garden of Eden, eh? Wise men do not make the same mistake twice. Forget this tailor's daughter, Thomas, for there are plenty more does in the forest.'

Tom's misery was written all over his face.

'Come now, Thomas, look not so sad! It displeases us and makes us think of our own sorrow. Lead us with a smile, bumpkin Verney, to the pretty boy in stone.'

As he had feared, within hours Tom's rejected request became the gossip of the court. Later the same day, as he was wandering through the garden on his own, unsure what to do or where to go, but keen to be alone, the olive-eyed Bishop Williams fell in step beside him. Thinking the figure to be a page or young gentleman of the bedchamber kindly come to sympathise at his misfortune, Tom did not immediately look up. It was only when the pragmatic cleric-keeper began to speak that he realised who he was.

'Are you a gamester, Verney?' It was an unusual way to begin a conversation, and had Tom not been so numbed by what had happened earlier in the day, he might have detected the warning ringing through the Welsh lilt.

'My lord, I crave your forgiveness. I did not see you

beside me,' he muttered, inwardly cursing the man for sneaking up on him when he had no wish for company.

'I asked, Verney, whether you are a gamester.' The tone was cold.

'Yes. I have wagered much on dogs and horses and cards, my lord. I enjoy the sport.'

For a while they walked on without a word. Where an ancient oak marked the frontier between formal garden and parkland, they turned left down a narrow path between some bushes, wide enough for only one person at a time. Williams went first, lifting the hem of his gown in places where the track became muddy, and addressing Tom over his shoulder. Evening was closing in and the wind had dropped. The birds were largely silent. Only the swish of clothes against the undergrowth and the squelch of boots through the patches of mire disturbed the stillness of the balmy spring evening.

Eventually Williams resumed his questioning.

'Are you irate, Verney, when something you wager much on fails you?'

'Sometimes, my lord,' said Tom, beginning to suspect where this was leading.

'So am I.' He stopped and turned round rapidly. 'I wagered on you, Verney. As did my lord treasurer. We believed you had comely looks, sharp wit, understanding and subtlety of manner sufficient to win the favour of His Majesty and retain it for favour of yourself and those who stood behind you. But we were mistaken. In that catalogue of qualities you have but the first listed – why, I do believe you would open your own front door with a ram if you were told it was a key!

'My lord of Middlesex and I are displeased. Do you grasp my meaning, or do I have to spell it out in country terms for you, blockhead?'

Tom could hardly believe his ears. Was it fair to kick a man while he was down? He had suffered enough for one day and although something told him he should respond, the fight had gone out of him. Standing impassively, he let the torrent of invective wash over him. After all, he reflected, it was only words. Yet more depressing words.

'I see you are dumb as well as stupid,' continued Williams. 'Well this is the end. Today you are the jest of the court and neither the treasurer nor I wish to have association with a fool. Look no more to us for favour, boy. Nor, I suggest, to anyone with half the wit of a camel. Verney, you are the leper of Royston. Get you gone!' With this final flourish of scorn, he stomped off down the path into the gathering gloom.

Before the bishop had completely vanished from sight, Tom recovered his composure sufficiently to shout after him, 'Farewell, you cheese-tongued mountain sponge! Go off into the devilish dark where you belong, for there is more of Christ in these trees than in your hellish heart. God rot you black!'

The unwise outburst raised Tom's spirits for a while. But as he stumbled back towards the palace he could feel melancholy, like a monster of the night, silently closing upon him from behind. Its breath clouded about his head, obscuring his vision. Its arms pulled him back, so that as he walked the warm and distant lights drew further away, not closer. Finally, in a glade beneath a spreading beech, it cast him down and left him weeping on the damp ground.

'Oh, God!' he sobbed, digging his fingers into the soft moss. 'It is at an end! Lucy, my love, what have I done to you? And my father and mother?' His tears fell like the waters of the palace fountains, though not so sweet. 'Almighty Father,' he groaned, 'have mercy on me, I beseech you. Help me, I pray. Help me. Oh, oh!'

iv

Sir Edward Conway, sometime soldier, now a principal secretary of state, was not pleased at the way things had been developing in council of late. Although he was aware of the man's faults, he admired the Marquis of Buckingham and resented the way Keeper Williams and Treasurer Cranfield were trying to take advantage of the favourite's absence by chipping away at his position. He realised that the marquis was almost certainly safe unless the king had a violent change of heart, which was most unlikely. Nevertheless, he felt that the magnates' attitude, patently based on nothing but ambitious self-interest, was damaging to the political health of the nation at this delicate time. For the last week or so he had been racking his brains in an effort to find a way of getting back at them.

On 12th April Conway was told an amusing story of how, the previous afternoon, a naive young courtier had tried to get the king's permission to marry a tailor's daughter. Initially Sir Edward had passed the tale off as just another piece of court tittle-tattle. But when he learned that the unfortunate young man was a student of Clement's Inn, where, he remembered, both Williams and Cranfield had relatives, he decided to follow the matter up. There was just a chance, he reasoned, that this young unfortunate, whom he knew from previous encounters to be no fool, might be able to give him some useful information. Moreover, he was old and wise enough to realise when told that Master Verney was sick in bed that the young man was probably suffering from nothing more contagious than embarrassment and melancholia. So he called round to see him straight away.

To Conway's surprise and delight, the meeting proved more fruitful than he had dared imagine. The most difficult part was getting Verney to admit him to his room. But when that had been done and he had won the lad's confidence by showing that he was prepared to listen to his difficulties with a sympathetic ear, he was given information that he could not have bought from all the professional spies in the country. Verney revealed that the treasurer's son, James Cranfield, was the leader of a band of young Roman Catholic zealots whose foul proceedings, which involved mocking the king and acts of extreme lewdness, were clearly treasonable. Equally useful was the fact that Keeper Williams' nephew, Leoline, was an active member of the same gang. The story, backed with dates, names and places, was almost certainly too well substantiated to be false. Conway felt like a card player who had been dealt a hand of aces. If it should ever come out that close relatives of two of the king's senior advisors were playing with treason, however flippantly, the careers of those ministers would be seriously blighted. As long as he used the information carefully, Conway knew, not only would he be able to keep Williams and Cranfield at bay, but he would also further his own career by demonstrating his usefulness to the favourite.

Politician he might have been, but Conway was also a just man, and in his delight he did not overlook his informant. By way of reward, he undertook to do Tom a number of favours. Firstly, he promised to get Cranfield and Williams to maintain their backing for Tom and to join the secretary of state in praising him before the king. This, Conway said, ought to mean a greater share of court perquisites coming Tom's way. It might also help persuade James to reverse his decision about the marriage.

Such was the king's obstinacy in such matters, however, Sir Edward doubted whether anyone but Buckingham or Prince Charles would be influential enough to effect such a change. The secretary of state's second undertaking was to get Williams, as Lord Keeper of the Great Seal, to order Justice Fuller of Stokenchurch to call off his persecution of Verney and one 'Great John', both innocent men unfairly under suspicion. Finally, and with a laugh, Conway agreed to persuade Williams that he had not heard what Verney had shouted at him in the palace grounds forty-eight hours previously.

Three days later Conway sent Tom a letter. In it he said, somewhat cryptically, that preliminary enquiries had shown all Verney's 'peculiar information' to be correct, and that his requests had been met, 'save for the relief of he who has no family name, for I am assured crimes of his magnitude may be pardoned by one man only.' Tom's disappointment at his failure to get help for John was alleviated somewhat by the presents which accompanied the communication: a heavy gold chain and a purse containing fifty pounds.

When Tom emerged the day after his meeting with Conway saying that he was fully recovered from his sickness, he was relieved to find the attitude towards him was already changing. This was partly due to the outbreak of a fresh and delicious scandal involving a captain in the king's bodyguard, a leek and the twin teenage daughters of one of the head cooks. More important was the way Tom was now being spoken of by certain members of the council.

Percipient as ever, James soon noticed this and asked, 'We see, Master Verney, that ye have of late discovered some power to make tongues wag in your favour. It is a great gift, and one we would ye passed on to your king, that he might get all his subjects to love him equally.'

By way of reply, Tom had been unable to say more than that he did not know what power he had, and that surely the king did not require it since all British subjects loved him with all their hearts anyway. Laughing the matter off, James had asked whether he still loved his tailor's daughter and, if he did, did he love her as much as he loved his king. The question, to which Tom managed to find a suitably flattering answer, raised his spirits somewhat. James had clearly not forgotten the marriage business, but neither was he angry about it. Indeed, his bantering manner suggested that in time there was just a possibility that, if caught in the right mood, he might give Tom his blessing.

Thus encouraged, Tom stayed on at Royston longer than he had intended. Every now and again, when he felt the moment apposite, he threw in a light-hearted remark about Lucy – still known only as the 'tailor's daughter' – until she became a topic of some good-hearted amusement at court. In this manner, carefully and as tactfully as he knew how, he prepared the ground for a new sowing. And as each day passed he felt more and more confident that when he let the seed drop, this time it would find fertile soil and take root.

But it was not to be.

On 25th April he received a letter from Lucy begging him to return to London at once. It was written in such pitiable terms that he did not have the heart to refuse her.

'Tom o' the wisp on his travels again?' complained James when Tom came to bid him farewell. 'Back to the tailor's daughter, no doubt. We warn ye, young Verney, that one day that lassie will be the ruin of ye. And when it comes to pass, do not come hither for our help.'

THIRTEEN

STRATTON AUDLEY MANOR

i

The letter bearing Tom's refusal to return home reached Stratton Audley Manor on Wednesday 6th April, the very day that Justice Verney had proclaimed that his elder son would be arriving. News that the gallant young courtier would not, after all, be putting in an appearance blew swiftly round the village. During the course of the afternoon a heavy cloud of disappointment crept over the Manor, enveloping it from the chimney pots to the floor flags. Like a pestilence, it seeped into every room, every corridor, every closet, until by nightfall there was not one member of the household, neither family nor servants, who had not been smitten by its finger of wretchedness. Of the Verneys, only the absent Tom and his younger brother Lucius, away at school in Banbury, remained untouched.

The cook presided over a grim and silent kitchen, the two housemaids were sullen, the stable boy long-faced.

Everyone was subdued with disillusionment. Even the talk in the servants' attic, normally a ripple of ribaldry and good humour, degenerated into back-biting and discontented grumbling. Eight-year-old Anne Verney, who had hardly slept the previous night because she had been so excited by the prospect of seeing her elder brother again, burst into floods of tears and was sent to bed early. Too concerned for weeping, Mary Verney and her daughter Elizabeth, now seventeen, sat together by the fire in the small parlour and talked far into the night. With John Verney's illness making him more irascible and difficult to talk to, mother and daughter had recently drawn closer together. They were worried about Tom, of course, wondering what he was up to, but their principal concern was for the justice, whose precarious health they feared would be further damaged by the shock of his son's blunt disobedience.

On receiving Tom's letter, his father had not exploded in a roar of anger, as those who knew him might have expected — rather, he had crumpled, as if his bones had suddenly been turned to paper. Fortunately, at the time he had been standing near a chair and his wife and daughter, waiting eagerly to see what Tom had to say, had helped him into it. There he had sat for the better part of an hour, bowed forward with his head in his hands, his thinning grey hair hanging about him like the isolating curtain of his misery. This was the moment he had always dreaded, but which all along he had known would come — the time when his son refused outright to obey him. At the back of his mind he knew he had been wrong to bring matters to the test like this, but it was too late now. Battle had been joined, and he was not going to be the loser. When finally he pulled himself together, he announced that he was taking himself to bed early — the following morning he had to leave for London at first light, 'to bring that damned renegade son of mine to heel'. His wife and daughter knew better than to protest, but as they gazed at his pallid face and watched the unsteady way he walked from the room, refusing all offers of assistance, they had serious doubts not only about the wisdom of his decision but also about his ability to carry it out.

Their doubts were well founded. The following morning John Verney did not get up at first light to ride to London. In fact he did not get up at all that day. Nor the next. For ten days he lay sick in bed, complaining of pains in the chest and singing in the head. He was fed on broth and bled heavily, on one occasion an opened vein in his arm releasing a whole milk jug full of heavy red blood. When semi-delirious, he asked after Tom. But as soon as he began his slow recovery, his former animosity returned. By the middle of the month he was once more preparing to journey to the capital, and on 16th April, against the advice of his family and doctor, he hauled himself into the saddle and, accompanied by a single manservant, rode from home towards Thame and the London road.

Travelling in easy stages, Justice John Verney reached the outskirts of the capital in three days and spent the night of 19th April at the Bull Inn near St Giles. The following morning, accompanied by his man Stanley, he rode to Clement's Inn and after the usual prolonged wait, managed to get Callow to emerge from his lodge.

'Is this the way London porters are accustomed to treat visitors?' enquired Verney huffily.

Callow looked at him through bleared red eyes and said nothing.

'Deafness,' the justice went on, turning to his servant,

'is common in these parts, Stanley. As is incivility.'

With a shrug, Callow turned to go. He had not been summoned from the boozy warm interior of his lodge just to be insulted.

Verney called after him, 'Stanley! Do you have the shilling I gave you yesterday to reward those who help us?'

Callow stopped but did not turn round.

'Here, sir,' said Stanley, fishing for the coin in his purse and handing it over.

'Good. I believe we will soon have need of it.' Callow swung slowly round. 'Now, fellow,' continued Verney, 'see here. I have a shilling. It is for you, if you will help me.'

'Help?' muttered Callow.

'I am Justice Verney of Stratton Audley, county of Oxford.' The porter's face showed no sign of recognition. 'I am come here to meet with my son, Thomas Verney, who was lately of this Inn. I wish to know where he may now be found.' He held up the shilling before him.

Callow spat at his feet and growled, 'Shove your shilling up your arse!'

Leaning forward, purple in the face, Verney roared, 'What did you say, rogue?'

With a hint of a smile, Callow turned to Stanley. 'Deafness,' he said, mimicking the justice's Oxfordshire accent, 'is common in these parts, Stanley.' Then he stomped back to his lodge and slammed the door.

Verney had forgotten that his son's manservant was the porter's grandson, and he assumed that his hostile reception at the gate had been due entirely to the low esteem in which Tom was now held at his former place of study. Wary of the power of assembled lawyers and fearing further embarrassment or even rebuke if he pressed his enquiry at the Inn further, he decided to call on his Oxfordshire neighbour Lord Banbury, whom he knew to have seen Tom recently. He did not like the pompous baronet, but for the moment circumstances obliged him to place necessity above pleasure. The last thing he wanted was to return home without his son.

On arriving at Pickering House, Verney was asked by the footman to wait in the tapestry room until his lordship had finished his afternoon prayers.

'His what?' asked Verney, scarcely able to believe his ears for the second time that day.

The servant smiled. 'His prayers, sir. Of late Lord Banbury has taken a good deal to praying and other matters religious. Since the accident.'

'The accident?'

'His lordship shot a young lady, sir, the daughter of Justice Fuller.' Verney winced at the mention of another man he did not care for, and he hoped the mean-minded puritan was not at Pickering House. 'My master says Almighty God directed his gun,' the footman went on, adding in a lower tone, 'there are strange things afoot, sir.'

'So it seems,' Verney replied, dismissing his informant and settling down to wait for the baronet to appear. After what he had heard, he was quite looking forward to meeting the man. A reformed Lord Banbury was as beyond his comprehension as a generous Scotsman.

Certainly the peer looked different. As he entered the room, dressed in uncustomary black, Verney noticed that he was both thinner and less flamboyant than when they had last met. He sounded different, too. Gone from his speech were most of the oaths and smutty innuendoes; in their place floated a flotsam of prayer and half-remembered scriptural references. The only time the baronet showed anything like his former uninhibited vigour was when he spoke of his wife or Roman Catholics. Almost at once Verney suspected the influence of Fuller, to whom several references were made in their introductory conversation.

After about ten minutes Verney managed to bring the conversation round to the purpose of his visit.

'I am come to London, my lord, to take home my son Thomas.'

'Very wisely done, Verney, if I may say so,' Banbury sighed. 'That son of yours is a probigal son, a true probigal. A lost sheep. And you, sir, like the good shepherd, are come with crook to take him home to the fold. At which there will be greater rejoicing in heaven than if ninety-nine had gone missing. You are a saint.'

Verney had no wish to discuss his son, particularly not in distorted Biblical terms. 'I fear I am no saint, my lord. Though it is kind of you to say so. No, young Thomas has seen enough of the great city and he must now return with me to the country.' Banbury nodded. 'But first I must find him. Your lordship may know that he no longer resides at Clement's Inn. Perhaps he has told you where he may be found?'

'Blackmore Street, by Drury Lane,' Banbury blurted out, then halted, uneasy at having revealed the address so readily. He was worried at what Fuller might say. The man was so clever, he thought anxiously, capable of seeing in a flash things that would never have occurred to himself, even if he lived to be as old as Methuselah, or whoever the old man of Genesis was. He felt certain that Fuller would come up with a reason why he should not have told John Verney where Tom lived. Consequently, the baronet determined to say no more on the subject, leaving his visitor to find out for himself what else his son had been up to. Having reached something of an impasse, therefore, and with the justice eager to get to Blackmore Street straight away, the interview was soon over.

Half an hour after Verney's departure, Fuller came down from his room, where he had been writing letters to fellow magistrates in various parts of the country asking them to keep an eye out for 'one who goes by the name of Great John, a very rogue, cutpurse, thief and murderer'. When Banbury told him that Justice Verney had called and he had told him where his son Tom lived, Fuller leaped as if kicked by a horse.

'Argh!' he yelped. 'You did not do well, my lord.' Banbury's heart sank. 'I beg your pardon, but that information had a value — it was not right to give it away for nothing.' Banbury looked blank and racked his brains to understand where he had gone wrong.

'Does Thomas wish his father to know where he resides?' asked Fuller, speaking slowly as if to a child.

Unused to being criticised and patronised in the same minute, the Toad was rather put out. But he was so in awe of Fuller that it did not occur to him to complain. Why, had the man not perceived a sign of heavenly benediction where others might have seen only a killing?

With a pathetic attempt at dignity he replied, 'No, I do not suppose Master Verney wishes his father to know where he lives.'

'And so, my lord,' Fuller explained, 'would it not have been better to wait until young Verney had returned from court? Then we might have explained to him that unless he revealed to us the whereabouts of that devil John, we would tell his father of his marriage.'

Banbury gave a low moan. 'Ah! I see. I was a peck generous, was I not?'

'You were, my lord. But I forgive you, and so, I'm sure, does God. We need to fasten every rope we can find onto this younger Verney or we will not hold him. He has already used his new connection with Keeper Williams to sever our legal grip over him. Such cunning serpents, made more slippery by covering themselves with popish slime, are not easily trapped.' His twitch became more pronounced. 'Sometimes only the cleansing fire can destroy them!'

Banbury shuddered. Suddenly he remembered something. 'But Justice Fuller,' he announced, 'you have forgot! We can still threaten Master Verney with telling the king of his marriage, can we not?'

Fuller's eyes narrowed. 'I had not forgot that, my lord. We can and we will, when I give the sign. Be patient, I pray you, my lord, until then.'

ii

John Verney and Stanley dined at the Angel, the inn where Princess was stabled. Finding the place agreeable, the justice took rooms there before proceeding to Blackmore Street later the same afternoon.

He was somewhat nonplussed when the door of the house where his son was staying was opened by a young boy who, without asking his name, politely showed him into the parlour and bade him wait while he fetched his mistress. Verney's confusion mounted when a pretty young woman in the early stages of pregnancy entered and asked him what he wanted. For a second he thought his son had taken up residence in a brothel. But when he was asked to step through to the tailor's workshop, he realised his mistake and said with a laugh, 'Nay, good wife, it is not the services of your husband I require.'

'It is as well, sir,' Lucy replied, confused, 'for he is not at home at present.' She looked closely at the stranger as if trying to remember where she had seen him before.

'That is of no matter. It is not yourselves I seek, but a young man lodged here with you. One Thomas Verney.'

Lucy jumped inwardly. Was this the prelude to another search? It was unlikely, for this man with the vaguely familiar voice seemed too civil for a common constable. Nevertheless, to be safe, she decided to go along with his misunderstanding.

'Thomas Verney is not here either, sir.'

'Oh!' he said with obvious disappointment. 'Pray, when will he return?' The inflexion in the man's voice gave it away. Suddenly, with a thrill of horror and delight Lucy realised to whom she was talking.

'I do not rightly know when he will be back, sir,' she stammered, wishing she had chosen to put on a more becoming gown that morning. 'Pray be seated,' she continued, drawing up a chair. 'Sir, I must explain at once, it is I who live here with Tom Verney — there is no other husband.' Half smiling, she waited anxiously to see what his reaction to the revelation would be.

Unfortunately, in her nervousness Lucy had not expressed herself clearly. At least not clearly enough for Justice Verney, who had heard only what he had wanted to hear. He had been almost certain that an obsession with this tailor's daughter, to whom Tom had referred in his letter, was the main reason for his son's difficult behaviour. The phrase 'live here with Tom Verney' had confirmed what he wanted to know, and he had scarcely heard what had followed. As he saw it, the picture was simple — his son was living in this house with his pregnant mistress who, fearing she would be left destitute if he returned home, had persuaded him to disobey his father's command.

John Verney's initial reaction to Lucy's statement was one of anger. He frowned across the table at her — the strumpet who had seduced his son away from the bosom of his family. But when she met his look with a winning smile, devoid of scorn or defiance, his heart went out to her. She was a pretty, kindly looking wench, he told himself. Tom could have done far worse than set himself up with such a becoming little jade. He thought of his own youth, and sighed.

'Pray do not sigh, sir,' said Lucy, delighted that his disapproving look had disappeared so swiftly and scarcely able to believe her good fortune. 'It is nothing terrible we have done.'

'No, woman, it is nothing terrible. It has been done before more times than there are stars in the sky. And no doubt it will be done again as often. But Tom has been in London long enough. He must return home now.'

Lucy thought it odd that he managed nothing more endearing than 'woman' for her. 'I am Lucy, sir. And your request is no burden to us. We will be on the road for Stratton Audley the very hour Tom returns from court.' She sat back and laid her hands across her stomach and smiled. 'But we will not, I fear, be able to travel as speedily as we would wish.'

The frown returned to John Verney's face. 'Mistress Lucy, it is not you I expect, but my son.' Seeing her face fall, he added, 'Come, you did not think, for all your pretty looks and winning ways, you would hold him for ever, did you? I will see you are left with enough for yourself and your child to live in comfort, I promise you. I am not a harsh man.'

'You are too cruel, sir!' cried Lucy, standing up and stamping her foot. 'You cannot say that! I will not be bought off like a whore, and I know my Tom will stand by me. He will never return home without his wife!'

He stared at her. 'His what?'

'His wife, sir! Do I have to write it on a slate and hold it up for you to read? As I told you, I am his wife. We are married in law.' Her face flushed with anger, she stood leaning against the table, panting.

John Verney stared at her for some time, scarcely able to believe his ears. A thousand thoughts flashed through his mind. Not even Mary Verney, for all her pessimism, had reckoned on this. Legally married – then where was the paper? He had been betrayed. By the one he loved most, his own first-born son. How dare this trollop do this to him? She was to blame. No! It was Tom. It was his son, Tom. How could he have done this to him?

But first he had to be sure that this was no wanton's trick.

Clenching his fists, he said slowly and quietly, his voice hoarse with repressed emotion, 'If you are my son's wife, madam, where is the marriage license?'

Lucy went to a cupboard, brought it out and laid it on the table before him. In the course of his duties as a magistrate he had had many dealings with such documents and he could tell a forgery in an instant. This was not one. There may have been some irregularities over the banns, but the marriage had taken place, performed by a priest of the Church of England in a house of God. He might challenge its legality in the church courts, but that would involve considerable expense and, worse, massive public humiliation. And even if the union were eventually declared false, it did not reverse the fact that Tom had entered it freely, of his own accord, knowing that it was against the wishes of his family.

John Verney ran his fingers over the license as if he were blind, feeling every wrinkle and elevation in its surface. Here, in his very hands, was written proof of his son's perfidy. He took a deep breath. No more evidence was needed. If Tom wished to lead his own life, abandoning his family, so be it. But the severance would be total.

He stood up and turned to Lucy. Not knowing what had been going on in his mind and hoping that sight of the formal license had finally persuaded him to accept her, she stepped up to him and laid her hand on his arm.

'Father . . .' she began.

It was the worst thing she could have done. Until now, John Verney had managed to keep himself under control. But the gentle touch of Lucy's hand and the pleading in her voice were more than he could bear. Pulled in pieces by conflicting emotions, he surrendered to the only one capable of subsuming all the others.

He roughly brushed away her hand and bellowed, 'Take your tainted hands from me, harlot! And if you dare call me "father" again I will have you whipped from the Tower to Ludgate Hill!'

Lucy was speechless. Fearing he was about to hit her in his rage, she covered her face with her hands and shrank back into a corner of the room. There, crouched crying in the shadows, she remained until he had gone.

Verney refused to acknowledge the pity welling within him and strove to smother it with still more vicious fury. 'Listen, whore! Tell Master Thomas that I accept his marriage to a snivelling tailor's daughter, and I wish him well of it. Tell him I hope he and his bitch live long and are blessed with many children – I see they have not been slow in that factory of lewdness. But tell him, too, haggard, that he has made his bed of bawdiness and he must lie in it.' He beat his fist upon the table. 'Never, never will I see him or speak to him again! Henceforth his ways are not my ways. And if he dares come creeping back to me with his tail between his legs like a beaten cur, by God! I will smash his brains to custard!'

iii

Lucy had written to Tom at Ralston after her disastrous confrontation with John Verney. It was not a long letter, nor did it spell out precisely what had happened, but the simple phrase 'I have met with your father' – delivered without explanation or elaboration – was enough to make Tom realise the urgency of her request for him to return to London.

His mood on the road home fluctuated as wildly as the weather, which swung capriciously between rain and shine. First he was depressed. The late April countryside, bursting with renewal and hope, seemed to mock him from every branch, bush and nest. Whatever way he looked at it, he had failed in his mission. His marriage remained a thing of shame, to be hidden beneath the sheets, not flaunted upon them. It should not be like this, he said to himself time and again, remembering the rhyme Great John had once used: 'When Adam delved and Eve span, Who was then the gentleman?' Who indeed? But that was in Eden, he reflected miserably, and this is the world after the Fall, a corrupt and sinful place.

However, at that moment a pair of magpies, chequered flashes of good fortune, flew across the road and settled beside each other on a bough of a young elm tree growing in the hedge to his right. That's luck! thought Tom, a sign that maybe all is not for the worst. Like the black-white plumage of the magpie, there will always be shadows and sunlight in the same scene. I must learn to look on the former, not the latter, for it appears that happiness stems not from what is, but from how one regards it. With a conscious effort, he began to list all the positive things in his life. Owing to the good fortune of falling in with Sir Edward Conway, his Royston visit had not been a complete disaster – he still had his official post, he had been saved from the prying suspicion of Justice Fuller and he did not lack money. He was, in short, well-to-do, well connected, in excellent health and married to a lovely young wife who was expecting their first child. What more could a man wish for? Moreover, he did not know for certain that his father had rejected Lucy. Why, perhaps he had fallen in love with her himself, as his son had done, and Lucy was keeping his approval of their marriage as a surprise for when he got home? That was just the sort of innocent, impish trick she would play! He leaned forward, stroked Princess's neck and began to whistle a jaunty air he had picked up at court. 'Aye!' he said to himself out loud, breaking off the song with a grin and imitating the voice of the king, 'It is a question, wee Master Verney, of how ye regard the world, not what is in it!'

Tom's high spirits lasted for about five miles. By the time he had reached the village of Puckeridge his worries had begun to close in upon him again. Whenever he thought clearly, he saw that much of his happiness rested on a perilously insecure foundation. He simply could not go on living a lie indefinitely, holding the two halves of his life apart. Someone was going to find out what was going on, sooner or later. Sooner, maybe, if his father had discovered Lucy was his wife and rejected her. And if he was honest with himself, this was by far the most likely intimation of her letter. Then Stratton Audley would know in a matter of days, then Lord Banbury, then the court, where Tom had already made implacable enemies of two of the most influential ministers, then the king ... And after that? It did not bear thinking about.

Throwing back his shoulders, Tom decided to be positive and make a plan of campaign. First, assuming his father had been hostile, he would comfort Lucy. Then, using the ample resources available to him from Conway's gift and the final instalment of the first year's profits from the Helford farm, they would move from Blackmore Street, with its host of unpleasant associations, to somewhere more respectable, with a maid as well as House Martin to attend on them. Finally, he would return to the king and pick up his campaign for recognition where he had left off.

Once he knew what to do, Tom felt much better. Eager to begin putting his scheme into operation, he urged Princess forward, south towards the capital and the sun.

For three or four minutes Tom and Lucy stood with their arms clasped around each other, not saying a word. Eventually, she lifted her head from his chest and said quietly, 'I do not need to ask, do I, Tom, whether the king has given his consent?'

'No,' he replied, burying his face in her hair. 'And my father? Do I need to ask whether he has consented to our marriage?'

'No, Tom. You do not have to ask.'

He stood back with his hands on her shoulders. 'Was he very unkind, Lucy, my dearest?'

'At first I liked him, Tom. I believed him a good man, and I thought ...' She lifted her head and laid her arms along his, so that they stood like two sleepwalkers who had inadvertently met head-on. 'Then he changed. He said such horrible things to me, Tom, such cruel, horrible things.'

For the next half an hour they told each other their adventures. Lucy prepared some supper which they ate before the parlour fire while they discussed the consequences of what had happened. Before long, stabs of criticism slipped into their conversation.

'Did I not say, Tom,' Lucy remarked, 'that you should have been more certain with the king's undertakings? It was not well done to raise my spirits so high, before vanishing like a swallow in September, sending me no word of your failure.'

The last word stung Tom deeply. 'Failure? Is that not unkind, Lucy? I was on the point of success when a feeble woman pleaded and begged with me to leave off my enterprise and return home. Then she scorns me for having failed! Fie, Lucy Simpson! You do me wrong!'

Lucy's eyes blazed. 'One, Tom Verney, I am not Lucy Simpson but Lucy Verney, whom it is your God-sworn duty to protect. And don't you forget it. Two, Tom Verney, I have a feeling in my bones that the king will never consent to your request. You are deceiving yourself, and me in thinking otherwise. Three, Tom Verney, I am a woman, yes. But not feeble, nor a pleader, nor a beggar. I have faced the tiger from which you have often fled, I believe?'

Tom laid down his knife. 'God's blood! My father is no tiger that he would have eaten you, wife. He is a man. And as such you should have won him to our cause with your charms — or are you faded already, like the many who paint themselves into an altar piece then let the pigment peel when the ceremony is done?'

'Why, Tom Verney,' she answered, her eyes narrowing, 'are you so blind that you need me to answer for you?'

Tom was tempted to storm theatrically from the room. Six months previously he would probably have done so.

But now he held himself in check, fixed to his chair by the weight of responsibility bearing down on him. He leaned forward with his elbows on the table and rested his forehead on his clasped hands. 'Lucy,' he said in a voice he hardly recognised as his own, 'what is this? Why are we fighting when I am only just returned? Surely we must support each other at this time, not pull ourselves to pieces!'

His words damped the fire in her eyes as swiftly as it had arisen. With a sigh she stood up and came round to sit on his lap. 'I know, Tom darling. I know.' She put her arms round his neck. 'Perhaps we fight because we are frightened? I am fearful of what lies ahead.'

'I am too,' he said, holding her to him. 'It will be a long and treacherous road. Come, we must not squabble again. Promise?'

'I promise.' She kissed him. 'Are you not tired after your journey, my love?'

'I am weary. But not so weary that I cannot go to bed.'

'Then I think we had better go to bed, Tom.'

The following few days were not easy. The squall that had blown up so suddenly after Tom's return from Royston had not blown itself out completely, and from time to time it gathered new force and roared about the house for an hour or so before dying down. It arose largely because Tom was bored. His scant interest in tailoring was balanced by a considerable interest in making love. If he had his way, he would have spent the better part of each day in bed with his wife. But even in the best of health that had not been what she wanted, and now, stressed and uncomfortably pregnant, her desire had waned still further. She wanted the comfort of Tom's presence, but little else. At the same time, although it was not necessary for financial reasons, she insisted on working long hours at her business. She did so out of affection for her departed father and as a way of maintaining her independence. Seeing her busy while he lazed about all day, Tom grew still more fractious. The bold plans he had made on the ride from Royston advanced no further than the first stage, comforting his wife. Although she agreed that Blackmore Street had brought ill-luck, it was the only house she had ever known. She had been born there and wished her child to be born there. After that, she assured him, she would seriously consider moving. Tom had little option but to go along with her wishes. As for the third phase of his scheme – returning to court – after what had happened the last time he had gone away, such a move was out of the question for the moment.

So Tom passed his days in doing little more than waiting for something to turn up. He kicked his heels about the house and burned up his frustration by taking Princess out on long gallops into the countryside. It was following one of these rides that Spid, who had been keeping a watchful eye on the house for the last fortnight, saw him return home. After this it was only a matter of time before something did indeed turn up.

iv

Elizabeth Banbury was finding it harder than she had anticipated to piece together what had happened at Pickering House on the day of Sarah Fuller's death. From casual remarks dropped by her husband, she gathered that the man fleeing from Sarah's room had been a Roman Catholic named John. It was in pursuit of this man, whom Fuller said was guilty of numerous crimes, including robbery and murder, that the magistrate had come to

London with his daughter in the first place. Elizabeth was disturbed by his accusations and wished she had been able to ask Sarah about them before she had died. In the course of their brief conversations the girl had made no more than oblique references to her lover and had never once suggested that he was in any way a criminal. Yet the discovery of the thief in the hall had provided strong circumstantial evidence to the contrary. Although all this was very confusing, Elizabeth could not credit that anyone as honest as Sarah would have become involved with a true criminal, let alone a killer.

The only other explanation for Fuller's charges, she realised, was that they were the false creations of a mind distorted by hatred. As his behaviour grew still more eccentric — almost deranged — with each day that passed, Elizabeth knew that this was a plausible alternative. She was coming to understand that the puritanical Fuller, like all fanatics, was a very dangerous man. And by implication the mysterious John was less of a rogue than a misunderstood, almost romantic victim of injustice and bigotry. Consequently, she decided that if ever it was in her power to do so, she would try to help him. Particularly if it meant thwarting the vicious Fuller.

This much Elizabeth concluded in a matter of days. But she had still made no progress on the two questions that really interested her — the possible relationship between John and Tom, and how Fuller and Lord Banbury had known where John was going to be on that ill-fated Monday. Fuller would give nothing away. She had hardly spoken to him since the incident over Tom Verney's hat. Her husband, too, was unusually unforthcoming. In the past she had normally shown little or no interest in what he did with his time, and when she did ask what he was planning to do — usually in order to find out when he would be out of the house – he had never been slow to tell her. But recently he had become too frightened to reveal anything. She knew the explanation, of course – Fuller. Since the shooting, the unscrupulous magistrate had played on her dull-witted husband like a huge, soggy bagpipe, so that now he had only to suggest something for Banbury to accept it as the score he too should follow. It had not taken the puritan long to work out that beneath his bluff and arrogant exterior, the baronet was not a confident man. For many years he had drawn strength in equal parts from drink and possession of a beautiful young wife. But neither of these had supported him in his hour of greatest need as powerfully as Fuller's narrow Christianity, which had poured into Banbury's ear, hour after hour, like a drug. Under its influence he had been converted from a blunderer who had committed manslaughter into a hero, a standard-bearer at the head of Fuller's crusade against sin and popery, both epitomised in the figure of John the seducer, John the thief, John the murderer, John the Catholic.

Worried that Fuller might undermine her hold over her husband still further, one evening, partly for amusement and partly because she needed to know where she stood, Elizabeth decided to put her powers to the test. Changing into a gown which did little more than offer a token covering for her ample breasts, she broke her usual routine and joined the men after supper. Sitting sprawled on a couch beside her husband and innocently adjusting her skirts to display an elegant ankle and lower calf, wet-lipped, wide-eyed and pouting, she stared at each of the men in turn. Every so often, in a manner which said 'bed' more clearly than any spoken word, she gave a little yawn and stretched out her arms like a cat. Fuller frowned and sweated, and tried hard not to look at her. Nevertheless, despite threatening himself with unspeakable pain each time he failed, his gaze was drawn inexorably towards her body, like a plant to the light.

His defensive monologue on the sinfulness of Eve fell on deaf ears. Fidgeting uncomfortably and alternating inane grins at his wife with solemn glances at his spiritual mentor, Banbury was pulled between hell and heaven. It was no contest. When she was sure the bobbing of her float was a catch and not just a nibble, Elizabeth finally rose languidly to her feet and, gazing straight at her husband – but not at his face – she announced that she was going to bed. Shooting out of his chair like a partridge from the nest, Banbury said that he was doing likewise.

Hell had triumphed.

As Elizabeth took her husband's arm and led him from the room, she called over her shoulder, 'Good night, Justice! I beseech you, remember us in your prayers!'

Sure of her husband's ultimate loyalty, Elizabeth still did not find him willing to speak on what he termed 'matters of holy import'. At one point, while she was torturing him with her charms, he almost begged her not to demand more information from him. Seeing how frightened he was and concerned lest he should report her questioning to Fuller, she took pity on him and desisted in favour of another tactic.

Since the start of her investigation she had always wondered how John had got into the house. Either Sarah had let him in – which was virtually impossible since she had been locked in her room; or Tom had let him in – a possibility, particularly in the light of his quip about knowing 'secret ways' when she had asked how he had entered; or someone in the house had helped him. And might that person not have assisted Tom, too? She rubbed her hands together in anticipation. Why had she not thought of this before?

Moving to her writing desk, she made a list of all the servants in Pickering House. Over the following forty-eight hours, she found out roughly where they had all been at the time of the break-in and crossed out those who for whatever reason could not have helped the intruders. Six names remained, two men and four women. Next, deciding that the most likely points of entry were either the front door or the servants' garden door, she arranged the names according to possible proximity to the two points of access. The result almost jumped from the page at her. Peter the butler! His parlour lay across the only route to the rear door. Casting down her pen, she ordered her maid to bring the man to her without delay.

Elizabeth had once trusted her husband's butler. On one or two occasions in the past she had even employed him to help a friend make a clandestine entry into Pickering House. But when, after one such incident, he had approached her with something sounding suspiciously like blackmail, she had had nothing more to do with him. Since then all she had learned about him had been gossip from her maid — that he had a bitter hatred of women and preferred the dumb company of dogs to that of other human beings.

'You sent for me, my lady?' he enquired as he stepped noiselessly into the room.

'I did, Peter. I have one question to ask. Answer me swiftly and leave. Where were you at midday on Monday 4th April? You remember the date, I suppose?'

'I do, my lady. I was here.'

'What? In my rooms?' Her tone was angry.

'Ah-ha! No, my lady,' he corrected, clearly playing for time. 'I was in Pickering House.'

Biting her lip, she stared at him with eyes of flint. 'Peter, answer directly or I will see you suffer. In which room of this house? In your parlour?'

There was a long pause. In the end Peter replied, 'No, my lady. I was in the cellar. Below ground.'

Resisting the urge to dismiss him, Elizabeth asked one further question. 'Is that the customary hour for checking the cellar, Peter?'

'No, my lady. But it seemed the correct place to be at that time on that day. Now, of course, I know I was mistaken, my lady. I am full of repentance—'

'You may go.'

'Yes, my lady. Thank you, my lady.' He slid out of the door like butter on a hot tray.

Thank you, said Elizabeth to herself when he had gone. But who had persuaded Peter to hide himself away at that crucial time? And how had Fuller known what was planned? Had Peter betrayed the trust placed in him? There was only one way to find out.

She summoned her maid again.

'Come hither, Tilly, and stand before me,' she commanded as soon as the girl entered. She did as she was bidden. 'Now, Tilly, are you sincerely attached to your mistress?'

Chosen for her common sense and reliability rather than her skills, after two years in Lady Banbury's service Tilly Wood had grown very fond of her lively and amusing mistress. She had been well paid and kindly treated, even receiving lessons in basic literacy as part of her training. She had no misgivings, therefore, in replying to Elizabeth's question in the affirmative.

'I am pleased to hear that, Tilly,' the baroness continued, 'for I am about to ask you to undertake a matter of great importance and secrecy. It involves Justice

Fuller—' the maid winced. 'You do not care for the justice?'

'No, my lady. I cannot say that I do.'

'That is just as well, for neither do I.' She smiled and placed her hand gently on Tilly's arm. 'Listen, this is what I would have you do ...'

v

Tom and Lucy were standing together in the workshop when House Martin let the visitors in. On hearing their voices, for a second or two Tom could not work out what was happening. It was unreal, like a dream, two completely disparate parts of his life suddenly thrown together. Before he had time to react, the door was pushed open and Lord Banbury and Justice Fuller walked slowly into the room.

Tom stood motionless. Instinctively brushing back a wisp of hair, Lucy stared at the arrivals in bewilderment. Lord Banbury coughed and gazed about the room, his face fixed in a vacuous smile. Only Fuller knew precisely what to do.

'Mr and Mrs Verney, I presume?' he asked with a sneer.

Tom hesitated but Lucy answered immediately, 'Yes, sir. May we be of assistance?'

Fuller snorted. 'You have been already, good wife.'

'My lord,' cut in Tom, moving to take Banbury by the hand, 'welcome to our humble home!' The baronet turned away awkwardly.

'That was wisely done, my lord,' said Fuller. 'The hand of the ungodly deceiver is surely tainted.'

'Sir!' shouted Tom, laying his hand on the hilt of his sword. 'If you have come here to insult me, for your safety leave before I drive you out!' He turned to Lucy. 'These men, my love, are Lord Banbury and Justice Fuller of Stokenchurch. The former is an ennobled acquaintance of our family. The latter is a psalm-pinching puritan weasel.'

Fuller's eyes narrowed. 'I will not forget the kind things you say of me, sir. Nor will I leave until you have furnished me with what I want.'

'You will get nothing from me or anyone else in this house!' snarled Tom, taking a step nearer the magistrate and drawing his sword a few inches from its scabbard.

'Tut! Master Verney, think you it wise to threaten a justice of the peace and a peer of the realm? Put in your sword! Listen to what I have to say.'

Realising that violence would not serve his ends, Tom sheathed his sword and went back to Lucy's side. 'Very well,' he hissed. 'Speak! Then go!'

'I will,' said Fuller. His lip began to twitch more rapidly. 'Where is the criminal known as' – he paused, as if hating the name so much that he dared not utter it – 'John?'

Tom felt like a man in the middle of a frozen pond who hears an ominous cracking all about him. There was no way to solid land. An icy cold started to come over him. He said nothing.

Enjoying his victim's torment, Fuller waited a long time before repeating his question. When eventually he did so, he added, 'We pray you tell us, Verney. Or we shall be obliged to inform His Majesty of your marriage. Would he be pleased to hear that he has been deceived?'

Tom was submerged and struggling. He looked at Lucy standing at his side, her face pale and frightened. She looks so small, so fragile, so vulnerable, he thought. It was not fair to do this to her. Royal approval was their last hope of avoiding future penury and shame. If James was told now his fury would be awesome. Tom knew that he would lose everything: his position, his reputation, his connections, his future. Nothing would be left.

But betray John? The man who had twice saved him and whose life had already been all but destroyed by this vile magistrate? How could he do such a deed? It was a terrible decision, like asking him to chose between cutting off his own leg or arm.

'I am waiting,' said Fuller. 'The criminal or your wife? Decide.'

'Neither.'

Fuller turned towards the door. 'Shall we depart, my lord? There is little joy to be had here.' Banbury looked first at Tom and then at the magistrate, unsure what to do.

Lucy started to speak. But Tom interrupted her, afraid that her intervention would only complicate matters further. 'Justice Fuller,' he began, 'yours is a false title if ever there was one! There is as much justice in you as there is milk in a river. I believe, no, I know you to be a wicked and evil man, a serpent in clothes of holiness. I despise you, sir, and I despise myself for what you are forcing me to do.'

He took Lucy's hand and pulled her close to him. 'But you give me no choice. I hate what I do, but to preserve hope for my wife and family I will tell you what I know.' He felt Lucy's fingers stiffen. 'I believe the man you seek, a worthy fellow and not the villain you would paint him' – Fuller gave a sour grimace – 'was making for Moseley Hall, near Wolverhampton in Staffordshire. And if you find him there, may he strike you dead!'

Even as he was speaking, tears welled up in his eyes. 'Now go!' he shouted, hammering his hand on the bench before him. 'Get out of this house! Go!'

With Banbury muttering something ridiculous about 'the pain of true justice', the two men left the room and were shown out into the street. As soon as the front door had shut, Lucy, her head bowed, walked past Tom without saying a word and went upstairs.

'Here, House Martin!' called Tom. 'Go and fetch wine for your mistress. She is not well.' He gave the boy some money and climbed the stairs.

Lucy was lying face-down on the bed, crying quietly. 'What is it, my love?' he asked, sitting beside her. He laid his hand on her back.

'Don't touch me!' she cried, rolling away.

Tom was hurt. He did not understand. 'Why? What now? God's eyes! I have done what I could for us, for you. You saw those curs. You heard what they said. What else was there to do?'

She sat up and casually pushed the hair away from her cheeks. There was a look on her face Tom had never seen before, a look of resolution and disdain.

'Tom Verney, I love you,' she said. 'But there are times when I fear I do not like you. What have you done? You have betrayed your family. You have betrayed the church. You have betrayed the king. And now, to your eternal shame, you have betrayed your friend.'

Tom stood up and leaned with his back against the wall.

'What did it matter,' she continued, 'if the king knew the truth? He would have discovered it one day, as the whole world will yet. You have stretched out your lie so thin it cannot but break. And now, for the sake of a shameful deception, this man, this John – from what you say a good and kindly fellow – will likely suffer. He may even die on the gallows. If so, he will be killed for your lie, Tom, and his blood will be on your hands.'

'Lucy, do you not understand? I acted as I thought best for you. That was my only guide.' His voice was thin and uncertain.

'Then why would you not let me speak? Had you done so, you would have learned what I wanted. But no, you did what Tom Verney wanted. It was always thus. And you did not think, you blundered like a blind ox. And I am married to you and I am carrying your child.' Breathing heavily, she gazed across the room at him with eyes of profound sorrow.

For a full minute he stood in silence, staring down at his feet. Then he raised his head, took a deep breath and said firmly, 'Then there is but one course left open to me.'

A shadow of fear passed across Lucy's face as she asked, 'And what is that, Tom?'

'I must ride to Staffordshire before them. I must warn John.'

Lucy thought for a moment. 'Yes,' she said finally, getting up from the bed and smoothing down her gown, 'that is what you must do. You must leave at once. I will prepare some things for you.'

As she collected together food and other items her husband might need, and he packed his clothes, they spoke not a word to each other. Only when all was ready and he stood by the door with his bags at his feet, did she come up to him, put her arms round his neck and say, 'God be with you, Tom Verney.'

He held her tight, feeling the swelling of her womb against his thighs. 'And with you, Lucy Verney. Take great care of yourself. I will be with you again soon.'

'I hope so, Tom.'

He dropped his hands to her waist. 'You hope so? What are you saying?'

'I am saying that it is a dangerous task you are undertaking. You may be a long time. You may be taken or wounded. And I will be here alone, not in the best health. Oh, you know what I am saying! Who can tell what God has arranged for us?'

'Who can tell?' he repeated wistfully. Kissing her one last time, he picked up his bags and turned to go.

'Farewell, Tom,' she whispered.

'Farewell, Lucy, my darling.' He opened the door and looked back into the room one last time. 'Forgive me.'

A minute later he was out in the darkening street and walking briskly towards the stables of the Angel Inn, Princess and the open road.

PART III

OUR BELOVED SUBJECT

... it is found by daily experience that many of His Majesty's subjects that adhere in their hearts to the Popish religion, by the infection drawn from thence, and by the wicked and devilish counsel of Jesuits, seminaries and other like persons ..., are so far perverted in the point of their loyalties and due allegiance unto the king's Majesty ..., as they are ready to entertain and execute any treasonable conspiracies and practices ...

Act for the Better Discovering and Repressing of Popish Recusants, 1606.

FOURTEEN

GODINGTON GRANGE

i

Silas watched Tom's hurried preparations with open-mouthed anxiety. He had grown very fond of Princess during the three months in which she had been in his care, and the prospect of her young master taking her on a long and inevitably dangerous night ride filled him with horror.

'Not often gentlemen sets out for the country at this time, sir,' he commented pointedly, scratching his chin.

'No?' muttered Tom. He was so preoccupied with checking the horse's girth and reins that he hardly heard the question.

The ostler persevered. 'You in great haste, sir?'

'I am. Great haste. I have to cross England to save a man's life.'

Silas's jaw dropped open. Shutting it with a snap, he let out a long, low whistle. 'Adventuring,' he whispered, glancing nervously about him. In the ostler's vivid imagination one dramatic sentence had transformed Tom from an idle young student, on whom so beautiful a mare as Princess was wasted, into a mysterious hero whom it was a privilege to serve. He longed to know more. But terrified lest he learn something for which one day he could be racked, he bit his tongue and kept quiet.

Tom fastened his leather bags behind the saddle and felt in his purse for a coin. 'Here, Silas,' he said, holding out the money, 'take this for your pains. Be sure you are here to tend Princess when I return. She will be exceedingly weary.'

'Thank you, Mr Verney, sir. I'll be 'ere, sir, when you returns. From your – er – quest.' With a heavy wink that caused his mouth to fall open again, he added, 'And God grant you saves him, sir.'

'Saves him?' asked Tom, hauling himself into the saddle.

'The man as what you are so hot to rescue from whatever it is, sir.'

'Ah yes! Thank you, Silas. I pray God I will not be too late.' As he was turning Princess towards the stable-yard door, a thought struck him. 'Silas,' he asked, 'do you know the Staffordshire road?'

'Where, sir?'

'The road to the county of Staffordshire.'

The ostler looked thoughtful for a second. 'No, sir,' he answered slowly. 'Yet I reckons it's north. Or maybe more west than north. The truth is, sir, I can't rightly tell the countries of Staffordshire and Suffolkshire and Sussex-shire apart. They're all foreign to me, sir.'

'To me, too,' laughed Tom. 'But no matter. I will enquire further. Farewell.'

He touched Princess's flanks with his spurs and trotted swiftly out of the inn yard, across Wych Street and right up Drury Lane. With a wistful glance down Blackmore Street as he rode by, he proceeded quickly to Holborn, where he entered the Bear to enquire which road he should take out of the capital. Impatient to be on his way, he was detained for almost a quarter of an hour as carters and coachmen earnestly discussed the advantages and disadvantages of the various routes north. While some were in favour of travelling via Oxford, the majority advised the Coventry road, via Aylesbury, Bicester and Banbury, suggesting that he seek further directions when he entered Warwickshire. The mention of Bicester, only a ten-minute ride from his home village, decided the matter. With the first seed of an idea forming at the back of his mind, Tom said that even if there were a more direct route than the Coventry one, he would not take it. He thanked his guides for their advice, threw a coin to the tapster with instructions that he was to buy them all ale, and leaped back into the saddle. Twenty minutes later he had turned right at Tyburn and was riding hard up the Edgeware Road towards Paddington and Hendon.

His frantic pace could not last. By the time he reached the windmill on Shoot Up Hill, the sense of desperate urgency which had fired him when he left home had largely burned itself out. Struggling up the incline towards the hamlet of Cricklewood, he eased Princess to a walk. Away to his right the wooded domes of Hampstead Heath blazed like copper shields in the setting sun. Now that he was travelling more slowly, he could feel the warm and enervating evening air wrapping him about in a cloak of calm. His senses came alive again, and he started to think more rationally about what he was trying to do. It was virtually impossible for Fuller to have set out before him, he reasoned. Besides, having no authority outside his own district, to remain within the law he would be obliged to get the support of a like-minded magistrate in the vicinity of Wolverhampton before beginning his search. At the soonest, Tom concluded, it would be several days before John was in danger.

Much more relaxed, he allowed his mind to return to the plan which had first occurred to him in the Bear. The more he thought about it, the more important it became, so that by the time he reached Hendon, where he decided to spend the night, it was dominating his thoughts like an obsession. And he was still wrestling with it — unsure whether it was feasible, let alone sensible or fair — when he dropped off to sleep.

A night's rest brought the issue no nearer resolution. He worried over it while he was dressing, during breakfast and for the first hour of his journey. In the end, believing he would go mad if he did not resolve the matter, he managed to put it out of his mind for the moment. He would, he told himself, take it up again when he was nearer home and a decision could not be put off any longer.

The remainder of the day's journey was a delight. A gentle south-westerly breeze brought an alternating canopy of billowing cloud and blue sky. Rather than spoil the effect, the occasional showers only fed the sense of well-being swelling in his heart. The wind on his cheek, the natural music of the field and wood, the thick, pungent smell of sun on the countryside after rain — all these told him that he was travelling towards more than a physical home. He was rediscovering his existence as a creature of the earth, for whom the rolling cycles of weather and season, crop and harvest, were vital milestones along the road of his life. He felt refreshed, like a snake which had sloughed off an old skin and now slithered clean and bright into a new existence.

Sometimes he thought of Lucy and of what she had said before they parted. But he did so with neither bitterness nor sorrow. It was as if she belonged to a different part of his life, a part which, now that he was out of London, no longer seemed of such vital importance, and his mind soon drifted to other matters. By midday, as he left the River Gade at Two Waters and swung north-west into the Chilterns along the broad valley of the Bulbourne, he was more concerned with how he should break the news of Sarah's death to John than with his own domestic troubles. Just beyond Tring he picked up Akeman Street, an old Roman road, and made good progress through Aylesbury towards the Oxfordshire border. The countryside became more and more familiar with every mile he rode. Finally, when he crossed the River Ray and saw the mound of Blackthorn Hill rising before him, he realised that he could no longer avoid making the decision he had been putting off all day. Anxiously biting his lower lip, he dismounted. For five minutes he stood beside the deserted highway, gazing about him and listening to the steady chomp of Princess grazing by the roadside. Eventually, taking a deep breath and smiling to himself, he climbed wearily back into the saddle and resumed his journey.

But less than a mile further on, instead of continuing down the Bicester road, he turned right along a rough track. It was now dusk, and by following field paths known to him since his childhood, he skirted round the handful of cottages and farms of Launton hamlet and rejoined the track heading north-east. Turning left before Field Farm, he made for the clump of marshy scrub known as Poodle Gorse.

By now it was almost completely dark. The wind had dropped away to the merest breath, leaving the whole countryside as quiet as a cellar. Even the birds were silent. Occasionally a dog barked anxiously at a shadow, then was still. On the hour, with the sound of pebbles clanging into an iron pail, the cracked bell of the church clock rang out across the fields. Painful waves of nostalgia surged through Tom's heart.

Tying Princess to a tree, he sat on a fallen bough and waited, motionless. Time passed slowly. Once, its twitching nose sharp as a pen, a fox came stealing by. Tom saw the creature before it saw him, and whispered into the darkness, 'Well met, old friend!' For an instant the animal froze — an ebony statue — before fleeing silently into the darkness. Princess gave a whinny of surprise.

One by one the flickering lights of the distant village went out. It began to grow cold. Needle-bright stars and a thin sliver of moon lit up the sky. The clock struck ten. Half an hour later, judging that everyone would now be asleep, Tom rose and whispered in Princess's ear that he would be back shortly. Then, pulling his cloak about him, he set off like a thief across the glistening fields towards the dark shapes of the houses and barns of his native village.

ii

Guided by the sombre shadow of the church, Tom made his way cautiously into Stratton Audley along a roundabout route from the west. From the fields he picked his way through cabbage-clumped cottage gardens as far as the Marsh Gibbon road. Keeping out of direct moonlight and bearing right about fifty yards from the green, he cut though the churchyard, ran over Fringford Lane and vaulted the wall surrounding the manor grounds. Hiding among the trees beside the drive, through his spectacles he could just discern the familiar outlines of the building which had housed the Verneys of Stratton Audley for the last two centuries. Indeed, as he was so painfully aware, it was much more than just a home — it was a symbol, a monument, a tangible, living record of his family's history.

To the left, half hidden behind the boughs of a spreading beech, stood the oldest wing of the house, originally a separate three-storeyed manor of stone, brick and timber, erected by Tom's ambitious fifteenth-century ancestors – yeomen who had prospered during the economic turmoil following the Black Death – as a proud manifestation of their new status. In the reign of Henry VII a small stone hall, topped with an elegantly beamed roof, had been built beside it. Apart from the addition of five spiralling brick chimney pots and various internal alterations, the building had remained unchanged until, following the accession of Queen Elizabeth, Tom's great-grandfather, Henry Verney, had drawn up plans to add new wings to the north and south of the hall, the latter replacing the original medieval structure. The resultant building, Henry declared proudly, would resemble a capital H. Unfortunately he had died two years later, aged twenty-eight, when the walls of his north block were only a few feet high and the southern counterpart not even begun. As his heir, Thomas Verney – after whom Tom had been named – was a mere baby at the time, the project was neglected for many years. When it was finally taken up again architectural styles had changed considerably and Thomas had a fresh set of plans prepared. Work on the north wing was resumed during the second year of the new century and completed in 1607, a year before Thomas's death. As the southern wing had never progressed beyond the design stage, Thomas was not slow to point out that the building now resembled a T rather than an H. But when his son John, the present owner, suggested that the scullery projecting behind the medieval building made the whole more like a J, the old man snorted and said that even if that were true, which it was not, the J would stand for King James, not John Verney.

And all this, thought Tom, staring at the moonlight gleaming white on the blind eyes of the windows, was one day to have been mine. The house, the gardens, the lands, the servants, the tenants, the history, the memories and the dreams. But now, because of love, because of duty, because of Lucy, it would not be. He sighed, and with the eye of imagination tried to look through the walls at his family asleep in their beds. He wondered whether any of them were dreaming of him. For a second, he considered marching up to the front door, hammering the household awake and announcing that he had come home, alone. But even as the idea passed through his mind he knew it to be foolish. Not only was it most unlikely that his father would accept him, but he recognised that he would never be able to live with himself if he added the most precious name of all to his list of betrayals. A cold gust of wind blew down the drive and he shivered. 'Farewell!' he whispered to the chill night air. 'Farewell, Father, Mother, Elizabeth, Lucius, Anne! God bless you! Tom has not forgotten you, and he never will, as long as there is life in his body.' Blowing a kiss into the night air and looking back at the house one last time, he turned and walked away, wiping his eyes on his sleeve.

Once over the wall, Tom retraced his steps to Poodle Gorse, collected Princess and followed the bank of a brook running north-east through the fields as far as a low ridge. Reaching the Poundon road, he did not ride west to rejoin the main highway north of Bicester. Instead, he turned right down the narrow track running along the wooded spur pointing like a finger towards Godington, a hamlet which lay on low, marshy ground beside a tributary of the Great Ouse.

A mile or so down the lane he crossed a small stream and entered the churchyard. The tiny church, no larger than an ordinary barn, loomed before him in the darkness. Tethering Princess to a yew tree, he continued on foot, walking stealthily along a path between the graves to an orchard. The rich scent of blossom hung in the still night air. Beyond the trees he could make out a high wall, with the blue-black outline of a large house behind it. Swiftly he ran across the orchard, his boots swishing in the long, damp grass, and climbed the branches of a trailing pear to the top of the wall. Now level with the first-storey windows, he scrambled along till he drew level with a small casement closed with shutters. By holding fast to the stones on the top of the wall with his left hand, he was just able to lean over the gap and reach the shutters with the fingers of his right. He pulled.

Nothing happened. He pulled again. Securely fastened from the inside, the shutters would not move.

God's eyes! he thought. To come so close and not see her — it was impossible! He changed his grip on the wall, leaned even further over and gave the shutters a more vigorous tug. Still they did not budge. But the stone he was using as an anchor broke free and tumbled to the ground with a crash. Clinging to the wall with his legs, as if he were in the saddle, he just managed to stop himself plummeting after it.

Muttering under his breath, he hauled himself upright and took stock of his situation. It was no good, he realised. Short of taking an axe to them, the shutters would remain closed and he would be obliged to resume his journey without achieving the purpose of his detour.

He clenched his teeth together in frustration and decided that he simply could not go without leaving some mark of his having been there. A written note was out of the question. He had no distinctive button or piece of jewellery to push between the slats of the shutter. So what could he do? Taking out his knife, he bent down and started to scratch a message on the soft limestone of the wall. He worked directly opposite the window, so that anyone looking out would be certain to see what he wrote.

He had finished the T of his name and was struggling to complete a recognisably circular O, when a voice whispered out of the darkness, 'I would not do that, Tom.'

Startled, he sat up. 'Anne!' he exclaimed, almost dropping his knife. 'What are you doing there?' His pulse was racing.

'What am I doing? Surely, Tom, it is you who should answer that. As this is my bedchamber, am I not entitled to be in it? What I wish to know is why a married man, supposed to be in London, is sitting on a wall opposite my window in the middle of the night, carving his name like a coat of arms for all the world to see.'

Tom hardly knew what to reply. He peered into the darkness at the pale face framed between curtains of long black hair and muttered, 'I wished – no, I needed to see you.'

'Needed? Your last letter was a farewell.'

'It was, but—' He was suddenly struck by the ridiculousness of his position. 'Anne?'

'Yes?' Her voice was calm and reserved.

'May I climb off the wall?'

'Certainly you may. Where will you go?'

He hesitated momentarily. Unable to see her face, he was not quite sure whether her obtuseness was real or feigned. 'I would like to come over into your room,' he answered finally, trying to sound mischievous and wounded at the same time.

There was a long pause. In the distance an owl hooted. The apple blossom, gleaming with phosphorescent brilliance in the moonlight, rustled against the leaves of the trees.

Eventually, Anne broke the silence. 'Tom Verney, you have not changed. Thank God.' Her tone was softer now, almost sad. 'Yes. Climb over if you are able. But mind you do not fall.'

Leaning across the gap, he held onto the window-sill, let his legs drop, then pulled himself quietly into the room. Anne was sitting on the side of the bed, dressed in a long night-gown with a shawl over her shoulders.

'How did you know I was there?' Tom whispered, tiptoeing across to her.

'I was not asleep. When I heard a noise at my window, I thought it must be a squirrel, so I went to see.' She held out her hand. 'Here, come and sit beside me and tell me what it is that brings you here. If you are seeking reconciliation with your father, I fear you will have little joy. He is, they say, consumed with fury at what you have done.'

He sat on the bed and put his arm round her shoulders. 'No. The squirrel is here to see you, Anne, not my father. I am journeying to Staffordshire – on business.'

'What business, Tom? I know so little of what you have been up to these seven months, except that you have married and been more welcome at court than at Clement's Inn. Come, it is not yet struck midnight. Tell me all.'

And so, sitting in the dark and holding tightly to one of his oldest and dearest friends, he recounted everything that had happened to him since he had left home. Unlike his conversations with Lucy, or even with John, with Anne he felt he had nothing to hide. As a result, he was obliged to confront truths about his behaviour and motives which hitherto he had been unwilling or unable to recognise. It was an exhausting experience. When he had finished, feeling as if a huge boil had been lanced and poison drawn from his body, he took his arm from round Anne's shoulders and flopped back on the bed with a sigh.

'Well,' she said, turning and lying on her front beside him, 'I would be a foolish person if I tried to pass judgement on that great pudding of adventures, Tom!' Her words were light-hearted, but her tone was streaked with despondency. When he stretched out his arm to make a pillow, she rolled over without a word and lay beside him.

Staring up at the dark ceiling, she whispered, 'You know, do you not, that I would you had done otherwise?'

'You need not say it, Anne. At times I wish so myself. It is like that even now.'

'You must not say that,' she scolded, without conviction. 'It will make matters worse. What is done, is done.'

For a minute or two they lay without speaking, each reflecting on the depressing truth of the maxim.

'And now, it is your turn to listen,' she said with the determined air of someone who had been unsure whether to talk or not. 'I have news of my own.'

Inclining his head towards her, in the gloom he could just make out the distinctive nose, high forehead and soft chin of her profile. 'Tell me your news,' he asked, running a finger down her cheek.

'You will not be angry?'

'I am too tired for anger, Anne.'

'Then listen. You know Sir Nicholas Morrison of Steeple Aston?' Tom grunted assent. Who in the district did not know Sir Nicholas, the genial old buffer with a penchant for pretty faces? 'Next year,' Anne continued, so quietly as to be almost inaudible, 'in the summer, I am to become his wife.'

'His what?' cried Tom, sitting bolt upright.

'Shhh!' she hissed, grabbing his coat and pulling him down again. 'You'll wake the household. You heard right enough, Tom. I, too, am to be married.'

'Oh, Anne! Why?'

Her answer was bitter, almost a rebuke. 'If it displeases you, Tom, remember you have yourself to blame.'

'Myself? How is that?'

In a voice thick with emotion, she explained how over the last few years an unpleasant quarrel had arisen between her father and Sir Nicholas over the possession of some extensive water meadows beside the Great Ouse. Recently Sir Nicholas had threatened to take the matter to court where, given his superior wealth and connections, he was almost certain to win, thereby depriving Toby Hutchinson of the best part of his estate. Shortly after Anne had heard of Tom's illicit marriage, Sir Nicholas had made a surprise visit to suggest a way of reconciling the Morrison-Hutchinson disagreement. If Anne would consent to being his third wife, he had promised to sign papers making over all the disputed water meadows to the Hutchinsons.

Toby Hutchinson cared deeply for his daughter. Initially he had been so shocked by the proposal, which, he said, asked him to sell his daughter like an African slave, that he would not even agree to put it to her. But in the end, after much persuasion, he had changed his mind and acquainted Anne with forty-eight-year-old Sir Nicholas's offer. He made it quite clear that he knew what her answer would be and that this would not disconcert him in the slightest. To his complete surprise, however, she did not reject the proposal out of hand, but asked for time to think it over. Two days later she announced her decision to her astonished family.

'I told them,' she explained, 'that since Sir Nicholas was a good man and a rich one, a girl could do worse than take such a one for a husband. And if by so doing she could help her parents, it was a doubly sensible match.'

Tom was so downcast at hearing her story that he could hardly speak. 'Anne, did you believe that, truly?' he asked.

'I did, Tom, at the time.'

'And now?'

'You know my answer before you ask. Like you, there are moments when I wish the wind had blown from another point of the compass.'

He turned his head to find her face barely an inch away. Gazing into the moonstone whites of her eyes, he felt the zephyr of her breath playing across his cheek. For the first time since his arrival, he was aware of the powerful animal magnetism which had always drawn them together. 'Is this one of those moments?' he asked, searching for her hand.

'My answer cannot be given in words, Tom,' she said, slipping her hand round the back of his neck and drawing him closer still.

With his lips brushing against hers, he teased, 'If not with words, then how?'

'Ah, Tom,' she whispered mischievously, 'that is for you to guess, is it not?'

'Maybe like – this?'

In reply, she closed her mouth softly over his and nestled against him.

As if they had discussed the matter beforehand, they both

knew instinctively the boundary which they could not cross. It was, Anne whispered as she turned reluctantly away from him, a mutual penance for past impulsiveness. Yet another ill-considered action would only make matters harder for them both.

A while later the events of the long day finally caught up with Tom, and he fell asleep. When Anne gently shook him awake the first yellow light of dawn was brightening the sky and there was no time to lose if he was to get out of the district without being recognised. Having washed his face at a basin in the corner of the room, he turned and took Anne in his arms for the last time.

'This time it is a true farewell, Tom,' she said. 'We must be strong, for we have chosen other paths and need to follow them.'

He kissed her gently. 'I know,' he said. 'I am learning, but I would it were not such a painful lesson, my love.'

'What did you say?'

'I said I would it were not so painful.'

'No, after that.'

'I called you "my love".'

She rested her hands against his chest. 'It is an easy phrase to say, Tom. But not so easy to mean. We each have others to love and must not play with their hearts as we play with words.'

Silent and motionless, they stood looking into each other's eyes, wondering whether they saw another person or a reflection of themselves.

A cock crowed in the yard at the back of the house.

Without a word, Tom hurried to the window, crouched on the sill and jumped nimbly over to the orchard wall. Turning and looking back at the window, he asked, 'Anne, was it right to come?'

'Yes. It was. We have something to remember. Always. It will sweeten whatever bitterness lies ahead.'

'Will it? I fear it has served to make the future more painful still.'

'You must not think that. Promise me?'

'I will try. Farewell. My dearest friend.'

'Oh, Tom! Will you—'

He heard no more. Alarmed by the clanging of milk pails in the dairy, he dropped into the orchard and ran to collect Princess. By sunrise he was five miles away, nearing Stoke Lyne and the highway to the north.

iii

Utterly fatigued, Tom reached Moseley Hall early that evening. He had no difficulty in finding the place, a huge, gabled, half-timbered building standing on a remote stretch of the road running north from Wolverhampton. Everyone he asked knew of 'the late Mr Pitt's new hall' which, before her marriage to the fortunate Thomas Whitgreave, had made lovely Alice Pitt the most sought-after heiress in the hundred, if not the county. Sliding down from Princess's back and staggering like a drunk, Tom made his way slowly to the wooden-pillared porch and, praying fervently that John was within, beat feebly at the door with his fist.

A maidservant appeared. 'Yes, sir?' she enquired, staring in apprehension at the red-eyed and travel-stained figure who leaned against one of the pillars for support.

'I am seeking one John, a large fellow with a beard. Might he be found here?' His voice was flat and tired.

'John? No man of that name here, sir. My master is called Thomas, the cook is Peter, the groom—'

'Do not list the household, I pray!' snapped Tom, too

fatigued for civility. 'Listen. I am here on weighty business. I have ridden directly from London' – a shadow passed across the girl's face – 'and need to find this John. If he is here, I beg you do not conceal him from me.' He lurched towards the door.

The girl put out her hands to stop him. 'Help!' she called loudly over her shoulder, 'To the door! There is a stranger here says he would speak with one John. He is making to force his way in!'

As Tom struggled to get round her, there was a clatter of footsteps in the hall behind. A pistol barrel was pushed into his face.

'Stand back, villain!' Tom did as he was bidden and squatted down on his haunches, too tired to remain upright. He looked up to see a well-dressed, stockily built man of about thirty-five staring down at him with eyes as blue as sapphires. 'If you move, sir,' the stranger said, lowering his pistol to Tom's chest, 'I will put a hole through your heart.' He glanced round at the small crowd of servants peering over his shoulder. 'Do I speak the truth, men of Moseley?' he asked with a flourish, as if making a play out of his confrontation with the intruder.

'Aye, aye!' came the muttered reply.

The pistol-carrier smiled. 'Now, strange rider,' he continued, shifting his attention back to Tom and resuming his stern expression, 'you are come here to find a John?'

'I am.'

'Why?'

'I have important news for him. It might save his life.'

'Your name?'

'Tom Verney, of Stratton Audley, Oxfordshire.' Tom closed his eyes. He was fast approaching the point where he would be too tired to care whether he found John or not. All he wanted to do was sleep.

His questioner called into the house, 'Alice, my sweetmeat! There is an Oxfordshire fellow at our door who says he seeks one John.' He turned back to Tom and asked, 'John who, blockhead? John of where? What John? Which John? Why there must be more Johns in England than sheep! Speak I true, men of Moseley?'

Again the chorus gave their soloist unanimous support.

'I know him only as John,' said Tom with a yawn.

'Ha!' retorted the bright-eyed inquisitor. He shouted inside again. 'Alice! It is a simple John he seeks. No other name. Odd, eh? Shall I shoot him, Mrs Whitgreave, my love?'

A female voice called from somewhere upstairs, 'First ask him his name, Thomas. Or else we shall not know what to carve on his headstone.'

'Sharp, my precious! Sharp! His parents named him Thomas, like me. But he prunes it to Tom, lest he forget it!' A cackle of laughter broke from the onlookers.

'Tom what, husband dear?' The voice was sparkled with good humour.

'God's chest! I have forgot.' He gave Tom his full attention. 'Dirty horseman, before I end your life and give Sally here the merry task of washing your blood from our doorstep, tell me your name again.'

Tom's head had sunk to his knees. He was hardly listening. 'Eh?' he grunted. 'What was that?'

'Afore God! What spirit!' cried Thomas Whitgreave — jolly sapphire-eyes was indeed the master of Moseley Hall. 'Here's no coward, for he sleeps when faced with the most cruel of deaths.' He nodded towards his servants and asked, 'Surely, men of Moseley, I am a fiendishly frightening fellow?'

This time the chorus was divided. Those who instinctively knew their parts mumbled in the affirmative. The majority, however, disagreed.

'Damn me!' said Whitgreave with a laugh. 'Then I needs become yet more vicious, more harsh still. I shall begin with this worm.' He gave Tom a poke with his foot. 'Fellow! Sleepy scoundrel, what did you say your name was?'

'Thomas Verney.'

'Alice angel,' called Whitgreave, 'our visitor says he was baptised – if ever holy water touched his sweaty skin – with the name of Thomas Verney...'

A tremendous roar burst from within the house. 'By the blessed bowels of our saviour! Tom Verney? Here, let me see him! Make way, there!'

Tom was taken up in a great wave of relief. He had come neither to the wrong house, nor was he too late. Smiling, yet more asleep than awake, he allowed John to lift him in his arms and carry him into the house like a child.

Over the next two days the atmosphere of Moseley Hall was a contrary blend of honey and onions. The sweetness came from Thomas and Alice Whitgreave. Tom had never met such a warm and genial couple, nor had he ever set foot inside such a happy and relaxed household as the one over which they presided. Ignoring the fact that he had come to Staffordshire only because he had betrayed John's whereabouts, they treated him as a hero, apologising profusely for the way he had been received initially. The reason, Alice explained, was that while John was sheltering with them it was essential to be wary of all strangers. They had established the routine to which Tom had been subjected as a way of checking for spies and fanatics.

Alice was a Roman Catholic, her husband an Anglican.

'Alas,' she said with a shrug, 'I fear we have been born with no brains, Tom, for we can find nothing in this to squabble over. Thomas and I are going to the same place by different roads, that is all. We are too stupid to see that this is good reason to burn or torment each other.' She stood beside her husband, smiling and holding his hands. 'Yet my Thomas is such a wild and contrary beast that every day I seek reason to slay him, do I not, my love?'

'You do, Alice,' he replied, kissing her fondly. 'And likewise I wake each morning in the hope that I will find an opportunity to rid myself of the wicked papist to whom I have the misfortune to be wed.'

As Tom watched the matched and contented couple, he thought of Lucy and was filled with sadness.

On the evening of his arrival, after he had been taken into the house and fed, Tom had told John that Fuller would almost certainly come looking for him, and suggested he flee into hiding elsewhere. To his surprise, neither John nor the Whitgreaves would hear of it. They all agreed that even if Fuller managed to get into the house to search for John, he would never find him. 'You see, sir,' whispered Thomas Whitgreave, 'when Alice's father had the Hall built some twenty years ago' – he dropped his voice still further – 'he took the wise precaution of seeing that it contained a pair of useful "devices".' Mystified, Tom enquired further, but was told politely that the matter had to remain a secret until such time as it might be required.

At this point the Whitgreaves glanced at each other and retired, taking the servants with them, leaving Tom and John to talk. It was the moment Tom had been dreading ever since leaving London. He had hoped to put it off until he had rested and felt better able to bear the strain. But as soon as the door closed John laid a hand on his arm and started asking him what he knew about the events of that fateful day at Pickering House, about the shot he had heard and how his dear Sarah was. He cursed himself, he said, for fleeing and leaving her to the mercy of her cruel father. 'Tell me, Tom,' he insisted, leaning forward urgently, 'that spike-thighed, snake-eyed puritanical devil did not hurt her, did he? By Christ's holy beard, Tom, tell me that. Tell me she is not being tormented for what I did.'

Raising his young eyes, circled with the grey rings of tiredness, Tom gazed into his friend's anxious face. 'No, John. Sarah's father did not hurt her.' He swallowed. 'Nor is she being tormented. She ...'. He stopped, unable to continue.

But what words did not say, his tone and expression announced with the clarity of a proclamation. John's powerful shoulders hunched forward. His head hung down and, slowly, like a great beast shot through the heart, he sank to his knees. 'Tell me, Tom Verney,' he said, clearly and deliberately, 'my beloved Sarah, the dearest creature on this earth, she who means more to me than my own life, tell me, is she dead?'

Tears poured down Tom's face. He tried to speak, but his dry throat would not respond. When John looked up at him, all Tom could do was shut his eyes and nod, like a dumb ass in a collar.

As if torn bleeding from deep within him, a truly terrible sound issued from John's lips – a low, infinitely long howl of lamentation, part cry, scream, moan, wail, sob and sigh, combining every anguish the human voice could articulate in a quiet resonance of unbearable sadness and despair.

A shudder of fear ran down Tom's spine. Without quite knowing why, he now realised that there would be a great deal more suffering before the feud between John and Fuller had run its course.

Fighting his tiredness, he quickly outlined how Sarah had died. Then he kept his stricken friend company for as long as he could hold his eyes open. The last thing he remembered was being gently shaken awake and told to go to bed. Reluctantly agreeing to do so, he slept longer and deeper than at any time since his childhood.

The next day, Wednesday, there was no sign of John. When he eventually appeared on Thursday afternoon, he surprised Tom by seeming to be his old vigorous, outspoken, and generous self, as much a part of the benevolent Moseley Hall community as the Whitgreaves themselves. Not once did he refer to Sarah's tragic death, and when Tom attempted well-meant words of condolence, he sharply bade him 'hold his tongue and talk no more of yesterdays'. Only once, when he caught sight of his friend sitting alone by the fire, was Tom given a glimpse of the struggle raging within John's heart. As he slapped one fist into the other, he silently mouthed the same word over and over again. Even without his spectacles, Tom knew the word. It was a name. The name of the girl neither of them would ever set eyes on again.

iv

Warning of Fuller's arrival in the vicinity came on the 11th May. The cook and her boy returned from Wolverhampton market with the news that a strange magistrate from down south was staying at the Queen's Arms, where he had met with the puritanical local justice, Mr Accepted Coalpit. Immediately, a lookout was established in the attic window overlooking the main road, and at night two watchmen were kept permanently patrolling the grounds. Drawing Tom aside after dinner, Thomas Whitgreave led him to the top of the house. There, under the rafters, he showed him a little chapel, neatly painted and simply furnished. 'You may think it strange,' he explained, 'to find a place of worship so far from the ground, like a bird's nest. But it is a Catholic chapel, built by my father-in-law, and it is not always wise to make a show of such features.

'Now come,' he went on, taking a tall stool from the chapel and proceeding further into the attic, 'I will show you one of Mr Pitt's devices, of which I spoke when you first arrived.'

So saying, he walked past the chimney to the small garret, which was serving as a lookout, dismissed the watch, placed the stool by the door and climbed up onto it. Tom watched in amazement. Releasing some hidden catch, with a careful sliding movement Whitgreave lifted off part of the lath and plaster wall between two crossbeams to reveal a small hiding place beneath the tiles.

'There!' he said, stepping off the stool and bidding Tom take a look for himself. 'Is that not the very trimmest lair as ever a fox could hide himself in?'

Tom peered into the dark, stuffy space. 'Is this what they term a priest hole, Mr Whitgreave?' he asked, pulling himself up and pushing his head and shoulders through the opening.

'It is. I believe Mr Pitt ordered its construction for the concealment of massing stuff from the chapel. But it will serve for a man of your size well enough.'

'Am I to hide in there if Fuller comes to search?' Tom asked apprehensively. If threatened, his instinct would be to make for the open and trust to Princess's speed rather than creep away to a hole in the roof.

Whitgreave saw the doubt on his face. 'Do not fear,

Tom. You will be as safe in there as in the Tower of London.'

As the Tower had probably meant death to more subjects than it had saved, Tom did not find the remark particularly reassuring. Nevertheless, he trusted Whitgreave, and rather than question his judgement he resolved to use the priest hole if Fuller came to search.

He did not have long to wait.

The alarm was sounded by Will the ostler at about nine o'clock on Monday morning, the day before Tom was planning to leave for home. Frantically waving a small hand-bell round and round his head, he bounded down from the attic crying, 'I spied Coalpit! Mr Whitgreave, I spied Coalpit!'

'Are you certain, Will?' asked the master of the house, hurrying from the library. 'Think carefully now.' Hearing the noise, John and Tom had already gathered at his side.

'Aye, Mr Whitgreave. No missin' he. Little black man on a big white horse. With another black man I dunna know.'

'Two black men?'

'Black clothes, I min.'

Whitgreave turned to his guests. 'That sounds like them, sirs. To your places.'

John and Tom embraced warmly, then John lumbered off to his 'device' to hide. Having sent his steward round the house to remind everyone of their duty, Whitgreave accompanied Tom to the attic.

'I do wonder sometimes, Mr Whitgreave, why I am doing this,' reflected Tom with a laugh as he was eased feet-first into the hole.

'Rather late now, sir, for such thoughts,' grinned Whitgreave. With his handkerchief he cleaned the wall where Tom's foot had left a dirty mark. 'Yet it is simple enough, surely? If you are seen here, they will understand that John is here too.'

Tom had wriggled backwards so that only his head was still projecting from the hide. 'Yes, I understand,' he answered. 'But to risk my position for a man like John – well, is that wise?'

'I understand your worry, Tom,' Whitgreave smiled. 'Yet for all that has happened, Father John is a good man.' He took up the panel which covered the entrance.

'Father John?' gasped Tom.

'Yes. I know we are wrong. Yet we still call him that at times. We – my wife in particular – like to remember his former days. Before – you know.'

'Tell me—'

'Enough, Tom! Fie, what a chatterer you are! It is dangerous to talk further now.' He lifted the door and held it before Tom's head. 'You did pass water before coming up here, as I said? It can be very uncomfortable otherwise.'

'Yes. I would not soil myself, even for Father John.'

'Very good. I would not wish our justices to believe we had a leaking roof. Farewell.' Whitgreave put the panel in place and secured it fast. Seconds later his footsteps echoed away down the stairs. Craning his neck to one side, Tom looked about his cramped, incense-perfumed hiding place. Made solid by the dusty air, thin shafts of sunlight flooded in between the tiles to cast bright patterns down his body. He closed his eyes and lowered his head onto the oak boards. Above him a bird hopped along the ridge. A bee buzzed in through a gap in the tiles and tasted the lifeless air before flying out again. It was so peaceful.

Then, from far below, came the sound of knocking.

*

Acting according to a carefully prepared plan, Justices Fuller and Coalpit decided to make no secret of their visit. Moseley Hall was known throughout the district for being a contented and close-knit community, so there was little point in their being heavy-handed. At least, not to begin with. Besides, until they had more concrete evidence to act upon, they could do no more than make preliminary enquiries.

Welcoming his visitors with his customary politeness, Whitgreave led them to a panelled reception room on the ground floor. Here, after they had both refused offers of refreshment, Coalpit explained the purpose of their visit. 'My friend Justice Fuller of Stokenchurch, Oxfordshire,' he began, speaking very quickly and without pause, as was his wont, 'tells me that a notorious papist rogue whom he is pursuing may have come hither from London in the past few days to escape the arm of the law and should you have set eyes on such a creature or have heard anyone even a servant of the humblest degree speak of him we ask you to send and move such knowledge in the direction of those charged by His Majesty King James with upholding godly justice and Christian ways in this great realm of ours.'

Whitgreave, who throughout this peroration had sat with his head back and eyes closed, now opened one eye and looked at each of the justices in turn. They really were an odd pair, he thought: the local man a tiny, almost dwarfish thing, with a nose hooked like a scythe; the stranger a tall, lean fellow, always twisting about as if he had a nest of vipers in his belly. He let them wait a little longer, then replied, 'No!' and shut his eyes again.

Fuller, who had sat twitching and wriggling ever since coming into the room, could contain himself no longer.

'Mr Whitgroove—' he began.

'Whitgreave,' corrected Thomas without opening his eyes. 'Do not be ashamed. I will not have you whipped, for it is an easy error. Many make it.'

'Mr Whitgreave—' spluttered Fuller.

'Ah! That is it! Well done! For the future, may I suggest a simple device? When you set eyes on me, you may recall that I am so lacking in *wit* that you must *grieve* for me! Ha, ha! Neat, sir, is it not? A device of my wife's making. Her family – the Pitts – were full of devices.'

'No. You said no in answer to the question of my colleague, Justice Coalpit,' said Fuller, so relieved at being able to get a word in that he cast aside all formal politeness. 'What did you mean, sir?'

Whitgreave looked at him closely. 'No, sir, means no.'

'No to which question, sir?' asked Fuller growing angry.

Having tested Fuller and found him as unpleasant as he had been led to believe, Whitgreave decided it was time to stop playing. 'I crave your indulgence, sirs,' he said brightly, standing up and moving to the fireplace. 'I have been dreaming. No, I have not seen any criminals. And yes, if I do meet with any such I will inform the authorities.'

Fuller did not like this answer, but before he could comment Coalpit said, 'We thank you, Mr Whitgreave, sir, for so firm a denial of complicity with those who stand on the opposite bank of the stream of law, a statement which we will record and keep for posterity to admire and read when they see fit.' Rising to his feet so that his head was now level with Fuller's, he walked round to the back of his chair and peered at Whitgreave over the wheel-spoked back. 'And now, sir, before we depart to pursue other matters in other places may we ask you to conduct us briefly about this fine hall which your father-in-law erected and which is much talked of as an example that even a papist may commission fine work if the Lord directs him aright. Ha! I have even heard say,' he went on, trotting round the chair and contorting his face with a look of contrived jocularity, 'that during the construction of Moseley Hall, Mr Pitt – ha! – ordered the placing of secret holes – ha-ha! – for the concealment of Romish priests and their popish stuff but I suppose this is mere fanciful rumour, is it not? Ha-ha!'

'It is,' said Whitgreave bluntly, feeling Fuller's black eyes burning into him. 'But, please, allow me to show you Mr Pitt's handiwork.'

The tour did not take long. Only once, when they paused before a small door which, when asked where it led, Whitgreave dismissed as 'merely a minor way to the attic', did Fuller and Coalpit show much interest. An hour after their arrival, the justices had made their formal farewells and were riding back towards Wolverhampton.

'Well, Justice Fuller,' asked Coalpit with unusual brevity, 'did you learn what I learned from our visit?'

'I did, Justice Coalpit. I did. That man Whitgreave does not like us. Yet God has revealed to me that my man is there, or has been there. I feel it in my bones. Praised be His holy name!'

'Amen!' chirped the smaller man.

'And Justice Coalpit—'

'Yes?'

'We know the place where we must search for him when we return, do we not?'

'We do, Justice Fuller.'

'The attic,' they chorused.

With the gleam of anticipated triumph shining in their eyes, they rode on in silence towards the distant town.

FIFTEEN

MOSELEY HALL

i

Like all obsessive puritans, Justice Fuller was mean and cautious. Before departing for Staffordshire, he had not only locked his room in Pickering House and taken the key with him, but he had also left everything of value in a large box which he had secured with an elaborate lock and chained to a leg of his bed.

The resourceful Tilly had no difficulty with the first line of defence – she simply stole a spare key from Lord Banbury's steward, Robert, and let herself into the room late one evening when no one was about. Instructed to bring her mistress anything that might throw light on what Fuller was up to, she held her candle before her and peered about the room in surprise. The place was not at all as she remembered it. Wherever possible, stark discomfort had replaced ease and beauty. The rugs and mats had been rolled to one side to reveal hard, bare floorboards; the pictures had been taken down from the walls and stacked neatly in the corner, leaving tomb-like expanses of whitewashed plaster; the fire in the hearth had never been lit; and a sack of coarse wool had been drawn across the soft linen sheets of the bed. The pockets of the magistrate's clothes were empty. As far as she could tell from a quick look round, there was nothing secreted in cupboards, drawers or behind the wainscot. Apart from the chained box, which was too heavy for her to lift on her own, the only other moveable object was a large leather-bound Bible, lying on a table by the bed. Seeing it was embellished with hand-written margin notes and a longer piece penned on a blank page after chapter twenty-two of the Revelation of St John, she gathered it up and left the room, relocking the door carefully behind her.

'And so, your ladyship,' the maid concluded with a slightly downcast look, 'that is all I can report. Room all strange and cold, this big box and this scribbled Bible here.' She pointed to where the volume lay on the table.

'Why so downcast, Tilly?' Elizabeth asked with a smile, rising and giving the girl a coin. 'You have done all I asked of you. When I have read the man's commentary on Holy Scripture, you will return his Bible to where you found it. And not a word to anyone.'

'No truly, your ladyship. And now, I pray you excuse me. I must replace the key before Robert becomes suspicious.' As she turned to leave, she glanced down at her reward and said, 'I am most grateful to your ladyship.'

'It is I who am grateful, Tilly. And tomorrow,' she added, deciding on her next move, 'tomorrow you will send Walter to see me.'

'Walter, your ladyship?' the girl asked in some bewilderment, wondering what Lady Banbury could possibly want with her husband's head coachman.

A mischievous grin tripped the edges of Elizabeth's lips. 'I have lost the key to one of my jewellery boxes,

Tilly,' she said. 'I believe Walter will find me a locksmith who may be trusted.'

Tilly nodded. 'We need a man who may be trusted, don't we, my lady?' she replied, entering into the game with enthusiasm. 'Who knows what may be found in there?'

'The very truth, good maid,' Elizabeth beamed at her. 'Now remember, fail not to send Walter.'

'No, your ladyship.'

'Very good. You may go.'

'Good night, your ladyship.'

'Good night, Tilly. And Tilly—'

The girl looked round. 'Yes, your ladyship?'

'This is the best adventure we have played yet, is it not?'

'It is, my lady,' Tilly smiled. 'It is the best I have ever known.'

When the girl had gone, Elizabeth sat down to look through Fuller's Bible. The comments, scattered throughout the book on almost every page, were in two versions of the same hand. One, obviously written after the other, took the form of amendments or afterthoughts. All were more dogmatic, more passionate than the original commentary. For example, beside where St Luke gave Christ's words on breaking bread at the Last Supper as 'This is my body which is given for you: this do in remembrance of me', the first note, neatly executed, had said simply, 'Here the papists take the words of Our Lord awry.' At a later date this had been vigorously crossed out and replaced in a larger, more untidy hand with 'Was the Saviour of the World a *Cannibal* of the Indies that he should bid us devour him???? To understand thus is the foulest heresy spewed forth from the bowels of the Beast of Rome.'

As Elizabeth was wholly unsympathetic towards Sir Christopher Fuller's spiritual pilgrimage from the moderate to the extreme puritanical wing of the Anglican Church, where she understood them she found most of his comments rather tedious, even distasteful. What held her attention was the fascinating, even frightening manner in which the man's thinking had changed so radically, swinging inexorably from the reasonably logical to the extreme, and then on to the bizarre. Where would it end? she wondered. Some of the remarks towards the back of the volume were so eccentric and disjointed as to be almost incomprehensible. What, she wondered, could he have meant by his untidy heading to the First Epistle of St John: 'Name of God, Name of S***n – sent to test – which which – damned wolf in wool of sheep – watch and pray, wch & py, wch & py – then strike – hard deep long hot burning iron fire to very soul of Antichrist?'

As it was already quite late by the time she reached the last page, she was about to set the Bible down and leave the final, longer passage of annotation to the morning, when she happened to catch its title, 'Revelation of C.F. 1st day of January. One thousand six hundred and twenty-three years since the birth of Our Lord.'

The Revelation of Justice Fuller! There was no way she could go to bed now. Fascinated, she read on.

The magistrate's mystical prophesy took the form of an extraordinary story, written rapidly in the same scrawly hand as the amended commentary in the rest of the Bible. It told how God raised a man, 'deserted by women', from the depths of a stinking pond and charged him with saving his nation from a dragon. The creature, part beast and part human, had 'seven wings scaled like breastplates' and a bearded, plague-breathing head, fashioned like an elephant and bearing three eyes, 'two as God has given us and a third, set upon his forehead, brightest and deepest of all, cut in the form of the legs of the Whore of Rome with the ball socket placed where all men lust and fall.' Riding upon his back was 'an old man from the north, whose forked tongue spoke strangely of his love for God, while in his black heart all he wished was to conquer for Satan and the Whore of Rome.'

The tale explained that when the man from the pond arose, covered in sores and foul smelling, he saw, 'through eyes bestrewn with weeds and spawn', the deceitful rider taking 'his terrible steed to the ranks of the ungodly, that from them he might gather strength with which to cast the faithful into the pit of eternal damnation, fire, poison, torment and pain.' The pond hero gave chase. Eventually, after a long struggle which concluded when the dragon and its master were consumed in carefully directed holy fire, he was taken up into heaven to sit at the right hand of God.

Having read the passage several times without making much sense of it, other than imagining that Fuller probably saw himself as the pond-man 'deserted by women', and the dragon as popery, Elizabeth went to bed and dreamed that Tom Verney had come to see her, flying in naked through the window of her room on the back of a bearded dragon.

Walter said he knew of two locksmiths who could help: Ector of Thames Street, who was 'fresh', and Zachary Hughes ('known to those as is close with him as plain Zak'), who was 'salt'. Lady Banbury looked blank. As they were not fish, she asked, what was the difference between a 'fresh' locksmith and a 'salt' one? In a profession more accustomed to working against the law than within it, Walter explained, the great majority of practitioners, usually the better craftsmen, were criminally inclined, or 'salt' – like most water. The honest minority were 'fresh'. Saying that she was quite sure 'fresh' Ector would be capable of dealing with a simple jewellery box, Elizabeth bade Walter bring him to her two days hence.

The same afternoon, under the pretence of needing to make a tour of inspection of the whole house, she had Tilly bring her the keys of all the rooms. The key to Fuller's room was duly removed from the bunch and the rest returned to the unsuspecting steward a few hours later. That night, grinning like eleven-year-olds creeping down to the kitchens for a slice of midnight pie, Tilly and her mistress made their way to the justice's bedroom. First the maid replaced the Bible exactly as she had found it. Then they lifted the leg of the bed round which the chain was wound and pulled it free. Finally, as quietly as they could, they grasped the box between them and half dragged and half carried it to Elizabeth's rooms, where it was hidden beneath a pile of discarded gowns.

Short, angular and elderly, Ector the locksmith had a key-shaped head and patchwork face that looked as if it had fallen off his skull and been stuck back again in a hurry. Accompanied by his daughter Kitty, he arrived at the time appointed and began to examine the box. The reason for Kitty's presence was apparent as soon as he set to work – despite donning a pair of spectacles with lenses as thick as four piled sovereigns, he could hardly see. He worked with his hands, calling to his daughter every now and again to pass him an instrument or show him where to place his fingers. At one stage in the operation, finding his own fingers too thick and unsteady, he stood behind Kitty and operated through her, using her arms and hands as an extension of his own.

Though the couple's method of working was unusual, it proved effective enough, and within five minutes the lock was free. At this point, thanking Ector for his work and telling him to report to Steward Robert for payment, Lady Banbury stepped forward to raise the lid herself.

'Nay!' the craftsman insisted, blocking her path. 'Op'nin' boxes is not your work, my lady. Might be 'splodin'.'

Startled at his effrontery, Elizabeth bade him stand aside. Still he refused, his scarred face set like a repaired plaster bust.

Just when it looked as if a nasty scene might ensue, Kitty intervened. 'It is yourself my father is guarding, your ladyship,' she explained, looking lovingly at the old man and taking his hand. 'Mr Ector did once find 'is way into a trap-box. One what 'ad been made for another, not 'im. Filled with gunpowder it was. Not made cleaver – the work of the likes of Zak most probably – so it only 'alf 'sploded. Yet burned off Father's face and most of 'is eyes. As you can see. That's why 'e 'as to open all boxes 'iself what 'e works on. Lest they be 'splodin'.'

Disconcerted, Elizabeth said, 'I am indeed sorry to hear that. But I assure you my jewellery box will not explode. Come, I will open it myself.' She took a step forward.

'No, you won't!' cried Ector. 'I knows a jewel box when I feels it, and this ain't one of 'em!' With a quick tug he pulled back the lid.

There was no explosion.

'There! My work is done,' he said with evident relief. 'Now I may go in peace, not in pieces.

'Good day, your ladyship,' he cackled as he was led

towards the door, 'and I 'ope as you find what you is lookin' for.'

When the locksmith and his daughter had gone, Elizabeth took her maid by the hand and approached the box. 'Now, Tilly,' she said, her voice eager with anticipation, 'let us see what surprises this wretched justice has left behind to delight us.'

ii

'Should I run like a fox,' said John, looking earnestly at Thomas Whitgreave, 'as sure as the Lord will send his soul for kindling, one day his cur's nose will raise the scent and he will be on the chase again. And I will run again. And he will chase again. And I will run again – until I turn, and bite his head off! Ha!' With a furious laugh he snapped his teeth together and banged his fist on the table.

The company jumped in their seats and stared at him, momentarily shocked into silence. Then, seeing the twinkle in his eye and grin on his lips, they relaxed and joined in his laughter.

'A toast!' called Thomas Whitgreave, raising his glass and climbing to his feet. 'Here's to John's appetite for puritan morsels!'

The others stood and echoed the cry: 'John's appetite!' Then, following an initiative from Tom, they added, 'And his freedom!'

It was now more than twenty-four hours since Fuller and Coalpit's visit, and the discussion round the dinner table was whether the pair would return and, if they did, would it be safer for John to hide or to leave the district. Alice Whitgreave and Tom had urged him to move on. Thomas Whitgreave and John himself, as he had just announced, thought it wiser to stay put. Certain that the justices would be back, they argued that it would be better for the trail to run cold at Moseley Hall, leaving the pursuivants no clue where their quarry might be, than for so conspicuous a figure as John to take to the roads and risk being identified, or even persecuted because of his brand.

'Moreover,' concluded his host, 'the men and women of Moseley do not wish him to depart from hence. His leaving us would impoverish the whole commonwealth of the Hall. Thus, for our welfare as well as his own, we implore him stay.'

'Bravely spoken, my love,' said Alice quickly. 'My sentiments entirely. I pray you not to think, John, that my counselling your departure was for any reason other than concern for your safety. I would not have you believe—'

John's face clouded with affectionate concern. 'Sweet Alice,' he interrupted kindly, 'say no more. I know that you have my welfare at heart as much as anyone here. By the mass! The love manifested by yourself and those of this place dissolves my choice as sun disperses the frost. I could not go now. Though every mincing, tight-minded, smile-killing, Sabbath-blackening puritan in the land come to draw me forth, here I will remain until they fret themselves to bones in the heat of pursuit, and creep in broken despair back to their unhappy, narrow hovels of bigotry!'

After a round of applause at this announcement, the meal was concluded in the best of spirits. Afterwards, Thomas Whitgreave re-established his security measures and arranged for a trusted manservant to ride into Wolverhampton each day to gather what he could of the movements of Justice Coalpit and his fervent friend.

★

About noon the same day a letter arrived at the Queen's Arms addressed to Justice Fuller. The single page of scrawl was as direct as it was illiterate:

> LUNDIN
> Onord Justiss in God –
> Vurney is gon from Lundin sum say norff.
> Yure humbel sarvint in the Lord,
> Spid

Fuller wrote at once to Lord Banbury, asking him in words which amounted to a little less than a command, to 'open the plan we conceived hitherto'. He then hurried round to Coalpit's house. Within an hour the Wolverhampton magistrate's men had received instructions not only to watch for a large bearded fellow with a brand on his forehead but also to ask whether anyone had seen a good-looking young stranger of about twenty, riding a fine horse, who may have arrived in the neighbourhood within the last week. Knowing where he was heading and keen to leave no trace of his arrival, John had travelled the last few miles to Moseley Hall at night. Tom, on the other hand, had ridden through Wolverhampton in broad daylight and twice stopped to ask directions. It was the sort of event idle town-gossips remembered, and, sure enough, at about the time Whitgreave was preparing his defences, Coalpit and Fuller were learning that someone exactly fitting Tom's description had been seen in the town asking the way to Moseley Hall.

The report, which confirmed that John lay almost within his grasp, sent Fuller into a twitching paroxysm of delight. His eyes flamed. He seethed in his chair, like a man in a fit.

'Now, Coalpit!' he cried as the informant left them. 'We must descend this very instant. The Lord has given the beast into our hands at last. Strike, Coalpit! The Lord tells us to strike!' Tensing his arms like gun hammers, he brought his fists together with a series of loud reports.

Unmoved, the diminutive Coalpit looked at him suspiciously. Bigot though he was — celebrated locally for having the entire menfolk of the village of Over Pen whipped for playing football on the Sabbath — even he was taken aback by some of Fuller's more extreme behaviour. 'Nay, Fuller,' he replied, folding his arms with deliberate slowness, 'we will wait until the morrow when I shall gather a small band of loyal men to help us search for this villain whose proximate presence brings you to the very edge of dangerous and perpetual motion.'

'We will approach at dawn,' urged Fuller, who had almost burst with impatience as he waited for Coalpit to conclude his serpentine sentence.

'No, sir!' retorted the local man. 'Mister Whitgreave is a prosperous gentleman and respected in these parts who had he a mind for such matters would be justice in my place and thus it is not for me to roar into his house like a lion in pursuit of popish prey. We must be careful, Justice.'

Although tormented by what he regarded as Coalpit's deferential cowardice, Fuller knew that he must not alienate the man. 'Very well,' he said with a sigh, 'I will be guided by your knowledge, sir.' Then, sitting quite rigid and staring out of the window, he added in an undertone, 'Matters might not be so hard if we had a king who cared in his heart to rid this land of popery.'

Coalpit turned his head rapidly and stared at his colleague. 'Justice Fuller,' he asked, shocked into brevity, 'did I catch your words aright? Did you speak of the king?'

Fuller realised at once that he had misjudged his man. Shaking his head as if clearing his ears of water after swimming, he answered vaguely, 'Eh? Oh, it was nothing, Justice. I said nothing.' He went on, struggling to cover his position, 'I sometimes speak as in a dream, Justice. Heed not what I say. It was mere foolishness.'

'I am certain that it was,' said Coalpit, still eyeing his colleague carefully. 'But take care, sir, lest others less wise than I hear you and understand your words at the meaning given to them in the common speech of this land. Though my ears are not what they were in my youth when I was known – ha! – throughout the county as the fellow who might pick out the arrival of the London post before the horse crossed over into Staffordshire, I believe I heard words from your lips that came close to, well, treason.' He pushed his beak-like mouth into a smile. 'Treason from a magistrate! Ha! It will never do, never do! Ha, ha!'

Though Fuller did his best to join in the laughter, both men knew that their false mirth hid nothing. From this time forwards a marked strain entered their relationship, and co-operation between them became increasingly difficult.

Tom had intended to return home as soon as he had delivered his warning to John. Princess had been fit enough for the journey by the time of the justices' visit and he was eager to get away before they returned, as everyone now seemed to think they would, to make a thorough search of the building. Two matters delayed him longer than he had planned. One was a feeling of uncertainty as to how things stood between Lucy and himself. Her confession that she did not always like him and the tense, almost tragic atmosphere of their parting still haunted him. His fleeting encounter with Anne Hutchinson and the harmony of Moseley Hall both fed his vexation, increasing his reluctance to go back to what he knew would be a less restful life. Then there was the business of Whitgreave referring to John as 'father'. Tom was loath to leave until he had solved that mystery.

He found an opportunity to talk with John in private on the morning of 15th May. Seeing his friend slip outside after breakfast, he followed and discovered him walking carefully round the intricately laid gravel paths of the shrub garden, staring down at his feet as if worried that they would go their own way if he did not watch them.

He looked up when he heard Tom approaching and said with a smile, 'Brought to bay at last! Thomas warned me that he had let slip something which might have been better kept close, and that you would most likely be pressing me for more.'

'Yes, John, you rogue!' said Tom. 'You know what he called you?'

'I might guess without bursting my brain.'

'Then, Father John, explain yourself.'

Taking his young friend by the arm, the bearded giant led him from the narrow path, where there was hardly room for them to walk beside each other, towards the small spinney which lay about four hundred yards from the house. 'Very well,' he began, 'but first you must answer my question.'

'I will.'

'Why are you here, Tom?'

'You know full well, John,' said Tom lightly. 'I came here to warn you of Fuller.'

'I know why you came here, Tom,' John replied slowly. 'But I asked why you are here now.'

Somewhere to their left a thrush filled the morning air with loud, innocent song. John stood motionless and listened. Eventually Tom spoke. 'I enjoy Moseley Hall,' he said unhappily. 'It overflows with a happiness that is rarely to be found.'

'Not in London?'

'Not when I departed thence.'

John stopped and leaned his broad shoulders against the mossy green trunk of a giant beech. 'Do the words of your prayer book say of marriage that it is "not to be taken in hand unadvisedly"?'

Tom nodded.

'And, by Jesus, you did not take it in hand unadvisedly, did you?'

Tom nodded again.

'Well, Master Verney, dally no longer. No man wins a battle by running away. Furnished with what you have witnessed here – a fleeting picture of God's sweet bliss wrought in an earthly home – return to your Lucy and build likewise, else you break a sacred vow made before your Maker.'

'I know you speak the truth,' said Tom, bending down to pick up a stick. 'But the truth is heavy and hard and sorrowful.' He hurled the stick far into the wood, where it landed in the undergrowth with a crash.

'By the Lord's jerkin, Tom! Do you think our mortal life is anything other than heavy and hard and sorrowful? If it were otherwise, where would heaven be?'

'You are preaching,' Tom grinned, walking up to his friend and tapping him gently on the chest. 'Which brings to mind my question. You have put me to the test. Now I will do the same to you.' Standing back and folding his arms in mock seriousness, he asked, 'Answer the court, stranger! Who are you? What sort of creature are you? And whence do you come?'

With an exaggerated groan, John placed his hands over his chest and groin. 'Woe is me!' he laughed. 'For I am to be undone! Pray, good sir, do not uncover my nakedness!'

'We have no mercy. Speak, slave!'

'Alas! I have no choice!' John's tone became more serious. 'Very well,' he said, lowering his hands. 'I will answer you. Thomas Whitgreave called me "father" because I was once a priest of the Roman Church.'

Tom whistled. 'Hey-hey!' he exclaimed with a chuckle. 'So this is what you have been hiding in the cupboard! But when? And why "once a priest"? You have raised more questions than you have answered.'

John pushed himself away from the tree. 'Come, walk with me and – by the mass! – I will tell you such a tale as you never heard before in your life.'

'I would walk to Africa to hear what you have to relate, you barrel of mystery—'

Suddenly both men were aware of someone running through the wood towards them. Seconds later a servant of the house burst into view, panting heavily. 'Gentlemen,' he cried, 'Mr Whitgreave begs you return at once! Searchers is coming back!'

'Then we will stay in the woods,' said Tom. 'No one will find us here.'

'That'll no do, sir,' replied the man, shaking his head imploringly. 'There's so large a band on the road riding hither. They'll look all places, for certain.'

'What he says is right,' said John, turning towards the house and breaking into a lolloping run. 'Besides, a search may endure many days. I have lived long enough in the woods not to wish for more nights on damp leaves.

'Come, Tom. It seems you will not be leaving to see your Lucy today after all.'

iii

Whitgreave only just managed to get Tom into the garret priest hole in time – even as he was securing the hide's outer panel, a fearful hammering was already audible from the front door. So as soon as he had checked that there was no sign of Tom's presence and that all evidence of Catholic ceremony had been removed from the chapel, with a whispered 'God be with you!' he hurried downstairs to face the pursuivants.

Tom's ordeal began with long hours of silence. To begin with this was not unwelcome. He collected his thoughts, said a short prayer, cleaned his fingernails and made sure he could remember the birthdays of Lucy, Anne Hutchinson and the members of his family. But by mid-morning he was bored and beginning to feel distinctly uncomfortable. Not only were the boards he was lying on uncompromisingly hard, but he was determined to last out his imprisonment without resorting to the goatskin bottle which Whitgreave had handed him as he squeezed into the hide. By noon, however, he could endure the discomfort no longer and managed to urinate with a reasonable degree of accuracy into the narrow neck of the bottle. Then, to his dismay, he found that the receptacle had no stopper and one of the seams leaked. For about half an hour he lay there holding the foul-smelling, dripping skin by its neck and wondering what to do with it. In the end, by twisting to one side and pulling a thread from his sleeve with his teeth, he managed to tie the offensive bag to one of the roof slats. The presence of a skin of acidic stench dangling a mere twelve inches from his face made the rest of his captivity considerably more disagreeable.

Time passed infinitely slowly. As morning slid imperceptibly into a long, hot afternoon, he lay baking under the tiles like a loaf in a bread oven, tormented by thirst and bathed in sweat. Greedy flies, attracted by the reek from the goatskin, flew in through the gaps between the tiles to feed. The oppressive heat, the smell and the incessant buzz of the insects turned his stomach and he knew that unless he did something he would be sick. At the risk of dislodging it and sending it crashing to the ground, he levered up a tile. Raising himself slightly on one elbow, he put his face to the hole and drew deep breaths of fresh, sweet air.

By early evening, as the temperature dropped, he was aware of new miseries. When he had entered the hide that morning, Whitgreave had thrust a piece of bread, a slab of cheese and a bottle of wine into his hands. He had devoured the bread and cheese long ago, and now his stomach was grumbling for more. His thirst was far worse, and his mouth and throat felt as dry as blotting sand. But recalling what John had said about searches lasting many days, he was unwilling to finish the wine just yet. The sound of cows lowing as they were gathered together for the second milking floated up to him from the distant fields. In his mind's eye he saw buckets of cool milk in clean dairies. He put his fingers in his ears and grimaced. At least I now have some idea, he reflected in his extreme discomfort, what it is to be tortured. It was grim consolation.

The short summer night brought little relief. The hide became bitterly cold and he slept little. As the first light of dawn filtered through the tiles, aching all over, tired, cold, tormented by hunger and thirst and suffering from excruciating bouts of cramp in his legs, he began to question why he was putting up with this hardship for the sake of a Catholic priest. Like a pain, resentment for John and his friends gradually swelled within him. Why had he been left cooped up for so long? Surely, he told himself, Whitgreave could have managed to slip upstairs with some food? As such thoughts took root, he found himself longing to be back in London with Lucy. He missed her straightforward homeliness, her instinctive cheerfulness and her common sense. Smiling, he thought that if she could see him now she would probably laugh at the ridiculousness of his predicament. He thought, too, about the baby she was carrying and blamed himself for having shown her so little concern. Finally, seized by a fierce cramp, he rolled over and hit his head against the goatskin. A sprinkle of stale urine fell into his hair and over his face.

'That is my limit,' he muttered under his breath. 'What is all this for? I have done nothing wrong, and even if Fuller and the other fellow see me, that will prove nothing. John will be safe.'

Suppressing a cough, he decided to count to five thousand, at the end of which, if he had not been rescued, he would force open the door of his hide and go down into the house to open his bowels, wash and collect some more food and drink. He took a deep breath and started counting.

Somewhere between two and three thousand he dozed off. Rarely, he thought later, could innocent sleep have had such momentous consequences.

He was awoken by the sound of footsteps on the garret stairs. Shortly afterwards he was able to distinguish two voices. Fuller's he knew well. The other, he soon gathered, belonged to Coalpit. He had not heard many words before he realised that the justices were quarrelling. Fuller, speaking keenly and quickly, was urging his colleague to adopt more stringent techniques. It was all very well, he was saying, to post men in the grounds and go through the rooms of the house one by one, but that way he would never detect a well-concealed fugitive. What was needed, he explained, clearly not for the first time, was to remove everyone – Whitgreaves, servants and all – from the house, then to set about looking for hiding places by tearing off the panelling, measuring, pulling up the floorboards and poking spiked rods into the plasterwork.

Coalpit would have none of this. He pointed out that, unlike his colleague, he would have to live in this county after the search was over. Life was going to be difficult enough for him as it was; wrecking the house of one of the district's best-loved families was hardly going to make things any easier. Besides, he went on, using sentences that Tom thought would never end, the current Privy Council had not been strong advocates of religious persecution. Fuller's ruthless tactics might have been acceptable in Elizabeth's reign, or even around the time of the Gunpowder Plot, but nowadays they were neither justifiable nor desirable.

Judging by their comments and the direction of their voices, Tom reckoned that the two men were now browsing around the chapel, looking for signs of popish ceremony.

'Justice Coalpit,' continued Fuller, 'you are too fearful for your reputation. God will protect you should you come to harm in pursuit of your duty.' Coalpit snorted. 'Come! We must let the Lord guide us. Did we not say that it was here, in the attic, that we would find our quarry? Can you not smell popish incense in the infected air?'

'The odour of piss is all that reaches my nostrils,'

Coalpit squeaked, 'and although I warrant we did believe this garret to be a likely place for a knave to hide, now you say there are two villains I fear we have passed over one in the rooms below for there is scarce room to hide a dog up here—'

'Ha! Dogs they are, too!' sneered Fuller. 'But I have already given the fellow Verney – the accomplice of whom I spoke – cause to regret his acquaintance with the devil John.'

Tom stiffened. Eager to catch what followed, he eased his head towards the entrance to the hide.

'And how is that, sir?' asked Coalpit.

'The young fool did of late find some favour at court. He also contracted a foolish marriage which he kept secret from the king. Yesterday, when I learned that the cur was here, I instructed Lord Banbury to inform His Majesty how young Verney had deceived him. That will end his vaulting ambition right enough. No king takes kindly to being deceived – I would not be surprised to hear that our Verney is taken into prison for his insolence. Hee-hee!'

The sound of Fuller's thin, muffled laughter drifted up to where Tom lay, but he hardly noticed it. Turning over in his mind what he had heard, he concluded that this was the end. There could be no reprieve. His proud hopes and ambitions, his devices and schemes for surprising his family and delighting Lucy, his position, his livelihood – everything had vanished like dew before the morning sun. He had built his house on the foundation of royal favour, and now, like so many others erected on that insubstantial ground, it had utterly fallen. With a wry smile he considered his present position – alone, tired, hunted, desperate for food and drink, incarcerated in a stinking hole scarcely larger than a coffin – a fitting allegory on his folly.

His thoughts turned to Lucy. Fuller's action had finally drawn a curtain over her dreams, too. Dreams that all along Tom had assured her, against her better judgement, were sure to come true. If the news was cruel for him, he thought, how much more so would it be for her. He must join her at once. John was right: he had a duty before God to love and protect her, and now, more than at any time, she would need him. Silently praying for the pursuivants either to find him or conclude their search and leave, he lay back to listen once more to the conversation floating up from the chapel.

The exchanges between the two men had now become quite heated. Fuller was urging his accomplice not to slacken in their quest for the evil one. This was followed by a long speech from Coalpit, full of self-pity, in which he bemoaned the fact that he had ever listened to Fuller's hare-brained scheme, since all it had brought him was distress. For a full day now, he complained, they had searched the grounds and every room in the house, finding nothing. There was no trace of this mysterious John, and no one in the household – neither master, mistress nor servants – had heard of him. With each minute that passed, Coalpit said, he felt more and more of a fool.

'I am like a sightless man proceeding into a quagmire,' he groaned, 'my sense tells me to return but still I go forward knowing that with each step I sink deeper into the slime until it is too late to crawl back to the firm land from which I ventured so ill-advisedly. All will be lost!' The remark was followed by a sound which sounded distinctly like a sob.

If sob it was, then nothing could have been more certain to annoy Fuller. 'Justice!' he cried. 'Take hold of yourself! Here, on the threshold of victory, you talk of withdrawal?'

'Unhand me, sir!' screeched Coalpit. A chair crashed to the floor.

'Why,' shouted Fuller, his voice rising higher and higher, 'there is no more of the Gospel of Jesus Christ in you, sir, than there is in a whore's lap! Call yourself a justice? Pshaw! You are a mere shrunken dwarf of a time-serving friend of Rome. I know you now, sir. The Kingdom of Heaven is to you no more than a goat's teat! If there were a whole host of papist vermin secreted within these walls, you would not stir your pigmy frame if it meant losing your precious position in this scurvy-ridden county! I see Accepted Coalpit is no more than an accepted elfin servant of the Roman traffic and her poxy Scottish handmaiden sent to seduce us—'

'Justice Fuller!' screamed Coalpit, whose equanimity, like Fuller's, had finally broken under the strain of the last twenty-four hours. 'This search is undertaken in my name and it is now at an end for you have so pressured and pricked me these last few days that I know not whether I walk on earth or fry in hell! It is at an end because I now know you to be a fool – nay a mad man – whose brain has been twisted by some devilish force which God alone can fathom into a muddle of scripture distortion false-hood fanaticism fury forgery...'

Coalpit's shrill denouncement faded into silence as, still shouting, he made his way down the stairs and closed the door behind him.

For about five minutes Tom lay with his head pressed against the door of his hide, trying to work out whether Fuller had followed his disgruntled colleague out of the attic. Just when he believed he had and the path was clear for him to descend, he became aware of a strange noise outside. To begin with he was not sure what it was. But as he listened, he realised that it was the sound of a man praying. Hardly daring to breathe lest he miss a word, he strained every fibre to hear what was being uttered.

Quieter now, though more menacing, the voice was unmistakably Fuller's. Sometimes, when his emotion got the better of him, the words were clear and distinct. At other times they were no more than a murmur.

'... Almighty God,' Tom made out, 'take Thy unworthy servant Christopher Fuller and make him ... instrument of Thy will on this earth ... to drive all sin from this land of England, even though it be in the highest places of all ... for ... one true king, and He is in heaven ... all others being pretenders to that one throne ... so give me strength ... in Thy name ... drive out popery, beginning with the corrupt governor, to which end ... Fire! Fire! Fire!' There followed a hollow hammering sound, like that of a club being beaten on a broken drum.

Not long afterwards, Tom heard Fuller slowly descending the attic stairs. When, a few minutes later, the sound of hoofs drifted up from the road outside, he knew at last that his ordeal would shortly be at an end.

iv

Having locked the door, Elizabeth and her maid began to remove the contents of Fuller's box and gingerly lay them on the table. First came some sort of plan or design. After a cursory glance, Elizabeth set it aside and turned to see what Tilly was holding in her hand.

'Look, mistress!' the girl laughed. 'Mr Fuller is so afraid lest he be called out riding without his whip, he has a spare one laid in his box!'

The baroness smiled. 'No, Tilly. I fear that whip is not for the mortification of any horse.'

'How so, your ladyship?' asked the maid, staring

innocently down at the leather handle and thongs. 'Why does he keep it then?'

'It is for beating himself. He has not asked you to assist him?'

Tilly gave out a little cry. 'Himself! Oh no, your ladyship!' She placed the instrument of penance on the table, watching it intently as if it might turn and bite her. 'What odd creatures men are, my lady!' she said when she was sure it was safe.

'Even so,' replied Elizabeth, lifting a small bag of money from inside the box and laying it beside the whip. 'Though not all men are as mad as this one.'

By the time they had finished, beside the whip, the drawing and the money lay five sheets of paper covered with names and addresses, a bunch of keys, a much used commonplace book, and two small packets. Inside these Elizabeth found two locks of hair, one dark, the other fair. The first was labelled simply 'Jane Fuller RIP 1605', the other 'Sarah Fuller RIP 1623'.

Swallowing hard, she carefully wrapped them up again and replaced them as they had been found. Recalling the pond-man 'deserted by women' of the Revelation, for the first and only time in her life she felt pity for Fuller. She also felt guilty, as if she had desecrated a shrine, so that if at that moment Tilly had not drawn her attention to something in the commonplace book, she would almost certainly have put everything back in the box and returned it whence it had come.

Her charity vanished the moment the maid spoke.

'See here, your ladyship,' she said, pointing to an entry near the back of the book, 'he has written the name of your friend Mr Verney.'

'Tilly!' Elizabeth snapped. 'Give that to me now!' She held out her hand. 'It is not for you to read!'

Abashed, the girl handed over the book at once. 'It were nothing wrong, your ladyship,' she murmured. 'Just a name. Besides, I can't read much more than that.'

'I know. I was too sharp. But I fear, Tilly, that this matter may run deeper than we think. You may go now. And make sure that Ector and his daughter are here tomorrow morning to lock up this box again. We must be sure to replace it before Mr Fuller returns, or he may have us both in the Fleet!'

Sending a message to her husband that she was unwell and did not wish to be disturbed, Elizabeth settled down to read Fuller's commonplace book. Between the well-worn, black pigskin covers were almost three hundred pages of the magistrate's thoughts, observations, memoranda and other random jottings, stretching back over the past five years. It was a most extraordinary compilation. Many of the entries, particularly in the front half of the book, were taken up with the routine business of a country justice of the peace, dealing with those who refused to pay their parish poor rate, settling squabbles over damage done by stray cattle, and so forth. After this came a section devoted almost exclusively to Fuller's vendetta with the mysterious John, listing when and where the man had been seen and the charges levelled against him, each carefully set out with dates, times and witnesses. Towards the end of this part of the book the name Tom Verney appeared, first in the context of the report he had given of his brush with John in the woods the previous September, then more frequently. Elizabeth soon realised that as far as Fuller was concerned, John and Tom knew each other well. In which case, she reasoned, the sooner I get hold of Master Verney and ask him what he knows, the better.

She resumed her reading.

Scarcely five minutes later she gave a start and lowered the book to her lap. 'Well, well,' she said quietly. 'Now you really do have some explaining to do, Tom, don't you?'

The last entry in this part gave the name Moseley Hall and a date. Beside this was written 'Wolverhampton, county of Staffordshire — from list, Accepted Coalpit'. Checking the sheets of paper covered with names and addresses, she saw they were arranged by county. Sure enough, on turning to Staffordshire she found the name of Accepted Coalpit. Underlined. Next, she went through the Oxfordshire list. Although some names were familiar to her, none were friends. This confirmed her suspicion that the list comprised most well-connected puritans throughout the country, men whom Fuller could expect to assist him in his hunt for John. Elizabeth shuddered as she imagined the passionate energy which the man's twisted hatred had engendered in him.

The last fifty or so pages of the book were taken up with religious matters. Some of the entries were rather dull. Others, particularly the pages in which Fuller had listed his sins and beside each had written the number of lashes he was to give himself after committing it, afforded her considerable amusement. She was surprised how frequently he was obliged to chastise himself for emulating Onan, and delighted to see that after her recent seduction of her husband in their guest's presence, he had been obliged to give himself fifteen lashes, 'for committing adultery in my heart'.

Five pages later she came across the heading 'SODOM AND GOMORRAH', heavily underlined and spread across the top of two leaves. Beneath it was written, 'Revelation 1st January, one thousand, six hundred and twenty-three'. Under this came '1 19 24 together 44. The time of the fire.' There followed a list of all the months of the year, with '1 19 24' repeated against January and other three-figure numbers beside February, March, April and May.

All this meant nothing whatsoever to Elizabeth. But feeling that some of it might be of value later on, especially the material relating to the day Sarah had died, she copied out all the entries she felt to be significant, including the Sodom and Gomorrah table. Next, she wrote out a summary, as best she could remember it, of Fuller's Revelation. Finally, she replaced everything back in the box in the same order as it had been removed. Before closing the lid, however, she glanced again at the sheet of paper with the diagram on it. Absorbed by her researches, until now she had forgotten it completely. The picture appeared vaguely familiar. By odd coincidence, she thought, it was almost a cut-away drawing of the very box lying before her. The only difference was that the one in the drawing was equipped with what appeared to be a most elaborate locking system, consisting of several springs and what looked like a piece of stone. At the bottom left-hand corner was the name Hughes. Surely, she said to herself, I have heard that name recently?

Unable for the moment to remember where, she made a brief sketch of the diagram, replaced it in the box, closed the lid and went to bed.

At about three o'clock in the morning she was awoken by a disturbance in the street outside. For a while she lay awake thinking over the previous day's discoveries. The more she thought, the more certain she felt that she had inadvertently stumbled across something more than just Fuller's fanatical desire for revenge on the man who had seduced his daughter. But she could not for the life of her work out what it was. There was a clue, she was sure, in the hand-written Revelation in Fuller's Bible and in his Sodom and Gomorrah table. She knew well enough what the sins of Sodom had been – she had even on occasion experimented rather unsuccessfully with them herself – and she remembered that the Biblical city had been destroyed by fire and brimstone. But what were all those numbers? Why the diagram of a box? And where was it that she had heard the name Hughes? Still turning questions such as these over in her brain without reaching any conclusions, she eventually dropped off to sleep again.

The first answer came only six hours later. The moment she saw Ector and his daughter, whom Tilly had warned not to pry into what was going on, returning to relock the box, Elizabeth remembered where she had met the name Hughes. Of course! He was the 'salt' locksmith, known as Zak, whom they suspected of making the exploding box which had removed most of Ector's face. Exploding box? Elizabeth sprang forward and seized Kitty by the hand.

'Child,' she said urgently, 'I need you to help me further. Wait here and bid your father stay his work until I am ready.'

As the girl took Ector to one side, Elizabeth went to the box and drew out the diagram. 'Here,' she called, standing by the window and holding up the paper, 'what is this?'

Kitty came over to her side and looked down at the drawing. She let out a loud gasp of horror.

'What is it, daughter?' called out Ector anxiously.

'No matter, Father. Just a piece of fine work what 'er ladyship 'as shown me.' She turned to Elizabeth. 'I beg your pardon for my forwardness, my lady,' she said, gazing down at the plan again, 'but where 'as this come from?'

'That is not your concern, child.' She lowered her voice to a whisper. 'Is it what I think it is?'

'Aye,' replied Kitty, speaking softly so that her father would not hear. 'God preserve us! It is a picture of one of Zak's 'splodin' boxes. It is a wicked thing, my lady, the very devil's handiwork!'

'What would it do to he who opened it? Blind him?'

'God's blood! Blind him? If it fired aright, blow 'is 'ead off. And the 'eads of all others near as spittin'!'

Without further questions, Elizabeth replaced the paper in the box and ordered Ector to lock it up again. As he was doing so, she asked him whether, to save his being called every time she wanted to put on her jewels, he could provide her with a spare key for the box.

'Easy as fartin', m'lady – if you'll excuse the sayin'.'

'Very good. I'll take two. Have them brought round here as soon as they are fashioned.'

Elizabeth and her maid had Fuller's box back in his room by nightfall. There, chained to the leg of the bed as before, its secrets were once more safe from the prying eyes of all but his most determined opponents.

Dismissing Tilly and returning to her private dressing room, Elizabeth re-read the notes she had taken on the box's contents, then added a few words to the copy she had made of Zak's diagram.

And that, she said to herself as she laid down her pen, is as far as I can proceed for the moment. Now I need to speak with that whoreson married monkey, Tom Verney!

V

Tom had intended to leave Moseley Hall as soon as possible after the departure of Fuller and Coalpit, but a violent attack of dysentery, almost certainly brought on by the conditions in the hide, detained him for the remainder of the week. Although he gave an amusing account of the quarrel between the two justices, and even managed to joke about his problems with the goatskin, for most of the time his hosts found him distracted and uncommunicative. Putting this down to the illness and an understandable desire to be back home with his wife, they ignored his occasional incivilities and did their best to nurture his speedy recovery.

Only to John did Tom explain himself further, revealing that Fuller had told the king of his marriage, thereby ending all hopes of family approval for the match. His friend was sympathetic but urged him to look at the situation positively: now, for the first time in his life, he was a free man. His only responsibilities were to God and his wife. He had looks, youth, an education, money and boundless energy. Why, John concluded, in a year or so he would be wondering what he had worried about. For a time Tom was heartened by his friend's optimism. But when he started contemplating the practicalities of restoring the harmony missing from his relationship with Lucy, his heart drifted back into its former torpor.

On the afternoon before his departure, he told John about the snatches of Fuller's prayer he had overheard. For some reason, he said, they had stuck in his mind like undigested food in the stomach. When John made light of this, Tom tried to explain that it was not so much the words themselves as the tone in which they had been uttered that had worried him most. He agreed with John that Fuller was probably going mad, but that did not make him less dangerous, he suggested. If anything, it made him more so.

In the end, John remained unimpressed. He advised Tom to forget Fuller for the time being and devote his energies to rebuilding his life. Nevertheless, he did undertake to call on him in London when the present danger had subsided, promising then to tell the full story of his past and discuss the magistrate's strange prayer at greater length.

For once, Tom heeded the wise advice he had been given. By the time he reached London he had come to the conclusion that the troubles between Lucy and himself had been largely of his own making. He had made up his mind to confess as much to her and promise to try harder to understand her needs and wishes. Brimming with fresh hope and charity, he did not make his way directly to Blackmore Street, but rode on to the city to find her a present. An offering of peace. He chose a large gold ring – more expensive than he could afford – to be the symbol of their new beginning. Having left Princess with Silas at the Angel, he strode towards home feeling better than he had done for a long time. Deception was now a thing of the past. Before him, full of honest opportunity, lay a bright future. Whispering a prayer to God for bringing him safe through adversity and teaching him the way to true happiness, he was almost running by the time he arrived outside his front door and hammered eagerly upon it.

There was no reply.

He tried again. Still no response.

'Hell's teeth!' he muttered to himself, listening to the hollow sound of his blows echoing round the house. 'She must be out visiting. And just when I was in such spirits, too.' He turned to go and wait in a tavern until she came home. As he did so, he almost knocked over House Martin, returning with a meagre basket of provisions.

'Well met, lad!' cried Tom, seizing the boy cheerfully by the shoulders and laughing. 'When will your mistress be home?'

House Martin averted his eyes and muttered something inaudible.

'Speak louder, Bird! Have you lost your voice since I have been away?'

'No, sir. But I don't wish to speak, sir.'

For the first time a wave of unease crossed Tom's mind. 'Don't want to speak? You must. When did your mistress say she would return?'

'No time.'

'You mean she did not know when she would be home?'

'No, sir. She went out more than a week ago. All she said was that she would not be coming home. Never.'

SIXTEEN

OLD TAILOR'S HOUSE

i

Two letters lay on the parlour table.

For a long time Tom stared at them, unable to decide which to read first. Then he asked House Martin to bring him drink.

By the time the first bottle was empty, the letters were still untouched. What had John said? he reflected. That he was now a free man with responsibilities to God and his wife alone. Huh! That double yoke had not lasted long! Calling for another bottle, he finally reached over and took hold of the larger of the letters, a scroll of heavy paper sealed with the royal coat of arms.

The wax cracked like bark at his touch and fell in pieces to the floor. He took a deep breath. Biting his lower lip, he unrolled the paper and cast his eye over its contents.

It could have been much worse. In fact, all the letter contained was a rebuke for not informing the king of his marriage — 'What marriage?' muttered Tom bitterly, momentarily glancing round the empty room — and a couple of brief official paragraphs. One stated that

'Thomas Verney of Stratton Audley was henceforth required and requested not to show his person at, or within five miles of, the royal court', and the second deprived him of his post of Deputy Receiver of Customs for Helford. The signature at the bottom, certainly not the king's, was indecipherable – probably that of some silly, smooth-tongued clerk, thought Tom, picking up the document and throwing it against the wall.

'God's great eyes!' he swore, watching the roll rocking backwards and forwards on the floor. 'To hell with court!' But behind the bravado lurked despair and the sure knowledge that he had only himself to blame for his misfortunes.

Refilling his beaker, he picked up the second letter, a simple folded sheet of paper with his name written across the front in large, bold characters. To his surprise, he found it even shorter than the first.

My dearest husband Tom,
  I do not know which will bring the greater pain, my writing this letter or you receiving it. I pray you believe that I do not act lightly or without long hours of thought.
  The truth is that over the past week I have not been in good health and I fear for our child. This has arisen, I know, from the thorny hedge which of late has grown between us. Now you are gone yet again – without a letter or a message to cheer me – I am obliged to leave this house. The dwelling once so fond is now become a prison or a desert, where, with an almost empty purse, I am alone and unloved. It is no longer a home. Not for a mother and her first baby. Even though Mary had but a stable, she did have Joseph to comfort her.

Sometimes I am angry, sometimes I am sad. Yet when my brain is clear I do not hold fault, but believe we started along a rocky path too young.

In time, God willing, all will be well. Of that I am certain. But until you have burned away the fire of your youth, I am riding to Rochester to live with my aunt, Mary Cooper. Come and see me when your world has stopped its spinning. Then we can begin our journey afresh. And you will find that I still love you – as I always have and always will.

Your fondest wife,
Lucy

Carefully, he folded the paper and absent-mindedly tried to press it into the inside pocket of his jerkin. But there was something already there, blocking the way. Raising his hand to remove it, he felt a small cloth packet tied with string. For a second he did not know what it was. Then, even as he was drawing it out, he remembered. The ring! The ring he could not really afford. The ring he had bought her that very afternoon. The ring he had intended as a symbol of their new beginning.

He took up the letter again and unfolded it. After he had re-read it, very slowly, he rolled it into a scroll over which he slipped the ring. Finally, he wrapped both in the cloth and retied the string.

Getting up and taking off his jerkin, he called for House Martin. When the boy appeared, he bade him take the packet and the jerkin into the workshop and get Jack to sew the little bundle into the jerkin's lining.

The boy hesitated.

'Go on with you, Bird,' said Tom.

'If you please, sir,' the lad stammered, 'it can't be done. Jack is left too.'

'What! Gone where? Why?'

'Gone to another master, sir. There was no work 'ere. No money neither.'

Tom sat down. 'Holy Mary Mother of Christ! Lucy gone, Jack gone, no work – what is to become of us, eh, Bird?'

'I don't rightly know. Maybe as I could work a bit, sir?'

'No, we are not come to that yet. I have money in my purse still.'

'I thank God for that, sir. Now I will go and sew Mrs Verney's letter into your jerkin. I can 'andle a needle right enough.' He turned to go.

'Bird?' Tom called after him.

'Yes, sir?'

'How did you know you had Mrs Verney's letter?'

The boy looked at him with large, sad eyes. 'What else would it be, sir?'

'What else, indeed?' Tom sighed. He gave the lad a wan smile. 'You will not leave me, will you, Bird?'

'No, sir. Not till I dies, or you sends me away.'

'That I will never do. I promise. Now, go and play the tailor, there's a good lad.'

Sometimes sitting morbidly alone in the parlour and sometimes pacing up and down the street in the warm evening air, before the day was over Tom had experienced as wide a range of emotions as a leading actor would be called upon to portray in a whole season of plays.

He began calm, logical and sensible. Lucy was, he admitted, quite correct in seeking somewhere safe and secure to stay for the birth of their child. After all, he had not been exactly the most caring of husbands. Then, little by little, reason was driven out by anger. At first, walking blindly down the middle of the road, he directed his fury towards his wife. How could she have left when she had sworn to be with him for the rest of her life? Her behaviour only confirmed what scripture had told him to expect from the weaker vessel. But within minutes, like the swirling blast of a tempest, his fury had swung round to blow full against himself. What a weak fool he had been! When her husband had not been considerate enough even to write her a single letter while he was away, who could blame her for seeking consolation elsewhere? 'Damn Tom Verney!' he cried out loud. 'Damn him! All he touches turns to pain and dross!' As if to prove the point, he inadvertently bumped into an errant juggler and brought a rain of heavy wooden clubs crashing about his head.

Retreating to the solitude of his front room, the scene of many of his most tender memories of Lucy, his fury subsided into self-pitying misery. He promised himself that in the morning he would ride down to Rochester and beg her to return. But the idea evaporated when he realised that even if he did persuade her to and she did come back to London, which was doubtful, there would be no joy in living with a woman whose confidence in him had been so totally undermined. To make matters worse, despite his bragging to House Martin, he now had very little money and almost no idea how to get any. A while later, temporarily cheered by a passing musician's jolly air coming in through the open window, he entered an optimistic, practical phase. Calling for House Martin to join him, he explained to the bewildered boy how they would shortly be leaving by ship for the New World, where, 'far from this backbitten country of meagre curmudgeons', they would find a pure, Godly life and fruits of the earth in abundance.

But neither this nor any of the other swirling feelings that assailed him in such rapid succession lasted more than a beaker or two. And finally, too drunk, confused and drained to care about anything any more, he emptied the last bottle, balanced it precariously upside down on the table, and made his way upstairs to bed and a long and infinitely troubled sleep.

ii

Having learned from Fuller's commonplace book that Tom lived in Blackmore Street, Lady Elizabeth lost no time in sending Tilly to find out the precise house. After a morning's reconnoitre, the girl returned with the information that Mr and Mrs Verney rented a small, two-storeyed dwelling with a workshop behind, about halfway down the street on the left-hand side as one approached from Drury Lane. As the only house in the vicinity with a tailor's sign outside and a freshly painted, blue front door, it was readily identifiable. At present, however, neither of the Verneys were at home and the house was being looked after by their boy. When she heard this, it occurred to Elizabeth that the simultaneous absence from London of both Fuller and Tom might not be simply a coincidence.

Thereafter, every two or three days, the baroness sent her maid to discover whether Mr Verney had returned, saying that she needed to see him on urgent business. Throughout she insisted that Tilly speak to no one about what was going on. Although the girl did not know exactly why her mistress was so keen to make secret contact with Mr Verney, she remembered having seen his name in Fuller's book and guessed, half correctly, that it was connected with Lady Banbury's need to share her discoveries with him.

While she was waiting for Tom to get back, Elizabeth took advantage of Fuller's absence in Shropshire to see more of her husband than she had been doing of late. She did so partly to wean him further from Fuller's influence and partly to see what additional information she could get out of him. The baronet was both delighted and alarmed by his wife's attentions.

'Oooo, Bessie!' he cooed on one occasion when she had afforded him the rare privilege of a visit to her bedroom. 'This is just as the day we were wed.'

'Precisely, my plum pudding,' she replied enigmatically. 'Some things in life never change.'

But others did. Deprived of Fuller's shoring, the puritanism which Lord Banbury had built around himself soon began to crack. Elizabeth went straight to its foundations, referring endlessly to Sarah's death as an accident and praising her husband's excellent marksmanship. Almost certainly, she explained, his shot had hit John. It had most likely passed right through him and hit Fuller's daughter standing behind. It was a terrible misfortune, but nothing more. Though Banbury was attracted by this suggestion, Fuller's interpretation of the same events – that he had been an instrument of the divine will – was even more flattering, and it was one he would not yield easily.

Other parts of his defences were not so secure. One morning Elizabeth made off with the drapes covering the naked statue in the hall. Not knowing who had sanctioned their removal, shortly afterwards her husband ordered a servant to replace them. Coming downstairs the following day he was startled to find that the statue had disappeared. Mystified, he went back up to his wife's rooms to see if she could throw any light on the matter. Pausing before her dressing-room door, he knocked and waited patiently for permission to enter. When this was granted — by no means a foregone conclusion — he pushed open the door and went in.

'My honeycomb—' he began.

'Shut the door!' snapped Elizabeth.

Promptly doing as he was commanded, he turned and looked about him. To his surprise he saw the missing statute, unclothed, standing on a chair in the middle of the room. He was even more surprised to see his wife, equally naked, taking up precisely the same modest pose on a chair beside it. For some time all three figures were so still — one through shock, one out of choice and one because it had no choice — that an intruder would have found it hard to distinguish the real people from the imitation.

Eventually, Banbury uttered the obvious. 'Darling rose petal, you have no clothes on.'

A shadow of scorn flashed across Elizabeth's face. She relaxed her posture, but remained standing on the chair. 'And do you like that, my latter-day Samson?' she asked, making sure that he had a clear view of her obvious attractions.

'I do. Oh yes, I do!' he exclaimed, stumbling towards her.

She allowed him to place a hand on her thigh. 'Well, wicked Banby dearest,' she said, removing his hand and pointing to the statue, 'why do you demand that we cover this pale imitation of real beauty?' She climbed down from the chair and stood before him.

'It was Justice Fuller's suggestioning, my lamb. He declared it to be — what was the phrase? — "an in-juice-ment to immortality".'

'Immorality?'

'Ah, yes. That was it. Immorality — that means lewdness, my love.'

'Though I am innocent, my sweetest pear, I do know the meaning of immorality.' She smiled at him and put her hands round his neck. 'Hercules, am I an inducement to immorality?'

'Oh, my fircone! Never!' His knees began to shake.

'Then how can a stone copy of one who is surely far less alluring than me be a threat to Man's virtue?'

'Well, I suppose it cannot,' he stammered.

'Of course not, my buck. Not even so mighty a lover as yourself could threaten the virgin chastity of a statue, could they?'

'It is most unlikely,' he muttered, shrinking at the very thought of sexual intercourse with a piece of marble.

'Then, my bull, shall we call the servants and have them carry it – naked as the day it was made – back to the hall?'

'We shall, Bessie. But after you have put on your clothes, my love?'

'Of course.'

The following day, the coverings were also removed from the *Sabine Women*. No one objected.

Lady Elizabeth managed to slip away to visit Tom on the morning of 23rd May, the day after she had heard of his return. Unusually, she went on foot, wrapped in a large, anonymous cloak for fear of recognition. She was let into the house by House Martin, who bade her wait in the parlour while he went upstairs. A minute later he reappeared, told her ladyship that Mr Verney would be with her directly and let himself out through the front door.

Tom looked dreadful. The dashing, shiny-haired, flush-faced lover had been transformed into little better than a beggar. The skin of his unshaven cheeks was pale yellow, his eyes red and sunken, his hair matted and his breath smelt as if he had breakfasted on a pint of sewage. Any plans Elizabeth might have had to chastise him for deceiving her went by the board as soon as she saw him – this man, she told herself, looks as if he has had more than enough trouble for one day.

Over the course of that morning's conversation the relationship between them moved onto a different plane. The former lusts were not abandoned – a wash, a change of shirt and breakfast soon restored Tom's vigour – but henceforward they were less the driving force behind their friendship than an integral part of it. For a long time, intervening only occasionally to ask a question, Elizabeth listened as Tom outlined what he knew of the John-Fuller vendetta and the tragic events of 4th April. He confessed that it had been he who had arranged with Peter for the rear entrance to Pickering House to be left clear for John and himself. But he assured her that he had no idea how Fuller had come to hear of the plot, unless Peter had told him, and he was equally mystified when Elizabeth informed him that the first shot had been fired by Fuller at a thief in the hall. With a rather sheepish look he said that he had planned to tell her all in due course, but events had forestalled his good intentions. Smiling, she said she believed him, though in her mind she was not sure that she did.

Having thanked her profusely for her part in the hat episode, he went on to recount his trip to Staffordshire, his ordeal in the priest hole and Fuller's prayer. Finally, he explained about his marriage and the letter he had found on his return. He felt oddly at ease telling Elizabeth about Lucy, as if her presence were a balm to his wounded heart.

As soon as he had finished, she stood up and went to stand by the fireplace. 'Hey-ho, Tom Verney!' she said with a grin. 'Two fish in the same pond!'

'Which pond?'

'Oh come now! You were wed before you had years enough to know what it was you did. I was wed before I had years enough to know what it was I did. You find pleasure outside that union. So do I.' For the first time that morning, Tom smiled.

'Yet there the resemblance ends,' Elizabeth went on. 'The world being what it is, a man may more easily make light of his marriage than a woman. Besides, you made a wiser choice than me. I married an old fool. A rich one, mind, but a fool nonetheless. You, from what you say, have married a most sweet and knowing young girl. Yes, she knows you better than you do yourself. She has done the only judicious thing open to her, for what woman with child would choose to ride an unbroken horse?

'So, Thomas, cease this melancholy! You should not have wed, as you yourself understand full well if you are honest. But since what is tied cannot be untied, thank God that He has allowed you your freedom back again. For a while, at least. He was not so generous with me!'

At the end of this speech, Tom was not sure whom he was more fond of, Elizabeth or Lucy. He had never thought of his predicament in this light before, and now Elizabeth pointed it out to him in such a matter-of-fact fashion, his self-obsessed misery began at once to wane. How strange, he thought, that it should have taken Bess – as he now fondly called Elizabeth – to show him Lucy's merits! For a second or two all he wanted to do was leap into Princess's saddle, gallop to Rochester and throw himself on his knees before his wife, begging her pardon and confessing how much he loved her. But as he looked at Elizabeth, leaning elegantly against the chimney breast, another thought came into his mind.

He stood up and kissed her, laying the palms of his

hands against her hips. With a conscious effort, she stepped aside.

'No, Tom. There will be time anon for our games. But it would not be right at present. Besides, I believe you now have more important matters to get on top of.'

'Very well,' he grinned, returning to his chair with feigned resignation.

'Listen—' she said.

And so, remembering as best she could the notes she had taken from Fuller's writings, she outlined what she had discovered over the past three weeks. At first Tom was distracted by the thought of making love with Elizabeth in the bed upstairs, and he did not pay much attention to what she was saying. But as his ardour subsided and he was able to concentrate better, the import of her findings gradually dawned on him.

'God's blood!' he exclaimed when she had finished. 'What have we here, Bess?'

'You tell me, Tom. I have squeezed my brains dry, trying to get sense from it, and all I can find is, well, a mad man who hates papists, your friend John most of all, and maybe wishes to destroy him with an exploding box.'

Tom thought for a while before saying, 'Sodom and Gomorrah – fire – exploding box – "the corrupt governor" – the "poxy Scottish handmaiden" of Rome – is there an ugly pattern there?'

Elizabeth frowned. 'I know what you say. But as yet that is mere fancy. What sense does it make of the box?'

Tom stood up and stretched. 'Nothing. Maybe it is all just fancy – we hate Fuller, so we imagine him planning hateful deeds. Come, if we continue like this we will be as mad as he is before nightfall.' He came round to where she sat and held out his hands. 'No more thinking today, I pray you.'

'Yet if it really be an issue of much importance,' she replied, unwilling to let the matter drop just yet, 'ought we not inform someone?'

'Fine sentiments! But who would believe me? And how are we to explain that we have acted together in this? No, Bess. Until we stand on firm ground, we must look into the matter on our own. First we need to examine what you wrote, together, for two heads are better than one. Will you come again, for I dare not show my face in Pickering House?'

'I will bring all I have written. And when Justice Fuller returns, I will send you word and watch for anything untoward.'

Grasping her outstretched hands, he pulled her to her feet. 'I must return home now,' she said, walking over to where she had hung her cloak.

He put his arms round her from behind. 'Now?'

'Yes, Tom, now. I have been here too long.' But feeling him aroused and pressing against her, she changed her tone. 'Sinner — tongues will wag.'

He cupped her breasts in his hands. 'Will mine?'

'I hope so,' she answered lubriciously, leaning her head back against his shoulder.

Fuller returned from Staffordshire late at night on the 25th May. Elizabeth did not hear him arrive, but when she went downstairs the following morning she guessed instinctively from the sour looks on the servants' faces that he was about. She could almost feel his presence in the repressive atmosphere hanging over the household. Her fears were confirmed when she noticed coverings, even more ridiculous than usual, once more adorning the hall statue. Furious, she stormed into the dining room where Fuller and her husband were breakfasting.

'Lord Banbury!' she shouted, ignoring the magistrate completely. 'A mean-minded, lewd-brained servant has dared reclothe the lady in the hall. What is more,' she went on, screwing the knife further into Fuller while she had the opportunity, 'the insolent cur has hidden her beauty beneath a dirty dull handkerchief and a man's cloak, thereby admitting to a narrowness of intellect which would make Calvin of Geneva appear pope and to the artistic taste of a hog in a ditch!'

Her tone softened. 'If you love me, dearest Banby, you will dismiss the slave at once.' Hands on hips and breathing heavily, she stood facing her husband with her back towards Fuller.

'My holly berry,' spluttered Banbury, trying to pick a fish bone from his teeth as he spoke, 'it grieves my heart to see you so agitated. I did not see the piece of in-solence when I came down, else I would have dealt with it myself.' She could tell from the way he refused to meet her eyes that he was lying – he had, in fact, seen the handkerchief and cloak but, recognising them as Fuller's, had not dared remove them.

'You will see to the matter now, my giant? And have the rogue dismissed?'

'Er, yes, my love. That is, if I can discover to whom the investments belong.'

'Surely that will not burden a brain such as yours, Banby dearest. Few of our servants would dare walk out in such dull, drear, mean apparel.'

Goaded beyond endurance, Fuller finally spoke. 'And if it should prove to be the clothing of someone other than a servant?'

Elizabeth turned very slowly to face him. 'Justice Fuller! I did not notice you! What a pleasure it is to have you amongst us again. I hope you will stay long, for so far this year you have graced our house no more than a few months.'

'I thank you, Lady Banbury,' he replied, half rising. 'His lordship has already shown such Christian charity as to invite me to reside here for as long as it suits my purposes.' The sour cream of his face was vividly offset by the dark hollows that held his eyes.

Elizabeth could not resist a further barb. 'You have been away hunting, Justice? If so, I trust you had good fortune.'

Fuller stared at her. His expression shifted sharply from incredulity to understanding and then to hatred. Excusing himself abruptly, he rose and left the room.

'These men of God are somewhat vole-tile, my love,' explained Banbury. 'They are so near to heaven that they do not always see what is on earth.'

'Ah! That is so?' answered his wife distractedly. 'Which men of God, Banby?'

'You know, sweet pickle. Men such as Justice Fuller.'

'Justice Fuller, of course. Such a holy man!'

Later that morning Elizabeth wrote a brief note to Tom telling him that Fuller had returned and that she would come round to see him when she had more news to relate. On a separate piece of paper she enclosed the mysterious numbers written against the first months of the year in Fuller's commonplace book. The papers were then entrusted to Tilly, who took them to Blackmore Street directly.

The door was opened by Tom. As he was wearing his spectacles, at first the maid did not recognise him.

'I have a letter here for – Oh! It's you, Mr Verney. The letter's for you, sir. From Lady Banbury.'

'Thank you, Tilly.'

The girl smiled, gave a neat bob and walked back down the street. For a second or two Tom watched her go. He was on the point of closing the door when his attention was caught by a small man on a pony slowly riding past in the opposite direction. I know that mount, he thought. It is the one used by the fellow who tried to follow me a few months ago.

As the horse moved from shadow into sunlight, he stared more intently. And unless I am much mistaken, he realised, I know the rider, too. And he was following the girl Tilly, curse him!

iii

Elizabeth's visit spurred Tom into making a real effort to get to grips with his new situation. By selling most of the surplus jewellery and finery he had collected at court, he found he had almost sixty pounds – far more than he had imagined and more than enough to last him for at least a year, as long as he was prepared to live like a hard-up gentleman bachelor rather than a courtier. When he first realised how much he had, his instinct was to take most of it to Lucy. But then he thought that she might not appreciate his turning up so soon; besides, if he came bearing large sums of money, it might look as if he was trying to bribe her to return to London with him. So, by way of compromise, he sent House Martin on a reconnaissance trip to Rochester with instructions that he was not to return until he had located the Coopers and handed over to his mistress the long letter and thirty pounds which Tom gave him.

Next, as part of a programme to prove to himself (and indirectly, therefore, to Lucy) that he could be a responsible citizen, husband and father, he visited his neighbours and re-established contact with George Cowley at Clement's Inn. He explained Lucy's absence by saying that a doctor had recommended that at this important time in her life she should go to her aunt's at Rochester, where the country air would be beneficial for her health. It was, he convinced himself, something very like the truth. And now that he had made the opening move and shown the suspicious residents of Blackmore Street that he was not the haughty young wag he sometimes appeared to be, they took to calling in on him. In Lucy's absence some of the more matronly women even felt sorry for him, bringing him cakes and other sweetmeats. The 'Old Tailor's House', as locals dubbed it, rapidly became one of the busiest and most sociable households in the neighbourhood. Despite his lack of years, Tom was a generous and attentive host. He delighted in seeing others enjoying themselves under his roof, taking particular pleasure in the company of George and a student friend of his named Will Speed. On several occasions the three of them sat up late into the night, discussing the Inn, the law, the Prince's trip to Spain and any other matter, legal, political or religious, that took their fancy. They were some of the happiest times Tom had known since arriving in London. But when his companions left and he climbed slowly upstairs to bed, his thoughts invariably turned towards Lucy. He missed her dreadfully. Lying there alone, staring out of the open window at the sky alive with stars, he tried to imagine her in Rochester, gazing up at the same sky and thinking the same thoughts. At such moments he ached for the morning, longing for Bird to come home with news from his absent wife.

On 1st June, a week after House Martin's departure, Tom received a letter. At first he thought it must be from Lucy.

But on looking at it more carefully, he saw that it was addressed in an older, altogether more familiar hand.

Mary Verney had written, she said, without Justice Verney's knowledge. He had forbidden anyone, family or servants, to mention Tom's name or try to contact him. But unable to bear the thought of severing all links with her son for ever, whatever he might have done, she was prepared to disobey her husband for the first time in her life. She hoped the letter would find Tom, for she was not certain where he lived, neither did she know how she was going to get the letter delivered without his father knowing.

In the circumstances, what followed was in some ways rather odd, at first even disappointing. The spirit of profound affection which had inspired the illicit communication was implicit rather than obvious. There was no reference to Lucy or her encounter with her father-in-law, nor to court business. Instead, there was page after page of family and village news, interpolated with anxious questions about her son's health, diet, clothes and future. Justice Verney had been unwell again but was now recovering, Anne Hutchinson was to be married to a much older man, Tom's brother Lucius continued to be the cleverest boy in his school, three people had died of the plague in Banbury already this year — it was, Tom thought as he read it through for the third time with tears in his eyes, as if she were sitting beside him in the Manor garden on a summer's evening, chatting gaily about the first thing that came into her head. Ultimately, it was unimportant that the subject matter was largely trivial. That only made the letter more immediate, more genuine. Nothing else she could have written, no grand phrases or passionate pleas, could have told him so convincingly that, for all his deceptions, foolishness and misdemeanours, his mother still loved him as strongly as the day he had been born.

Fuller's number codes — if that was what they were — made no more sense to Tom than they had to Elizabeth. Without giving their background, he tried them on George and Will Speed, without success. It was after they had failed to crack the mystery and Will was pressing Tom to give him more of the context that he casually mentioned the figures might have something to do with religion.

'Then try a priest, numskull!' cried Will. 'George and I, and you too, no doubt, know little more of theology and Holy writ than our catechisms. Yet I wager twopence a priest will conclude your puzzle before you can say Nebuchadnezzar!'

And so it was, at nine the following day, that Tom made his way a second time to York House to ask a favour of Canon Chillingworth. Although he had made no contact with anyone of courtly status since his rejection by the king and consequently was a little apprehensive how he would be received, he was looking forward to seeing the pale and eccentric cleric again and felt sure that if his acute, offbeat mind could not make sense of the numbers, then no one's would.

Very little progress seemed to have been made on York House or its grounds since his last visit. A swarming army of workmen were still engaged on sufficient digging, sawing, measuring, glazing, painting, plastering and planting to establish a complete new town, let alone a single mansion. Fascinated by the activity, Tom picked his way down corridors open to the sky, across planks and through courtyards strewn with bricks and blocks to Chillingworth's chambers. To make sure he was heard above the noise of construction going on about him, he knocked heavily on the door. There was no reply. He was just about to try again when a workman staggered past carrying a huge slopping bucket of pale blue paint.

'Canon Chillingworth?' asked Tom.

'God's pox!' cried the man, setting down his burden with a grunt. 'Maybe you've seen a canin carryin' paint, but I ain't!'

'Stone head, could you think I would mistake you for a priest?' laughed Tom. 'No, I wish to know where the canon might be found.'

'Little foam-faced squeaker?'

'That may be him.'

'In the chapil.' Tom shrugged his shoulders questioningly. 'Out into courtyard wiv coat o' arms on top, through door on far side, up steps, over 'all and there she is.' Without another word, he picked up his paint and continued on his way, leaving a trail of duck-egg splashes behind him.

'I thank you,' called Tom, walking off in the opposite direction.

When he entered the chapel, Chillingworth had his back to him and was talking to a carpenter engaged on setting up the reredos. Instantly recognising the man's distinctive black-draped figure and high-pitched voice, Tom went forward to greet him.

'Canon Chillingworth!' he cried, advancing down the nave. 'Well met!'

Hearing his name, the canon turned to see who was calling him. He recognised Tom at once, blinked, frowned slightly, shook his head and resumed his conversation. 'And I am certain, Master Joseph,' he said, looking straight at the workman, 'that my lord of Buckingham and his Heavenly Maker would appreciate it just so. Not a tittle to the left, nor one jot to the right. Just so.'

'Canon,' blurted Tom, coming up to him and taking him by the elbow, 'it is Tom Verney, of Stratton Audley.'

Carefully, Chillingworth lifted the young man's hand from his arm. 'Verney, did you say your name was?'

'Canon—'

'Yes, I recall the name. Yet, er, I believe the Almighty has never afforded me the pleasure of your company on a previous occasion, young sir. Never before. Now, if you would stand aside, I have God's business to attend to.'

Tom was dumbfounded. For a moment he stood staring at his erstwhile friend, unable to believe his ears. Then, growing desperate, he cried, 'Canon! What is the meaning of this?'

The carpenter laid down his measure and stepped forward menacingly. 'Shall I put the vermin out of doors, Canon?' he asked gruffly.

'I thank you, Joseph, but I believe that will not be necessary. After all, this is a House of God, not a bear garden, and I believe this persistent yet misguided stranger is wise enough to depart without further ado, eh?'

Tom looked blank. 'Come sir,' Chillingworth continued, 'I will lead you back to the wide world whence you came.'

So saying, he steered Tom down the nave towards the door. Just before they reached it, he slowed his pace and spoke in a soft undertone which Joseph could not possibly have overheard. 'Master Verney, are you come here by daylight, plain as Gospel truth, to pull me down beside you into the pit of infamy? Do you not see? Among those who would grace the court you are become as a man with the plague. The plague, sir. I would not catch of you, or anyone. I am sorry for your, er, plight. Verily, I am. I have in the past, I believe, done what lay in my power to assist you, but now that you have foolishly cut off your own nose, I can do no more. No more. What is gained if one man drown trying to save another, eh?'

'But friendship?' muttered Tom, too shocked by what he had heard to think clearly.

'Friendship?' the canon repeated as he laid his pale hand against the door and pushed it open. 'Friendship is a whore.' He raised his voice. 'Farewell, sir. Think on what I told you. Heaven is where your mind should be, Verney. And, God willing, you enter there by your own conduct, not riding on the shoulders of friends. Good day, strange sir. I have enjoyed our brief meeting. Enjoyed it.'

The door of the chapel clicked shut, leaving Tom standing outside alone.

iv

Three days later, as Tom was getting ready for bed and wondering whether in his prayers he should not try to find a charitable word for Chillingworth, there came a violent knocking on his front door. Thinking it was some rowdy young fellow come to drag him off to the tavern, his first reaction was to open the bedroom window and tell the fellow to shog off. But not feeling particularly tired and in need of a little jollity, he changed his mind. He descended the stairs, pulling on his cloak as he went, lit a fresh candle and drew back the fastenings on the front door.

No sooner had he slid the last bolt across than the door flew open, knocking him backwards and extinguishing his candle. A man stumbled heavily into the room, bringing with him a strong smell of drink. Tom felt for his knife.

'In the name of Holy Mary and all the apostles, what sort of reception is this, Thomas Verney?' called the intruder, fumbling his way about the room in the dark. 'I am – by the devil's breeches! – accustomed to being greeted with trumpets and shawms and dancing virgins tripping their sprightly figures before me like does in the park. And what do I find? I find a silence deeper than that which hung over the world on the first day of Our Lord's creation and a profound darkness such as I have met before only in the souls of unbelievers.'

Tom began to laugh. 'John, you great bear,' he cried, closing the door and feeling on the floor for his candle, 'of course it is dark if you gallop in here like an Egyptian chariot and throw the light to the ground.' He located the candle. 'Now, what is the meaning of this attack?'

John looked about him as a yellow, glimmering light slowly illuminated the unfamiliar surroundings. 'Attack?' he said. 'This is no attack, by Jesus! It is a peaceful embassy.' From somewhere within the voluminous folds of his cloak he produced two large bottles and laid them on the table. 'I am come to visit you, Tom. You and your pretty young wife.'

Having spent most of the day in various taverns, John was in better spirits than Tom ever remembered having seen him. Unfortunately for his host, this manifested itself in such bellowing and roaring and laughing that after a quarter of an hour Tom was driven to telling him that unless he quietened down, he would have to spend the night in the street. Although John muttered dire curses against the 'icy-hearted citizens of the parish who could not abide the thought of men enjoying themselves', he did as he was asked and in fact grew quieter as the night wore on.

For long hours the conversation slipped hither and thither, far and wide, like a seagull over the waters. During its course Tom explained about Lucy's absence, House Martin's mission of reconciliation and his letter of banishment from the royal household. At one point he began to talk about Fuller and what Elizabeth Banbury had discovered in the man's secret box while he was away. But when he noticed that mention of the magistrate reminded John of Sarah and made him maudlin, he changed the subject, deciding to leave the matter of the numbers until morning. A while later, however, he remembered the man on the pony and warned John that the house was almost certainly being watched. 'Zounds! If that be so,' laughed John, 'then, unless the watcher be as blind as Barnabus, we will be dead men in the morning!'

'How is that?' asked Tom, growing alarmed.

'Why, Tom, I was so in my cups that I came down Drury Lane and your street like Herod's army, singing and calling out your name for every watchman and spy in London to hear. God swat them flat, peeping flies!'

'Was that wise, John? Fuller is likely to have a man posted hereabouts.'

'Wise? What is wise? Listen! If that devil-black, pinched-up seed of a magistrate sends a man here for me, I will break him into pieces with my own hands and feed him to the crows!'

'Very well,' said Tom, realising that with John in this sort of mood, even if he had been seen, there was nothing Tom could do about it now. Nevertheless, for his own sake as well as his friend's he determined to get him out of the house as soon as they awoke.

He then asked the question he had been waiting to ask ever since the refugee's arrival. 'Now John – sometime priest of the Roman Church, sometime thief in the woods, sometime goodness knows what else – your past. You promised.'

'I promised, by thunder! What did I promise, thumb-screw?'

'To tell me who you are and whence you came.'

John cleared his throat, refilled his beaker and sat back. 'Well, do you have an hour?'

'I have till cock-crow, when you must leave.'

'Then give ear to this ...'

What followed was truly, as John had said, a tale the like of which Tom had never heard before.

It began in July 1544, when Henry VIII had crossed over to Calais to take nominal command of the English army fighting in France. Although by now a gross and sickly old man, he insisted on maintaining the formalities of his younger years, one of which was that while on campaign he should never sleep alone. To satisfy his vanity, therefore, a beautiful French mistress named Francoise was found for him. To the amazement of the small circle who knew what was going on, the girl's kindly charms and skills succeeded where the somewhat mirthless queen had failed, and before the self-satisfied Henry returned to England he ordered that Francoise be given sufficient funds to provide for herself and the royal bastard she was carrying. Shortly before her baby was due, she entered a convent near Montreuil, where she told the sisters who the child's father was. Sadly, she died a week after giving birth, leaving a healthy baby boy, Pierre, to be cared for by the nuns.

Pierre was raised for revenge. In his youth scarcely a day went by when the sisters did not remind him that his father was Antichrist and the only way he could save his soul was by fighting for the true church against all its enemies, wherever they might be found. The combination of Tudor wilfulness, Catholic indoctrination and his mother's sweetness produced an unusual man. Part Catholic knight, part soldier of fortune, part kind-hearted rogue, Pierre travelled around Europe selling his sword to the highest bidder. He married at least twice, fathered countless children in and out of wedlock, made and lost three fortunes, fought the Dutch in the Netherlands, was wounded by Sir Francis Drake on the Spanish Main and finally, in 1588, at the age of forty-three, went aboard Philip II's Armada bound for England.

Like so many of the fine galleons which sailed up the Channel so proudly that summer, Pierre's ship, the *Santa Maria*, never returned home. The Spanish fleet was battered by gunfire, scattered off the French coast by enemy fireships at night, and finally, no longer in a fit state for a long voyage, driven north by storms. With his vessel leaking badly and half its crew either dead or dying, the captain of the *Santa Maria* beached in Loch Dunvegan, at the north-western tip of the Isle of Skye, and told those on board to fend for themselves as best they could. As far as Pierre knew, he was the only survivor. Every other member of the scurvy-ridden crew who managed to reach the shore was either killed by the men of the island or died of exposure in the hills.

Pierre himself was more fortunate. A few years previously he had served in a Spanish regiment alongside a Gaelic-speaking Scottish mercenary. Having some interest in languages, to pass the time during a winter camp he had paid the scrawny red-headed man from the north to teach him his strange native tongue. Consequently, when challenged on the beach beneath Dunvegan Castle by warrior henchmen of the Macleod, to their amazement he was able to greet them in their own speech. This, together with his massive size and upright bearing, immediately set him apart from the others who came ashore, and his life was spared. When, that night, he explained that his father was the great-great uncle of Scotland's king, James VI, his status rose even further, and he was invited to stay with the rough but open-hearted clansmen for as long as he wished. Having nowhere else to go, he accepted the invitation gratefully.

Almost without his noticing it, the refugee's stay among the Macleods extended from days into weeks, then into months and finally into years. The chief found him a house and a wife, and for the first time in his life Pierre found peace. And in time Pierre Macleod, 'the giant from the sea', became something of a local legend, so that when he died in 1609 his body was not buried but taken out into the loch and returned to the waters whence it had come.

Pierre's wife Oonagh bore him four children, three girls and a boy, John. Believing fervently that God wished his family to continue their struggle to revenge his mother's shame, though by peaceful means, not force, when his son was eight his father sent him to Ireland to be raised as a priest. From there, at the age of sixteen, he was ordered to Spain to complete his education. Ordination followed five years later and the young man entered the church with a view to gaining experience before coming to England as a Catholic missionary.

In a small village outside Santander John did gain experience, but not the sort which mother church expected or approved. As he admitted himself, in those days he had too much of his father and grandfather in him to be a good priest, and within six months his bishop had received so many complaints of his immoral and riotous behaviour that he was compelled to move him to another diocese. Ten months later he was moved again. A third compulsory change of parish followed before the year was out. Finally, aware that if he did not begin his mission soon he would probably never be able to do so, John sailed to Dublin with Spanish wool merchants. From Ireland he traversed the narrow sea to Scotland and met up with his sisters on Skye. Refreshed and in good heart, he then moved south, crossed the border into England and began his ministry. Within a few months he had been eagerly adopted by the Catholic community of the west Midlands, which was how he first met the Whitgreaves.

Unknown to John, however, his reformation had come too late. The Vatican, which had been taking evidence on his case for several years, finally decided to defrock him in 1618. The official papers reached him at Moseley Hall the following year. For a while he was not sure what to do. He went back to Skye but was soon bored by the isolation and returned to England. Here he tried his hand at various jobs, and although none of them suited him, they began to open his eyes to what he believed to be the manifold corruptions and injustices running like rot through English society.

'And that, Master Thomas,' said John with a yawn, 'brings you to as near the present as you will get.' He peered into the bottles on the table. Finding them both empty, he folded his arms and settled back in his chair.

Tom hardly knew what to say. Like the first story John had told him, this one was so strange, so unusual that his initial reaction was to disbelieve it. An illegitimate grandson of Henry VIII? Sisters on some remote Scottish island? Educated in Ireland and Spain? It all seemed too fantastic.

'John,' he began, 'would you tell me—' Before he could say anything further, he was interrupted by the sound of heavy snores. Lying prostrate in his chair, his arms hanging loosely by his sides and his mouth sagging open like a cave, John was sound asleep.

Far off in the city, the clocks began to strike. God's blood! thought Tom. Three o'clock! And we must be up at dawn. Too tired to climb the stairs, he lay down on the hearth and pillowed his head on his arms. Just before extinguishing the candle, he remembered the portrait of Henry VIII he had seen at Hampton Court. He looked up to where John, large and powerful, sat sleeping beside him. Yes, he thought, I suppose it is possible.

The sun was already streaming in through the window when Tom awoke. For a second or two he did not know where he was. Then he remembered. John – drinking – the extraordinary story. He rubbed his eyes and started to stand up.

'Stay there, Verney!' The voice was harsh and vaguely familiar.

Tom raised his head and looked about him. By the door, barely two yards away, stood Justice Fuller and Spid. Both held loaded pistols pointing directly at him. John was still asleep in his chair.

'What is the meaning of this?' Tom asked hoarsely. Disturbed by the noise, John began to stir.

'The meaning? You were a student of God's law, were you not? I am arresting you for sheltering a criminal. And your slumbering friend I am arresting on the charge of murder.'

SEVENTEEN

THE BLEEDING STAG

i

It was another five minutes before John was fully awake.

'By the Holy Virgin of Nuremberg,' he exclaimed, stretching out his arms and yawning like a lion, 'that was a night to enjoy, was it not, Tom?'

Fuller, who was still standing motionless beside Spid with his back to the door, interrupted in a voice as cold as the dawn. 'Slave of Rome, it gives me great pleasure to hear that you enjoyed your last night on this earth. In the place to which I will shortly send you there are nothing but long nights of torment.'

For a full minute, his arms outstretched and his mouth wide open, John did not move. He stared at the wall in front of him, trying desperately to stir his drink- and sleep-befuddled brain into action. Eventually he lowered his arms and looked down at Tom, still sitting on the hearth. 'Do my ears deceive me, Tom?' he growled. 'Or has the black serpent of bigotry come sliding in here unawares while we slept?'

Fuller had moved round to face him, leaving his

accomplice by the door. Once again he cut in before Tom could speak. 'Spotted and lost souls, you are the prisoners of God. He will not accept that you speak profanely of those who do His work. Therefore you are not to speak. If you do, you will suffer.'

Without taking his eyes off his captives for a second, he called to his henchman. 'Spid!'

'Yes, sir?'

'Will you be so kind as to show the bearded papist dog what befalls those who cannot control their tongues?'

'I will gladly, Mr Fuller,' Spid replied, relishing the opportunity for a little violence. Walking up behind John, who was sitting with his back to the door, he hit him hard on the jaw with a pistol butt. John winced and made as if to rise.

'Don't move!' screamed Fuller, rushing up to him and pressing the muzzles of both his pistols into his face. 'The Almighty does not wish for your death now, but He will accept it rather than your escape. And I will be His agent. I will kill you, do you hear? I will kill you!'

John had only to glance into the fanatical black eyes flaming before him to realise that his captor meant what he said. He raised a hand to his cheek and felt the deep cut inflicted by Spid's blow. His mouth, too, was bleeding and a tooth at the back of his jaw was cracked. Staring back at Fuller, he slowly lowered his hands and held fast to the seat of his chair in an effort to control himself.

'That is very good,' said Fuller, taking a step backwards. 'Very good. You see I am a man of my word. Now, we must prepare.'

With his master keeping guard, Spid went to the back of the house and returned with a length of heavy cord which he used to bind the wrists of Tom and John. They were then taken through to the workshop and made to sit on the floor. In this position they were gagged and tied to either end of the heavy oak workbench.

Scarcely had this been completed than there was loud knocking at the front door.

'Pay no heed,' snapped Fuller. But when the noise did not stop and a voice began calling 'Mr Verney! Mr Verney!', he untied Tom's gag and asked him if he recognised who was there.

'It is my boy, Martin,' said Tom. 'But please do not harm him. He is but a young lad.'

'God has ordained his end, not me. But if you do as I bid, I will not cause him hurt.'

'Very well.'

'When we have unfastened you, go to the door and tell the boy that you are tired and have no need of his services today. My pistols will be at your back. If you say other than what I have told you, you will die.'

Against the background of House Martin's continued knocking and calling, Spid hastily unfastened Tom's bonds. Then, with Fuller's pistols pressing against his kidneys, Tom walked through the parlour to the front door. 'Open but an inch,' demanded his guard.

Tom did as he was ordered.

When he saw the door move, House Martin gave a little cry of relief. 'Oh, Mr Verney,' he gasped, 'I feared you was took sick! I am returned from Rochester—'

Eager for news of Lucy, Tom was desperate for him to continue. But the message of Fuller's pistols, now being dug harder into his spine, was obvious. 'I am tired, Martin,' he obtruded, 'and am in need of rest. I do not require your services today.' He tried to open the door a little wider so that House Martin could see him wink. Fuller held it fast with his foot.

'Not see me, sir?' asked the incredulous boy. 'Not after where I have been?'

'No, Martin. Tomorrow. Come tomorrow. Farewell, and God be with you.'

Fuller pushed the door shut and locked it. He then led his captive back to the workshop. As he was being trussed up again, Tom wondered whether House Martin had realised that his master was in trouble, and, if he had, whether he would know where to turn for assistance. After thinking the matter through, he came to the conclusion that there was little hope on either score. The boy was far from stupid, but one brusque interview on the doorstep was hardly sufficient evidence for summoning the law. And were the prisoners not in the hands of the law already? Eventually Tom decided that such speculation was pointless – he would know soon enough whether help was on the way. If the lad had raised the alarm, someone would be round within an hour at the latest.

When nothing had happened by noon, he gave up hope of rescue and concentrated on trying to work out what Fuller was planning to do.

It was already obvious that this was no ordinary arrest. Under normal circumstances the accused would be behind bars by now, awaiting trial. Instead, John and he were bound up like chickens in the market and kept out of sight. And now he came to think of it, what had Fuller meant by saying that John had spent his last night on earth? The more Tom thought about his helpless position, the more frightened he became.

He was given the first inkling of what was happening when, in the early afternoon, they were joined by Moses and Ben, the thugs who had assisted Spid in his previous search of the premises. As they walked straight in without needing Fuller to open the door from the inside, Tom guessed that they, like the magistrate, had their own keys to the house. That meant that Fuller had probably been planning this raid for some time, waiting only for John to appear to put it into operation. Tom began to blame John for having made his arrival so conspicuous. But thinking the matter through, he realised that he was just as much at fault himself for having let his friend stay overnight in a house that he knew to be watched. As that made him even more depressed, he gave up wondering what might have been and turned his attention to his guards.

The new arrivals had each brought with them a large canvas bag. Having talked to them in hushed tones for a while, Fuller opened the bags to check their contents. Immediately he did so a strong smell of lamp oil and tar filled the workshop. He grunted his approval, and saying he would be back shortly and did not expect the guards to take their eyes from the prisoners for a second, left the house.

Stranger and stranger, thought Tom. What do they want with lamp oil?

A terrible thought seized him. What had the last words of Fuller's prayer been? 'Fire! Fire! Fire!' No! Surely not even a man as mad as Fuller would set alight to the house with his victims inside it? That would not be justice. There had to be a trial. Besides, you could not burn a man alive for offering hospitality! It was all wrong! No! No!

Panic-stricken, he began frantically wriggling about and moaning through his gag. Moses heard the noise and stood up. Walking over to him, he threatened, 'Lie still, you whoreson papist scab-sucker, or I'll break your neck!'

Tom looked up at him with terrified eyes, but continued to struggle hopelessly to free himself. Moses kicked him hard in the ribs, twice, knocking the breath from his body. He slumped forward in his bonds, uttering muffled groans.

As the bully raised his foot to strike again, Ben called out with a laugh, 'Don't kill him now, Moz. Justice is saving him for the fire.'

Moses shrugged. 'Mercy costs,' he muttered, bending down and emptying the contents of Tom's purse into his own.

The workshop was a long, narrow room with windows down the left-hand side. Beneath the windows and running almost the full length of the room was the bench to which the prisoners were secured, Tom at the far end, John nearer the door. Unless they twisted their heads right round, which drew inevitable blows from their gaolers, they could not see each other. After the assault from Moses, Tom passed most of the rest of the day in silent, fearful prayer, preparing his mind and soul for the coming ordeal. Occasionally, he raised his head and stared out of the window to his left. In the foreground was a low brick wall. Behind it, above the rooftops, he could just distinguish the hazy outline of a neighbour's cherry tree against the summer sky.

Fuller returned in the early evening, shortly after Tom's small patch of blue sky had started to brighten with streaks of orange and gold. He inspected his captives in turn. With his arms wrapped about his lean body, he stared down at John for about ten minutes, saying nothing, but rocking slowly backward and forward with a thin smile on his lips. He then moved on to his second victim.

Seeing Tom gazing out of the window, he remarked, 'So, arrogant Verney has noticed the fire in the sky, has he? All things begin on high and descend to earth. It was ever thus. God sent fire to serve man, to cook his food, to purify the souls of sinners and infidels so that they might become acceptable in His sight. You do know, do you not, Verney, that you will burn tonight?'

Still staring out of the window, Tom nodded. The rays of the setting sun were glinting on the leaves of the cherry tree. Glinting on leaves? questioned Tom. How odd! Momentarily distracted from his misery, he tried screwing up his eyes to see more clearly. When this proved ineffective, he gave the matter no further thought. He had more important matters on his mind than the science of reflection.

Meanwhile, Fuller had set his men to work preparing for the conflagration. They unravelled rolls of cloth and strewed them about the workshop and the parlour. From their bags Ben and Moses drew out twists and small bales of flax, soaked in oil and pitch. These they placed at strategic points about the ground floor of the house. Finally, a string fuse was laid to one of the largest of the bales.

It had been dark for almost an hour when all was ready. Fuller called his men to him and bade them kneel in prayer. To begin with there was silence. Then the voice of the crazed justice became audible, first as a mere whisper but gradually rising to a frenzied shout.

'Dear Lord Jesus Christ who taught that there is but one true way and one true church, look kindly on thy servants Christopher, Spid, Ben and Moses. Grant, we pray, that their work to rid Your world of sinners be blessed with success. Grant also that the black, defiled and wicked souls of the bearded murderer, his henchman Verney and other such villains be cleansed in the fire of righteousness which we will light. Let their evil vanish in the fire! Burn them, O Lord! Burn them!'

As soon as the others had added their muttered amens, Fuller rose to his feet and said in a brisk, business-like manner that the time had come to finish the matter. 'Come, Ben! Come, Moses!' he ordered. 'For one last time make sure the offenders are secure.'

Tom watched Moses lumber towards him and kneel to check his knots. All of a sudden, he heard a series of muffled thuds. The man's body quivered and convulsed, and his jaw dropped open like a frog. His left hand groped for the edge of the table. A gurgling sound came from his throat. He coughed violently, sending gouts of warm, bright red blood splashing onto the floor and over Tom's chest. Then, very slowly, he toppled forward and lay quite still. One arm and part of his heavy torso rested over Tom's legs. The cruciform hilt of a large knife, straight as a stanchion, projected from his back, and around that grim and miniature calvary sluggish blood oozed from several holes in his doublet.

Above the corpse, looking impassively down at his handiwork, stood Fuller.

Spid's voice came from the other end of the room. 'All well, Mr Fuller?'

'Moses is gone. Ben likewise?'

'With his maker, sir.'

'May God have mercy on their souls. Come, Spid, we must away. The flint.'

Seconds later Fuller had lit the end of the fuse and left the building, his parasite hard on his heels.

By craning his neck round, Tom could just see the flame making its way inexorably down the string towards the highly inflammable bundle at its end. He saw, too, that John was looking in the same direction. Their eyes met. John signalled something with his head, tossing it furiously.

Simultaneously, he tried to stand by lifting the bench with him.

The fuse had about three feet left to burn.

Kicking the body of Moses from him and tucking up his legs, Tom strained with all his might to lift his part of the bench. He felt the other end move as John's massive strength came to bear. He glanced round.

Two feet to go.

He tried again. His whole body ran with sweat. The cord bit into his wrists. His fingers went numb. Knees shaking with the strain, he heaved upward. The bench lifted a fraction. As it did so, John's weight forced it down the room, pinning Tom against the far wall. He looked at the fuse.

Nine inches.

Terror seized him. He kicked and wrestled. Tears of frustration sprang from his eyes. His wrists started to bleed. But all was in vain. He was stuck fast.

With a roar the flame reached the bale of flax. Within seconds the room was filled with thick, black smoke. Red and yellow flames crackled and danced towards the ceiling. Tom felt their heat on his face. His eyes were stinging. From the other end of the room, where the fire was already burning fiercely, he heard John's racking cough as the smoke entered his lungs.

With a crash, the leaded panes of the window above him burst inward, sending slivers of glass into the room. At first Tom thought it was the result of the heat. Then, as he peered through the smoke, he saw a figure climbing into the room. A small, familiar figure. Scarcely more than a child.

House Martin!

A sharp blade cut through Tom's bonds. As soon as he was free, he grabbed Moses' purse and, bending low to avoid the worst of the smoke, led his rescuer to the other end of the room. The heat was intense. John had already lost consciousness in the suffocating fumes. Suspended by his bonds, he hung like a corpse from the bench.

House Martin cut the body free and the two of them dragged it to the other end of the room. Somehow, they lifted it onto the bench. From there, half blinded by the smoke and scorched by the flames, they rolled and pushed it through the broken window, and carefully lowered it onto the cool, damp grass outside.

ii

'I pray pardon me, my lady,' Tilly whispered, leaning over the bed as far as she dared, 'but I have news.'

Her mistress opened one eye and closed it again. 'News?' she asked huskily, unaccustomed to being woken at this hour of the morning. 'What but ill tidings can come at this time of the day?'

'I don't rightly know whether it be good or ill, my lady,' said Tilly enigmatically. 'But I believe it may come from Mr Verney.'

'Shh!' Elizabeth hissed, opening both eyes and sitting up. 'Quietly with that name in this house. Now, be quick, what is this mystery?'

Tilly explained that when she had left the house early that morning to buy some thread with which to mend the dress her mistress wished to wear, she had seen a small boy standing on the opposite side of the street. She could not but notice him, she explained, because he looked so forlorn, as if he had been kept awake all night in an ash pan. His eyes were red with tiredness and his face, hands and clothes were covered with soot and burn marks.

To her surprise, she went on, as she walked off the boy

had started to follow her. At first she had thought he was a beggar and had taken out a penny to give him. But as soon as they were out of the sight of Pickering House, the lad had come up to her, and asked apologetically if she knew of a maid called Tilly. When she had said that she was Tilly, the boy, glancing nervously about him, had given her this message: 'Tell your mistress not to worry when she hears of the fire. Mr V and his friend are safe.' The grimy messenger had then vanished down a side alley.

'Was that all?' asked Elizabeth. 'He did not say what fire?'

'No, my lady.'

'How mysterious!'

Elizabeth had to wait only until dinner time for the mystery to be solved. The servants had just cleared away the roast goose and two of them were staggering in under the weight of a magnificent leg of pork, decorated with sprigs of rosemary and swimming in a bath of succulent juices and spices, when Fuller, who through the meal had been less acerbic than usual, said in a nonchalant, conversational manner, 'I am told there was a fire in Blackmore Street last night, my lord.'

Without taking his eyes from the sizzling joint, now being carved into platter-sized slices, Banbury asked, 'Blackmore Street? Is that not where young – I mean, well, I once knew a man in Blackmore Street. I pray God he is not harmed!'

'Then I fear that I may have ill news,' said Fuller in a voice that had become strangely jubilant. 'You recall young Verney, my lord?' Listening intently, Elizabeth stared at her plate and picked at her meat without eating anything.

'Aye, I do, Justice. Why, do you not remember that only a while ago I informed the king—' At that moment Fuller upset his wine glass, sending a thin river of red stain sliding across the table towards his host. Alarmed, the baronet pushed back his chair. One of its legs broke under the strain and he tumbled to the floor. Fuller and several servants rushed to his assistance.

By the time the justice had apologised profusely, a new chair had been found and his lordship dusted down and set in his place again, the original topic of conversation seemed to have been forgotten. But not by Elizabeth. Having noted all that had happened, she waited until order had been restored then turned to Fuller and asked, 'Now, Justice, before your little clumsiness I believe you were about to impart some ill news?'

'Ill news?' Fuller scowled.

'The fire? Blackmore Street?'

'Ah! I thank you, my lady, for reminding me.' He turned and looked straight at her. As she stared back at him, she wondered again what he had made of the information that Tilly had been seen calling on Tom. She had to be careful.

'I was informed by my trusted Spid,' Fuller went on, 'that the fire started in the very house where Master Verney is staying. All night the conflagration roared like a furnace of hell itself, consuming not only that house but several around it. By the morning nothing was left but dust and ashes. And a scattering of burned bones.'

'Oh no!' cried Banbury. 'The Lord preserve us! Not bones! Not burned bones!' He licked in vain at a rivulet of grease flowing from the corner of his lips. It ran down his chin and onto his shirt front.

'Alas! yes, my lord. Bones! Charred bones!' Taking his eyes off Elizabeth for a moment, Fuller lifted them to the ceiling in a gesture of theatrical piety before lowering them again to his hostess. 'So great was the blaze, the officers could not tell how many had perished. Two, three, four – only the Lord knows. Yet Verney is not to be found, my lord. I fear he has gone.'

Banbury look blank. 'Gone?'

'Gone to hell – or heaven,' Fuller explained. 'Dead, my lord.' He twitched more pronouncedly than ever as he strove to control the smile forcing its way onto his lips.

'May the Lord have mercy on his soul,' muttered Banbury. 'That is sad news, Justice, very sad. For all his sins – and I warrant he had many – he was a good young man. This sorry news will break his father's heart.' He continued his meal in silence.

Knowing that it would be closely observed, Elizabeth planned her reaction to Fuller's announcement most carefully. To begin with she neither did nor said anything. Then, as if the full horror of the Blackmore Street fire was dawning on her in gradual stages, she stopped eating, hung her head, stifled a sob and finally, saying that she was not well, left the table for her rooms. As Fuller watched her go, his face glowed with satisfaction.

After she had closed the door, Banbury sighed, 'A woman of such fine sensintivities, Justice. I believe she would weep at the decrease of a fly.'

'I do not recall her being as distressed at the death of my daughter,' observed Fuller slyly. Having seen the way Elizabeth had reacted to the report of Tom's death, he was sorely tempted to follow this bitter remark by sowing seeds of doubt about the baroness's virtue in Banbury's mind. But deciding that the man was too valuable to risk alienating, he said without enthusiasm, 'Yet God be praised! She is a fine and honourable woman!'

Banbury, who had been thinking of his wife, replied

with a loud 'Amen!' and called for another wedge of beef.

Just as he was about to force it into his mouth, he stopped, set down his knife and said, 'I have just remembered. He was married.'

'Who was married, my lord?'

'Verney. It was at your suggestion that I informationed the king that the youth had wedded in secret, though His Majesty did not take kindly to the news, nor, I believe, did he regard me highly for being the bearer of it. We saw Mrs Verney at the house, did we not? A pretty wench.' He sniffed. 'And to think, Justice, that the sweet creature is now no more than a handful of black dust.' His eyes began to water. 'I would I had not told the king, Fuller. It was not a Christian deed.'

The magistrate looked alarmed. 'Lord Banbury, you are the finest Christian in all England! You did your holy duty, that was all. You uncovered a cheat—'

'But a cheat that is now dead. So is his wife. And your daughter. Oh, Fuller! Death is following me, and I do not like it. I am sore afraid.'

'My lord, listen. The honest and worthy Spid brought me news of the fire. He saw the ashes and talked to the officers. They told him that all the bones they found were of too large a size to be of women. The girl is safe, but it is not known where she is.' Banbury stopped snivelling. 'Take cheer, my lord,' the justice continued with a slight laugh, 'and join with me in thinking on large bones.'

'Thinking on large bones? I do not compre-hend.'

'Who has – had – large bones?' asked Fuller patiently.

The baronet scratched his ear. 'I know not. A donkey?'

'Very close, my lord. Not a donkey but a dog. The cur we were pursuing. The cur you shot at. The cur they called Great John. The papist slave we hated more than the devil himself!' Unable to control himself any longer, he stood up and began hopping around the room. 'Big bones! Praise the Lord! He is burned! Consumed in fire! Gone, gone, gone!'

'You are certain he was there, Justice?' enquired Banbury, staring in amazement at the unprecedented performance from his spiritual mentor.

Fuller stopped gallivanting and approached the peer so closely that he could smell the food on his breath. 'Yes, my lord,' he said with a dreadful intensity, almost spitting out each syllable. 'I am as certain as if I had seen him with my own eyes. He was seen entering the house.'

'Very well,' Banbury shrugged.

As if remembering something, Fuller stood back and clasped his hands together. 'Lord God,' he prayed, 'I praise You and thank You with all my heart and soul that You did look kindly on the first part of my holy mission.'

After an appropriately reverential pause, Banbury asked in some alarm, 'First part? Surely there is not more?'

A lean smile cut across Fuller's mouth. 'Thank the Almighty, no more for you, my lord! Just a pleasing request.'

'Oh yes?'

The puritan's voice fell to almost a whisper. 'I am so taken up with holy delight at our success in ridding the world of the Beast of Rome, my lord, that I have decided to show my loyal gratitude by presenting our great sovereign and his son with precious gifts. To make the giving more of a delight, I would my Christian intentions were known only to you and me. Until the time that my gifts are presented, I trust you will keep the secret, my lord?'

'I like the plan, Fuller. It shows your noble spirit in a goodly light. Therefore, I give you my word as a Pickering that your secret is safe. We have no need of swearing, surely?'

'God must witness,' Fuller replied sharply. He set two table knives in the shape of a cross and placed Banbury's hand over them. 'Swear by Almighty God.'

'I swear by Almighty God to keep Justice's Fuller's secret,' said Banbury. Irritated by the way he was being treated, he made to remove his hand.

Fuller held him back, prompting, '—Or may your soul burn in hell.'

'Or may your soul—'

'Come, my lord,' Fuller corrected, '*my* soul.'

Banbury sighed with exasperation. 'Or may *my* soul burn in hell. There! It is done.' Clearly annoyed, he complained, 'Sometimes, sir, I believe you almost too sharp in your observances.'

'Ah! But forgive me. The best is yet to come, my lord. His Majesty was displeased with you when you told him of Verney's – God rest his soul – deception?'

'As I aforementioned, Fuller, he was not well disposed towards me, no, sir,' answered Banbury, still feeling cross and wondering where all this was leading.

'Then,' cried the magistrate, 'you shall win back the king's favour by taking my gift to him, while I travel to Spain similarly to honour the prince.'

'You do not wish to see the king yourself?'

'I do. But he knows me not, and, besides, I must to Spain. You are such a man about court, so welcome there that you will be able to press my gift even into the hands of the king himself. I could not do that.'

'No,' mused the baronet, puffing out his chest, 'you could not. Then, to be of Christian assistance to an old friend, I will do as you request, Fuller. Really I will.'

'Lord Banbury, you are a true Christian knight,' cried Fuller, grasping him by the hand. 'But remember, I pray, my design is secret. I wish to surprise the king.'

The baronet smiled. 'So you shall. I shall not reveal the gifts, not even to my Bessie. To tell the truth, Fuller,' he went on confidentially, 'I was weary of that priest hunting. Too much blood and fire. I am glad that all will now end happily.'

'So am I, my lord. To cite the adage, "All's well that ends well", eh?'

'Precisely, Justice. We must, I suppose, thank God that all is now well.'

iii

All was not well, however, in the upstairs room of the Bleeding Stag on Blackheath, the run-down and ramshackle inn to which the three escapadoes from the Blackmore Street fire had dragged themselves. House Martin, wrapped in a grey blanket, was asleep on the floor. Struggling as best he could to bind the suppurating burn on his left forearm, Tom sat beside him, every now and again casting anxious glances at the figure on the bed. John had scarcely recovered consciousness since his rescue. As they were hauling him to safety, a large piece of burning timber had fallen across his head, cutting open his scalp and singeing his hair. His lungs were an even more serious cause for alarm. Lying prostrate on the straw mattress, his eyes closed and his great frame as loose as washing on the line, his breath came in long, painful and infinitely slow groans, each rumbling and gurgling round the room like a wave gathering along the pebbled shore.

Tom could still not fully grasp what had happened. After the rescue his first instinct had been to get as far away as possible without being seen. Had it not been for House Martin's formidable knowledge of the paths and byways of the district, this would have been impossible.

Somehow supporting John between them, they had groped their way through two gardens, over a low fence and found themselves next to the cherry tree that Tom had seen from the workshop. Here the boy had paused to explain that they were now in the yard of an unoccupied house and that he had been using the tree as a lookout post. Then, like a wraith, he had vanished into the night to fetch Princess. Until his return, Tom had cradled John in his arms and watched the fire gradually take hold of his house, then spread to another downwind of it. By this time, alarmed by the sound of church bells, the whole parish had woken up. The deep and awful roar of the blaze, quite audible from where Tom sat, had been punctuated by the shouts and cries of terrified citizens.

After the boy had helped him set John on Princess's back, Tom had offered him tearful thanks for all he had done. He had then instructed him to go home and rest, but to be sure he was up at first light to deliver a vital message to Lady Banbury's servant, Tilly. After that, he was to join John and himself at the Bleeding Stag, a suitably undiscriminating hostelry he had remembered from his days with Williams and Corbet. Only after the lad had gone and he had been leading Princess through the city towards the bridge, had Tom remembered that in all the excitement he had not asked about the trip to Rochester. House Martin had not mentioned it either. Had the boy forgotten? he had wondered as, too tired to walk any more, he had pulled himself up behind his unconscious friend. Or had House Martin kept to himself news he did not want to impart? On arriving at the inn the following morning House Martin had still said nothing. He had simply announced that he had given Tilly the message, then fallen asleep.

Tom feared the worst.

★

House Martin woke up at about two o'clock in the afternoon. After they had eaten, saying that he needed to get some fresh air in his lungs, Tom suggested they take a short walk on the heath. Raised between city walls, the boy did not trust open spaces, but he agreed to his master's proposal and five minutes later they were ambling side by side through the long grass.

To begin with they talked about the rescue. House Martin had thought that something was wrong, he said, as soon as Tom had opened the door. 'And when you called me just "Martin", like I was my grandfather,' he smiled, 'then I knew as things had gone bad.' The trouble was, he went on, that as he did not know the nature of the difficulty he had no idea what to do about it. His family were all taken up with a cousin's wedding, and seeing Ben and Moses – whom he had encountered previously as law officers – enter the house, he had not dared go to the authorities. So he had decided to find out more. To that end he had snooped around until he had located the empty house and its cherry tree, and then settled down to watch and see what happened. Having seen nothing all day but a few figures wandering about the workshop, the fire had come as a complete surprise and it had taken quite a hold before he had realised what had been going on. The rest of the story, he concluded, his master already knew.

Tom sighed. 'And one day,' he said, putting his arm round the boy's thin shoulders, 'when I am rich, I will reward you as you ought to be rewarded now. I owe you my life.'

'I owe you mine, sir.'

'Eh? How's that, Bird?'

'You was good enough to take me on when I was

nothing. Or else I would have taken to livin' by thievin' and such like. And ended on the gallows, so 'elp me God.'

'Never! There is no gallows low enough for you. Besides, your grandsire would not have let you sink to ill living.'

'He would not 'ave knowed,' the boy shrugged. 'I am good at being secret.'

Tom stopped and turned to face him. 'Well, my secret spy, what did you find in Rochester? Come, Bird, do not hold back. I know she did not speak well of me, or else you would have told me before now.'

'Well, sir, she did not speak well of you,' he replied hesitantly, 'but she did not speak ill of you neither. She did not speak of you at all.'

'Silent anger?' suggested Tom sadly.

'No.' He paused, then suddenly blurted out, 'She said nothing because I could not find her!' Pulling out the money he had been given for Lucy, he pressed it into his master's hands and clung sobbing to him like a distressed child to his father.

It took Tom a while to settle the boy down, and even longer to get him to tell his story. But when he eventually did so, his admiration for the lad rose to even greater heights.

House Martin had reached Rochester easily enough and had no trouble finding Mary Cooper and her husband. They were well-known and kindly people, and when the visitor had explained who he was they had welcomed him into their home and given him food and lodging. But they confessed that they had not set eyes on Lucy for years – indeed, they wished they had, for they had fond memories of her. But if, as the boy said, she had left London to come and stay with them, she had certainly not arrived. The news had devastated the diminutive ambassador. The next day he had taken it upon himself to follow the London road out of Rochester, stopping at all the inns to ask if anyone had seen a young woman answering to his mistress's description. No one had. After five days of fruitless search, fearing that Tom would be sick with worry at his delay, he had returned home.

In the light of his recent experiences, Tom's first assumption was that Fuller was behind Lucy's disappearance. Leaving House Martin to look after John and beginning with the Bleeding Stag itself, he spent two days asking after his wife at every inn between Blackheath and those checked by his servant. Once again, no one remembered seeing her. He then rode on to Rochester and called to see the Coopers. They had been making enquiries locally, they said, but had come up with nothing. Lucy had simply vanished.

In normal circumstances Tom's next course of action would have been to write to or visit all the magistrates of the parishes through which Lucy might have passed. But knowing that this would inevitably lead to Fuller hearing of his whereabouts, he decided to delay doing so for the time being. So, as he rode disconsolately back to join his companions, he considered what options remained open to him. His sheltering of John, his fall from favour at Clement's Inn and at court, and his rift with his father had left him perilously vulnerable. As Chillingworth had demonstrated only too plainly, he no longer had any friends of wealth or influence – apart from Elizabeth Banbury, and even that relationship was illicit. He could not hope to challenge Fuller before the law, for he had no proof of the man's criminality or that he planned further mischief. The contents of the mad justice's box, even if they could be shown to be treasonable, which was extremely doubtful, could not be made public without risking Elizabeth's ruin. No, he concluded, the only course of action left open to him was somehow to find conclusive proof of Fuller's guilt and bring the man to trial. That way he would probably be able to clear his own name, if not John's, and so involve the authorities in the search for Lucy.

As he rode up to the Bleeding Stag, Tom was surprised to see a familiar head poking out of one of the upper windows. 'No, by Mary's pomander,' the head shouted down to him, 'this is no ghost you see before you, young Verney! It is the flesh and blood rogue of the seven seas, restored to health by the tender ministrations of this Bird of yours. Come up, long face, and drink to my blossoming health!'

Tom had to smile.

Over the following twenty-four hours the two friends worked out a plan of campaign. First they had to find out where Fuller was and what he was doing. Once they had checked that he was not engaged on anything immediately dangerous, they then had to see if they could make sense of his secret scribblings. As Tom's notes had been lost in the fire, it was essential for him to see Lady Banbury again. She would also know what Fuller had been up to. But when Tom said he would ride into London the next night and make his way into Pickering House under the cover of darkness, John immediately objected.

'Tom, Tom,' he groaned, 'since our meeting I have brought nothing but pain and misery upon you. Were I sure that all would be well with you, then – by our Dear Lord Jesus Christ! – I would leave this God-forsaken island for the New World tomorrow, for that is where I have determined to begin my worm-eaten life afresh. Yet I will go only when this war with Antichrist is won and you are happy again. Until such time, we fight together. Your way is my way, Tom, so I cannot let you venture unaccompanied into the city. We enter the lion's den together, or not at all; there I will shield you even as you have shielded me.'

Tom was deeply touched by his friend's offer. But thinking it over, he could not accept. The wound on John's head was not yet properly closed, and his lungs were still so clogged that every now and again he was seized by violent fits of coughing that left his vast handkerchief stained with black bolts of blood and tar. Pointing out that a night adventure would slow his companion's recuperation and might, if he was taken with a coughing fit at the wrong moment, even jeopardise the mission's success, Tom insisted on going alone.

Only later did it occur to him that John might have wanted to visit the place where Sarah had died.

iv

It was a bright summer night and Tom had no difficulty in directing the ferry to the small jetty that had been erected exclusively to serve Pickering House. Explaining that he was engaged on an assignation with a 'devilishly fair servant girl' with whom he planned to elope, he paid the boatman to wait for his return. 'And mind you do not sleep,' he warned, 'for if I am pursued by the girl's master, I shall need to be away in a trice!' The oarsman gave Tom a broad wink and, taking up his pipe, assured him that as long as he got his money he would be quite happy to stay until dawn. Initially, he had been suspicious of Tom, particularly as his fare's burned clothes and bandaged left arm made him look more like a discharged siege-gunner than a gentleman. But once Tom had explained that his mission was romantic rather than criminal, and that he was prepared to pay handsomely, the man had mellowed and entered into the spirit of the adventure with a will.

A high wall surmounted by iron spikes protected the southern flank of the grounds of Pickering House. On the day of the April shootings, Tom had cleared this obstacle easily enough by scaling a tree, swinging along a branch till he was beyond the spikes and dropping down onto the river bank. However, on getting out of the boat he saw to his dismay that since his escape the ground on either side of the barrier had been cleared. Having walked up and down the wall several times, inspected the defences of the properties on either side, and tried the massive wrought-iron gates, he was forced to conclude that without a ladder his mission was impossible. He cursed himself for not having planned his visit more carefully. Returning to the gates, he pressed his face against the bars and gazed into the orchard. In the distance the vast bulk of Pickering House loomed out of the darkness. As he stared, he noticed a movement barely ten yards in front of him. A figure appeared, walking quietly between the trees. The watchman! Tom slipped quickly out of sight behind the wall.

Looking round the gatepost to see if the man was still there, he had an idea.

A couple of minutes later he returned to the boatman and explained what he wanted him to do. Once again the fellow was reluctant to get involved in anything underhand. But Tom's gold and impassioned entreaties finally won him over, and, slipping the coins into his purse, he sat back in the stern, withdrew a bottle from under the seat and cleared his throat.

Tom disappeared into the shadows beside the wall and whistled quietly. In a piercing and high-pitched flat tenor voice that carried far into the night, the ferryman started to sing.

'She said to me as she closed her eyes,
As she closed her eyes in the meadow,
"O come, kind sir, it is no surprise..."'

Alarmed by the din, the watchman came hurrying down to the gate to see what was going on.

'Who's there?' he cried, peering into the river mist. Continuing his passable imitation of one who had been carousing for several hours, the tuneless boatman paused, belched and explained that he was on his way home after seeing his brother-in-law released from Windsor gaol and had moored to take a little refreshment.

'Private mooring!' barked the watchman, clutching his staff. 'If that hellish caterwauling wakes his lordship, I will be shent! Silence! Or I'll shoot!'

Knowing it was highly unlikely that a humble watchman would be carrying a firearm, the boatman thought for a while. 'If you shoot, you'll miss the mark and wake 'is lordship. So 'old your fire. I have an 'appier dream. Give ear, watch!'

A couple of minutes later the guard opened the gates and went down to the river to share the trespasser's bottle. As soon as he was in the boat, Tom slipped unobserved through the gates and into the gardens of Pickering House.

If Elizabeth was surprised when she heard Tom scratch at her door and call in a whisper to be admitted, she did not show it. So many strange things had happened in her world recently that a clandestine night visit seemed almost normal. She pulled on a loose gown and opened the door. But when she stood back with her candle to see how her lover was, she could scarcely forbear to cry out. 'Why, Tom!' she gasped. 'You sent word that you were unharmed by the fire. If you were not injured, then I would fain see one who was.' She went up to him and kissed him, running her fingers over his bruises and cuts. Asking tenderly about his arm, she eased him into a chair. Then, seated on the floor by his side with her head resting on his leg, she bade him tell her all that had happened.

When he had finished she said kindly, 'I am truly sorry about Lucy. I am sure you will find her one day soon' – she hesitated – 'if that is your wish.'

'Yes,' Tom answered quickly, 'that is my wish. At least, that is my wish most of the time. I truly miss her, Bess, yet know that were she back with me we would quarrel before the day was out.

'But enough of this maudlin gossip! I have not crept through the night to talk about my heart.' Running her fingers over his knee, she glanced quizzically up at him. He smiled. 'At least, not my married heart, Bess.'

'Unless he is the very serpent of deception, that murdering justice believes you and John to be – dead,' she laughed, allowing her hand to slip further up his leg.

'Dead? Do I seem so to you?'

'Let me see ... No! I have scarcely met a man more alive – and upright.'

'And you, Bess, have you been touched by the dryness of the final vault since last we met?'

'I have practised no vaulting, Tom; but I believe the spring still flows.'

'Shall we see? I have forgotten. Is ... this ... where the source lies?'

'Mmmm! It is.'

'Then, Bess, there is no drought.'
'No, I think not. Tom?'
'Yes?'
'My knees are – Oh! – growing weak. I must sit.'
'Then sit here, Bess.'
'Is it sufficiently – firm?'
'I believe it will hold up. If I move ... And you place your ... Ah-h!'
'Slowly – yes – Oh, Tom! I am glad you were not burned.'
'It was my – agh! – luck ...'
'Luck! Oooo! Such l-luck! More!'
'Ah-h-h! More luck?'
'More – everything! Oh! Tom!'
'Bess!'
'Quick!'
'Yes!'
'Oh-h! Oh-h! Oh-h!'
'Ah! Ah-h-h!'

Holding Elizabeth tightly to him, Tom whispered into her hair, 'My beautiful Bess ...'

'Mmm?'

'What would I do without you?'

'The same as me without you,' she replied, stroking the back of his head.

'And what is that?'

'Nothing.'

He laughed. 'You are my oasis. But before we drink again, should we not put our heads together over Fuller's papers?'

'Yes, we should.'

As she was fetching her notes, Elizabeth told Tom that she was certain Fuller believed John and him to have died in the Blackmore Street blaze. Yet she was equally certain, as they had previously surmised, that his self-appointed mission was not yet finished. His mood of triumphant good humour following the fire had soon passed, and now, as he had done ever since his arrival in London, he was for ever slipping furtively in and out of the house, muttering to the disgusting Spid and giving knowing winks to her husband. If anything, he was becoming more obsequious towards the baronet with each day that passed, and by involving him in some new and secret scheme, he had even managed to win back some of the ground he had lost to Lady Elizabeth. When she questioned her husband about what was going on, despite her most audacious blandishments to date, all he would say was that she must not worry her pretty head over what Fuller and he got up to: it was nothing but a merry idea to bring happiness and favour to everyone. He announced this with such clod-headed innocence that she was sure he believed it. What really worried her was the knowledge that to Fuller the 'merry idea' was bound to be altogether more sinister.

For almost an hour Tom and Elizabeth sat at the table poring over the various clues: the figures, the drawing and the snippets of annotation, prayer and Revelation. Certain aspects of the matter were plain. Fuller was consumed with hatred for the Roman Catholic faith and its adherents. How or why this had come about, they had no idea, although it had certainly been fanned by Sarah's love for John. This tragic liaison was also likely to have reawakened the pain he had felt at the loss of his wife. It was therefore safe to assume, Tom concluded, that the wretched pond-man 'deserted by women' was Fuller, as seen through his own eyes. This would tie in with his preoccupation with sexual sin. It was also clear, both from the man's writings and from the way he had tried to kill Tom and John, that he was convinced fire was the only way to cleanse the world of papists. It was known, too, that he had plans for an exploding box, presumably to kill some unfortunate Catholic. But they did not know the intended victim of the trap, nor whether it had been built or delivered. Perhaps it had been intended for John and was therefore no longer needed? If that was so, then what was Fuller up to now?

At their last meeting, alarmed at where they were going, the couple had refused to follow their thoughts through to their conclusion. But now, convinced that Fuller was both mad and a dangerous killer, they knew they had no option but to press on, however dreadful the destination might be.

Elizabeth made the first move. Taking up her pen, she began to use her notes and the conversation and prayer which Tom had overheard at Moseley Hall to compile a list of references to the veiled target of Fuller's loathing. From the Revelation she discarded the bearded dragon with three eyes, 'one cut in the form of the legs of the whore of Rome', as that was plainly a reference to John. Instead she wrote, 'old man from the north – forked tongue spoke strangely – conquer for Satan and the Whore of Rome.'

She paused and looked at Tom.

'Continue, Bess,' he urged. 'We cannot stop here.'

'Very well. But I am afraid. Think if these words were seen. It might not be Fuller on the rack, my handsome one, but us.'

Writing very slowly, she added to her list: 'time-serving friend of Rome – the Roman traffic and her poxy Scottish handmaiden – even though it be in the highest places of all – one true king, and He is in heaven – the corrupt governor – Sodom.' By the time she had reached the end her hand was shaking so much that she could hardly hold the pen. Putting his arm round her shoulder to comfort her, Tom could feel her heart thumping heavily against her ribs. Thus they sat, staring down at the paper, without moving or saying a word.

'Sweet Jesus Christ protect us!' whispered Tom eventually.

'Amen to that,' Elizabeth replied, placing her hand over his. 'Yet we may have misunderstood—'

'Is that what you believe, Bess?'

'No.'

'Neither do I. The late Queen Anne was of the Roman faith – the family of Lord Buckingham's wife are the same; the king will not commit his country to fight beside the Protestants on the Rhine; Prince Charles and Buckingham are in Spain to woo the Catholic Infanta – I tell you, there is business afoot sufficient to disturb a broken mind such as Fuller's.'

Elizabeth stood up. 'Tom, come stand beside me and tell me I dream.'

'No, sweet Bess,' he said, rising from his chair. 'You do not dream.'

'Then one of us must say it.' She lowered her voice until it was barely audible. 'Tom, is it true that Justice Fuller wishes to murder the king?'

'It seems so.'

'But when? And how?'

'We do not know. I must take the Sodom and Gomorrah numbers to John. He may find in them what eludes us.'

He crossed to the table and started to copy out the figures. Elizabeth stood behind him with her hands on his shoulders. 'Tom,' she said when he had finished, 'you know why I am so afraid?'

'I do. We have stumbled against the blackest treason.'
'It is more than that.'
'More than treason?'
'No, not more than treason. But more than Fuller's treason. I am frightened that the villain has an accomplice – a stupid but innocent man who cannot see what he is engaged in.'
'Spid? He is no innocent—'
'No, Tom. Not Spid. My husband.'

EIGHTEEN

THE FOUR TUNS

i

Before Tom left Pickering House, Elizabeth arranged with him that House Martin and Tilly should meet at Charing Cross at eight o'clock each morning to exchange messages from their employers. In the meantime, bearing in mind that Fuller had been told of Tilly's presence in Blackmore Street and therefore probably still mistrusted the girl and her mistress, she agreed to keep as close an eye on the justice as was possible without raising suspicion. For his part, Tom undertook to lay the Sodom and Gomorrah numbers before John when he returned to the Bleeding Stag, and let her know at once if anything important materialised. Their farewell was prolonged and unusually emotional. Afterwards, tired, elated and frightened, he slipped out of the house, passed through the garden gate with a key she had given him and reached his boat before the tide had turned.

After breakfast the next day, 10th June, Elizabeth tried once again to get her husband to discuss the 'merry idea' which he and Fuller were hatching. To begin with she was off-hand and casual, as if to suggest that the matter was of so little importance that he might as well tell her as not. When that tactic failed, she became injured, telling him he was cruel to have secrets from his wife, and that if he really loved her he would explain what was going on directly. Although he was clearly suffering acute mental and spiritual anguish, to her intense irritation and frustration he still refused to talk.

'Don't you see, my scented piece of silken flesh, that I have sworn an oath? If I break it, my internal soul will burn in hell. Justice Fuller made me swear to that. I beg you, Bessie love, do not let me burn in hell!'

Unfortunately, the sight of the Toad grovelling before her brought back all Elizabeth's old distaste for him, and rather wishing at that moment he would burn in hell, she could not prevent a note of scorn from creeping into her teasing. 'Oh, false Banby!' she cried. 'So you love a puritanical justice more than your little wife, do you? I tell you, you are a weak man who knows not what he is about!' She had rarely before spoken to him so harshly – or so honestly – and overcome with a welter of emotions, she left the room. What irony, she thought as she took a turn about the garden to settle herself, that the only time she had ever quarrelled with the stupid man was because, for once, she had been trying to help him.

Back in the house, Banbury padded disconsolately towards the Crimson Closet. Staring down at his splayed feet and muttering gloomily to himself, he did not see Fuller gliding downstairs as noiselessly as a spectre to intercept him before he reached his haven.

'How now, my lord,' he said with an oleaginous grin, 'not in the best of humours?'

'No, Justice, I am not! I am going to my Closet to get away from your oaths and my wife – before they pull me in two pieces like, like a walnut!'

As the baronet tried to push past him, Fuller laid a hand on his arm. 'Lady Banbury is seeking to know our little surprise?' Banbury nodded angrily in reply. 'Then may the Lord bless you, sir, for being a strong man!'

The peer hesitated. 'A strong man? My Bessie says I am a weak man.'

'Oh, mighty Lord Banbury, blessed of God! You are wronged!' cried Fuller, standing back and raising his arms in a theatrical gesture of horror. In silhouette against the brightness of the window he looked like an enormous vulture. Banbury shrank back against the wall.

Fuller lowered his arms and bent forward, metamorphosing the vulture into a spider. 'Our secret is safe?' he asked Fuller with a confidential leer.

'Of course. I do not wish to pass my eternity in a furnace, burned up like poor young Verney.'

'Then who can call you weak, my lord? Verily, even Samson, the mightiest of all God's chosen, could not withstand the wiles of a woman. But not so Lord Banbury! Not all the perfumed charms of the most beautiful woman in London – nay, all England – could make him forswear his oath. In time, my lord, the world will see him for what he is – the prophet of his generation.'

'That may be so, Fuller,' said Banbury with a frown, 'but it is not easy being a prophet. I am still inclined to re-tire to my Closet.'

As Fuller watched his host waddle off down the corridor, his small eyes contracted still further into tiny cauldrons of contempt.

The following morning, when Tilly called to collect her message for delivery to House Martin, Elizabeth could think of nothing to write other than that her husband remained strongly ensnared by the villainous puritan.

'You have heard no whisperings yourself, have you, Tilly?' she asked as she handed over the note.

'Well, my lady, Walter did tell me as he had heard Justice Fuller's man, that Spid, was seen visiting Zak. You remember, the locksmith—'

'I remember full well who Zak is, Tilly. Here, hand me the letter.'

Taking back the paper, she broke the seal and added at the bottom: 'I am told that F's man has seen Zak – the locksmith. The old fox is up to a new trick, for certain. I like it not.' She then renewed the seal and sent her maid scurrying off to Charing Cross to meet with House Martin.

An hour later the girl returned bearing a letter from Tom. Elizabeth opened it eagerly and read through the contents. When she had finished, she turned to Tilly and asked if she had visited Castle Lane, in Blackfriars.

The girl looked bemused. 'Not as I remember, my lady. I never had cause to.'

'Well now you do, Tilly, for that is where we are going this morning. Come, my cloak!'

ii

As Elizabeth had feared, no sooner had she and Tilly stepped into her husband's barge and ordered it to pull towards the city, than Spid and Fuller appeared on the landing stage and asked if they might accompany them, as they too had business in the city that morning. Elizabeth knew that she ought to agree to their request, then slip away when they landed. But the thought of sitting with Fuller in the narrow confines of a boat was more than she could bear, and she replied, vaguely but firmly, that she wished to travel alone as she was about a private matter 'of concern only to women'. The justice and his servant, she concluded, had to find a boat of their own. Of course, if he needed money for the fare, she would be only too happy to oblige.

Fuller turned away in fury. The unspoken truce was now broken. From this time onwards the relationship between them, hitherto overlain with a veneer of formal cordiality, moved rapidly towards open war.

Realising that Fuller was bound to ask the oarsmen where they had taken their passengers, Elizabeth disembarked at Puddle Wharf. From there she walked quickly to Castle Street and the Four Tuns inn, where Tom was waiting for her near the door. As soon as she entered he led her upstairs, asking Tilly to remain below with House Martin to keep watch. On the landing, out of sight of prying eyes, he welcomed Elizabeth with a kiss and explained that since their last meeting he had taken a room in the inn, a discreet hostelry tucked away between Castle Lane and the old city wall beside Bridewell Dock, so as to be nearer Pickering House. Heavily disguised, John and he had travelled there from Blackheath the previous evening.

Tom had been awaiting the meeting between John and Elizabeth with some trepidation. Not only were they strong personalities with widely different religious and political views, but, on a more personal level, their coming together would force him to recognise, if not reconcile, two separate strands of his life.

On leaving home, he now realised, in order to cope with independence he had divided himself into compartments, each featuring a different Tom Verney – the student, the lover, the wastrel, the courtier, the husband

and the – well, he was not sure into what category one put the friends of Great John, but it was certainly different from all the others. Sometimes he had allowed his true identity to disappear behind the part he was playing. Over the past few months, however, partly through chance and partly through his own actions, one by one his roles had been reduced and their masks cast aside. With the disappearance of Lucy only two remained. But he was afraid that their removal would reveal something he despised or, even worse, nothing at all.

He need not have worried. John was captivated by Elizabeth's looks and charm the moment she entered the room, while for her, after years in the company of the fops, bloodsuckers and nincompoops that largely made up her husband's circle of friends, meeting John was like travelling to another continent. He was an unknown and exotic land, exciting, dangerous, fascinating. Within minutes of their meeting the two were talking together like old friends. And when, speaking with obvious sincerity, each told the other of their deep affection for Tom, he was not so much flattered as profoundly relieved. Listening to the easy conversation between two of his dearest friends, he realised that he was now almost a single person again.

Elizabeth was the first to raise the subject of the Sodom and Gomorrah numbers, asking John if he had been able to make sense of them.

'Sense, my lady?' he retorted with a good-humoured guffaw. 'To one of my training such devices are as common as blackbirds. But, by the Holy Virgin's spotless veil, had Europe but kept faith with the old church and its cloak of the Latin tongue, such things would never have arisen!'

'How so, sir?' asked Elizabeth. She was sitting flanked

by John and Tom at the head of a heavy table. Her chin was cupped in her hands.

'Holy scripture is like fire, Lady Banbury. A blaze tended with care cheers the heart, warms the body and cooks the food. But in the wrong hands it changes from a friend into a dangerous foe which may destroy the whole house. Do we allow children to make a fire? No. Then no more should we permit those unskilled in its interpretation to look into the Holy Bible. Latin is a guard round the hearth of scripture, keeping out meddling fingers that might else be burned. Fuller – may God forgive me for uttering such an accursed name – is such a meddler. Like a monkey with a pistol, as like to shoot its mother as a viper, his ignorant and untrained mind has played with what it does not truly comprehend and produced an evil tragedy.'

Elizabeth, who was far more interested in the meaning of Fuller's numbers than in the relative merits and demerits of translating the Bible into the vernacular, had grown impatient towards the end of John's Catholic homily. Now she leaned forward and asked urgently, 'Yes, yes, I am sure what you say is true. But come, sir, you forget the numbers! What is their meaning?' She drummed her fingers on the table.

John grinned. 'Zounds! When the subject is close to my heart I prattle like an old dame at a wedding feast. Tom said the pages were headed "Sodom and Gomorrah" – is that correct?'

'It is.'

'The story of God's destruction of those two cities is told in the nineteenth chapter of the Book of Genesis, the first book of the Bible. Now, after a brief visit to St Andrew's in the Wardrobe, where he read the words for himself, young Tom tells me that in the version of scripture authorised by

King James, and twisted by the vile Fuller, the twenty-fourth verse of that chapter runs thus:

> Then the Lord rained upon Sodom and Gomorrah brimstone and fire from the Lord out of heaven.

'You see? The twenty-fourth verse of the nineteenth chapter of the first book of the Bible tells of the destruction of evil people, by fire too, Fuller's favourite element.'

'And he had written alongside the month of January: one, nineteen, twenty-four,' Elizabeth said slowly. 'These he had totalled, I assume correctly, to forty-four. Thus much I understand. But surely we learn nothing from this, nor from the numbers against the other months?'

Tom could not resist intervening. 'But we do, Bess! We do! John believes Fuller opens his Bible at random each month and reads a text. The position of that text in the Bible — its book, chapter and verse — gives him the numbers for that month.'

Laying her hands flat before her and looking down at them intently, Elizabeth said, 'Yes, Tom. You have explained how things stand at the present, and done so very prettily. But,' she went on in a quieter tone, 'we are talking of what seems to be a treasonous plot. Do Fuller's number games tell us what lies ahead?'

'It may be that he is waiting for something,' Tom answered, laying his hands absent-mindedly over hers. 'Did you find the totals of the numbers for the other months?'

'Tom! My pen would serve me better picking my teeth than messing at arithmetic. I cannot find the total of any number larger than my ten fingers.'

Tom explained, 'February was fifty-eight, March thirty-eight, April forty-seven, May forty-two.' Remembering that they were not alone, he withdrew his hands and glanced at John to see if he had noticed. The answer was a broad wink.

'Yet if he chooses these numbers from a random text,' Elizabeth continued, unabashed, 'is it not strange that they are all so close to forty-four. Closer, truly, with each month that passes.'

John chuckled. 'Your arithmetic, my lady, is sharper than you allow. The answer, I would wager, is that this wicked justice cheats the Holy Bible as he cheats everything else he meets with. He wants and needs the number forty-four again. Therefore, he will deceive himself to get it.'

'But why another forty-four? What good will it do him?'

'It will do him no good, my lady, nor anyone else,' said John grimly. 'Yet I believe when he finds forty-four a second time – repeating the number which signifies to him the destruction of wickedness by fire – then he will think God has given His blessing for the justice to strike at evil again. It is not the cities of the plain he will burn, nor a branded priest and his friend, but – well, you have uncovered his intended victim, and I incline to agree with you.'

There was a long pause. Eventually Elizabeth said in scarcely more than a whisper, 'Yet I read his book in May. It is now June. If he has chosen his number for this month and it is the second forty-four, then God have mercy on all of us, for we may be too late! Now I understand why your letter bade me hasten hither without delay. Even now he may be – yet he was at home this morning – his man had seen Zak—'

'My lady?' John interrupted.

'Yes? But hold! I know your request before you make it.'

'You do?'

She smiled. 'I may not excel at arithmetic, but I am no fool in other matters. We must be certain. To that end, I will return directly to Pickering House. Having a key to Fuller's secret box, the very instant he leaves it unguarded my maid or I will to his room and there discover the number he has written for June.

'And gentlemen,' she concluded, rising to her feet, 'let us pray God it is not another forty-four.'

iii

Tilly paused outside Fuller's bedroom and listened. Apart from the noise of her master entertaining old friends in the dining room – a gesture of independence against both his wife and Fuller – the house was quiet. The magistrate had departed half an hour before, excusing himself to attend a prayer meeting which would detain him until near midnight. Spid had gone with him. As soon as they had left, Lady Elizabeth had retired to her rooms. Her husband would not be up for some while. Tilly glanced nervously about her. The way was clear.

The lock on the bedroom door turned silently and easily. Slipping into the room, she closed the door and locked it. She put the key into her pocket and drew out the smaller one made by Ector for the box. Her hand shook with fear.

Through the window came sheets of clear white moonlight, as bright as December sunshine. The corners of the room were hidden in purple shadow. As she looked about her, the girl shivered. She was not cold, but about that hard, clean, chamber there was an unearthly feeling of permanent winter.

She tiptoed across the room and knelt down. The box

was still there, chained to the leg of the bed as before. As quietly as possible she pulled it out and tried the key in the lock. A perfect fit! She raised the lid.

Far away on the other side of the house she could just make out the muffled noise of Lord Banbury's revels. Outside in the Strand a woman screamed. Otherwise, all was still.

Quickly, turning over the papers with deft fingers, she found the commonplace book. She moved over to the window where the light was brightest and began to flick through the pages, seeking the heading she had memorised. It was somewhere towards the back, she remembered. Ah! There it was, 'SODOM AND GOMORRAH'! The months, with the figures next to them, were just as she had been told they would be. She glanced down to June, then across to the space next to it.

There were no numbers, only writing. Telling herself not to panic, she held the book up to the light and read:

> Be not far from me; for trouble is near;
> for there is none to help.

She read it through again, then lowered the book and stared out of the window. It did not make much sense to her. Probably from the Bible. Her mistress would be disappointed. She re-read the passage and tried to commit it to memory: "Be not far from me; for trouble ..." She glanced momentarily down at the sentence. With her lips silently mouthing the words she was trying to remember, she watched the figures in the street below. To her left a woman, presumably the one whose scream she had heard, was reeling unsteadily in the direction of the city. A coach rolled by, throwing up a cloud of dust. As it settled, a tall angular figure carrying a lantern walked up to the front door of Pickering House. His deportment was familiar. Tilly's heart leaped. Fuller! The justice had come back!

Rushing over to the box, she replaced the book where she had found it and slammed the lid. The sound of the front door bell rang through the house.

The key! Where had she put the key? Fumbling in her pocket, she found it and drew it out. She then locked the box and pushed it back under the bed. Now for the door.

But before she had taken a single step, there came the sound of long-striding footsteps ascending the stairs.

She was too late.

Terrified, she pushed the box key down the front of her dress. She wanted to hide, to call for help, but found she couldn't move. A cornered creature petrified with fear, she stood motionless in the middle of the room, staring at the door, waiting to be caught.

A key clicked quietly in the lock. There was a slight pause. The handle turned, the door opened and, preceded by a pool of candlelight, Fuller stepped noiselessly into the room.

He uttered a slight gasp when he realised someone was there, and reached for the knife at his side. But recognising the intruder, he lowered his hand and walked forward into the moonlight.

'Well?' His voice was flat and hard.

Tilly opened her mouth. No words came. She was quivering uncontrollably.

'Explain, wanton drab, why you come creeping into a gentleman's bedchamber at night?'

'If you please, sir ...'

Fuller set down his candle and came up to her. 'If I please, eh, callet? I may please, or I may not. When a man enters his room at night and finds a dark figure there, he does not wait to see who it is. He strikes first and looks later. I will kill you.' He put his hand on the hilt of his dagger.

'Oh! I pray you, sir—'

Her plea was cut short by a blow from Fuller's fist which left her clutching the side of her face. 'Silence, strumpet!' he hissed. 'If you are not to die, then I will need two things. One is the truthful purpose of your being here. As for the second, even a camel of your dull wits may guess that.'

Terror-struck, Tilly looked at him in disbelief.

'Very well. I take your silence as consent. We will talk.' He turned to close the door.

'Indeed we shall, Justice. We shall hold a little parliament – or will it be a court?' Standing in the shadow of the doorway, the tall figure was unrecognisable. But not so the voice.

'Lady Banbury!' said Fuller slowly. 'What brings you here at this time of night? A man is certainly fortunate when two haggards come to warm his bed!'

'You dung-tongued snail! A woman would rather give herself to a baboon than creep between your putrid, inadequate and loveless sheets! Come, Tilly! We must leave the justice to his solitary pleasures.' The maid took a step towards the door.

'No!' growled Fuller, grabbing her arm. 'I will not let her go until she tells me why she was here.'

'That is not your concern.'

'But it is. I wish to know. Just as your husband would wish to know why she called on your young companion in sin, the late Mr Verney.'

'Do not mock the dead, sir!'

'Very well. But why was this drab in my room?'

'A drab, Justice?' said Elizabeth with an icy smile. 'Ha! A jest, surely? She is no more a drab than you are a justice!

If you would know, my maid was here on my order. I sent her to clean the room. It is strange, sir, but every time we look in here we find a trail of chill and stinking slime, as if a great slug had taken up residence within these walls. You have noticed it yourself, I do not doubt, but are too polite to mention it. Or perhaps you have a cold in the head and cannot smell? I tell you, the whole house is poisoned by the stench – even our visitors complain – and it was because the vile infection prevented me from sleeping that I dispatched Tilly to wash it away. Did I not do well, sir?'

By the time she had finished, Fuller was shaking with rage. His face twitched, his hands trembled and his eyes blazed black hatred. For a second or two she believed he was going to strike her. Then, somehow taking a grip on his fury, he said in a hoarse and sinister whisper, 'Curse you, Elizabeth Banbury! May the great God Jehovah who made this world, the God of Adam and of David, look down from heaven at your unrepentant and lustful soul, and curse you to a life of eternal torment.'

Tilly felt her blood run cold. Although quietly spoken, such was the intensity of Fuller's words that she felt they must be audible in every room of the house.

Elizabeth, however, appeared unmoved. 'Kindly unhand my servant, dear Justice, lest she bite,' she replied coolly. 'Now, stand aside and let her pass.' Without taking her eyes off the man for a moment, Tilly moved to her mistress's side. 'Has the lizard harmed you?' Elizabeth asked.

'No, my lady.'

'Then we will bid the creature good night—'

'Lady Banbury!' Fuller interjected.

'Yes?' She turned to Tilly and sighed. 'It seems we must endure one more blast of foul air before we may retire.'

'Lady Banbury, I will leave this house at my earliest convenience. But you shall be punished, that I promise you. You – shall – be – punished!' With these words, he sprang forward, pushed Elizabeth and her maid into the corridor and slammed the door shut in their faces.

Back in the safety of the baroness's rooms, it took a large glass of strong ale before Tilly felt calm enough to talk about what she had discovered. Then, when she was ready, Elizabeth sat at the table with her pen poised and began by asking for the June number from the Sodom and Gomorrah table.

The girl looked down into her empty glass and made no reply.

'You did find it, Tilly?' her mistress enquired, trying to conceal her anxiety.

'Oh yes! I found it easy, my lady. But June had no numbers – just writing.'

Elizabeth's face fell. 'But Tilly,' she cried, 'this is a matter of great consequence. You did look carefully?'

'I did, my lady,' answered the maid, close to weeping, 'I read it all. Three times. First there was the numbers, as you said, by the other months. But I swear June had words, just words. I took the book to the window so as I might see it better in the moonlight – that is how I saw the justice returning.'

'He did not see you at his box?'

The girl wrung her hands together. 'No, my lady. He did not see me. And I put everything back careful. As before.'

Elizabeth was filled with admiration and pity. 'Tilly?' she smiled.

'Yes, my lady?'

'No one in the world, no, not even the king himself or

the Great Khan of China, could be blessed with a servant such as I have.' Stepping forward, she kissed the girl fondly on both cheeks, saying, 'Tilly, you are my angel!'

Already stretched to near breaking point by what had happened in Fuller's room, the girl was totally overcome. With a plaintive cry she threw herself on Elizabeth's breast and sobbed like a tiny child.

When the hapless maid had settled down and taken a second glass of ale, Elizabeth returned to the table and urged her to try and remember what she had read.

'I know how it began,' Tilly said. 'It was like Bible words. "Be not far from me", it started.'

Elizabeth wrote the phrase down. 'And then?'

'I am not so clear after that, my lady. It was about there being trouble but no one to help.'

Try as she might, Tilly was too shaken, and perhaps a little too tipsy, to recall exactly what she had read. In the end, hoping that a night's sleep would refresh the girl's memory, Elizabeth put her to bed on the couch in her dressing room and retired herself. Until Fuller had left the house for good, she decided, it would not be wise for either of them to sleep alone.

She was woken at about four in the morning by the sound of Tilly crying out. Fearing the worst, she lit a candle and hurried next door. To her relief, she saw that apart from the maid, who was obviously having a nightmare, the room was empty. She walked over to the couch with the intention of calming the troubled girl, but just as she was about to wake her, she recognised the words she had taken down earlier that night: ' ... not far – from me.' She stooped down and put her ear close to Tilly's lips. ' ... Far from me,' the sleeping girl repeated. Then she rolled over and cried out, 'Trouble is near and there is none to help!'

Hoping that these phrases might be part of the missing sentence, Elizabeth jotted them down and went back to bed.

Both mistress and maid rose early. Between them, using the words Elizabeth had written the previous night, they came up with as accurate a copy of Fuller's June sentence as Tilly could manage. It ran, 'Be not far from me, for trouble is near and I have no help.' When this was complete, they wrote Lord Banbury a message stating that they had gone to call on a French milliner newly arrived in town, and left by coach for the Four Tuns.

From the window of Fuller's room, Spid and the magistrate watched them leave.

'You did not wish me follow, sir?' asked the henchman.

'No. You do as I say, which is the way of the Lord God.' His lips tensed into a hard crease. 'The time has come. The whore is away, so we may act. Go at once to Zak and bring back with you the presents he has made for me. Cover them with a blanket lest they be seen. We would not want the happy secrets revealed before their time, would we Spid?'

Spid looked blank. 'I do not know, sir.'

'Good. It is best I alone know. Then nothing can go amiss, can it? Be gone!'

iv

John recognised Fuller's June sentence as soon as Elizabeth laid the paper on the table. 'By the mass, a psalm!' he cried. 'A psalm of David! Though not in the tongue in which I am accustomed to seeing it, I believe it to be the twenty-second psalm.'

'No numbers?' asked Tom, shaking his head.

'Ass!' retorted John with a laugh. 'We are not so dull that we cannot write our own numbers. We have the second already: twenty-two. When we have found the other two, then we will know whether we may sleep in peace or not.

'This is how it must be done. The first may be uncovered as easy as baking pigeon pie – I will undertake that. The second, Master Tom, you must bring to us. Hasten with the speed of Mercury, I pray you, once more to St Andrew's church. Peep into that heretical translation of yours at the twenty-second psalm. Then return with the number of this verse.'

'Were you priest or sergeant before I met you in the woods?' Tom asked with a grin. 'You command like Hannibal with an ache in his belly!'

'Enough, quibbler!' said John, waving his arm imperiously in the direction of the door. 'We have no time to lose.'

Clapping his friend on the back and squeezing Elizabeth's hand, Tom pulled his hat down over his face and left the room.

As soon as he had gone, John reached for the ink and quill that stood on the table and began to list the books of the Bible from memory. Against the first, Genesis, he wrote the figure one, then so on down to the Book of Psalms, which was number nineteen. 'There,' he said when he had finished, 'we are safe for the present.'

'Safe?' asked Elizabeth.

'June is not the month.'

The baroness looked at him incredulously. 'How does your list allow you to say that? Must we not wait for the third number which Tom will bring?'

John laid down the pen. 'Lady Banbury,' he began, 'did

Tom tell you that I am – or rather I was – a priest of the church of Rome whose ministry is no longer required by his holiness because it did not accord with the example set by the blessed apostles?'

'Tom did explain as much.'

'Good. Now, when I was a child, my father trained me for my calling by dipping me in the Christian faith as deeply as Achilles was dipped in the Styx, except that my weak spot was not my heel, but somewhere more private. Thus, as you have seen, I can recall the books of the Bible, and know that the Book of Psalms is number nineteen. Fuller's verse is taken from the twenty-second psalm. The total of those two numbers is forty-one. If we are to manufacture forty-four, the number we dread, then Tom must return to say that the verse is number three. But, I warrant, he will not, for I remember the psalms sufficiently closely to know that the verse is eleven or twelve – unless in rendering the Latin into English the king's scholars have taken it into their heads to turn the word of God upside down!'

Elizabeth sat in impressed silence as John checked and rechecked his list. When eventually he looked up, recalling his grumbling about vernacular translations of the Bible she said, 'We are playing with fire, John.'

'We are,' he grunted, looking steadily towards her. 'Why?'

She shrugged. 'I do not believe there is one reason. To be with Tom; to save my husband; to preserve the king; to fight evil – all those, yet none. And you? Tom says you have no love for the order of our state. Why do you risk your life to help preserve it?'

John replied without hesitation. 'To keep us from something worse, Lady Banbury. It is true I do not like what is, but I have seen with my eyes and felt in my heart what the world might become should men like that pebble-hearted justice become our governors. God forbid that we should ever suffer under a King Puritan and his council of the elect! I have known the silent, grey and mean cities where such men hold sway, my lady, and it freezes my soul to think on them. I tell you, in the lands of the Presbyterian and the Baptist and the Adventist and the Brother and the Calvinist, the spirits of God and man are wrapped about so tight with Thou-Shalt-Nots that even the little children have forgot how to smile. The devil take all Sabbath-hawking, scripture-screaming, marble-hearted misers of delight! Why, such crusaders of cruelty would have us all as black as ravens, on our knees more than our feet, and – what is worse – swinging from the gallows for the merest twist of an eye towards a handsome face or a pretty ankle!'

'And that,' said Elizabeth with a smile, 'would not be a world for you or me, would it, sir?'

'It would not, my lady. Verily, it would not.'

As their eyes met Tom came panting into the room. 'Eleven!' he puffed as soon as he had shut the door. 'Eleven. What is the sum of the numbers, John?'

'Fifty-two.'

'Fifty-two?' cried Tom. 'It cannot be. That is greater than the last. We are in error. Let me see your list.' John handed him the paper on which he had written the books of the Bible. 'One, two, three ...' Tom counted, '... eighteen and nineteen. Damn the man's eyes! There is no logic in him.'

'No,' said Elizabeth. 'We must watch and wait. It may not be easy, for he said he was leaving Pickering House.'

'Leaving?' repeated Tom. 'If, as you fear, your husband is his key to the court, why should he leave? He needs Lord Banbury if he is to get near to His Majesty – unless he plans some highway ambuscade, like those which John commanded. Or perhaps he has abandoned his design? Or is he nearer to its discharge than we believed?'

John leaned across the table and retrieved his list.

'I am sure it is not abandoned, Tom,' said Elizabeth. 'But how? And when?'

'With an exploding box which he will leave in the king's presence,' suggested Tom. 'And in July, at the soonest.'

'No,' muttered John without looking up. He had picked up the pen again and was placing brackets round some of the names on his paper and writing new numbers alongside them.

'No to what?' asked Tom.

'To July.'

Elizabeth tried to see what he was doing. 'August then?'

John sat up. 'Not August, Lady Elizabeth. Nor September. Nor any month but the one we are in. June.'

'You are mistaken,' pleaded Elizabeth. 'Pray God you are mistaken!'

'No,' answered John solemnly. 'Look here.' He pushed the paper across the table to where Tom and Elizabeth could see it. Pointing to a circle he had drawn round the books of Genesis, Exodus, Leviticus, Numbers and Deuteronomy, he explained, 'Here are the first five books of the Bible, otherwise known as the single Book of Moses. Number one.'

Tom gasped. Glancing at him, Elizabeth reached over and took his hand.

John indicated a second circle round the two books of Samuel and the two books of Kings. 'And these four are sometimes called simply the Book of Kings. If we were to do so, they would not be the numbers between nine and twelve, as I had written, but all of them number five. Do likewise with the two Books of Chronicles, and what do we have?' He pointed to the new figure he had written beside the world 'Psalms'.

'Eleven books, not nineteen,' read Elizabeth softly. 'O God!'

Tom muttered, 'Eleven and twenty-two and eleven ...' His voice trailed into silence.

John finished the sentence for him. 'Yes, forty-four. He will strike this month. Thirteen days have passed already. Surely we have not long to wait.'

The rest of their meeting was taken up with deciding what to do. Once again they discussed whether there would be any point in taking the whole business to someone in authority. Tom even considered approaching his father. But in the end they came back to the same problems as before: who they were and the flimsiness of their evidence. As their case rested on nothing more substantial than uncorroborated personal experience and obscure stolen private papers, a criminal and an outcast in league with another man's wife could not hope successfully to charge a well-connected justice of the peace with murder, arson and treason. Spid might talk under torture, but they had no means of getting that far. Their only hope, they concluded, was to catch Fuller in *flagrante delicto*. In his case that meant seizing him in public in possession of his dreaded box, at a time when he was known to be on the way to visit the king. The best place for such a denunciation would be in the Strand, outside Pickering House, in the presence of Lord Banbury, the servants and passers-by. However, to effect such an interception it was essential that Lady Elizabeth learned of all her husband's movements in advance and relayed them immediately to Tom and John. For this purpose, they agreed to increase the Tilly–House Martin letter exchange to four a day. The men undertook to find accommodation even nearer Pickering House and to recruit a couple of reliable helpers. All would be in place by the following morning.

After that, they would just have to watch and wait.

v

Spid came back in the middle of the afternoon, driving a small cart. Once in the grounds of Pickering House he sent a stable boy to find Fuller, who appeared almost at once, hurrying into the stable yard like an ostrich. Without a word to Spid, he went straight to the back of the cart and lifted the blanket. There, fashioned in rare tropical teak and inlaid with delicate bands of brass, lay the two boxes. Fuller stretched out his hand and stroked the gleaming woodwork like a lover.

'Zak gave me these,' said Spid, holding two keys before him.

Fuller seized them eagerly, enquiring, 'Are they locked? Which is for which box?'

'Both locked, Justice. Box with brass peacock on lid has key in form of that bird. Box with tree on top has key in form of tree. Clever, eh, Mr Fuller?'

'God guides his servants with infinite skill, Spid. Now, carry the peacock box to Lord Banbury's coach and leave it under the seat. I will take the other to my room. When that is done, tell his lordship's servants to prepare their master's coach for a journey on the morrow. Order them, on pain of a flogging, not to touch the interior. When that is done, lie low. Come to my room at dusk.'

★

Spid knocked at Fuller's door at about seven o'clock that evening. Expecting a reward, he had taken the liberty of arriving earlier than he had been instructed. He was told to enter and found his master sitting on the bed with the second box on his knees.

'You have done as I said?' Fuller asked when Spid had closed the door behind him. He was clearly annoyed that the man had called so soon.

'Yes, Justice.'

'Then come and look here,' said Fuller, setting down the box on the bed and moving over to the window. 'Do you see that cross?'

Standing behind him, the diminutive Spid could see very little. 'I beg your pardon, sir,' he explained, 'but you are before me and taller, so I cannot see the cross at all.'

'We must all see the cross, Spid. Come, I shall step aside.'

He walked slowly round behind his servant and pointed with his left hand over the man's shoulder. His right hand dropped to his waist.

'Where is the cross, sir?' Spid was worried now. He screwed up his eyes and scanned the skyline. All he could see were towers, chimney pots and trees.

'You cannot see Our Lord's cross?' There was an ominous edge to Fuller's voice.

Spid started to sweat. His master's arm was not just resting on his shoulder, it was beginning to bear down on him oppressively. Wanting to get away, he cried out in false delight, 'Yes! There it is, sir!'

'Where?'

The arm grew heavier still and started to bend round his neck. 'Near the tree!'

'Near the tree? There is no cross near a tree, fool. You lie! You cannot see the true cross of Our Lord Jesus Christ because you are a false sinner!'

Realising that he was being slowly choked, Spid started to struggle to free himself. Suddenly, holding his victim firmly with his left hand, Fuller drew his dagger and struck. The long blade entered the soft tissue below the ribs, pierced the diaphragm and skewered the heart.

Standing back to avoid getting blood on his clothes, but keeping hold of Spid by the hair, Fuller lowered his servant's jerking body to the floor and stood watching until the last spasms of life had died away. He then tore off the dead man's shirt, which he used to mop up the blood, and pushed the corpse beneath the bed.

Fifteen minutes later, his hands washed and his gown changed, he was talking excitedly with Lord Banbury.

It was all going better than he had dared expect. Thrilled by the novel secrecy of the operation, Banbury had promised to slip away very early the next morning. The king was at the palace of Theobalds, Fuller told him, an easy journey from London. If he left at six he would be in plenty of time to give the gift to the king during the pre-dinner audience. The justice was most insistent that Banbury did not look into the box himself before he reached court, in case he spoilt the wrapping.

'But what is it, Fuller, that comes so neatly bedded?' he asked, hopping from one foot to the other with anticipation.

'Shhh! Secret, my lord! You will discover soon enough. All I will say is that I chose it with great care and, do not fear, the whole world will hear of your delivering it. That I promise you!'

He went on to explain at great length how the box had to be handled with the utmost caution and opened only in the close presence of His Majesty. On this point he was categorical, even suggesting that the opening might be done by James himself. To all this Banbury eagerly agreed.

'And you are going to Spain with a box like mine for the prince? Well, what a subject you are! And all because you believe that papist dead!'

Fuller smiled a thin smile and replied, 'Yes. I will leave for Spain in the morning, my lord. I will travel through France because I fear sea air might harm my gift. I will be at Dover tomorrow night.' He stopped abruptly, aware that perhaps it was not wise to talk of his plans too freely with a man whose tongue was normally as loose as court morality.

Banbury rubbed his hands together. 'Fuller, if I am to rise with the lark, I must to my chamber early tonight. What a game we play! Such a caper as I never dreamed of! And do not fear, your secret gift will be safe with me and, if I am able, I will press it even into the hands of the king himself. Oh, my Bessie's sweet face when I tell her that I won great favour at court with the presentationing of your gift! She will love me more than ever!'

Fuller inspected his fingernails. 'Indeed, my lord! She will love you with a burning fire that can never be quenched.'

On hearing that her husband had retired early for the night, Elizabeth decided that this gave her a good opportunity to question him about his plans for the next few days.

Quietly unbolting the interconnecting door between their apartments, she called softly into the darkness, 'Banby! Banby, my love!'

Normally such a direct approach would have brought Sir Julius bounding from his bed like a dog at feeding time. But tonight all that greeted her was the sound of exaggerated snores. Certain he was not asleep, she left the door ajar so that she could see where she was going and crossed the room. Stealthily pulling aside the silken hangings, she peered inside. In the gloom she could just make out the gross figure of her husband, night-cap pulled down over his ears, lying on his back with his mouth open. He was snoring like a horse. As gently as possible, inch by inch she pulled down the covers then raised his night-shirt and kissed him. There was no response from either end. She tried again. This time he could pretend no longer, and with several wide yawns he went through the motions of waking up.

'My Bessie!' he said eventually. 'I was asleep.'

'So you were, my pike. All over. I have come to wake you up.' With her right hand she did her best to raise his expectations.

On meeting with some success, she knelt over him, only to find that tonight, as on every other night, drink and anxiety ensured that the gulf between thought and deed remained as unbridgeable as ever. Banbury tried unsuccessfully and inexpertly to make up for his shortcoming with a podgy forefinger, explaining as he did so what had gone wrong. His pitiable excuses were the only masterpieces he ever produced.

'The truth is, my little fox cub, that, unusually, I am beset with a double vex-ation. First, I am exceeding tired. Second, I am all a-quiver with the thought of the surprise I have prepared for you on the morrow. These two have quite quenched my appetite for your charms.'

Elizabeth smiled to herself. 'I can wait, my stag, till your rutting time.' After all, she said to herself, what is another day when I have waited all these years?

'I will make it worth the wait, Bessie.'

'You will. But tell me, wicked man, about this surprise.'

'Not now. Wait till morning, my lamb. Wait till morning.'

Elizabeth decided that this was not the moment to press the issue, and after further desultory chat, she retired to think over what she had heard. A surprise, but no mention of Fuller. No talk of going to court either. In the end she concluded that whatever her husband had been jabbering on about, it was not Fuller's plot. Checking that Tilly was safely asleep in the other room and that the doors were securely fastened, she went to bed in the knowledge that, for the time being at least, Fuller would not be able to move without her knowing.

NINETEEN

THE WHITE CLIFFS

i

The screaming seemed to go on and on. Shuddering around the house, it rose and fell in intensity but never ceased entirely.

At first Elizabeth thought it was part of her dream. Then, realising with horror that it was real and was coming from somewhere on the ground floor, she stumbled out of bed in her night-gown and opened her door. In the corridor the noise was much louder and clearly distinguishable as the voice of an hysterical young woman. As she listened, not yet fully awake, there was a sudden shout, followed by a noise like clapping. Then silence.

Seconds later a footman came running up the stairs.

'John! What was that infernal din?'

'It was Kate, my lady. When she entered the room under what the justice sleeps in – to clean it – she found a big black patch on the ceiling and something all dried on the floor below. She called me in. I knew it the moment I set eyes on it. Seen it before, my lady. Blood!'

The baroness shuddered. 'Go, John, wake my husband and Justice Fuller.'

'I shall, my lady.'

By the time Elizabeth had woken Tilly and pulled on a more respectable gown, John was knocking at her door. 'I beseech your pardon, my lady,' he called. 'It is a matter of much importance.'

'Well?' she demanded, stepping into the corridor once more.

'Lord Banbury is not to be found in his rooms, my lady. It is said he went out very early. And the justice's door is locked fast. There is no noise from within and all the keys have vanished. There is a third strange happening, my lady. The servants say as last night none of them set eyes on the justice's man, Spid. He did not sleep in his bed.'

As Elizabeth listened, a haunting fear grew in her mind. The mysterious bloodstain and the simultaneous absence of her husband, Fuller and Spid must somehow be related. Had she failed to notice what had been going on beneath her very eyes and, as a result, missed the moment she had been watching for? Dear God, she prayed, I beseech You in Your mercy let me be mistaken!

She turned to John. 'Listen!' she ordered, surprised at her own decision. 'Send a man to the stables. See that all the horses and carriages are there. If they are not, ask who has taken them and when they did so. Let me know the answers with all possible haste. While that is being done, break open the justice's door and see what lies within.'

Three blows from a large hammer smashed the lock on Fuller's door. Elizabeth herself was first to enter, but remained only long enough to see that her presence was superfluous. From the smell and the noise of the flies she knew that whoever lay beneath the bed – and from the small, gnarled hand extending from under the valance she knew it was not Fuller – was well beyond any help she could bring.

Back on the landing, she called for a glass of wine. It arrived at almost the same time as Ned, who came scuttling in from the stables. Fuller and her husband had left almost simultaneously at around six o'clock that morning, he reported. Lord Banbury had taken his coach, saying he was going directly to the court at Theobalds but hoped to be back that night. The justice had taken his lordship's best horse, hung with a large saddle-bag. He had told no one where he was going. From the two men's cryptic conversation the stable lads had gathered that they were definitely not headed in the same direction. They had also told Ned that the previous afternoon Spid had arrived with a cart and put something into Lord Banbury's coach, after which no one was permitted to enter it.

For a moment Elizabeth despaired. 'Oh, my poor, simple Banbury!' she moaned, covering her face with her hands. 'What has that vile man done to you?' A tear slipped between her fingers.

'My lady?' asked Ned in embarrassment. 'Is all well?'

The question brought her down to earth. She thought of poor Sarah, of the burns on Tom and John, of Tilly's terrified face, and of the warning of what would happen if men of Fuller's ilk had their way. 'Yes, Ned,' she said, wiping her eyes. 'All is well. See that a horse is saddled for me. Now!'

'A horse, my lady?' Ned was amazed. No one had ever seen Lady Banbury in the saddle when she was in London.

'Would I ride a pig? I said a horse, numskull, and I meant a horse! I will be at the stables directly and expect all to be prepared.'

As she was being helped into the saddle Elizabeth remembered that she did not know where Tom and John could be found. They had moved the previous day to be nearer the Strand, but she would not know where until Tilly brought back the letter she had received from House Martin. She glanced up at the clock on the stable tower. Half past seven. To save time, she would ride to Charing Cross and meet the boy herself.

House Martin was late.

With each minute that passed, Elizabeth grew more and more anxious. She found it impossible just to sit and wait. In the hope of intercepting the messenger if he was coming from that direction, she rode back up the Strand. There was no sign of him.

She returned to the cross and tried the direction of the Hay Market. Still no luck. Then she caught sight of him, whistling perkily and dawdling along the side of the road in the early morning sunshine with a stick in his hand. Urging her horse forward, she galloped furiously up to him.

'Here, boy! Mount my horse behind me!' she shouted.

Mouth agape, he stared up at her, unsure whether to comply with her command or flee.

'I must find Master Verney!' she screamed, extending her hand. 'Get up!'

Somehow, half climbing, half pulled, he scrambled onto the creature's back and gingerly placed his arms round Elizabeth's waist.

'Now, direct me to your master!'

'Near Scotland Yard, my lady. Ahead.'

The horse reared up and sped off down the road towards Westminster. Clinging on for dear life, House Martin passed the short but exhilarating journey shouting occasional directions into the baroness's ear and reflecting on the extraordinary things he found himself doing for his incorrigible young master.

★

'The dog is fleeing!' cried John as soon as Elizabeth had finished relaying her news. 'Yet someone will have seen him go. Come, Tom, the hunt is on!' He took up his sword and prepared to leave the small ground-floor room off Scotland Yard which he and Tom had rented the previous evening.

She looked at him in disbelief. 'The hunt? And what of my husband?'

'I believe we are too late, my lady. The palace at Theobalds is some twenty miles hence—'

'Fifteen,' interrupted Tom. 'You forget, I was once welcome there.'

'Even so,' John said with a nod. 'Yet if his lordship departed at about six o'clock this morning, as your people say, then he will arrive at the palace before a rider can reach him. Lady Elizabeth, take strength in God's great mercy, for I fear your husband's cause is lost. We may still pray that the true nature of the box – if that is what the wretched Spid laid in the coach – is detected by the palace guards, or that it fails to explode. Like Man, such mechanical toys never work better than in the mind of their creator.'

'But even if the box fails or is discovered, the man bearing it ...' Elizabeth's lip was trembling so violently that she was unable to finish her sentence. Her eyes filled with tears. Turning to Tom, she laid her head against his shoulder and said, trying hard to control herself, 'You know I do not love my husband, Tom. But I have lived with him for many years now, and though I know him to be a fool and a braggart and many other things beside, I would not see him harmed through another's villainy. He has been kind to me. If they catch him with that box at the palace, well, what they will do to him is more terrible than I can imagine!'

Tom put his arm round her and looked steadily at John. Through the open door floated the chimes of a quarter to nine. Two hours to Theobalds, he thought, by which time it will be near eleven. If Banbury reaches the palace between ten and half past ten, then John may well be correct – the box will be with the king before we can prevent it. But if Banbury is delayed on the road and put to the back of the audience queue as he was at Hampton Court, then there is just a chance ...'

'John,' he said, 'you go to the coast if you wish. I know Fuller is the man you want. But come what may, I am riding to Theobalds.'

He went to the door. 'Bird!' he shouted. 'Fly to the stables and bring me Princess.' Coming back into the room, he took John by the hand. 'Well, Great John, what is it to be, the peer or the puritan?'

'I fear neither will grace the steps of the ladder to heaven, Tom. Yet neither will I. Is it better for my soul that I extinguish a sinner or save a man who has been kind to a lady?' He drew a deep breath and cried, 'By the blade of St Peter, I am with you, Tom Verney! The puritan can wait. Lead on!'

Moving quickly, Elizabeth put herself between them and the door. 'God be with you and keep you safe. And with all my heart, I thank you.' She kissed them both on the cheek and stood aside to let them pass.

When John reached the door, he hesitated. 'My lady?'

'Yes, John?'

'May I have use of your horse?'

Despite the gravity of the situation, she could not but laugh. 'For certain John, you may. Had I ten thousand horses, you might have them all if you could but save poor Banbury from the rack!'

ii

Tom had no difficulty in remembering the road for Theobalds. To begin with, as they cantered round the north-western outskirts of the city to avoid the clogged streets within the walls, he led the way. But once they were out into the open countryside, John brought his mare alongside Princess, and side by side the two men rode along the straight highway, smiling at each other for encouragement and exchanging the occasional snatches of shouted conversation.

At the village of Stoke Newington, just before the road picked up the high ground on the left of the Lea Valley, they stopped to water their horses. Although Princess was sweating heavily, she seemed in good shape. John was more concerned about the elegant-looking creature he had borrowed from Lady Banbury. Unused to such a heavy rider, she was already very tired and not certain to reach Theobalds if they maintained their rapid pace. In an attempt to save her, for the next half an hour they travelled at no more than a brisk trot, reaching Edmonton by about ten o'clock.

About a mile further on, John signalled for Tom to slow down. 'She will not make the journey,' he called, pointing to his horse's foaming mouth. 'You go on. I will follow as best I may.'

'Never!' Tom cried. 'Ride her till she drops, then come up behind me. Princess will not fail us!'

And so, sometimes trotting and sometimes breaking into a faltering canter, John spurred on his flagging mount for a few more miles. By the time they reached Enfield she could scarcely walk. Her sides were bloody, her flanks heaving. In the end, at the edge of a small wood, her legs gave way completely and she sprawled forward into the highway, twisting her neck beneath her. It was quite clear that she would never recover.

John borrowed an axe from a woodcutter working nearby and with a single swift blow put the sorry creature out of her misery. Then, telling the workman that the carcass was his to do with as he wanted, he clambered up behind Tom and they continued their journey as fast as Princess could manage.

Originally a modest dwelling known as Tongs, at the hands first of the Cecils and then of King James, Theobalds had been expanded with a series of brick and stone courtyards into one of the finest houses in the land. It stood at the end of a mile-long avenue of cedar trees within a huge wooded park. To keep out poachers, a high, spike-topped brick wall, regularly patrolled by armed gamekeepers, had been built around the estate. The entrance from the main road was through a pair of massive wrought-iron gates. It was guarded by soldiers and opened only to admit known visitors or those whose credentials had been carefully scrutinised.

About four hundred yards from the palace grounds, Tom turned into the trees beside the road and dismounted. Tying Princess to a tree, the two men crept through the bushes to a position from which they could observe the traffic passing in and out of the park. A few minutes later a single horseman rode up. Recognising him at once, the guards flung back the gates before he had reached them and stood back to let him through. No sooner had they closed them again than a carriage rumbled up.

Tom stared in disbelief. The horses, the livery, the coat of arms on the door – it was Banbury's coach! And there inside, lolling against the cushions in exactly the same manner as he had done when they had travelled to Hampton Court together, was his lordship himself.

How in the name of thunder did we miss him on the road? Tom wondered. At some point we must have ridden right past him without knowing it.

Eager to make the most of their good fortune, he started to move forward, thinking John would do the same.

A huge hand pulled him back. 'Fool!' John hissed. 'Would you have yourself shot? You think those guards will wait to hear your story when you come running out of the bushes at them? You would be as dead as Spid before you were fifty yards from the gate.'

Subdued, but relieved to know that at least they had not arrived too late, Tom sat and thought how they might get past the guards.

The next arrival at Theobalds Park was another lone rider. He was followed by a large and important-looking coach preceded by a pair of outriders. Just before the procession came within sight of the entrance, a third horse trotted out of the wood and, unseen by those in front, fell in at the rear.

The Bishop of London was a frequent caller at the palace, and the captain of the guard ordered the gates to be opened as soon as he saw his grace's vehicle approaching. He then stood back smartly to watch the little cavalcade pass. But as he looked, he realised that something was wrong.

He knew the outriders. He knew the coach. But who was that behind? Wait! It was not even a single fellow, but two on the same horse.

'Halt!' he yelled. 'Close the gates!'

The mysterious horse immediately pulled out from

behind the coach and made for the opening ahead. She was a fine creature, and despite her double load was already moving quite fast.

'Shoot!' screamed the officer.

Three of his men reached for the charged crossbows which were kept in constant readiness on a rack beside the gate. The intruders were level with them now, still gathering speed. Soon they would be through the opening and an impossible target among the broad cedars beside the drive.

The first two bows discharged simultaneously. Their operators had been too hasty, and the bolts whizzed harmlessly into the wood. The third man was more careful. Resting his machine against the gate, he took steady aim and fired.

The bolt hit the horse in the back of its neck and passed right through, emerging at the throat. The creature gave a horrible scream and fell to the ground. Blood spurted high into the air.

Jumping clear as the beast went down, the two riders, a young man with long brown hair and a larger, older one wearing a leather jerkin, fled into the trees. Two of the guards gave chase, but returned empty-handed a short time later to await further orders.

Moving as fast as the terrain would allow, Tom and John made straight for the palace. When it came into view, they turned right and followed the edge of the trees until they were opposite the elegant southern façade, noted for its range of tall leaded windows which extended almost the entire height of the ground floor. It was a warm day, and some of the lower panels had been opened to admit the breeze.

About one hundred yards from the house they found

a small hollow overgrown with alders where they lay down to rest and plan their next move. Having been shown over the building in March, when he had called with Canon Chillingworth, Tom knew that the chamber James used for audiences lay almost directly in front of them. But for the moment the heart-breaking loss of Princess was all he could think about. The horse had been his parents' parting gift, the last thread linking him to the world he had lost. What was more, apart from his mother and sister and House Martin, she had been the one living creature which had never failed him and in which he had had absolute faith.

And now she was dead.

He cursed the guards, he cursed the king, he cursed Lord Banbury. But most of all he cursed Justice Fuller and his damned boxes.

'I am more than ever resolved to see this business through, John,' he declared when his immediate sorrow and anger had subsided a little, 'even if it costs me my life.'

His friend, who for the last five minutes had been watching the guard walking back and forth before the palace, replied ominously, 'It may not cost you your life, Tom. But I fear it will cost the life of that poor soldier yonder. Time is not our friend. If we dally longer, by Christ, either your oily pumpkin will blow the king's head off or we will have the dogs on us! I will dispatch the guard – I see no other way.'

Horrified at what John was suggesting, for a minute Tom did not reply. He gazed at the sun reflecting off the hundreds of tiny triangles of glass and tried to imagine the scene behind them – the scented atmosphere, the opulent trappings of majesty, the eccentric, ailing king, the courtiers' whispered mocking of Lord Banbury as he struggled into the chamber with his box, the baronet's inane comments, his handing the box to the king ...

'If you must kill him, John, then you must.'

'Pray God it will not be necessary. But we must have a clear path to the windows, and he is stopping it.'

'Then hurry.'

John grunted. When the guard was at the furthest point of his beat, Tom watched his friend break cover and saunter towards a corner of the building that was not overlooked. Seeing a stranger emerge from the woods, the guard turned and walked slowly but purposefully towards him. John feigned ignorance of the soldier's presence. Kneeling before a flower bed, he took out his knife and started to trim a small honeysuckle.

Tom was glad that he did not see clearly what happened next. The guard was obviously annoyed by the supposed gardener's off-hand manner and prodded him with the butt of his halberd. Keeping his back to the man, John stood up. He turned abruptly. There was a scuffle and the two fell to the ground. Seconds later, it was all over.

Having checked that there was no one else about, Tom ran over to the house and crouched beneath the wall a short distance from his friend. Out of the corner of his eye he could see the body of the guard lying stretched out on the earth. On the front of his shirt, just below the heart, was a small scarlet stain.

Immediately, all Tom's old doubts about John came flooding back. If he had just killed so skilfully and with so little compunction, then might he not also have done so when he was on the run? Perhaps he really had intended to murder Tom in Stokenchurch woods? Indeed, had Tom any proof that this man – priest, charlatan, criminal, or some unholy combination of all three – had ever told the truth?

He shuddered. Then, realising that this was neither the time nor the place for such thoughts, he forced himself to concentrate on the matter in hand.

The first window of the audience chamber was about ten feet away, set into the wall he was leaning against. All its casements were closed. Keeping close to the brickwork, Tom crept along to the stone frame and, where a wide mullion made a natural spy-hole, peered in through the glass.

He found himself looking down the length of a rectangular, panelled room of a goodly size, sparsely furnished but crowned with an impressive ceiling of intricate plasterwork. James and several ministers and other officials were sitting with their backs to the window. A large crowd of courtiers lined the walls. At the far end of the room, flanked by four guards, was a broad doorway. As Tom watched, the door opened and a man and a woman entered, bowing low in the direction of the king.

Tom scuttled back and whispered to John what he had seen.

The best plan, they agreed, was for Tom to creep along the wall below the height of the window-ledge until he reached one of the open casement windows, and when the present suitors had left, jump quickly into the room. He would then have a few seconds before he was arrested to convince His Majesty of the danger he was in. Tom was sure that if he was given time to say even a few sentences, Banbury would be subjected to a precautionary search and the truth discovered.

Before moving forward, Tom checked the room once more and saw that the couple had already gone. Without further ado he squatted down, removed his spectacles and began scampering along the wall like a rabbit.

After a few yards he paused and cautiously looked over the sill.

A man was standing directly in front of him with his back to the window, blocking his view. Tom slowly moved his head to the right. Although he had no more than a misty impression of the scene, he could just make out that a new suitor had arrived and was standing in the centre of the room holding something in his hands.

Something in his hands?

Tom fumbled frantically for his spectacles and pulled them on. Yes! O God, it was Banbury! With a stupid grin on his face, the baronet was waddling towards the king, holding the box before him like a priest with a communion chalice. He was barely four feet in front of His Majesty.

Glancing to his right, Tom saw that the nearest open window was perhaps twenty feet away. Too far. He looked back into the room. Banbury was standing directly before the king. The box was between them.

Tom took three steps backwards, turned and launched himself like a cannonball at the window. There was a loud crash, followed by the sound of falling glass. Someone screamed.

Then all hell broke loose.

iii

Lord Banbury had enjoyed his journey to Theobalds.

Normally a late riser, he found the clear morning air surprisingly invigorating. Later, with his coach bowling swiftly along the road which ran smooth and straight from the capital to the palace, he thought how much he was looking forward to being rid of Fuller. With a chuckle he recalled that his wife had been particularly pleasant the previous night, too. Near Enfield he pulled off the highway for a hearty breakfast and continued in even better spirits than before, reaching his destination in good time.

The guards at the entrance to the park admitted him with a minimum of fuss, and when he stepped from his coach and felt the warm late-morning sun beating down on the back of his neck, he was sure it was a sign that this was going to be one of the more memorable days of his life.

His sense of well-being increased as he was ushered forward towards the audience chamber with uncustomary celerity. When he explained the nature of his gift to the ushers, it was nodded through with no more than a cursory glance. Although always anxious during his meetings with the king, particularly as they normally happened only when he had a favour to ask, he felt more relaxed this time. For once he was going to be the giver of largess and not the recipient. Furthermore, like a child on his birthday, he could not wait to see what was in the box. It was heavy, very heavy for its size; yet it did not rattle, no matter how hard he shook it. Was it glassware? he thought. Gold even? What an odd fellow that pious justice was! So cautious most of the time then, for no obvious reason, as generous as an emperor. Ah well! he sighed, resting the box on a chair in the anteroom, he would never understand men of God any more than he understood women.

His name was called. Picking up the box, he walked through to the audience chamber and fell heavily to his knees, almost dropping his gift. A titter ran round the room.

'Lord Banbury, is it not?' Although more frail than he remembered it, the king's voice still had the unmistakable ring of authority.

'Y – yes, Your Majesty.'

'We are delighted, of course. We see ye have brought a wee boxed chamber pot with ye, my lord.' Another ripple of suppressed laughter. One of the younger clerks was biting his tongue and trying not to look at the person next to him.

'I beg your pardon, Your Majesty, but it is a gift. For you.'

'For us? Oh, how kind you are, my lord! Bring it here at once for us to inspect. We are impatient.'

Banbury struggled to his feet. Explaining that the gift was not exactly from himself, but brought by him on behalf of another, he approached the king, trying to lift the lid with his thumbs. It would not move. Then he remembered.

He paused and muttered, 'I crave your humblest pardon, Your Highness, but it is keyed — I mean locked. If one of your intendants would be so kindly...'

A man stepped forward and held the box while Banbury rummaged around for the key. By this time almost everyone in the room was struggling not to laugh out loud.

'Here we are!' said Banbury, finding the key and turning it in the lock. 'Shall I open it for you, sir?'

'No, Banbury. That is our pleasure. We would be first to see what delights are ours. Come hither!'

iv

Tom landed on the floor about eight feet behind the king and sprawled forward onto his face amid a storm of broken glass. As he fell, he heard the sharp crack of his left arm breaking beneath him. Blood was already streaming from his head and hands.

He raised himself painfully onto his knees and cried,

'The box! A trap, Your Majesty! Do not touch the box!' Then he fell forward again onto the carpet of jagged splinters.

Most of the crowded audience chamber were too shocked to move or speak. Banbury stood rooted to the spot, holding onto his gift like a magus in a nativity scene. The king turned pale and trembled violently. He might well have fallen had Lord Conway not stepped up briskly and taken his arm.

A woman screamed. Then, gathering power like an avalanche, an inundation of noise and activity burst through the room.

Horrified officials quickly formed a hostile circle around Tom. Yelling orders to their clerks, ministers shuffled their papers together as if expecting a whirlwind. A disorientated mob of squires, chaplains, stewards, pages, secretaries, gentlemen of the bedchamber and other hangers-on milled about nervously, calling loudly to each other. Courtiers pressed forward eagerly to see what had happened, making it difficult for the soldiers to reach the other end of the room. The king, when he realised what had happened, exclaimed in a high-pitched squeal, 'Oh me! The mad bumpkin is returned!', before being escorted to a chair, where he sat and stared in fascination at the bloody intruder.

Only Banbury did not move. Still as a rock in a seething ocean, he stood mouth open, staring before him.

By the time the guards reached Tom, he had staggered to his feet. He was a dreadful sight. One arm hung limply by his side. His clothes were torn and bloodstained, and his body so cut that there was scarcely a patch of pale skin to be seen anywhere about him. All the while, spitting the blood from his lips, he continued to warn, 'The box is a trap! Beware the box!'

Pushing through the ring of servants, the first soldier rushed straight up to him, his boots crunching on the broken glass, and knocked him to the floor. The second grabbed him by his broken arm. He screamed with pain. Between them the guards hauled him to his feet and shoved him, whimpering in agony and slippery with blood, towards the king. Those who could see what was happening fell silent.

'Box!' Tom said feebly. 'Gift – Lord Banbury!'

All eyes turned to the petrified baronet.

'Well?' said the king, recovering some of his former vigour now that he believed himself in no danger. 'What do you say, Lord Banbury?'

To begin with Banbury's lips moved without making a sound. Then he said, 'God save me! I have seen a ghost!'

'Christ's eyes!' cried James. 'Another fool! Sergeant?'

'Yes, Your Highness?'

'Take that box from him and see what gift he brings us.'

Stepping smartly forward, the sergeant wrenched the box from Banbury's grasp and laid his hand on the lid.

'No! No!' screamed Tom, trying in vain to free himself.

The soldier took no notice. With a flick of the wrist he threw back the lid and looked inside.

For about a second nothing happened. Then there was a click, followed by the sound of flint striking on metal. Suddenly, with a tremendous roar, the box disintegrated and a sheet of flame shot up towards the ceiling.

The sergeant, whose face had been directly in the way of the blast, died instantaneously. Several others who had been standing nearby were wounded by flying fragments of wood and metal. A small fire started on the floor below where the box had detonated, but was soon extinguished.

To everyone's relief and joy, the king, who had been screened by the body of the unfortunate soldier, received not a scratch. More surprising was the lack of injury to Lord Banbury, who got away with no more than a cut on the cheek and singed hair. But there his luck ended.

What the wretched baronet escaped from the explosion, he received soon enough from the soldiers. Hardly had the noise died away before they were on him like wolves, pushing him to the floor where they kicked and beat him unmercifully. While he still had enough breath in his body, he managed to exclaim between his cries and groans, 'Mercy, I beg you! I am an innocent man! Fuller's box! Gone to Dover to kill the prince! Innocent! Mercy!'

No one in the room was listening.

Eventually Lord Cranfield managed to call the soldiers off. Bruised and bleeding and unable to walk, but still feebly protesting his innocence, Banbury was dragged from the room between lines of hissing and spitting courtiers. Once outside the door he was bound and taken away for interrogation.

Unfortunately for the miserable Banbury, the man who could have ended his torment at once had fainted shortly after the explosion. As the peer was being stripped and tied to a bench in the cellar, the unconscious body of Tom Verney was being gently laid on a bed in a room near the audience chamber. The king put his head round the door and wept. The royal surgeon appeared shortly afterwards and worked on the patient's wounds. When he left more than an hour later, he shook his head. He had done his best, he said, but he doubted whether that would be enough. The young man had lost too much blood. He would probably be dead before the day was over.

V

Amid all the excitement and noise, no one in the audience chamber had thought to look into the park to see whether Tom had been accompanied. Consequently, through the smashed window John had heard almost everything that had happened. In fact, not distracted by the spectacle, he had heard what others had not. He alone had listened to Banbury's pitiable protestations and noticed the word 'Dover'. It had galvanised him into instant action. Like a hound picking up the scent, he tensed, raised his head, and pausing only to pick up the halberd from the dead guard, bounded off towards the woods with huge, loping strides.

Once under cover he hesitated for a second in order to get his bearings, then strode off towards the park entrance. When he reached the line of cedars a few hundred yards south of the gate, he stopped again and listened. A coach was approaching from the direction of the palace, its wheels rattling on the cobbled drive. He slipped behind a tree and waited.

Widow Wormeley was distressed. Nestling her sixteen-stone bulk into the corner of her coach as it rolled slowly through Theobalds park, she told herself that no lady in all the kingdom could have been more unfortunate than her. For months she had bribed and cajoled and pleaded to be given an audience with the king at which she could raise the matter of her late husband's will. And then, when at last she had managed to get an appointment and was on the verge of entering the royal presence, all her plans had been – almost literally – blown up in her face by some ridiculous assassination plot. It really was too bad!

Without warning, the coach stopped. From the roof

came a strange thumping noise. 'Azariah!' she called out to the coachman. 'Have you fallen asleep?'

There was no reply, just a dragging sound followed by a dull thud. 'Azariah, you fool! What, pray, is going on?'

She lowered the window. As she did so the gleaming steel head of a massive halberd came through the opening, pointing directly at her ample bosom. 'We are going on,' said a voice she did not recognise. 'I am your new coachman, Beelzebub. I have eaten Azariah and I will eat you too should you utter one word, nay one syllable of warning. I will begin with the tender meat of your thighs!'

The halberd was withdrawn and the window closed from the outside. With the new driver in place, the coach rattled on towards the gate.

Two miles beyond Theobalds John pulled off the road into a small wood and drew the coach to a halt. Jumping down, he opened the door and told the widow to get out.

He looked at her carefully as she eased her vast frame through the coach door. 'Take off your gown!' he commanded.

A look of complete terror came into her face. 'No!' she whimpered, her chins wobbling like the teats on a pregnant sow, 'I pray you, Mr Beelzebub, do not eat me! I am but a poor widow!'

'Poor?'

'I am but a widow!'

'You are too fat. I will not eat you. But I order you to take off your gown!'

'Ohhh!' she wailed, fumbling with her laces. 'Not that either, I beg you!'

'Widow Gross-belly, no harm will come to you if you

do as you are bid without delay. But, by God's sacred beard, if you do not ...' He had no need to finish the sentence. A massive gown of turquoise silk was already floating down like a sail towards the mossy ground.

Five minutes later Widow Wormeley lay bound and gagged on the floor of her coach and an extraordinary figure trotted out of the wood on one of her horses. Dressed like a woman in a voluminous gown that billowed out behind in the wind, the rider sat astride the horse like a man. A female bonnet and scarf covered most of the head and face, but wisps of a very male beard showed at the edges. Some who saw the creature galloping by believed it to be a witch. Others thought it was just a young fellow playing the fool. But all agreed that whatever it was, witch or fool, it was riding as if its very life depended on it.

vi

In the official report of what became known as the Verney Case, presented to King James some months later, the Widow Wormeley incident was only the first of several bizarre and violent happenings attributed to John's relentless pursuit of his enemy that day. An ostler at the Black Swan in Enfield reported having been threatened by a 'monster of a lady in a green dress' who walked into the stable yard and demanded the best horse he had, or she would break his neck. Rather than test her resolve, he had handed over the creature right away. That night it was found beside the road near Clerkenwell, so broken that it had to be put down.

Other horses were stolen, usually with threats of violence, at different points along the road to Dover. Food was taken from the Queen's Arms in Bexley, where the landlord, who was unfortunate enough to challenge the thief with a cudgel, found his own weapon turned on himself and was knocked unconscious. A priest was robbed at knife point in Clerkenwell and the money used to buy a mare which burst a blood vessel at the southern end of London Bridge. While the requisitioned horses were being prepared, drink disappeared from inns at Chatham and Canterbury.

Although Widow Wormeley's gown was never found, it seemed most likely that John abandoned his disguise somewhere between Enfield and Clerkenwell. All those who saw him from that point onwards spoke of a large bearded man with unruly hair and a doublet of leather. The barmaid of the City Arms in Canterbury said she thought she had glimpsed some sort of scar on his forehead.

The last section of the report, assembled from a number of eyewitness accounts, was by far the fullest.

A tall, lean man with a twitching lip – assumed to be Fuller, but never conclusively proved to be so – arrived in Dover about midday. He was dressed entirely in black and carried a heavy canvas saddle-bag. Going straight to the quay, he said that he had to cross to France at once and was prepared to pay any sum for the privilege of doing so. On being told that a French vessel would be leaving for Roscoff that evening on the eight o'clock tide, he became angry and said he would ride to Deal or Folkestone to find a boat leaving sooner. When this produced only disinterested shrugs, he calmed down and tried to pay the captain to bring forward the time of his departure. Finally, when it had been explained to him that not all the gold in the world could hasten the changes in the tides, he took himself off to a tavern, where he hired a private room and locked himself away for the remainder of the day.

Emerging at six o'clock, he appeared very edgy. He spent the next hour walking about the ship telling the crew in broken French to speed up their preparations. In the end his unwarranted intrusions became such a nuisance that the captain ordered him ashore until the vessel was ready to sail. Clutching his saddle-bag, the passenger walked down the gang-plank and onto the quay, where he paced up and down like a caged tiger, sometimes calling to the sailors on deck to ask if they were ready, and sometimes staring up the valley in the direction of the main road from London.

At half past seven he unexpectedly left the quay. Outside the tavern where he had spent the afternoon he came across a boy, Joe Staley, to whom he offered a gold piece if he would go to the edge of the town and watch the main road for him. If any horseman appeared in the distance, he said, particularly one or more riding hard, the lad was to let him know immediately. Delighted with the offer, Joe plucked a juicy piece of grass, positioned himself on a gatepost with a clear view of all approaching traffic, and settled down to earn his reward.

At about a quarter to eight the captain called to the quay that he was almost ready for his passengers to come aboard. A young couple and a wool merchant emerged from the tavern and tried to engage the stranger in conversation. He made no effort whatsoever to respond to their overtures. Disgruntled, in a voice clearly intended to be overheard, the woman remarked to her partner that she had never seen a man with such a pronounced twitch, but she did not feel sorry for him because he was so ill-mannered.

The stranger swung round.

As he opened his mouth to speak, Joe came running onto the quay. 'Sir! Sir!' he called. 'I seen a horse coming at the gallop. Can I 'ave my coin?'

'Curse you for a thieving whelp!' growled the man between clenched teeth. 'What horse?'

Before the boy could reply, the sound of rapid hoofbeats was heard approaching through the town. All eyes turned to where the main street branched towards the sea.

The horse was a beast from hell, steaming like a cauldron, bloody-flanked, staring-eyed and covered in dust, sweat and foam. Its dirty and dishevelled rider, hardly less of an apparition, jumped down from the saddle and walked slowly towards the man in black. Afterwards witnesses remarked on the size of the new arrival. One spoke of a Goliath, others of a giant, and they were all struck by the fact that he had an unusually deep voice that rumbled, as the merchant put it, 'like breakers on the beach'.

'At last!' said the rider, stretching out his arms towards the twitching passenger. 'Justice for the justice!'

The man he addressed had turned as white as a gull's wing. 'You are not dead?' he muttered. His mouth was working furiously.

'Yes, dead! And returned from my grave for revenge!'

The eyes of the thinner man flickered towards the ship, then along the shore. Suddenly, throwing his canvas bag into the harbour, he darted past his enemy and started to run with short, stabbing steps in the direction of the grey-white cliffs towering out of the sea to the north. With a roar that sent birds screaming into the air all over the harbour, the giant turned and set off in pursuit.

Along the quay they went, then turned right and crashed along the shingle track that followed the high-water mark. While they were on the level the stronger man gained on his enemy. But when the stones gave way to chalk and the path began to rise, gradually at first but more and more steeply as it ascended the side of the cliff, the lighter figure drew away again.

News of what was happening had reached the town, and a small crowd gathered on the foreshore to watch the chase. At one point a stout constable set off in pursuit, calling on the two men to come back and settle their differences amicably before him. But by the time he had reached the climb the combatants were so far ahead that he gave up and returned to the quay to watch with the others.

On reaching the top of the first escarpment, the passenger had put a gap of almost fifty yards between himself and his pursuer. He paused momentarily on the crest to look back, then set off again with his neat steps along the undulating cliff path, scampering down into a fold, before slowing as he struggled up the other side. To his left stretched fields and scrub. A few yards to his right the white precipice fell abruptly into the sea.

All agreed that the decisive moment of the chase came when the leading figure was almost halfway up the second scarp. He fell forward without warning, clutching at his leg. A faint scream floated down to the town. Seconds later he got up and continued to climb, dragging his left leg behind him like a shackle.

The two men were now almost half a mile from the town, and growing smaller all the while in the eyes of the onlookers. To townsfolk emerging from their houses and seeing them for the first time, they were hardly human beings at all, but more like wooden figures in a distant puppet show, whose actions bore no relation at all to the real world.

The gap between the two closed. Finally, just below

the summit, the pursuer caught up with his prey and brought him to the ground. The struggle was brief and, according to those watching, surprisingly one-sided. It looked, they said, as if the man in black had been totally exhausted by the chase or had lost the will to fight.

When his vanquished enemy lay still, the giant seized him by the waist and raised him above his head. Holding him aloft like a trophy, he walked towards the edge of the cliff. On the brink, he paused.

At first the noise might have been mistaken for the cry of a gull. But when it rose to a peal of victory, then dipped into a wail before soaring trumpet-like to a final long note of ecstatic triumph, the watchers knew it was not made by any bird. Nor had they heard the like from any living creature, man or beast, either before or since.

As the sound died away, the giant bent his arms and tossed his victim up and out over the cliff. For a second the body hung at the top of its arc like a huge winged insect against the pink blue of the evening sky. Then it fell, silently turning in graceful circles and gathering speed until it hit the green waters below and disappeared from sight.

Several small boats immediately pulled from the shore to look for the body. But the light had almost gone by the time they reached the spot where it had fallen, and the tide was flowing fast. Neither the corpse nor any article of the murdered man's clothing were ever recovered.

Over the next few days parties of volunteers combed the cliffs and a close watch was kept for the bearded stranger at all the ports of south-east England. When there were no sightings, it was assumed that he had fallen over the cliffs in the dark, and the search was called off. Like the body of the man he had killed, the thunder-voiced giant had vanished without trace.

TWENTY

ST NICHOLAS, SOUTHFLEET

i

'Forasmuch as all mortal men be subject to many sudden perils, diseases and sicknesses, and are ever uncertain what time they shall depart out of this life ...'

He tried to focus on the words, but his mind was floating, drifting through clouds, and he could not concentrate. He felt weak and utterly helpless.

The voice droned on.

'Hear us, almighty and most merciful God and saviour. Extend Thy accustomed goodness to this Thy servant, Thomas, which is grieved with sickness: Visit him, O Lord ... and restore ... his former health (if it be Thy will) or else give him grace ... that after this painful life has ended, he may dwell with Thee ...'

'Life has ended' – the phrase triggered something in Tom's mind. Did it mean death? Whose death? A name had been mentioned, but he could not remember whose it was.

Then it came again – 'Thy servant, Thomas'. Thomas?

Why, he was Thomas! What was going on? Surely he was not dying?

He tried to open his eyes. The lids were weighed down and would not move. He tried again. A bright yet hazy light appeared. Through the mist he could just make out a face. Pale, almost bleached white. It was vaguely familiar. Something to do with rejection. Yes, that was it! The face had rejected him, and now it was doing so again, telling him to die.

No, he would not! He would not submit to the man. He would – not – die.

Chillingworth finished reading the service for the Visitation of the Sick. Quietly closing his prayer book, he glanced once more at the stitched and bandaged face on the pillow, sighed, made the sign of the cross in the air above the bed and left the room.

For several days after this Tom drifted in and out of consciousness. Sometimes he looked and felt remarkably well, sitting up in bed, eating, drinking and chatting with visitors. During the first of these periods of lucidity he related his version of the events leading up to the assassination attempt. Probably because he was overtaxing his still-fragile constitution, these bursts of activity were invariably followed by relapses, when he would slip back into coma. It was towards the end of his first week as an invalid, after a morning playing cards and drinking French wine, that he experienced the sharpest of these deteriorations. He ran a high fever, for which he lost almost as much blood to his doctors' leeches as he had from his cuts, and was unable to take more than a few drops of water. Once again his life hung in the balance. But youth and strength were on his side. He was out of danger after three days and thereafter began a quick and even recovery.

On 26th June, a date he would always remember, he called for a looking-glass. There, for the first time, he saw that even if he were allowed to, he would never be able to forget what he had done. Immediately after his leap through the window, with blood running off his body like sweat, many of the cuts he had sustained looked worse than they were, and when excellently set and splinted by an Italian doctor attached to the court, his fractured arm healed as straight as it had ever been. But several wounds, particularly on his knees, hands and face, had left broad, permanent scars. The most noticeable ran from his forehead, over his right eye, which, the surgeon said, had been saved by the spectacles, down his cheek to the back of his jaw. Puckered and bright pink at first, with matching stitch marks dotted at either side, in time the new tissue turned a pale yellow – except when Tom grew angry, when the scarlet flush returned. With grim humour, in public he called the scar his weather vane, because, he said, by studying it others could see when his storms were coming. In private he sat for hours running his fingers down its length and wondering whether the fame and fortune now being heaped upon him could ever compensate for what he had lost. He smiled wryly to himself when he thought how Blind Jane's phrase, 'Tom vain Verney', had taken on a new meaning. He had little cause for vanity now.

For almost three weeks, before he went south for a spell at Hampton Court, the attentions of the king on his earthly saviour verged on the absurd. First, having been told Tom was likely to die, he insisted on having the young man's unconscious body propped up in bed on cushions and knighting him then and there. 'We would our beloved subject, who in one crowded hour of glory rescued His Majesty and the whole kingdom from a most foul puritan plot, be remembered as the late Sir Thomas Verney,' he explained. The gesture was followed, once Tom was out of danger, by gifts of jewellery, clothing, works of art and a substantial pension for life. When the patient was well enough to talk, James made a point of coming to see him every day. Sitting on the edge of his bed and holding his hand, in a fatherly manner and with far more sincerity than he had ever shown previously, he asked him about his family, his upbringing and his village. Yet Tom noticed that there was one matter of personal interest which he did not raise, and assuming this was because it had proved so controversial in the past, he avoided it himself, too.

Following the example set by their master, courtiers and councillors flocked to see their new hero. As if he were some exotic beast newly imported from Asia or Africa, queues of men and women – particularly women – formed outside his door each morning to pay their respects. Some brought presents; some asked Tom's advice on matters about which he knew nothing, such as the most effective code for sending secret messages to Poland, or what to feed a war-horse on over the winter; some just stood and gawped. Most who had known Tom during his previous visits to court made out that they had always thought highly of him or, if they were more honest, that they had underestimated him. Conspicuous among the former was Keeper Williams, whose single call began with a nauseating display of false unction, deteriorated into a monosyllabic impasse and ended with a mutual understanding that it were best if in future the two men avoided each other whenever possible. Treasurer Cranfield was more straightforward. 'I confess I cannot but admire what you did, Verney,' he said, 'although, in truth, I do not like you any more than before. I once put money on your head and saw it lost. In politics a man soon learns not to wager twice on the same nag, so I will not do so again on you, even if you would take my backing, which I doubt. Yet I would be a foolish man were I to fall out with one of your reputation. I respect you for what you are as, I hope, do you me. I manage the kingdom, you – once in a while – save it. We are both invaluable. Therefore, if I may assist you in some way that is not too great a strain on the already rattling treasury, I trust you will ask. Good day, Sir Thomas.' With what might have been a flicker of a smile, he turned smartly and left the room.

When the chequered form of Canon Chillingworth slipped into the room one wet afternoon towards the end of the month, Tom was at a loss what to say. The memory of the rejection in the chapel of York House still stung. The priest, he soon noticed, was equally unsure how to proceed.

'Well, Master – er – Sir Thomas,' he faltered, 'the Lord has smiled on you – at last.'

'Which was more than many did when I was down, eh, Canon?'

Chillingworth looked at him straight. 'The way of the world, I fear, sir. The way of the world. Men such as I are but fleas of the church which is in turn a flea on the body of the state. We live off the blood of others, and must, I fear, feed where the blood is richest. Not from society's skeletons. In your new and high estate, you will find you acquire many fleas, sir. Many fleas.'

'And no friends?'

'Oh no! You will have friends—' He hesitated, realising that he had walked straight into the trap.

Tom tried not to smile, for his face still hurt if he moved it more than he had to. 'A man once said to me,

Canon, that friendship was a whore. Was he lying?'

For the first and only time, he saw a little colour come into Chillingworth's cheeks. 'Maybe,' he muttered.

'Come,' said Tom, 'not so downcast. I must thank you, for you saved my life.'

'I believe you are mistaken, sir. I do not recall saving the life of any man, or any woman. A few souls, perhaps, but never a life. Never.'

'When I lay very sick you prayed over me.'

'And my prayers saved you? Ah, they must be more highly regarded by the Almighty than I had believed.'

'No, Canon. When in my sickness I saw your face, darkly, as in a fog, and heard you talk of my death, I determined that you would not cast me aside a second time. I do not think your prayers saved me. But your praying did. Perhaps they are the same?'

'Perhaps. The ways of the Almighty are wondrous strange.'

Both men sat in silence for a while. Eventually Chillingworth said, 'I must be leaving, Sir Thomas. I am, er, truly glad that your health is returning, and that your valour has earned you such favour. Truly glad. We may meet again?'

'Maybe. But you will forgive me if I do not trust you, Canon?'

'Ah! The Lord has granted you wisdom to learn that lesson?'

'He has, I regret.'

'Good. By placing you in my path, he has taught me something, too …'

'Yes?'

'That one should not despise whores. One in particular. Farewell.'

'Farewell, Canon. I think we shall meet again.'

ii

Elizabeth Banbury and House Martin arrived at Theobalds the day after Tom had first seen his damaged face, when he was most in need of cheering. The boy, washed, wearing new clothes and somehow appearing larger and more confident than he remembered him, called first. Ignoring his master's changed appearance, he said that at present Tom was the most famous man in all London, and as a consequence his servant was brilliantly illuminated with reflected glory. The king had made him a present of one hundred pounds, for saving his master's life in the Blackmore Street fire. Clement's Inn had taken a collection in his honour, amounting to a further fifty pounds. Principal Edwards had also sent Tom a formal apology for the manner in which the Inn had treated him in the past, and hoped that he would return to continue his studies when his health permitted. Tom did not think the letter merited a reply.

Turning to House Martin, he asked, 'So, Bird, now that you are a rich man, what will you do with yourself?'

'As before, sir. If you will have me.' Tom stared at him. 'Or maybe you's wanting someone grander, seeing as you are Sir Thomas. I do understand, sir.' He gave a weak smile.

'Someone grander? Who could be more grand than my Bird? No, I was silent because I could not believe what you said. You will stay?'

'Like as I said afore, sir. Always.'

A short time later Elizabeth appeared, and the boy went off to find accommodation for himself, saying that he did not plan to go back to London unless it was at his master's side.

In a gown the colour of the summer sky, against which her hair glowed like autumn beech, Elizabeth looked as handsome as Tom ever remembered having seen her. Watching her walk towards him, her body radiating health, vitality and attraction, he instinctively raised his hand to his cheek.

Noticing the movement, she bent down and kissed him, first on the lips, then on the scar. He winced.

'It hurts still?' she asked. 'I am sorry.'

He took her hand. 'No, Bess, it does not hurt. It is just that, well, it feels strange.'

'No hero is without his scars, Tom. Besides, you were too baby-faced before. I like your new adornment – it makes a man of you, Sir Tom!' She laughed and kissed him again.

'If you like it, then I should not complain. I have more than enough to be thankful for. But come, you have much to tell me, Bess. Do you have news of John? I confess I told them something of him when the body of the guard he had slain was discovered. And what of your husband? And you – what do they know of you? And us – are we discovered?'

'Shh! Quietly! You bring on your sickness again. There is no hurry.' So saying, she drew up a chair beside him and settled down to tell him all that she had gathered.

She began by reassuring him that as far as she could tell, apart from the usual idle gossip, no one thought their relationship had been anything other than a working partnership occasioned by a mutual mistrust of Fuller. As for John, she knew no more than Tom. The man had vanished. Although not everyone had agreed with the wisdom of the gesture, the king had granted him a pardon for all crimes he may or may not have committed, including killing the unfortunate palace guard.

'I often think of him,' said Tom wistfully, 'for I still do not know what sort of man he was.'

'I have not met a man like him,' she agreed, 'and for certain never will. The looks of a bear, the charm of an ambassador, the heart of – what of his heart, Tom?'

'The heart of Great John? Mmmm. As wide as a church door, Bess, but with holes in it through which Christian compassion may sometimes slip without his noticing.

'And your husband, Lord Banbury? They say at the palace he is recovering from his ordeal but slowly.'

Under interrogation in the cellar of Theobalds Palace, Banbury had saved himself much further pain by admitting to everything which he had been accused of. He had, he said, been plotting to assassinate the king for a long time. The idea was, of course, entirely Fuller's and he was just a weak and foolish man who had allowed himself to be taken in by misdirected puritan zeal. As far as he could recollect, the enterprise involved not only the Stokenchurch magistrate but a hermit who lived in a cave near Ivinghoe, an emissary from Zurich with only one arm, and weapons from Zealand which were to be used in the general uprising following the announcement of the king's death. The baronet willingly gave names, dates, places and addresses, and signed a broad-ranging confession of his crimes.

It took the authorities only a few days to realise that virtually the whole of Banbury's story was false, the creation of a fertile imagination inspired by fear of torture. Fortunately for the baronet, by this time Tom had been well enough to give them his version of events, which was subsequently endorsed by Lady Banbury. The baronet was detained a while longer, then sent home to be nursed back to health. He had, the king told him, been saved by his wife.

As Tom knew much of this already – as did most of the nation with an interest in scandal or politics – Elizabeth did not dwell on the details. She went on to say that after his release, depressed rather than physically injured, her husband had seemed to lack the will to recover. He had lain in bed with the sheets pulled up over his head all day and night, neither eating nor sleeping. His wife had begun to despair of ever getting him back to normal, until one day she had gone to his room and whispered to the shapeless hump of bedclothes that she was with child. The transformation in him had been as total as it had been sudden. He had forgotten his misery and bruises immediately, and had passed every waking minute since then strutting about the house and garden as if he had just been told he was to inherit the throne. The only thing he would not do, he confessed, was visit Tom. He promised to make amends one day soon, but for the moment he was simply too ashamed to face him.

When she had finished, Tom asked, 'But, Bess, was that not a cruel trick?' He was somewhat dismayed at what he saw as her dishonesty.

'Trick, Tom? What trick?'

'Telling him that you were with child.'

She leaned forward and smiled sheepishly. 'That was no trick. It was God's truth.'

He could hardly believe his ears. 'But you told me he did not ... It is wonderful! But, but who?'

'Some questions we do not ask, Tom. I wished for a child. Lord Banbury wished for a child. Now God has granted us our wish. I explained to my husband that one night, when he was full of wine, I came into his bed and he managed what hitherto he had not. He did not recall the incident, of course, because he was too drunk. But he has my word that it is true. And that is enough.'

'But Bess—'

'Yes?'

'I am so very fond of you. We have been through so much together, and I thought, I hoped that we might ...' He was not quite sure what he hoped.

'And I am as fond of you as I am likely to be of any man. But I have a husband and you have a wife.'

'Yes. You are right.' He raised his hand to his face again. 'Tell me of Lucy, I pray. Why will no one talk of her?'

'They want your father to be the bearer of that news,' she replied, giving him a look he did not understand.

Justice John Verney entered the room and closed the door quietly behind him. The two men stood and looked at each other. If the brief pause before they spoke was a trial of strength, the last act in a rite of passage, then it was over almost before it had begun. Despite his splints and his scars, Tom exuded strength and new confidence. His father was a changed man. Illness had aged him rapidly and severely. The original colour was gone from his thinning hair, which hung about his ears in drab, grey locks. Sunken and sallow, his skin had lost its lustre. Several more teeth were missing, so that when he spoke he was inclined to whistle inadvertently. He walked with a slight shuffle and stood with a stoop. Only his eyes, Tom thought, brown and warm like his own, reminded him of the vigorous man he had been so in awe of such a short time since.

The older man was the first to move. With a cry, he stumbled over to his son and embraced him, kissing him on the cheeks time and again before standing back and examining him. The eyes of both of them were filled with tears.

'Tom,' the justice said, 'Tom, I do not know which to say first: that I am sorry, or that I am so proud of you!'

'Say neither, Father. The past is gone. And as for the business of the box, I did only what any man would have done.' He knew it was not strictly true, but he felt it was the correct thing to say.

'New modesty to go with the knighthood, eh, Tom? You do not have to pretend with your old dad! Tell me all, from the beginning, every jot. I have heard the story, of course, but not the true one, I'm sure. Not the way you tell it.'

John Verney glowed with paternal pride as Tom went through his story for what must have been the fiftieth time. When he had finished he spent the same time again answering a multitude of questions. At last, when he had given his father every conceivable detail of the whole adventure, from the type of rope used to tie up the prisoners in Blackmore Street, to what the king was wearing when he had first spoken to Tom after the assassination attempt, the older man was finally satisfied.

'So, so, so,' he muttered, 'and to think that the hero of all that was my son! God be praised! Did I not say many years ago that Justice Fuller was a rogue, eh, Tom?'

'You said you did not like him, Father.'

'That is the same thing, surely?'

'Probably. But, Father, I can speak of it straight to you now – what news of Lucy? No one will tell me. They all say I must wait for you. There must be news. Is it good or bad?'

With deliberate care his father placed his hands on his knees, first the left, then the right, one finger at a time. Seeing they were in place, he looked up.

'Bad.'

Tom knew that was what he had been going to hear.

He felt all along that Lucy had not been found, or if she had been—

'Father, what has happened to her?'

'The king lent men to help. On seeing what you had done to save his life, he was filled with remorse and sent for your wife that he might meet her and be reconciled with her. When she was not to be found, he learned from Lady Banbury – with whom, I gather, you have talked much – that Lucy Verney had gone to stay in Rochester for the birth of her child – my grandchild – but she had disappeared on the way there. Since then royal officers have searched high and low without joy.'

'She is still missing then? It could be worse.'

'It may be even yet, Tom.'

John Verney explained that during the enquiries a story had come to light which was, in likelihood, the explanation for Lucy's disappearance. Several travellers remembered seeing a young woman, heavy with child, walking from the capital in the direction of Chatham and Rochester at about the time Lucy would have been travelling that way. No one knew anything about her, where she came from or where she was going. She would not talk to those who addressed her and she refused all offers of help. Two days later she and her newly born baby were found dead beneath a haystack outside the village of Southfleet in Kent. Mother and child were buried in unmarked pauper graves in the churchyard of St Nicholas, Southfleet.

'The saint whom the Romans believe guards little children,' Tom muttered. 'He must have been asleep that day.'

'What was that, son?'

'It was of no consequence, Father. I thank you for telling me what you have heard. But the unhappy wretch you spoke of cannot have been my Lucy.'

'Are you so sure?'

'She left me a letter when she departed — I was at Moseley Hall to warn John of Fuller's intentions towards him — in which she wrote, I am certain, that she was travelling to her aunt by horse.' He picked at a scab on the back of his hand. 'I will tell you, Father, what I have not told others, except Bess — Lady Banbury, that is.' John Verney looked at him strangely. 'Lucy and I did not find perfect harmony in our wedded life. We — well, you may imagine.'

'I am sorry. Yet it is not unusual.'

'She went to stay with her aunt because she hoped for help in bearing and raising the child, help and comfort which I failed to bring.' He swallowed hard. 'But she planned to ride, of that I am sure. It was too far for her to have travelled on foot, alone and carrying a baby.'

'You have the letter?'

'Alas, no! The fire took all I had.'

'Even if she had started out on a horse, might it not have fallen? Or been stolen?'

Tom felt suddenly angry. 'Do you want her dead, Father? Have not enough people died already?'

John Verney chose not to reply, and his son said shortly, 'I beg you forgive me, father. I should not have spoken as I did, but my heart is so charged that I fear it will break.'

The justice came to where his son sat and laid a hand on his shoulder. 'You have taken too many blows for any man to bear, Tom. You do not need to ask my pardon. I am your father.' He looked out of the window at a deer gracefully sauntering by under the trees. 'You know I met Lucy when I came to London.'

'I do.'

'I will say now what then I would not say even to

myself. I thought her a kind, sweet girl, and I was very cruel to her.'

Tom hung his head and wept.

iii

By the second week of July Tom was strong enough to take walks in the park. With House Martin at his side, each day he roamed further and further until one afternoon towards the end of the month he came to the place where Princess had fallen. The rain had washed the grass clean and only a slight scoring of the turf remained to identify the spot. After gazing at the ground for a few seconds, he turned to his companion and said, 'Bird! I need another horse! I must think of what will be, not what was, or else I will become like the old soldier in a tavern, full of ancient glories and valour, but running to lock himself in the privy at the first scent of danger.'

'You might 'ave a coach if you wished it, sir.'

'A coach? After Princess! No, I want the wind and the speed, Bird. I want to ride, not wobble along like a cake in a box.'

He bought Prince a week later, a fine, bright-eyed piebald stallion. At the same time he bought House Martin his own first mount, a small, intelligent creature like his owner. Frequently riding out together in the security of the park to familiarise themselves with their steeds, Tom's strength gradually built up to the point where, comfortable though life at the palace was, he felt there was no longer any purpose in his remaining there. The doctor agreed, and having bade farewell to the servants who had cared for him, and written to his father explaining what he was doing, on the 10th August Tom left Theobalds in the company of House Martin and took the road south.

Travelling in easy stages, they followed the highway to the capital, then turned east to catch a ferry across the river to Gravesend. From there it was but a short ride to the village of Southfleet.

They arrived in the late afternoon. Having taken a room in the local inn, Tom walked out alone down the London road. It had rained recently and the soft surface of the highway still bore the footprints of those who had walked that way since midday. He watched how his own feet pressed imprints of themselves into the ground, and tried unsuccessfully to imagine Lucy's feet doing the same along the same stretch of road. When he reached the first milestone, he turned and retraced his footsteps, keeping his eyes on the scene ahead. This, he told himself as he gazed at the towered church and the cluster of buildings around it, is what she saw. Almost the last thing she saw on earth. He wondered where the haystack was. There were several in the fields around and he decided it must have been the one about two hundred yards away to his left, near a spinney of elms. He did not investigate further.

Originally he had intended to visit the churchyard that evening and leave in the morning. However, as he approached the wooden lychgate, he turned aside, moved by an unidentifiable feeling that she did not want him there then. He returned to the inn, took a quiet supper and retired early to bed.

Sleep was impossible. The air was hot and damp, and the mattress too hard. After tossing about for almost an hour, he got out of bed and walked over to the open window. In the dark he could just make out the church. A short distance from the western door, beneath an old yew, lay the dark mounds of recently dug graves. He closed his eyes. Lucy! he called silently into the night. Lucy, where are you?

The yew sighed gently in the light breeze. There was no other reply.

This time whispering the words out loud, he begged, 'Lucy, forgive me! Come back, I pray you. Please come back to me.'

The only answer was the rustle of thin leaves in the humid night air.

He fell to his knees. 'Dear God,' he prayed, 'I beseech you hear your servant Thomas when he calls to you. Forgive the many wrongs he has done, for which he is truly contrite. But above all, guard, protect, guide and save his wife Lucy, wherever she may be, in this world or the next. This he asks in the name of Jesus Christ, our only Saviour. Amen.'

He rose to his feet and went back to bed. Five minutes later he was asleep.

After breakfast Tom and House Martin walked together to the churchyard. Two of the recent graves had been dug a little apart from the others. They were plain humps of soil, already sprouting shoots of new grass, unadorned by cross, stone or tablet. One was the length of an adult. The other was scarcely three feet long.

Kneeling in the damp grass, servant and master prayed quietly for almost fifteen minutes. Then Tom rose and entered the church. Inside he met the priest and explained that the woman and the child who had recently been buried might have been relations of his. The priest, a kindly looking man of about fifty, was sympathetic and promised to make a special mention of the deceased and their family in public prayers. Before he left, Tom handed over some money and asked for a single stone to be raised at the head of the two graves.

The priest agreed to see that this was done, but added,

'I may not put names thereon, Mr Verney, until we are certain who is buried.'

'The name of the mother is known to God,' Tom said. 'That is enough. On earth she shall be remembered for what she was. Would you be so good as to have the mason carve these words: "Here lies a kind, sweet girl and her child. May they rest in peace at last."'

'It shall be done as you wish, Mr Verney.'

'Thank you.' Tom turned to go. 'And vicar?'

'Yes, sir?'

'Tell me, was the child a boy or a daugh – girl?'

'I believe it was a girl.'

'Ah! A girl. Thank you once more for your assistance. I assure you I will not forget it.'

Tom walked slowly out of the churchyard and signalled House Martin to join him. Without saying a word, he climbed into the saddle and set off in the direction of London.

As he was passing a cottage on the edge of the village, the front door suddenly swung open and a young child ran out directly into his path. Pulling hard on the reins, he brought Prince to a halt and watched carefully as she crossed before him. When she had safely reached the other side of the road, he smiled at her. She waved and called out to him, but he did not catch what she said.

Touching Prince's sides with his heels, he resumed the long journey home.

iv

Before taking the Oxford road, House Martin and his master spent a few days in London bidding farewell to family and old friends. Tom held a dinner at the Angel for George, Will and his former neighbours from Blackmore

Street, and called round at Pickering House to see how Elizabeth was coping with the prospect of motherhood. As her looks testified, she was in excellent health. When they were alone she confided with a puzzling look that her only concern was that her son – she was sure it was a son – might have too much of his father in him. Tom assured her that was impossible, as the stronger partner always overcame the weaker. She smiled.

Just as he was getting up to leave, the door of the tapestry room opened a little way and a voice called out, 'Master Verney?'

The accent was unmistakable. 'Yes, my lord?'

'Master Verney – Oh! I have blundered again! Sir Thomas, I meant – Sir Thomas, I am still overcome with such shame that I dare not appear before you in daylight. I do not supposition that you care to return at night, so that we may con-verse in the same room without my being seen?'

'It would be difficult, my lord.'

'As I imagined. Then I will speak thus, hidden like a lapwing on the furrow. All I would say, Mas – Sir Thomas – Verney, is that over the matter of Fuller and the box I was a blind fool. There! I have said it. Will you forgive me, sir?'

Tom looked in the direction the voice was coming from. 'I will,' he said with a grin, 'for your sake, for that of your wife and unborn child.'

There was a pause. 'You have been told?'

Tom glanced at Elizabeth. 'All London knows, my lord. Come, join us to celebrate the news!' He stood up and walked briskly across the room.

'No! I dare not! No!'

Before Tom reached the door, he heard the sound of heavy steps retreating up the stairs.

★

Tom's last visit was to House Martin's family. He wished to meet them so that he could get their formal consent to take on their son as his servant, something he had never previously considered. As, with some embarrassment, the boy had explained to him before they arrived that his home was not quite Theobalds, Tom was expecting the sort of dilapidated and cramped dwelling lived in by the most menial country cottagers. Even before they reached the place, however, he realised that he was wrong. They wound through mean alleys near the river, each more dark and dirty than the last, until at last they reached a small court. The stench of rot and ordure was unbearable. On three sides the buildings had virtually collapsed. Tom walked towards the one that was still standing, but House Martin called him back and pointed to a hut constructed within the wooden shell of a burned-out warehouse. Children blackened by playing among the charred timbers ran up to him and asked for money. Many of them were naked. Onto the pools and cracked beams of that little sink of forgotten life the summer sun beat down with cruel, mocking brilliance.

Picking his way through the rubbish, House Martin went up to a woman standing at the entrance to the hut and spoke to her. Scratching idly at her thigh, she did not look up. The boy returned and told Tom that his mother had agreed to his going with him.

'But will she not talk with me?' Tom asked in amazement.

'I think not, sir. She says as she's 'ad 'er bellyful of gentlemen, and I am only going back where I come from.'

Tom thought about the remark all the way back to their inn. Although it clarified some things, it obscured others, and certainly did not explain how so remarkable a Bird could have emerged from such a terrible nest.

Out of curiosity and nostalgia, they took the Oxford road out of London, entering the Chilterns shortly after Beaconsfield and climbing through the beech woods to Stokenchurch. Here, asking to be shown where Justice Fuller had lived, Tom was taken to a large, deserted building standing alone near a small dark copse of ash and sycamores. The house was in no way unusual, except that its front garden was dominated by an enormous wooden cross, as tall as the eaves. Tom's guide explained that the justice had turned strange when his wife had been killed in a fire at his previous house, and had put up the cross to remind him of her. Latterly, as he became stricter and stricter in the execution of his duties, he used the cross as a gallows. It was said that at night he used to sit at his bedroom window and watch the bodies of those he had condemned to death swinging back and forth in the wind.

Glad to get away from that sinister memorial to bigotry and cruelty, they rode the short distance to the Green Man for dinner. Robin Goodfellow, every bit as large, rubicund and hearty as Tom remembered him, welcomed them in and called for his wife to serve them.

'You will not stay, sir?' he asked. 'By Our Lord's sainted sandals! We are known in these parts as the inn that offers the traveller all the comforts – that is my motto, you know: "All the Comforts".'

'I know your motto, landlord,' Tom replied. 'And I know it to be true, for I have stayed here before and sampled your comforts. Yet even they cannot tempt me to stay the night here.'

'Very well, sir. You say you have stayed at the Green

Man before? I am not in the habit of forgetting a face. You are certain you were here?'

'Certain. But my looks have altered somewhat since then.'

'Ah!' said Goodfellow, glancing uncomfortably down at Tom's scarred and bespectacled face. He left to look for his wife.

A minute or so later he came hurrying back, more red than ever.

'Sir,' he cried, 'my wife believes she remembers your voice from your last visit. And your name, too. It has been on everyone's lips these last two months on account of the stories coming from court—'

'Landlord,' interrupted Tom, 'I am the same man as was here a year since. Treat me as such, I pray.'

'Yet you are Sir Thomas Verney?'

'I am. Now send your wife. My boy and I will perish of hunger if you do not. Is that all the comfort you offer?'

'Oh no! She will be here directly, Sir Thomas.' He rumbled off to tell the village who was dining with him that afternoon.

'I expect, sir,' said House Martin, 'as you sometimes wishes you was invisible.'

'I do,' Tom nodded, wondering yet again at the lad's remarkable prescience.

Rosy acknowledged Tom with the simplest of curtsies. 'Good day, Sir Thomas,' she smiled. 'I am glad to see you again, sir.'

'And I am glad to be here, Rosy,' Tom answered, surprised to feel that after all that had happened over the past year, the same instinctive concord was still there between them. 'It is fortunate,' he went on, 'that it is you who have come to serve us. The landlord said it would be his wife.'

'It is his wife, sir.'

Tom looked up sharply. 'You?'

'We are very happy, sir. Now, what will you and your boy be taking for your dinner?'

As an indefinable pang shot through Tom's heart, he realised that though the old vanity was dormant, it was certainly not dead.

To avoid excessive ceremony, Tom had deliberately not written to his parents telling them precisely when he would return. So the following afternoon, with House Martin trotting by his side, he was able to enter Stratton Audley unheralded. Roused by the sound of hoofs, old Job Barnet, too frail to work, looked up from his customary seat outside the inn. Failing to recognise either of the riders, he returned to his ale. From neighbouring fields labourers making a start on the harvest also glanced casually across at the fine horse, then went on with their tasks without comment. Pointing out to House Martin familiar landmarks and places associated with his youth, Tom passed the church and rode up to the manor gate. There he dismounted. Hardly able to believe where he was, he started to walk down the drive to the Manor.

Elizabeth was the first to see him. Sitting sentinel by an upper window, she uttered a little scream, ran down the stairs, out through the front door and straight into her brother's arms. For a while they clung to each other without speaking. Then came a torrent of questions and observations. Before he had time to answer even one, Mary Verney joined them. At the sight of her familiar, loving face Tom almost dissolved in the swirl of joy and contrition that swept over him. However, biting his lip, he succeeded in keeping some control over his emotions and so was led into the house with all the noise and excitement of a victorious general returning from campaign.

For the next three days there was such junketing and merry making at the Manor as had not been seen since the celebrations held to mark the delivery of the government from the Gunpowder Plot, eighteen years before. At their heart was a great feast. It began in the middle of the afternoon and ended only when the servants hauled the last guest out from beneath the table the following morning. The Manor was inundated with meat by the basket, bread by the barrow, wine by the barrel, every scrap and drop of which was consumed. There were songs and dances, interludes and games.

The high point of the occasion was probably Tom's speech. Standing between his mother and father, none too coherent but transparently genuine, he proposed the health of his parents twice and that of House Martin no fewer than five times. The low point of the celebration was probably the recitation by the fifteen-year-old Lucius, sober, earnest and precociously scholarly, of a poem he had written in honour of his brother's exploits. Prepared at the outset to give the youth a fair hearing, the audience was disappointed before he had reached the end of the first line. The paean was in Latin. Thereafter interest and comprehension dwindled rapidly. By the time he reached the forty-eighth stanza, in which he compared Tom with Alexander the Great, the noise of coughing, belching, snoring and other manifestations of boredom had become so great that his mother had to suggest that he stop and give the guests time to take in what he had delivered so far, leaving the rest – another fifty-six stanzas – for 'a time later in the evening'. Not surprisingly, the time was never found. A few days later, as a sign of his gratitude, Tom made the effort to read the poem right through. As his sojourn at Clement's Inn had shown, his command of Latin was not great, and he did not enjoy it.

After the feasting came the visitors. Tom had not believed there were so many people in the whole of Oxfordshire, let alone in his parents' circle of friends and acquaintances. He seemed to be forever clasping hands and answering questions. Seeing how weary he became and how difficult he was finding it to remain polite, Elizabeth joked that it would be easier for him to write his adventures in a book and sell it at the manor gate for a shilling.

'Yes, sister,' he replied, 'but then I might miss someone I wished to see.'

'I would have thought, Tom,' she replied, 'that you have seen everyone you wish to see twice over, and many more besides whom you did not wish to see.'

'Ah, but I have not seen everyone, Elizabeth.'

'Well, hero, if she will not come to you, then you must go to her.'

Thus prompted, after dinner on the fifth day since his return, Tom saddled Prince and rode down to Godington Grange.

The front door stood slightly ajar. He pushed it open and entered the hall. His shoes clicked on the stone flags. The scent of bread and polish hung in the air.

'Hello?' he called, looking about him at the family portraits in heavy frames, the weapons and other trophies hanging from the walls. 'Hello?' Again his greeting echoed through the stillness of the summer afternoon without drawing a response. Flies buzzed against the windows.

A door creaked on the landing above him. Looking up,

he caught a glimpse of dark hair and a gown of pale blue, trimmed with white lace. The figure was hidden behind the balustrade for a second, then reappeared at the head of the stairs.

'Tom?' The voice was as warm as the August air. She came slowly down the stairs towards him and stopped on the bottom step.

'I have been home since Friday, Anne. Why did you not—'

'You are a hero now, Tom. I am pleased for you. And proud of you. But heroes go about the country leaving behind them a trail of broken bodies – and broken hearts.'

'Is that why you did not come?'

'Maybe.'

She crossed the hall to the front door and passed out into the sunshine. Following, he fell in beside her and they walked slowly beside the stream running down from the churchyard.

'I am sorry you were wounded, Tom.'

He did not reply.

She stopped and looked down at the water by their feet. 'Is there news of your wife?'

'I believe she is dead. I visited the grave.'

For a moment all was still. Even the brook seemed to stop flowing. Her grey eyes grew heavy, like tiny storm clouds.

He took her arm and led her into the lane.

'May God have mercy on her soul,' she said eventually. 'You will tell me all, one day?'

'I will. One day.'

She spoke quickly, in a matter-of-fact manner. 'My wedding is appointed. The fifth day of December. When it is cold,' she added, without quite knowing why.

'Is the date certain?'

'Why, Tom!' she exclaimed, suddenly laughing. 'You of all people should know by now that nothing is certain. But I am to be the wife of Sir Nicholas Morrison, who loves me dearly and will care for me, on the first Saturday in December — unless, God forbid!, some great calamity strikes me before then.'

He took her hand. 'Anne, might I be a great calamity?'

After they had walked on a few paces, she paused and looked up at him.

'Sometimes, Sir Thomas Verney, I do believe you might be.'